The War Baby

by

Larry G. Johnson

A

Vabella Publishing
P.O. Box 1052
Carrollton, Georgia 30112
www.vabella.com

Cover photos by Lynn Wilkinson

Manufactured in the United States of America

ISBN 978-1-938230-25-7

Library of Congress Control Number 2012955297

10 9 8 7 6 5 4 3 2 1

Dedication

To my grandfathers, both named Walter, who modeled for me the difference between a human being and a human doer.

Episodes

PART I: W.O.W

Part II: The Ugly Duckling

PART III: THE IDENTITY DILEMMA

Part I: W.O.W.

> In war, truth is the first casualty.
> Aeschylus

> Wars begin when you will, but they do not
> end when you please.
> Niccolò Machiavelli

The Three Musketeers

"What do folks around here do for sin?" the city slicker asked the man at the filling station. The sign over the Coke machine said, "In God we trust. Everyone else must pay cash." The traveling salesman put a nickel in and pulled the lever.

The flatlander had a flat a few miles back, and his spare was as bald as J. P. Williamson's head. Tires were hard to come by with the country barely out of the throes of the Great Depression, and now embroiled in an all-out war.

Grady Robinson at the Texaco station dropped his four-way lug wrench, and it rattled a time or two on the concrete slab. The crusty old mountaineer did not flinch, however.

"We don't have all them temptations like you people in the big city. So we hast to use our 'maginations. We might live up here in the sticks, but don't you thank for one minute the preacher don't have nuttin' to preach about. We jest mind our own bidness, take keer of our own, and then pull the shades down when it gits dark."

Mason, Georgia sat right on the Tennessee border, literally. It was also near the junction with North Carolina. The little village was located in a picturesque valley with clear, cold streams running through it, teeming with native trout. The Blue Ridge Mountains were ever in the distance no matter which way a person looked. The air was clean, the water pure, and consciences were clear, for the most part.

It did not take much to entertain those who lived up in this little corner of the world. The banter at the barbershop always seemed to come back around to the antics of Dillard Porter and Dudley Peacock. Dubbed the Dubious Brothers by the locals, these ne'er-do-wells took turns being the town drunk and the village idiot.

The four main annual events in Mason were the high school

graduation in May, the community-wide Fourth of July picnic, the revival meeting at the Baptist Church every second week in August, and the Halloween Carnival in the fall.

At last year's picnic, some of the boys got into a deep discussion while sitting under a big old oak tree. They debated whether it would take longer to cut the tree down with a pocketknife, or to scrape the dirt road all the way to Mountain Home with a butcher knife.

Dudley Peacock got saved for the third year in a row at the annual meeting. This time he really meant business. He promised to stop boozin', gamblin', cussin', thievin', and being ugly to his wife. The penitent Peacock surprised everyone when he showed up for the baptizing in Tumbling Creek. After old "Dud's" sins were washed away, nobody fished in that hole again for several weeks.

Once the king and queen of the Halloween Carnival were crowned, local horse trader, George King, took the teenagers for a hayride on his modified ¾-ton GMC truck. Even though they complained of the smell of manure, the boys and girls climbed aboard anyway, in anticipation of some undercover hand holding beneath the quilts.

Some of the parents of these youngsters kept up with the news on the radio. Just about all families gathered around that wireless receiver on Saturday nights to listen to the Grand Ole Opry, live from the Ryman Auditorium in Nashville, Tennessee. That was about the extent of their connection to the rest of the world. Most kids had never even ridden on a train.

A stranger passing through the little settlement where Maude King and Todd Williamson grew up might call it idyllic. Agreements were sealed with a handshake, transactions were cash on the barrelhead, and a man's word was his bond. The husband was the head of his household, a woman's place was in the home, children were to be seen and not heard. Cats lived in the barn and dogs slept under the front porch.

Masonites went to bed with the chickens, and they got up with the rooster. They eked out a living as best they could in the rocky hills. These rugged individualists were wary of outsiders, and they had nary a notion that anybody owed them anything. The residents of this community never locked their doors at night, and if they happened to own an old vehicle, the key was always left in the ignition.

Whether it was ever read much or not, a Family Bible was a part of each home. A firearm hung over the fireplace, and the indwellers hid what little money they had under the mattress. Everybody feared God, and nobody worshiped the Almighty Dollar.

If folks were looking for a good wholesome place to raise a family, nothing could be finer even in Carolina, which was just up the road a few miles anyway. Even so, some people just don't know how to leave well enough alone.

Graduation weekend was like an area-wide homecoming for the people in Mason and its twin town just across the state line in Tennessee. Earlier graduates often held class reunions. Residents of the surrounding area then turned out for the commencement ceremony to salute the current crop, even if they had no kin in the bunch.

The townspeople also used this time of celebration to show their appreciation for the educators. Teachers worked diligently to keep students from dropping out. They labored tirelessly to make sure the ones who stayed in school met the requirements to get their diplomas. Sometimes they were successful. More than half the time, the teachers failed.

Boys often quit school to help their parents try to make ends meet. Todd Williamson did not finish the ninth grade. Some lads joined the army just as soon as they could get someone to sign for them.

Furthermore, many of these folks far removed from urban areas saw little benefit in a girl having much schooling. Those students who beat the odds were applauded vigorously.

George King wanted his children to get as much education as they could. When his son, Earl, graduated in 1933, he went straight to the recruiting station. There was no draft at the time, but he wanted to serve his country. Mr. King had no idea what his daughter Maude would do once she got her diploma. Neither did she.

Not many girls of her generation had a career. Some became secretaries. A few entered the field of nursing. Others were teachers. Most young ladies just got married and became homemakers.

Maude King had a hard time seeing herself in any of these roles. Getting additional training was out of the question where she lived. The girl had never been in love, and she saw no prospects of that changing anytime soon.

Nothing much was remarkable about the twelve boys and sixteen girls who made up the Class of 1941. They did have the distinction of being the inaugural group to walk across the stage in the new gym/auditorium. For the first time in the school's history, the basketball teams did not have to play outdoors.

With the big graduation ceremony just around the corner, Maude was struggling with her mixed feelings. Summers always dragged with nothing to do except help around the house. The girl grew weary of forever being under the critical eyes of her mother Ruby. It was hard for her to imagine an approaching autumn without the anticipation of school about to start.

More than anything, though, she was going to miss her friends. While a number of students had come and gone during her eleven years in school, one thing was constant. Maude King, Millie Mitchell, and Maggie McDonald started first grade together, and they had been steadfast friends ever since.

With their names all beginning with the same letter, they called themselves The Three Musketeers. The girls knew very little about what that meant, other than it was the name given to three warriors who vowed to band together, come hell or high water. They had also seen Three Musketeers candy bars at Morgan's General Store, but Maggie was the only one who had ever tasted one.

Maude closed out her senior year amid a flurry of activity. When the much-anticipated day finally arrived, the guys were expected to be in their Sunday best on graduation day. A couple of them would be fortunate enough to get a new suit of clothes. Those who could do no better had no shame whatsoever in marching across the stage in their best pair of overalls.

Each girl wanted a new dress for graduation. Sewing machines were humming all over the school district.

Maggie invited Maude and Millie for a sleepover on the night before the big day. It was understandable that these chums wanted to celebrate this milestone together.

Mildred (Millie) Mitchell was the smartest in school. There was never a doubt that she would finish at the top of the class. The studious one could always think things through. Although she was an attractive young woman with beautiful long black hair and a slim figure, boys shied away from her. Millie wondered if it was because she wore glasses.

Margaret (Maggie) McDonald was a free spirit. She had a tendency to throw caution to the wind. Whenever she came up with some wild, hair-brained scheme that might get the girls in trouble, Millie became the voice of reason. Taller than the other two, Maggie was also the one most well-endowed. Boys were mesmerized by her furtive and flirty dark brown eyes.

Maude King was the one easily led. She just went along for the ride. A couple of boys had been sweet on her in school, but she had never been out on an actual date. Local lads were too afraid of her father to come courting. Maude finished right behind Millie as the class salutatorian.

All of the girls wore lipstick on occasion. Maggie preferred outrageous deep red. She often painted her fingernails and toenails to match. Maude had no lipstick of her own, but her mother let her use her pink tube for special events.

When Maude went to her daddy to ask permission to spend the night with Maggie, George's response was a predictable, "No." While he had no problems with Millie, Mr. King had always been a little concerned about

Maude's friendship with the McDonald girl. He was afraid that she might be a bad influence on his daughter. This time he suspected boys were involved.

Maggie was not too surprised when Maude informed her of her father's verdict. She said to let her work on it. She went to her own daddy and asked him to do something. Raymond McDonald would do anything for his only daughter.

George King was a bit surprised when Raymond's car drove up in the yard. The two men shook hands. "Looks like our girls are about all grown up now," Raymond began.

George nodded in agreement, not sure of the nature of this visit.

Raymond then went straight to the point. "George, we've known each other for a long time, haven't we?"

"Yes, I can say that's true," Maude's daddy responded, still a bit puzzled.

"Well, George, here's the thing. Maggie tells me that you will not let your daughter spend the night at my house. My wife and I find that highly insulting. If you think that your girl is too good to stay at my place, I want you to just say so straight to my face."

That put old George back on his heels. "Well, Raymond, I never meant it that way. But, I guess I can see how you feel. Maude says that your daughter has been out on several dates. Maude does not have a boyfriend. Raymond, can you guarantee me that no boys are going to call on the girls that night?"

"George, you have my word on it," Maggie's father assured him.

"Then I would be honored for my girl to spend the night at your place," Mr. King replied.

Maude's dress was almost ready. She had tried it on three times now. Her mother always managed to stick her with a pin as she was making adjustments.

Maude wanted to go straight to Maggie's on the last day of school, but Ruby told her that she had to come home and try the dress on one more time. Except for leveling the hem just a bit, it was ready. George was happy with that arrangement. This would allow him to drive his daughter over to the McDonalds' house. Just his presence signaled that he was keeping check on things.

When Martha McDonald called the girls to supper, they tried to stop giggling long enough to eat. During his blessing before the meal, Raymond asked the Good Lord to guide these young ladies as they were about to go out into the highways and byways of life.

As the girls said their goodnights and went to Maggie's room, their emotions were at a fever pitch. No one remembered exactly how it started, but before long, the three were in a fierce pillow fight. They were letting off some steam. Meantime, the seam of one of the homemade pillows gave way. Feathers went flying. This took some wind out of their sails, as the girls had to stop and clean up the mess.

Millie was sleeping in the room with Maggie. Maude would spend the night in Little Ray's room. Maggie's brother volunteered gladly to go to his grandparents' house when he heard about the commotion that would be going on at his own.

Raymond came to the room a couple of times to try to restore order. The last time he said, "Don't you girls think it is time to get some sleep? You have a big day ahead of you tomorrow."

"In just a few minutes, Daddy," Maggie responded.

It was time for one more Three Musketeers huddle. Maude wanted the other two to assure her that they were not going to slip out and go meet some boys after she went to bed.

"Daddy would kill me if he were to catch us," Maggie responded. "Why would you ever think of such a thing?" she said with her eyelashes fluttering.

Then Millie took the lead. "Girls," she began. "We have been friends all through school. Who knows what the world is coming to, with this war going on and all? Who knows where we might wind up? Let us make a pact tonight. Let's pledge that we will always be there for one another, no matter what."

There was not even a moment's hesitation. The girls locked their arms in an embrace.

"The Three Musketeers today."

"The Three Musketeers tomorrow."

"The Three Musketeers forever," they chanted.

"One for all, and all for one," they vowed.

Maude soon made her way down the hall and went to bed. With her schooling now behind her, she lay awake for a long time wondering what her life would be like. Alone in the room, she fancied herself a secretary. The girl could type a little thanks to the commercial class, but she was not very good at shorthand.

Would she ever learn how to drive a car? Her mother had never driven one. Would she get to see the bright lights of a city? Would she even find a husband and have children? Or, would she be a spinster like her Aunt Lucy?

The one thing that should have concerned Maude more than anything was something that never crossed her mind. Not too far down the road, the youthful innocent vow that she had taken a few minutes earlier would come to dominate her whole life.

The house was quiet now. Through the open windows, the girls could hear the katydids and the tree frogs trying to outdo each other, with the crickets chiming in for good measure. What none of them could hear was the rhythmic sound of the swing squeaking solemnly, as Raymond McDonald sat on the front porch keeping an eye on things. Eventually, the girls all drifted off to sleep.

The Kings and the Williamsons

"Maude, lunch is ready," Ruby King hollered through the house. Maude had gone into her room and closed the door about mid-morning. Ruby was so preoccupied cutting out a shirt for her husband George that she had lost sight of her daughter. Maude's daddy had put on a little weight during the winter of 1941-42. His personal tailor was making some adjustments to the tattered old pattern accordingly.

"Maude, did you hear me?" Ruby called out. When she still got no response, she knocked gently on the door. All was quiet from the other side. She then tried to open it but found it locked. "That's strange," she mumbled to herself. Was her daughter asleep?

Ruby pushed cloth, scattered patterns, scissors, measuring tape, pincushion, thimbles, spools of thread, and the button box to one end of the table so she could put out the leftovers from Sunday dinner. She decided to go ahead and eat so that she could get back to work. Maude would have to do the best she could.

Ruby was worried about her daughter. Since graduating from high school, the girl was lacking in direction. Recently, she was keeping company with John Paul and Ethel Williamson's son, Todd. Ruby sure hoped Maude would not get carried away. George would not be home until later in the afternoon.

Ruby Moore King was an attractive woman with raven black hair. She wore little wire rim glasses. Standing only five foot three inches tall, her husband towered over her. She married George King in 1915, when she was only sixteen. Since finding a good husband was a girl's main objective, the sooner the better. Young George was a good catch for sure.

George was the son of a circuit-riding preacher man. His father dropped dead in the pulpit one Sunday while preaching a sermon on Heaven. Those in the congregation that day said he was so ready to go to glory that he just went on.

Maude's mother came from a big family. Ruby was second to the youngest, with two older sisters, three older brothers, and a baby sister the neighbors described as peculiar.

When George took his young bride home, he soon found out that she was more delicate than he presumed. A hearty and vigorous young man himself, he was often impatient with her. Ruby's brothers and sisters had no doubt spoiled her. He had to learn how to indulge and patronize his wife to get along with her.

The young wife had just turned eighteen when Earl was born. She almost died during childbirth. At least, she thought she did. The young mother then took to her bed for weeks. Fortunately for George, Ruby's sisters were able to divide their time staying with him and the baby. He did not know what he would have done without them.

Maude was added to the family in 1924, eight years after Earl's tumultuous birth. Ruby did not plan to have any other children. She did not want to go through that ordeal again. The woman also knew the best way to keep that from happening.

Every now and then, though, George was able to have his way with her. Ruby was fit to be tied when her tummy began to rise.

Maude King was a daddy's girl. Her mother just did not take a shine to her. Even though her daughter's birth was far less complicated than Earl's was, Ruby still milked it for all it was worth. Her sisters again came trudging over grudgingly to help until she could get back on her feet.

Maude was only nine-years-old when her brother, Earl, left home to go in the military. In many ways, he seemed more like an uncle to her. They were never close. With no other siblings, she mostly felt like an only child.

Maude's hair was dark brown like her father's, and she was a good three inches taller than her mother. Unlike her brother, she had a slender build. Ruby chided her daughter, telling her that no boy was ever going to pay her any attention unless she put some meat on her bones. It seemed to Maude that her mother became more critical with each passing year.

Her father, meanwhile, became overprotective. He could not stand the thought of anything bad happening to his baby girl. George was a man of considerable pent up passion. It was only natural that he assumed every boy of breeding age was lusting after his daughter.

"Where was Todd going in the car?" Ethel Williamson asked her husband when they sat down at the dinner table. John Paul said that Todd told him he was going to see a friend about to go off to the war.

"I didn't know he had the day off from work," she continued. "He didn't say anything about it to me."

"What do you make of that King girl?" she asked J. P. as they were eating their lunch.

"She seems to be a nice young lady, and the Kings are fine people," he answered her.

"Well, I don't like it," Ethel weighed in, although her husband had not asked her how she felt about the situation.

Todd's mother, Ethel Allgood Williamson, was often referred to as a stern woman. She came about that trait honestly. The Allgoods were strict Primitive Baptists, what some folks call, "Hard Shell." They were just simple humble folks, unpretentious when it came to worldly goods.

Ethel was the oldest of nine children. She was of sturdy stock, standing about an inch taller than her husband. The woman always wore her bonnet when she went outside. Not many people could ever remember seeing her smile. Ethel was a true Puritan in that she supposed anything enjoyable and pleasurable must surely be sinful.

Her only known vice was dipping snuff, so long as a person was not too particular with the use of the word "known." Neither of her children had any idea of her habit. J. P. was aware that his wife dipped because he could smell it on her breath, although in their marriage of more than two decades, they had never discussed it.

Those who did business with the Allgoods sometimes murmured among themselves. They said it seemed as if those of this clan were just a little too proud of their humility. Calvinists that they were, these stalwarts subscribed to the doctrine that some people are chosen by God to be saved, while others are predestined to be lost and doomed to Hell. They knew for sure which camp they were in.

The family name did not help either. They were not just good part of the time. The Allgoods were always good. Wanting her firstborn not to forget his heritage, Ethel made sure that Todd's middle name was Allgood.

Maude's father was a horse trader. Actually, he was more of a mule trader than anything else. Horse trader just sounded better to Ruby. He bought and sold the famous Tennessee mules, prized by farmers throughout the southland.

Mr. King set up a network of breeders. He then commanded their loyalty by giving them top dollar for these agricultural work animals. When farmers in his territory needed a good pair of mules, they knew who would treat them right.

George did not just trade horses and mules, though. In his travels around the country, he always had some spare change in his pocket. He often came home with clocks, pocket watches, jewelry, knives, tools, and of course, guns.

Mr. King could have just as easily been called a gun dealer. He was especially fond of 12 gauge double barrel shotguns. At any given time, he would also be in possession of a variety of rifles, pistols, and other firearms, some of them valuable antiques.

Country people were often willing to part with valuables during hard times. George prided himself in that he never tried to take advantage of anyone. While he did not always give them the original asking price, he made sure they got fair treatment in return for their goods. Sometimes they swapped with him for something they needed. George was after all a trader.

No one knew how many folks Mr. King had lent a helping hand to during some rough spots in their lives, not even Ruby. He read his Bible almost every day. George believed in not letting the right hand know what the left hand was doing when it came to being charitable.

Maude's father had gone to deliver a pair of mules the day she went missing. Ruby met him at the door when he got home. She told him that their daughter locked herself in her room, and then she slipped out the window. Her graduation dress was not in the closet. That could mean only one thing.

Maude King and Todd Williamson did what generations had done before them. When a girl came of marriageable age, she found a husband. At seventeen, Maude was actually a year older than her mother was when she and George tied the knot. The groom was usually a little older. Todd was twenty.

In the late 1930s and early 40s, jobs were scarce as hen's teeth. Most families around Mason were rather sufficient in that they lived off the land. Even during the hardscrabble days of the Great Depression, these folks had food to eat.

Todd was fortunate to get a job at the local feed and seed store. It paid just enough for the newlyweds to rent a small furnished apartment. They did not own a vehicle. Both of their fathers had an old rattletrap should the need arise.

Emma Louise was born less than eleven months after Todd and Maude stood before the justice of the peace. In the span of about a year and a half, Maude King Williamson went from being a high school student who was very much dependent upon her parents for everything, to being a wife, and then a mother. That was pretty much the norm out in this neck of the woods.

When war clouds started forming over Europe during the late 1930s, many boys from the backwoods made a beeline to the recruiting station. Others waited to see if Uncle Sam was going to request their services. Todd was among those in the latter group.

The Kings and the Williamsons were just ordinary, run of the mill, down to earth folks – what the Good Book calls the salt of the earth. People like them were not prone to think in terms of good times or bad. Ethel Williamson grew up hearing her father say, "There's no two ways about it. Things are just what they are. There ain't much of nothing nobody can do about it, neither. What will be, will be."

Not everyone shared in Mr. Othell Allgood's concept of fate, however. Others presumed that humans have a little more say so in their own destiny. Regardless of whether people live in poverty, or if they enjoy prosperity, when push comes to shove, the cream inevitably rises to the top, and dregs settle to the bottom.

If the going gets tough and the straits are dire, otherwise undistinguished individuals often rise above their circumstances. Because of their noble deeds and heroic efforts, a small number even have the accolade of greatness attached to their names.

When their backs are to the wall, the weedy, on the other hand, cower if epic demands are placed upon them.

When it is crunch time and everything is on the line, the seedy, eyeing a windfall, take advantage of those knocked off balance.

What's more, as the unwary come upon the proverbial fork in the road, they sometime stray into forbidden territory, erstwhile unimaginable.

When the smoke finally clears, and the dust settles, there are then those who have to live with the consequences of what they have done, whether it was in a moment of weakness, a fit of passion, or in the heat of battle.

A war is not really a war until somebody gives it a name. Those who understand that sort of thing occasionally show some originality, perhaps even cleverness. Mostly, though, names of wars are dull and drab. Early on, correspondents settled on simply calling this one World War II. For some folks in the sleepy little mountain town of Mason, December 7, 1941, was not the only day that would live in infamy.

People up in those parts still talk about how Mason, Georgia got its name. The folktale is handed down from one generation to the next.

After the Cherokee Indians were herded up and sent on their way to Oklahoma along the Trail of Tears in the late 1830s, the Norths were the first white settlers in the area. As a little community started developing along the road that connects Chattanooga, Tennessee and Asheville, North Carolina, the people needed their own post office. The town had never been formally chartered.

The Norths wanted to call the little burg North, Georgia. Strange as it may seem, the Souths were the next family to relocate in the area. They petitioned to have the place named South, Georgia. Officials down at the state capital in Milledgeville were not amused.

A survey team then showed up one day right out of the blue. The settlers thought they knew about where the state line was, but it had never been officially established. To the amazement of the homesteaders, the crew determined that the border was actually about a quarter mile south of where they presumed it to be. The boundary between Georgia and Tennessee split the settlement in two, cutting right between the Norths and the Souths. The Souths actually lived in Tennessee, and the Norths were north Georgians.

Time dragged on with the residents unable to come up with a name for the twin towns that both sides could agree on. The one room schoolteacher then had a novel idea. Since the state line was in effect separating the Norths from the Souths, he suggested one community be named Mason and the other Dixon.

The controversy was not over yet, however. Those on each side of the border preferred Mason. For generations, the men from these families had been members of the Masonic Order. Each clan wanted their town to pay tribute to this fraternal organization.

Alas, there was only one way to resolve the stalemate – the old coin toss. That lot fell to the preacher to do the honor. When the Reverend W. W. Rogers was asked to flip the coin, he refused until he was convinced that it had nothing to do with gambling.

The Norths won the toss, and the south side of town was recognized as Mason, Georgia. Not much would change for them. The Souths, now residents of Dixon, Tennessee, were no longer Georgia crackers. They had to get used to the idea of being east Tennessee hillbillies.

Most people simply referred to the twin towns as Mason-Dixon. State

Street now runs right down the middle. The residents decided years ago that it was not feasible for both townships to run a school. They combine their efforts to operate the Mason-Dixon School. It is located on the Georgia side of the street, but Tennessee agrees to recognize its graduates.

Maude's mother Ruby was a direct descendant of the Norths on her mother's side. Todd's mother Ethel's maternal grandfather was a South.

Ethel Allgood and John Paul Williamson met in 1919, at an all-day singing way out in the country at the Mt. Pisgah Primitive Baptist Church. Ethel seemed taken by the debonair young man who was actually there that day with another young lady.

One family created a minor sensation when it brought a tub of lemonade. Ethel saw the handsome young man heading toward it. She carefully positioned herself right beside the No. 2 washtub with her own glass. The young gentleman that he was, John Paul obliged her.

J. P.'s father was the village blacksmith. The next day when Ethel asked her own daddy if he had ever seen the smith's son about the shop, he responded in the affirmative. In fact, the lad had repaired a plow stock for him.

Girls were rather limited when it came to making advances in those days. Ethel Allgood nevertheless had a way of getting her way. When told that J. P. was also fashioning some pieces of furniture, she just happened to hitch a ride with Mr. Othell Allgood on his next trip to town.

Ethel then wandered into the blacksmith shop with a request of her own. The Williamson boy was summoned from the back. John Paul found himself looking into the eyes of the same girl that he had encountered at Mt. Pisgah.

"Can I help you?" he asked rather awkwardly.

With no show of emotion whatsoever, Ethel inquired as to whether he could make her a hope chest. The personable young man responded by telling her that depended on how much hope she had, and what she was hoping for. Ethel was for the moment sidetracked.

The young woman then made a quick recovery. "I'm hoping for an honorable man willing to marry me, and to provide a good home for me."

"Then, I'm not sure I have the tools to create that kind of hope chest," John Paul muttered clumsily.

"Well, you could try couldn't you?" she implored.

With that, Ethel did an abrupt about face. She then walked out with her head held high.

Soon thereafter, the Williamsons' old horse and buggy were making regular trips out to the Allgood place, with J. P. sitting in the driver's seat. Or, so he thought.

One by one, John Paul Williamson's older brothers went off to fight in World War I. After being in the "war to end all wars," and seeing the capitals of Europe, Mason, Georgia was too small for them. They settled in places like Atlanta, Nashville, and New Orleans.

The Williamson boys brought their families back to Mason for the annual family reunion every fourth Sunday in June. The men all had a ruddy complexion with reddish brown hair and hazel eyes. By the time each lad was in his early twenties, his hairline was already beginning to recede. Simultaneously, a little bald spot appeared. The men compared noggins to see who had the shiniest dome.

As John Paul was preparing for marriage, his father deeded him about ten acres from the family farm. Doing much of the work himself, a little bungalow house was ready for the couple to move into when they took their vows. It was at the edge of town near the main highway, and across the road from where his folks lived.

After their parents died, J. P.'s siblings all agreed that their younger brother should inherit the rest of the old home place, since he was the one who stayed home to take care of them. Most of the eighty acres were wooded. One stretch of bottoms along Tumbling Creek, though, was very fertile farmland. J. P. eventually tore down the old house and barn and used the materials to build a barn and woodshop on his side of the road.

John Paul was still trying to figure out how to make use of his son. The boy quit school a year and a half before he graduated. Todd was a good hand with the mules when things went to suit him. Mr. Williamson was delighted when the boy found a job.

J. P. was also concerned that Todd had shown little interest in members of the opposite sex. Then rather abruptly, he started keeping company with the King girl. The war situation was especially troubling to this father of a twenty-year-old unmarried son.

John Paul tried to make a living from his woodworking. He custom-made tables, chairs, dressers, headboards and footboards, bookcases, and even some rather fancy desks. Ethel said that he never charged enough for his work, and they barely scraped by. This master craftsman was pleased that many of his pieces would be passed down as family heirlooms.

As the country was finally getting back on its feet after the Depression, people discovered new ways to purchase things. Just about anything could be ordered from the Sears Roebuck Catalog. Big cities actually had furniture stores where they sold items that were mass-produced in factories. J. P. got fewer and fewer requests for his handcrafted items.

While one door was closing, another began to open. With more and more people taking jobs, they had less and less time to spend in their gardens. Supermarkets like A & P sprang up in small towns. Whether it was actually true or not, many people said they could buy their food as cheaply as they could raise it.

John Paul decided to expand his own gardening and sell fruit and vegetables to the public. The area had long been recognized for its tart and tasty apples. The Williamsons already had a big orchard that would now be enlarged. Those fertile creek bottoms from the home place could also be put to good use.

In the early spring of 1936, Todd's father bought his first Studebaker truck. After he dug his Irish potatoes, he then called on grocery stores. He went back again when the green beans were ready to pick.

As other vegetables matured, he proffered squash, corn, tomatoes, butter beans, okra, peas, peppers, radishes, carrots, cucumbers, cantaloupes, and watermelons. He grew turnip greens and collards in the fall. Sweet potatoes were dug just before the first frost. The Williamsons also produced several gallons of syrup each year from their sorghum cane patch.

J. P.'s produce was top quality. Store managers favored him to help keep their bins stocked. The humble woodworker returned to his trade during the winters, cherishing the hours he spent alone in his shop.

The family opened a produce stand down on the road when Todd was a teenager. All summer long, plenty of whatever was in season was available to passers-by. Pieces of J. P.'s woodwork were also on display.

The Williamsons did especially well during the late summer and early fall when the apples got ripe. In addition to selling them by the bushel and peck, they squeezed their own cider and sold it by the gallon.

Ethel was also famous for her fried apple pies. She always carried over some dried fruit from the previous year. It did not take long for the new apples to dry in the warmth of September days.

A Man on a Mission

Todd Williamson's father kept up with the news. As tensions mounted and hostilities escalated in Europe, he grew more concerned. J. P. and Ethel Williamson hoped that the United States could remain neutral. They had a son likely to be called up if it did not.

Like the other males in his clan, Todd started losing his hair soon after he was grown. This made him self-conscious. The boy did not have any great plans for his life. Like many of the youths his age, he saw little need for an education beyond the ability to read, write, and do simple math. About the only thing that concerned young Williamson was pleasing his mother. Ethel always knew what was best for her son.

Todd never had a girlfriend before Maude. He had been out on a couple of double dates, but he felt uneasy and awkward around females. He was still living at home with his parents and his younger sister Katherine.

When it seemed inevitable that the United States would be drawn into the war, Todd Williamson made the determination that single men would be the first to be called up. He, therefore, decided to look around for a wife. The young man also thought his chances of being drafted would lessen significantly if he had a child on the way. He went searching for work, and he started developing his strategy just in case.

Then came that infamous day in December 1941, when the Japanese attacked Pearl Harbor. Ready or not, the country was at war. Todd feared the worst. It was time for him to move forward with his plan.

When he went to register for the draft, his mother sent a letter along with him, instructing the board that her son did not have the disposition to be a soldier. She begged the officials to give him an exemption. The message was noted and placed in his file.

The young man decided that he could not rely on his mother alone, though, to keep him out of the military. For the first time in his life, Todd Williamson would not be able to confide in her. There was too much risk that Ethel Williamson would not approve of what her son was about to do.

Maude wanted to get a job after she graduated from high school, but nothing was available in the small town. Maggie got married almost immediately. Millie was now employed by the bank. If Maude found work, she would have to relocate.

No amount of persuasion could convince George King that his daughter was ready to be out on her own. Even if she could find a job in the county seat town of Mountain Home some fifteen miles away, Maude was not ready to drive to and from work.

The seventeen-year-old girl continued to live at home under her mother's thumb and her daddy's control. She missed school and the daily camaraderie of The Three Musketeers. Maude was convinced now more than ever that she was destined to wither on the vine.

Todd had never experienced any romantic feelings for a female. This was not about love, though. This was about war. He set his sights on Maude King, a neighbor girl that he thought he might be able to impress. He would discuss his strategy with no one.

Maude had known Todd all of her life. Both families attended the Mason Baptist Church. Instead of hanging out with the other kids, Todd always sat with his parents. She had never paid him much attention. He had certainly never given her a second look. This was why she was so shocked when he showed up at her house one day.

Todd anticipated that his biggest problem would be getting past Maude's father. He was right. Although his daughter had graduated from high school, George King still did not consider her to be raised. Besides, some of her friends were a little too wild for his liking.

With time of the essence, Todd struck quickly. Christmas was approaching, and he had saved enough money to buy Maude a watch. Maybe that would get her attention. First, however, he had to go courting.

The Kings' house was set off the road at the end of a long twisting drive. It had several large oak trees in the yard. Constructed of heart pine, the clapboards would not hold paint. As he approached it apprehensively, the large weathered house with a sprawling front porch was foreboding.

The nervous young man was relieved when Mr. King's truck was not in the yard late on that cold Friday afternoon. He climbed the steps quietly and tapped gently on the front door.

Maude was just inside in the living room. She was flattered that she had a suitor. Todd never came inside. He asked if she would like to go to the movies with him the next night in Mountain Home.

Of course, Maude wanted to go, but she was rightly concerned that her father would not let her. She suggested to Todd that they meet at the theater. She would try to talk her daddy into letting her go with Millie. Ruby was busy in the kitchen at the other end of the house and never knew anyone was on the place.

Not without some drama of its own, Maude was finally granted permission. After mulling it over, and since it was a family flick, George King eventually decided that this was a safe arrangement. Millie came by in her daddy's car and picked her up.

Todd was in the lobby when they arrived. The girls spoke, and he handed them tickets that he had already purchased. Maude's date did not go in immediately, but he watched to see where she was seated. After the lights were turned down, he came in and sat beside her.

The little theater was crowded. A few other couples were there on dates. Several families had brought their children to see Shirley Temple as "Kathleen."

Midway through the movie, Maude's admirer slipped his hand into hers. This was awkward, but like the actors up on the screen, Todd Williamson also had a script that he was following.

After the movie was over, the elated young woman thanked him for inviting her. As the lights came on, he slipped out into the darkness. Millie took Maude home, both of them giggling gleefully all the way back to Mason.

The man on a mission knew that he would soon have to confront the girl's father. On Sunday afternoon, Todd went and paid a neighborly visit. Normally, he would have been terrified at the very thought of such an encounter. By now his juices were really flowing, though not necessarily the ones normally driving a young man at this age.

George was polite but reserved. With some hesitation, he finally granted permission for his daughter to go out with Todd under tightly controlled circumstances. Maude's daddy knew the Williamsons to be good honorable people. He had never heard anything disparaging regarding their son.

The next Saturday night on their first official date, Todd took Maude to a barbershop quartet convention held in the new school auditorium. This time they would be seen together as a couple right out in the open. He was very self-conscious, imagining everyone staring at him. Yet, he knew there was no turning back. He had not told his parents that he would be sitting with a girl on either occasion.

The next day was the Sunday before Christmas, just two weeks after Pearl Harbor. Todd asked Maude if he could walk her home from church. Her father said it would be fine, and that he could stay for Sunday dinner. George King wanted some time to size up the young man who had taken such a sudden interest in his daughter. Todd hardly said a word at the table.

Maude followed him out on the porch and into the yard as he was leaving. He then reached into his pocket and pulled out a neatly wrapped little package. He suggested that she open her Christmas present right away.

The young lady was very surprised when she saw the gold-plated Elgin. She wanted so much to give Todd a hug, but she knew there was far too much risk that her father might walk out the door any second. This was the first watch the girl had ever owned.

Maude concealed the gift and the packaging under her clothing until she could get to her room. She said nothing about it to her parents. She secretly wore the watch when she knew they would not see it on her arm.

Looking back, Todd was still amazed at how successful he was in carrying out his plan. Was it his charm? That made him chuckle. What he had not figured on was just how badly the young woman wanted to get out from under her mother's roof and her daddy's restrictions.

Todd Williamson and Maude King eloped on Valentine's Day, 1942.

When Ruby King realized that Maude had slipped out that Monday morning, she feared the worst. George had gone to deliver a pair of mules. He had just gotten home and found out about their daughter's disappearance when the couple came driving up in the Williamsons' old Chevrolet. They told her parents that they went over the state line into Tennessee, and found a justice of the peace who performed their marriage ceremony.

Ruby burst into tears. She then went to her bedroom and closed the door. After expressing his feelings that he would rather they had waited a while, George wished the newlyweds well. Maude went to her room and started packing some things to take to the little furnished apartment that they had rented on Saturday.

The nervous groom's father-in-law took him out on the porch. Mr. King said he regretted that Todd was not man enough to come and ask for his daughter's hand in marriage. The young man just stood there with his head down.

"That's my baby girl. You better take good care of her," George added, with an expression on his face that communicated even more than the words he had just spoken. Young Williamson had no doubt that Daddy King would be looking over his shoulder.

The next stop was the Williamsons' house. This visit Todd feared even more than he did facing his new in-laws. Ethel was immediately suspicious when the two of them came in together. This was the first time Maude had ever been inside the house where Todd had grown up. The new bride tried to conceal the modest little wedding ring on her finger.

"Where's Daddy?" Todd asked.

His mother said that J. P. was out in his shop. The groom took his bride by the hand and said, "Let's go see what the old man is working on." Todd's little sister Katherine had not gotten home from school.

Mr. Williamson looked up in surprise as his son and his girlfriend entered the dusty outbuilding. He apologized to Maude for the woodshop being in such a mess.

"Come on, Daddy. Let's go to the house for a minute," Todd said to him. At that point, John Paul knew what was going on. He dusted himself off, and the three of them went up the path in silence. Once inside, Todd made the big announcement.

"Son, what have you done?" was his mother's only response. J. P. shook his boy's hand. He then gave Maude a polite hug, welcoming her into the family.

While Todd added his clothes to the backseat, Mr. Williamson imparted to his new daughter-in-law some kindly words of fatherly advice. The groom said that he would bring the car back the next day. J. P. then watched the newlyweds drive off to begin their life together.

When he went back inside, Ethel said to him with a deep scorn on her face, "I don't like it. I just don't like it at all." Her husband said that he did not like it very much either, but it was over and done with. They now just had to get used to it.

Not long after breakfast the next morning, John Paul Williamson showed up at the Kings' house. When Ruby came to the door, he asked to speak with George. Neither of them mentioned what had transpired the day before. Maude's mother told him that her husband was out feeding and watering the livestock. J. P. made his way to the barn.

"Hello, Mr. Williamson. What brings you over this way?" George greeted his neighbor.

"I think you and I need to have a man to man talk," J. P. answered. Mr. King nodded in agreement.

Todd's father began by saying that it looked like the two families were now going to be tied together. George again nodded his head in accord. J. P. then said he wanted the Kings to know that he and Ethel knew absolutely nothing about what their son and Maude were up to. "If we had known, I would have come here earlier," he continued.

George then added that J. P. could presume that he and Ruby were also in the dark.

Mr. Williamson continued. "I guess I should have suspected something when Todd mentioned at the supper table around Thanksgiving that he was thinking about going down to the Lipham's Feed and Seed Store and see if they needed any help. He said he figured that since Lloyd died last fall, Luther might not be able to handle everything by himself."

After stopping to reflect a moment, he then went on. "I was a little surprised that Ethel encouraged the boy to look into it. I'm sure she would have sung a different tune if she had any idea that her son was looking for work so he could get married."

George listened respectfully as J. P. continued. "I'll have to admit I was proud to hear that the boy had some interest in a job. I thought maybe he was about to show some gumption.

"Lord knows he was little help to me. All the boy ever does is make fun of me, and criticize whatever I am doing. Apparently, he does not think I know how to do anything, at least anything right. He won't listen to reason. I cannot remember that boy ever being wrong about anything in his whole life. More than once I have said to him, 'Sonny Boy, your old daddy might be a little smarter than what you give him credit for'."

Mr. Williamson dropped his head not knowing what to say next.

"Thank you for sharing these sentiments with me," George then injected. "Let me add that I have some equal concerns about my daughter. Maude has always been too easily influenced. Her mother and I have just never been able to get that girl to stand on her own two feet.

"Now, J. P., I am not saying that to reflect on your boy, or to imply that he coerced her in any way into this marriage. I hold both of them equally responsible. Maude was old enough to sign that marriage license. She has made her bed, and she will now have to lie in it, even if it is no bed of roses."

The two men stood for a few moments not knowing where to go next. J. P. finally broke the silence. "If what you are telling me is true, then that girl better start growing up fast. It is going to take a strong woman to stand up to Todd's mother."

Mr. King had some appreciation for what Mr. Williamson was telling him.

"One thing that does bother me is this war that is going on," John Paul continued. "Todd is likely to be drafted. If the two of them were so determined to get married, I wish they had waited to see what Uncle Sam has in mind for him. I certainly hope they are not planning to start a family anytime soon. They are married now, though, and I guess that is none of my concern."

"J. P., I'm so glad you came over this morning," George said, realizing that this conversation had gone as far as it needed to at the time. John Paul Williamson and George King then agreed that if either of them ever needed to speak with the other about something, that the door would always be open.

The two men shook hands. This was not the last time they would talk.

The news of the wedding spread slowly throughout the twin towns. When Maggie and Millie heard about it, they decided to go together and pay Maude a little visit. She looked surprised when they showed up on Saturday morning. The conversation was jovial.

The two old friends told Maude how romantic it was getting married on Valentine's Day. The new bride admitted that it was not really by design. It just happened to be the Monday after they rented the little apartment. She told them that Todd said there was no reason to wait since they were paying rent. He said the longer they delayed, the more likely somebody would find out.

"I know what he is doing. This way, he will never forget your anniversary," Maggie then said jokingly.

"And he will also have to get you only one gift," Millie added.

Neither of them acknowledged that they heard what Maude had said, and what she had not said.

It was time for some serious girl talk. Maude could not hide her anxieties about what she had done. It was as though she had gotten herself all caught up in a whirlwind.

"Oh, you will be all right," Maggie said, not half believing it herself.

"Of course you will," Millie agreed, not quite so sure either.

"Marriage is not so bad," Maggie added.

"That's easy for you to say since your husband is overseas," Maude replied, with doubt and concern written all over her face.

About that time, Todd came walking through the door on his lunch break. The new bride went scrambling into the little kitchen. Maude's friends extended to the groom their hands and their congratulations. He did not say much. They knew it was time for them to leave.

This was the last time the three former classmates would all be together for the next year and a half. So much had happened to these young women during that same span of time leading up to that moment. Nothing could prepare them for what was yet ahead. Neither was there any way for them to grasp the significance of the vow The Three Musketeers had pledged to each other the night before they graduated from high school less than a year earlier.

Wounded Pride

Todd could not have been more pleased with the way things worked out. Maude had only one menstrual flow after they were married. She then conceived his child just as he had imagined.

Sometimes the best-laid plans just do not pan out, however. In September 1942, Todd received his draft notice to report for military duty, even though he was a married man with a child on the way.

Todd Williamson's unceremonious induction into the army was nothing to write home about. Nonetheless, the new recruit was certain many of the others present that day did exactly that. What happened the day he swore his allegiance to defend the United States of America would haunt him the rest of his life.

The Kings and the Williamsons all met at the bus stop to see him off. George and Ruby said their solemn goodbyes to their son-in-law. Leaving Maude was more painful than Todd imagined, even though he was still having problems sorting out his feelings for his wife.

Then, there were his parents. John Paul shook his son's hand and wished him well. He then stepped aside. Todd's mother hugged her son with the stiffness of a wagon tongue in need of some axle grease.

The draftee took the bus to Chattanooga, and then the train through Atlanta, to Fort Gordon in Augusta, Georgia for his six weeks of basic training. Still in civilian clothes, the inductees were assigned to their barracks. They were told where to pick up their uniforms.

Orders went out for the new recruits to assemble for roll call at 6:00 a.m. the following morning. The motley group would then be sworn in as soldiers of the United States Army.

Todd's sleep was fitful. This was the first time he had ever been away from home. Like the others in bunks up and down the long narrow building, he wondered if he would ever see home again.

At 5:00 a.m. sharp, the soon-to-be-soldier was awakened by something that was about to become a routine part of his life. The platoon bugler shattered the silence with the reveille. Todd put on his uniform for the first time. It was a little loose on his thin frame. His shiny new shoes were a bit too snug.

At the appointed hour, the new recruits formed a line in front of the drill sergeant. He looked at his clipboard, and he then started calling out names. One by one, the ragtag bunch responded that they were present and accounted for.

The sergeant hesitated as he got near the bottom of the list. He looked at the next name again. He then blared out "**Toad Allgood Williamson**." An immediate roar of laughter went all up and down the line. The lieutenant standing beside the sergeant shouted, "Ten-Hut." Order was quickly restored.

Todd was panic-stricken. He stood paralyzed. The drill sergeant then repeated the mispronounced name.

"It is TODD Allgood Williamson, sir," the humiliated young man was finally able to say.

It seems that when the clerk was typing up the list, the ribbon on the old manual typewriter was just about used up. When he struck the first "d" in Todd's name, only the bottom part of the letter printed. His name looked every bit as if it were "Toad" on the form.

This north Georgia soldier boy was branded. To the adrenalin pumped bullies in his outfit, the private's first name was "Toad." If wounded pride mattered very much to the military, Todd Williamson would have been awarded a Purple Heart on the very first day.

Lucille Moore, Ruby's baby sister, had a special fondness for Maude. Like her siblings, Aunt Lucy did her part helping the Kings both times when Ruby was down after giving birth.

It did not seem to bother Lucille that folks thought she was a little odd. She never really understood why some boys got a whipping at school for calling her Looney Lucy. She rather liked that description of herself.

As she saw things, there were plenty of strange people in the world. Most were just not as open about their peculiarities as she was about hers. It was no disgrace to be a spinster, either. Some men and women were just not the marrying type. If busybodies wanted to call her an old maid, then she guessed they had a right to.

Lucille was a few inches taller than Ruby. Her hair was also black, but she began graying in her late 20s. The unmarried woman always kept it cut short.

More than a few eyebrows were raised when Lucille announced that she was moving to Jacksonville, about twenty miles west toward Chattanooga. While she had no prior experience, the local doctor agreed to train her to become his assistant. Over the back fence, the issue was discussed privately as to exactly what kind of assistance old Doc Elliott needed.

When Dr. Ross Elliott finished medical school, the Jacksonville townspeople put out a plea for him to locate there. The community was little more than a wide place in the road. The young physician knew that he barely passed his exams. He would never be comfortable in a big city with other more able doctors looking over his shoulder.

As an incentive, the community leaders agreed to purchase the old Jackson home place. They made the massive house available to Dr. Elliott for use as both a residence and an office.

In return, the physician pledged never to turn people away who were unable to pay for his services. Actually, that was already a part of his professional oath, but it made the pact sound more official. If Doc Elliott ever decided to leave Jacksonville, the facility already belonged to the town.

The Jackson place, dating back to around the turn of the twentieth century, was by far the most impressive building along the main road that went right through the village. Porches wrapped almost all the way around the house. The physician took the parlor off to the right and made it his office. Adjoining space was converted into an examining room and a pharmacy.

Many of the outbuildings were torn down through the years, but one good-sized structure that once served as the servant quarters remained. The physician fixed it up for his daughter Jane, but she soon moved back into the main house. Now, he was making it available to his assistant for her residence.

Maude gave up the little apartment after her husband was drafted. She moved back in with her parents, once again living in her mother's house. The Williamsons offered for her to stay with them, but she was never very comfortable around Todd's mother.

Maude's Aunt Lucy was just settling in about the time Todd went into the service. While he was in basic training, she sent word for her niece to come for a visit. Busses ran every day connecting the two towns.

Aunt Lucy's invitation provided a welcomed break. The expectant mother stayed almost two weeks with her aunt before going back to Mason. After Todd got a letter from his mother informing him of what his wife had done, he wrote to Maude expressing his displeasure.

When Todd boarded the bus that morning in Mason, it was still a little more than three months before Maude's due date. There were no leave passes while he was in basic training. After he was reassigned to Fort McPherson in Atlanta, he was able to go home once before his daughter was born.

When word got to his base via Western Union that the little girl had arrived, Todd's master sergeant gave him an immediate three-day pass. He took the train to Chattanooga, and then caught the last bus leaving for Mason. If the baby had come a little earlier, he would have been home for Christmas. Emma Louise Williamson was born on December 26, 1942.

Ruby's son-in-law was not prepared for what he encountered when he got off the bus. The baby was born at the Kings' house. Dr. Gilbert Worth from Mountain Home got there in plenty of time. Everything went about as routinely as giving birth to a child could.

That is except for the histrionics of Maude's mother. She fainted twice during the day. Ruby was now keeping watch and ordering everyone around. She was also serving as the gatekeeper to the room where mother and daughter were getting used to each other.

Todd was not granted immediate passage when he arrived. He was informed that his wife and the newborn were resting. About an hour later, the new father finally got in to see his baby girl.

Todd was overcome with emotion. For the first time, he had a bit of understanding for his own father when Katherine was born. Because just like that, Emma Lou did something that no other female had ever been able to accomplish. She stole Todd's heart.

Todd was hoping that he could shake the "Toad" image after basic training. It was not to be. While a number of the inductees were shipped overseas, about a dozen of them went with him to Ft. McPherson. The young recruit had never mentioned his moniker to any of his family members.

While his mother's letter to the draft board did not keep him from being called up, Todd's commanding officer had to agree with her on one thing. Ethel Williamson's son did not have the temperament to be a fighting soldier. He was therefore trained to be in a support role as a supply clerk.

Todd had illusions of remaining stateside throughout the war. He worked hard at his assignments. He tried as best he could to befriend those with authority over him. It did not bother him at all that his buddies called him a bootlicker.

Pitched from Pillar to Post

Doc Elliott was a widower. He was single when he moved to Jacksonville. The young physician soon became enamored with Mary Kate McWhorter, the church organist. More people were at the Jacksonville Baptist Church on their wedding day than anyone could ever remember, even for a funeral. A musician was borrowed from the Methodist Church to play "The Wedding March."

When the Elliotts' son Malcolm was born, Doc had enough time to get Dr. Gilbert Worth to come deliver him. However, when they were expecting Jane, Mary Kate went into labor one night almost a month before her husband thought she was due. She sent Malcolm running to fetch his father. Doc was playing poker with the boys, and they were taking a little snort after each hand.

The physician/husband got to the house to find his wife passed out on the floor. He was able to save the baby girl, but Mary Kate died of hemorrhaging. The next morning he could hardly remember what happened the night before.

The young doctor went into deep grief. He was in no way prepared to raise his children alone. Mary Kate's mother came to live with them for a time while he tried to find a nanny. In the course of four years, five nannies came and went.

The struggling father finally gave up and just hired a maid. Miss Liza soon became an indispensable part of the household. She had been with Doc for twenty-three years when Lucille moved into the old servant quarters.

The country doctor was not an imposing figure. He stood only five foot six inches tall, and he had let a few extra pounds gather around his waist. His eyes were still good, but he had to have glasses when reading, or examining a patient. Doc Elliot's shoulders had become more rounded with each passing year. He always began the day with a coat and tie, but his suits had begun to look a little seedy.

Maude and the baby were pitched from pillar to post for the next few weeks after Emma Lou was born. They divided their time between the Kings and the Williamsons. The teenage mother appreciated help, but she felt she was still being treated like an adolescent.

When Aunt Lucy again beckoned, Maude took Emma Lou and they stayed with her for two weeks during the spring of 1943. The house was small, but it did have running water. It also had an indoor bathroom. Both her parents and the Williamsons were still making use of an outhouse.

Living with Aunt Lucy did have a couple of other important benefits as well. Miss Liza kept the baby's diapers washed and folded. There were also leftovers from the meals prepared for the doctor and his daughter.

Todd was once again very unhappy with this arrangement. He found a little furnished apartment just off base as soon as he could. The army private went home on leave, and he took his wife and daughter back with him to Atlanta. This was the first time the three of them were able to live together as a family.

The soldier had regular hours, and he came home for supper every night. The little girl enjoyed her daddy's attention. Maude, on the other hand, was still struggling with her domestic duties.

Pvt. Williamson was holding out hope that he would be able to ride out the war where he was stationed. The Allies were not gaining any ground on the Axis Powers, though. Those at the base kept hearing murmurs about a big build up underway. The next year would be pivotal.

Todd got his orders soon after Emma Lou's first birthday. His outfit was being shipped to England as part of the support effort for the big push. During leave time before he deployed, he moved his little family back to Mason. He then told his wife emphatically that he did not want her spending time in Jacksonville with her aunt.

On February 22, 1944, Todd's family gathered one more time at the bus stop in Mason to say goodbye. This time Kathy got out of school to see her big brother off. None of them had any idea if or when they would see him again. In Chattanooga, he caught the train headed north this time toward New York City.

Leaving Emma Lou was especially difficult. Todd wondered if his daughter would even remember him when he got back.

The morning Todd boarded the bus, Ethel Williamson was not only carrying an ache in her heart, but a rather severe one in her right side as well. She mentioned the sharp pain to J. P. the night after their son left. Her husband was concerned, but he naturally assumed that his wife was experiencing some physical discomfort that corresponded to her emotional distress.

The next morning after Ethel was up and down all night doubled over, John Paul summoned Dr. Worth. The small town physician suspected that Ethel had appendicitis. If that were indeed the case, she needed attention as soon as possible.

The general practitioner went to Morgan's General Store, and he called the hospital in Chattanooga. He alerted the staff that he was bringing in a patient for emergency surgery. Dr. Worth drove as fast as he could. Ethel felt every bump in the road. J. P. comforted and consoled his wife as best he could.

By the time she went under the knife, her appendix had ruptured and peritonitis had set in. The physicians tried in vain to get some of the new wonder drug penicillin, but it was all being sent overseas to treat wounded soldiers. Ethel had only a fifty-fifty chance of survival. If she did, she would be laid up for weeks.

Mrs. Williamson's first word when she regained consciousness was "Todd." As she became more coherent, she more or less demanded that Dr. Worth send a telegram to her son's commanding officer with an urgent request for Todd to be released from the army as a hardship case. Unusually long for a wire message, the physician tried to explain the seriousness of his patient's condition, and the financial strain her family would be under due to the cost of her medical care.

Todd was surprised when he was pulled off the ship just before it set sail. His case was sent higher up for review. The panel was immediately skeptical when it opened the soldier's file and found the other letters his mother had sent trying to get her son discharged. The military authorities determined that the Williamsons' difficulties were not sufficient to overrule the hardship the country was experiencing at that time.

Todd could not help but wonder if his mother willed herself into this affliction. He knew beyond any shadow of doubt that she loved him so much that she would have deliberately inflicted the pain upon herself, if it might help him.

Todd was reassigned to another platoon shipping out in two days. While he had little money in his pocket, he was able to get out and see parts of the big city. He regretted that his mother's malady did not keep him from going to the battlefront, but at least she had done him a big favor. He would now be separated from those insufferable recruits in his unit who had treated him with such indignity.

After the unscheduled delay, Todd Williamson walked the plank to board the next huge liner about to embark with a boatload of soldiers. While there were some decent fellows in his first outfit, he would not miss any of them. He hoped never to run into even one of them again before he returned home.

Once on board, Pvt. Williamson was directed to his tiny room. He would share the cabin with another GI. One bed was stationary, and the other suspended above it with chains. He was hoping that he would be able to claim the lower bunk.

When he found the room, Todd noticed that the door was slightly ajar. He pushed it open to the drawl of, "Well, come on in 'Toad' and make yourself right at home."

Todd knew his roommate only by the name of Tex. It seemed old Tex came down with a round of nasty diarrhea the day they were supposed to set sail. While the medical officer suspected it was just too much partying and a case of nerves, he could not risk exposing a shipload of soldiers to some contagious stomach disorder.

Tex was all better now, and part of Todd's new unit. There was no way on God's green earth or high seas that he could prevent the good old boy from Texas from spilling the beans regarding that gawd-awful nickname.

Todd was seasick for the first two days on the high seas. On the third, he managed to get out and get some fresh air. He then returned to his little compartment, and he decided to write Maude a letter. He did not know when he would be able to post it, but it would be ready.

In his brief note, he mentioned his seasickness to his wife. He assured her this was unlike anything that he had ever experienced. Before he stopped and thought about what he was doing, Todd wrote to her about Tex, and the "Toad" thing. However, he made her promise not to share this bit of information with anyone.

Later that day, he noticed a mail drop near the mess hall. Todd decided to go ahead and put the letter in so that it would go out its next opportunity. Immediately after he let go of the envelope and watched it go down the chute, he regretted that he had said anything to Maude about his dreadful nickname.

Maude and Emma Lou once again spent a few days with the Kings, and then they would move in with Todd's parents for a while. Ruby ran the show when they were at her place. The young mother was ever under the watchful eyes of Ethel at the Williamsons' house.

When Aunt Lucy sent Maude a letter inviting her and the baby to come back for an extended visit, the young army wife did not know what to do. Todd made it plain that he did not want her staying with her aunt. The young mother, on the other hand, was now struggling to keep her own head above water.

Unable to make a decision on her own, Maude talked the situation over with her father. George understood her predicament perfectly. He offered to drive his daughter and granddaughter to Jacksonville, since she would need to carry along more than she could take with her on the bus.

Todd Williamson's new outfit pulled out of the New York harbor on February 26, 1944, and landed in Liverpool about a week later. The platoon then went by truck convoy to a base just outside London. The rail lines had been bombed, so no trains were running. The Allies were just trying to hold on. Rumors persisted of a big invasion in the works. Regardless of the outcome, it would likely turn the tide of the war, one way, or the other.

The soldier was now far from home amidst unimaginable destruction and devastation. Sirens often went on and off all night. Bomb blasts sometimes shook the buildings and lit up the night sky.

As a supply clerk, Pvt. Williamson mostly shuffled papers, and made sure the laundry was stacked properly. One of his more pleasant duties was that of being the mail handler. There was no way for him to know it at the time, but he was launching a career.

This job allowed the soldier to rummage through the parcels before mail call. Of course, he always looked for anything with his name on it first. He was able to read his mail before others got theirs.

It was no secret that Todd was not the most popular private in his unit. Neither was he above withholding mail for a few days from those that he felt were taunting him. During mail call, the clerk took pleasure in shaking his head, and looking pitiful when somebody he loathed insisted that there must surely be something in the bag for him.

Todd Williamson hated this bloody war. He found little ways to amuse himself. If his clandestine hobbies helped settle some scores, then so much the better.

Mercy Percy

Like his father, Earl King was a little on the stout side. The way he saw it, hard times were not going to last forever. He had learned a thing or two watching his daddy trading and bartering. Earl decided not to spend his life toiling to make a living through manual labor. He would follow in his father's footsteps, but what he had in mind selling would bring in more revenue.

When Earl went into the army, he never quite figured out how it happened, but somehow he became a mess sergeant stationed in Texas. When his three-year stint was up, he got his discharge.

The officer who helped him fill out his papers asked Earl if he was going to join the reserves. Trouble was already brewing in Europe, and most people believed that it was only a matter of time until war would break out. Earl respectfully declined. The man sitting behind the desk reminded him that he could still be called back up.

"Then you better send more than one man to get me if that happens," Earl responded. Sgt. King's separation papers were signed without further delay.

Earl did a lot of thinking while he was in Texas. He could foresee a time when mules would no longer till the soil. After his discharge, the army veteran pulled up his stakes and moved to Adamsonville, Georgia, county seat of Chappell County where cotton was king. The Central of Georgia Railroad came right through town. So did the Coosapoosa River.

Earl King put on his only suit of clothes one morning, grabbed his hat going out the door, and walked in unannounced at the new Adamsonville Savings & Loan Association. After a brief wait, he was escorted into the office of President Woodrow Coleridge.

Earl told Mr. Coleridge that he wished to open a tractor dealership in Adamsonville. The executive wanted to know what kind of collateral the young man had to back this venture. Earl was thrifty, and he had put aside most of his military pay. Yet, it was a paltry sum compared to what was required for a startup company. The aspiring entrepreneur was told that his loan application would be given consideration, but for him not to get his hopes up.

When the governing body met the following Monday, the votes were unanimous in denial. Then, Marvin Prince, one of the board members, started thinking about the proposal afterward. Adamsonville really did need a tractor dealership. The timing was right. He called Earl to come back in to discuss the matter with him privately.

Mr. Prince informed the winsome chap that the only way he would qualify for a loan was if he had a partner to back him. Earl certainly did not have within his circle of friends such a person. Marvin Prince then looked young King straight in the eye. He asked him if he was interested in the two of them working together.

Over the next few days, they hammered out all the details. Mr. Prince would largely fund the dealership, and Earl would run the day-to-day operation. Marvin decided to maintain an office in the business so that he could refer financing to the savings and loan.

Since Mr. Prince was considerably the older of the two, they agreed that when the business was profitable enough, the junior partner could buy the other out if he wished. Within three years, the King and Prince Implement Company was selling more putt-putt John Deere tractors than any other franchise in the State of Georgia.

Without missing a beat, Earl King made himself at home in Chappell County. Right off the bat, he started running into folks with his same last name. Kings were early settlers in the area. Their roots went deep.

The Atkins family over in the Naptowne Community bought the first John Deere from the King and Prince Implement Co. They decided to barbecue a shoat and invite all the neighbors to see their new tractor. The handsome and very much available young bachelor who made it happen was the honored guest.

Miss Frances McGuffey, Mr. Coleridge's executive secretary at the savings and loan, was one of the county's true blue bloods. She took Earl by the arm and introduced him around. Miss Fanny was the area's resident expert on everybody's business. She knew who the real Daughters of the American Revolution were, and those whose genealogy had to be stretched a bit.

While Miss McGuffey was enlightening the new resident as to who was related to whom, she was also sniffing around Earl's pedigree. He really did not know much about his heritage beyond his grandparents. He was, nevertheless, very familiar with the North/South controversy, and how the towns of Mason and Dixon got their names.

When Miss Fanny found out that Earl's great-grandfather on his mother's side was a North, she let out a big, "Mercy Percy!" Then she exclaimed, "The woods around here are full of Norths. And they are all good people." Miss McGuffey then got everybody's attention so that Earl could tell the Mason-Dixon tale to the entire group.

The young entrepreneur was so friendly and personable that the Kings and the Norths decided to claim him as kin, whether he actually was or not. Being accepted as family certainly had its advantages. The eligible young bachelor was invited to many social gatherings. On the other side of the ledger, some of his so-called kinfolks wanted family prices when they did business with him.

Marvin Prince, Earl King's business partner, had a daughter named Mary Elizabeth. The Princes were not paupers. When she graduated from college, they threw a big reception in her honor. Mary Beth was the first female on either side of the family to get a college degree. She took her first two years at Adamson State College, and then she finished at the Georgia Teachers College for Women in Milledgeville.

While Earl had heard all about Mary Beth, the two had never actually met. That is, until the night of the reception. Earl was smitten. Apparently, so was Mary Beth. They started seeing each other on a very regular basis.

Mary Elizabeth Prince had that all American girl look about her. Her medium length sandy hair blended in beautifully with her fair complexion and blue eyes. One of the first things that the young bachelor noticed was her pleasant smile. It was beckoning.

Earl and Mary Beth were soon the talk of the town. It was hardly a surprise to anyone when the two announced their engagement six months later. Earl jokingly said that instead of having to buy him out, it would be a whole lot easier just to inherit his partner's share of the business.

Baby News

May 1, 1944

Dear Todd,

(Lifting the pen from the paper, Maude wondered if she should have said "My Dearest Todd." It was too late now. The tablet was already thin.

Getting more writing paper would not be easy with the war going on. Everything seemed to be in short supply, especially money. She could not afford to waste a single sheet.

Besides that, Maude was not sure how her husband would react if she expressed emotion. As her father-in-law put it when they went by to tell his parents that they were married, "Todd is serious-minded." Apparently, that bit of advice was supposed to help guide the new bride as the couple began their life together.

She already had some inkling of what John Paul Williamson meant. During their brief courtship, Todd never actually told her that he loved her. While he seemed quite adept in expressing himself when things did not go to suit him, her husband seemed unable to say much of anything that involved a sentiment. If his wife reached out to him in a way that leaned toward tenderness, it made him uncomfortable. So, perhaps this was the correct way to begin this most significant letter to her man off in the war.)

> The weather has been nice here. After that late frost, it really warmed up fast. It is too early to tell if there will be any apples this year. Almost everyone has gardens planted by now.

(This kind of news would interest Todd. Even so, Maude felt a sudden knot in her stomach. Her husband probably already knew what she was saying. His mother wrote to him a couple of times a week. No matter what the young wife tried to do or say, she was smacked right in the face with the harsh reality that she was playing second fiddle to Ethel Allgood Williamson. Maude married a mama's boy, and there were no two ways about it.)

> Little Emma Lou misses you so much. You would not believe how much she is changing every day. She loves to hold your picture and say, "Da Da." I do hope this war is over soon, and you get to come home.

(Maude put the pen down. She had come to the moment of truth. Yet, truth had little to do with the unexpected news that this war bride was about to disclose. She had run it through her mind over and again, trying to find a way to phrase what she must tell her husband. Nothing sounded right. After walking around the room several times, she looked in on Emma Lou who was fast asleep.)

By the way, you are going to be a daddy
again.

Your devoted wife,
Maude
(Todd would certainly not hear this news first from his mother.)

Maude and Todd had exchanged a couple of letters while she was still
in Mason. They were getting used to correspondence moving at a snail's
pace. The brief note about another baby on the way was the first one that she
had mailed from Jacksonville. She knew her husband was not going to like
the return address. What concerned her more, though, was what his reaction
was going to be when he read what was inside.

Days passed as Maude and little Emma Lou settled into some routines
with Aunt Lucy. When she was not helping Doc, Lucille took in sewing to
make a little extra money. Maude's aunt was also giving her niece some
valuable lessons in the art of stitching on her old Singer Sewing Machine.

Ruby and Maude never bonded. They did few mother-daughter things.
With no one else in the family to help guide her, Maude did not learn much
about the art of homemaking. After they were married, she wondered what
Todd had seen in her.

Maude looked out one afternoon and saw the mailman pulling away
from the box. The clock was striking 2:00 p.m., and she had just put her
daughter down for a nap. Since Aunt Lucy was peddling away on the sewing
machine, Maude went to get the mail.

The army wife had been thinking about Todd all morning. She went
out the door wondering if he had received her letter telling him about the
baby news. Even so, not enough time had passed for her to receive his reply.
She could only imagine the look on her husband's face when he read that last
sentence informing him that he was going to be a daddy again. What had this
Musketeer gotten herself into?

The letter in the box was addressed to:
Mrs. Todd Williamson
C/O Lucille Moore
Jacksonville, Ga.
The return address said it was from Mr. & Mrs. J. P. Williamson.

Maude waited until she got back inside to open the envelope. The first
thing that caught her attention was a quarter and a dime taped to the page

inside. She carefully removed them before reading what it said:

May 13, 1944

Dear Maude,

> We regret that you are spending so much
> time with your family that we do not get to
> see our little granddaughter Emma Louise.

(Well, there was nothing subtle about that. Maude knew that Mrs. Williamson did not like her. Why would the woman even pretend they missed seeing her? She took some pleasure in believing that no girl was good enough for Todd, at least in his mother's eyes.)

> We know money is tight, so we have
> included bus fare so you can visit us soon.

(It was not even signed.)

Yes, money was in short supply. Since she had no permanent address, Todd's little government check was sent to his parents' house. Mrs. Williamson insisted on getting it cashed to save Maude the trouble. The soldier's wife was not even sure how much her husband was paid.

Getting the letter was not all bad news. Maude should pay her in-laws a visit. She needed to go ahead and tell them that another baby was on the way before they heard it from Todd.

She had not yet told her own parents, either. She would pay them all a visit very soon. With seemingly good news to share, Maude was, nevertheless, apprehensive about how it would be received.

On May 14, 1944, Todd Williamson went to meet the supply wagon. The soldiers were in urgent need of towels, soap, and especially disinfectant. These items were supposed to be in that shipment. He hoped a sack of mail was also on the truck. It was.

Without letting anyone see the bag, Todd took it and hid it in the barracks. After getting the supplies shelved, he started secretly rummaging through the parcels. This was the time that he most enjoyed his little sideline. Two letters would not be delivered from this batch. They would have to wait until the next mail call. The mail clerk felt so empowered that he could punish those guilty of mocking him.

Not far into the stack, Todd saw an envelope with his name on it. He recognized his name in Maude's now familiar handwriting, but in his haste, he did not even notice the return address. He put it aside.

Near the bottom, he discovered one from his mother. He tucked both letters away until he finished getting all the mail sorted. Pvt. Williamson then went into a closet, closed the door, and proceeded to open his mail. He would read the one from his mother first. Of course, he would.

May 3, 1944

My dearest child,

(Well that was certainly true. Todd was an only child for almost nine years. Then, a little sister showed up. He saw Katherine as nothing but a nuisance, siphoning off precious time that should be reserved for him. The only good thing about having a new baby around was that his father had something else to occupy his attention. At least his daddy was not on his case all the time.)

There is not much news since I last wrote to you. Daddy heard on the radio that the bombing of Britain has slowed a bit. I hope you are safe.

(Todd would get a letter off to reassure his mother again that he was not in a serious peril.)

We don't get to see much of Maude and Emma Louise. They stay mostly with the Kings. We have heard through the grapevine that your wife and daughter are spending most of their time with her mother's sister over in Jacksonville again. I don't like it. I know how much it concerns you that your daughter is under the influence of that crazy Moore woman.

(Todd was not pleased to get that news at all. His wife was defying him again. He could feel his blood begin to boil.)

Your daddy is busy getting the gardens plowed and planted. You know how he is. Every year he jumps the gun, and then he usually has to replant at least part of the vegetables. I am afraid the late freeze got the apples. They were in full bloom when it came. If the cold snap did not get them, then the worms will.

My side is finally getting better. The doctor said it is nothing short of a miracle that I survived. I can sleep most nights without much pain.

Ethel Williamson signed her letter as she always did – Your Mother. Nothing else was required.

Just as Todd was putting the single sheet of paper back in its envelope, an alarm went off calling all personnel to command their posts. Maude's letter would have to wait. He stuffed it in his pocket.

The distress signal created quite a stir. The company had to move out immediately. Intelligence reports came back that the Germans had discovered their location and warplanes were on the way. After hastily loading the supplies and grabbing his belongings, Pvt. Williamson climbed aboard a military truck. Mail call would have to wait.

Sandwiched between two burly soldiers, one of them asked "Toad" if he had enough room. The others laughed. He pretended not to notice, but he was taking names.

Todd tried to figure out a way to read the letter from Maude without anyone seeing him. Else, they would know that mail had arrived before they were forced to move out. He decided not to risk it. There would be time enough after they were relocated. It was almost dark anyway, and he had already read the important mail.

As the balky army trucks lumbered along through the night, the soldier boy so far from home tried to get some sleep. When he dozed, the vehicle hit a bump. Todd's mind began to drift. His plan to avoid being called to active duty had failed miserably. Since he was drafted anyway, he wished at times that he had abandoned his ploy. Then again, there was Emma Lou.

With no one to talk to, Todd tried to sort out his feelings for Maude. He remembered how excited he was watching his plan as it was unfolding. It amazed him how Maude went right along with his scheme.

She would not be one of those bossy wives. He was not worried about keeping her under control, although the news about his wife and baby again staying with her aunt bothered him. He was not at all concerned about Maude coming between him and his mother.

Todd's mind drifted back to their wedding night. As they prepared for bed, about the only thing that he had to fall back on was growing up around livestock. He had seen the bull mount the milk cow, and he wondered how it felt. He witnessed the hens submitting to the rooster. More than once, he had to separate the dogs when they got hung up.

He tried to imagine how humans actually do it. Fortunately for him, Maude understood that she was to lie on her back and open her legs. He figured out the rest.

Todd and Maude had repeated the act a number of times since. They went for weeks without doing it after Maude conceived, though. Todd did not want to do anything that might put the baby at risk.

Then, he was drafted anyway, and that created periodic separations. During the time they lived in Atlanta, he and his wife engaged in sexual relations at least a couple of times a week. He remembered the last time they were together, the night before he left for New York.

Todd had to admit he missed that part of being a husband. He had learned how to take charge. When he mounted his wife, he enjoyed how she was so submissive to him. He was the bull of the woods. He was the cock of the walk. He was in control.

Not once had Todd given even a single thought as to whether Maude was enjoying what they were doing. Except for keeping her eyes closed tightly, if she was, or if she was not, she had never given him any indication one way or the other.

After meandering along until just past midnight, the convoy finally reached its destination. The trucks had to drive without headlights so as not to be spotted by surveillance planes. Todd had no idea where they were other than obviously still in Great Britain.

It took all the next day for the GIs to get their gear unloaded and organized in their new quarters. Todd thought for sure that he would finally get a chance to read Maude's letter, but the sergeant called lights out before he had any opportunity.

The next morning in the makeshift mess hall, his commanding officer asked if any mail had caught up with the company. When the clerk answered in the affirmative, an announcement was made that mail call would follow breakfast.

For once, Pvt. Williamson did not get to read his mail any earlier than the rest of the soldiers. At least that was true of one letter. After the mailbag was emptied, Todd slipped back to his bunk. This time he did see the return address. As he opened the note from Maude with a grimace already on his face, he noticed immediately how brief it was.

His eyes quickly perused the single page, all old news that he had already heard from his mother. He then did a double take when he read the last line. What?

"And by the way, you are going to be a daddy again."

How could this be? Was it a cruel joke? This soldier boy was not expecting this kind of news. Just think. He had been carrying around this message for the better part of two days. Todd looked up at the top of the page and saw that it was dated May 1. May Day!

The young private's mind was suddenly in a whirl. He was visibly shaken. How could this have happened? He remembered well that she was on the rag on their second anniversary. They only did the deed one time afterward, and that was on the night before he got on the bus.

Much to his delight, his wife conceived within two months after they got married. Now she was with child again? This time it did not thrill him. To make matters worse, his wife and daughter were both back under the influence of loony Aunt Lucy. "Toad" Williamson was not a happy camper.

After reading his wife's letter, the strain of the day had taken its toll on Pvt. Williamson. He did not even notice the other GIs in his barracks watching him while trying not to be obvious. Todd had always been shy and reserved, but there was no place for modesty in the service. Slipping out of his fatigues, he knew even that old army cot was going to feel good tonight.

He reached for his pillow to pull down the covers. Yikes! A frog leaped on his bare chest, and then it went jumping in a panic across the room amid the pandemonium.

"Good night, 'Toad'!" a chorus of male voices rang out.

Uncle Sam's mail service was somewhat unreliable for a while after that.

Things did not go much better for Pvt. Williamson the day after the frog incident. He wanted to report the prank to his superior officer. In his mind, what those soldiers did was worthy of court martial proceedings. Even so, Todd knew that he would get no sympathy. To make things even worse, everywhere he turned, he was confronted with a devious face grinning like a possum.

Todd had only one fellow private that he considered a friend. Strange as it might seem, it was Tex. Even though he was usually right in the middle of the antics, the Texan usually came by later and apologized to Todd.

About mid-morning, Tex sought out the despondent soldier. His friend tried to get him to understand that these boys were all nervous and apprehensive about the dangers they were in and the unknowns ahead. They would not admit it, but most of them were scared to death. He further tried to explain that humor was a great release for their pent up fears. He encouraged Todd not to take everything so seriously, to join in, and to be a good sport.

Getting familiar with new surroundings yet again, these soldier boys had figured out that they were not in England to put down stakes. They would not call any place home for very long until they got back to their roots.

Todd was still trying to get a handle on the news from Maude. In his master plan, a child was just a necessary step to help him avoid the military. Now, another baby was on the way.

Maybe this child would be a boy. He had his heart set on a son when Emma Lou was born. He envisioned how this would make him feel more like a man. On the other hand, he worried that a son might be closer to his mother. He feared the two of them might shut him out.

If the next child were a girl, Todd had no idea what they would name her. His mother suggested Emma Louise, after her grandmothers. They already had an understanding if they had a son. He would be Todd Allgood Williamson, Jr.

As they were discussing this one day, Maude asked Todd what they would call the boy. She sort of liked Sonny, but he balked at that idea. He could imagine his son becoming a great leader. "Do you think anybody would vote for a senator or a governor with a name like Sonny?" he asked her.

Todd preferred Chipper. "You know, like a chip off the old block," he swaggered. "Now Chipper sounds like a Hall of Fame ballplayer to me," he told his wife.

Things began normalizing for Pvt. Williamson's company in their new headquarters. There was a lull in the fighting. When he had some off duty time, he went out and wandered the streets. He learned that they were in Manchester, a manufacturing area. The Germans had set their sights on the factories early in their assault on Great Britain. They had now moved on to other targets.

The devastation was sporadic. Most of the residential areas were left intact. The people were carrying on as best they could.

On a couple of occasions, Todd was invited to join some of the others from the outfit. He was finding that these boys were for the most part just a bunch of normal guys from rural areas and small towns.

Todd actually felt a little ashamed about withholding their mail when he came to know them better. They were just as anxious to hear from their wives, sweethearts, and parents as he was. That still did not mean he liked it when they called him "Toad."

About a week after the May Day missive, Todd received another letter from Maude. She included a snapshot of herself and Emma Lou. His wife mentioned to him where she was staying. She said that he just did not understand what it was like trying to live with either her mother or his. She told her husband that she talked the situation over with her father, and that he had taken her to Jacksonville.

Daddy King – Todd again had to contend with his old adversary.

One day when it was raining, the private decided to catch up on his correspondence. Before he began his letter to Maude, he put his pen down. It was inconceivable that he was married to her, and they were Emma Lou's parents. He found it particularly difficult to comprehend that another child was on the way. It did not help that he was an ocean apart in such a foreign land.

I Don't Like It

Maude decided that she could wait no longer to make the trip to Mason. The unpaved road from Jacksonville to Mason was bumpy. Emma Lou entertained herself looking out the open window of the bus. Her mother pointed out objects like cows and trees and clouds. The little girl learned so many new words every week. Not long into the trip, she fell asleep snuggled against her mother's side. That was fine with Maude. She needed some time to think.

The house where Todd was raised was only about a quarter mile from the bus stop. Emma Lou walked most of the way holding her mother's hand. The shadows were getting long. The two of them made a game of the daughter trying to stay in her mother's shadow.

The tot got tired before they got there, though. She pitifully begged her mother to tote her the rest of the way. Since Maude was lugging the small suitcase with their belongings, Emma Lou was an armful.

That was not the full extent of her cargo, either. The army wife was also carrying a heavy burden inside, the likes of which could not be weighed on a set of scales. Maude had no reason to believe that the load would ever get any lighter. The circumstances pertaining to the baby news involved a big secret, the mystery of which she had vowed to take with her to her grave.

Emma Lou was reenergized when she saw her doting grandfather. She ran and jumped into his arms. They danced around the room with glee. Maude's mother-in-law was not nearly as exuberant. She reached for the valise, and took it to Todd's old bedroom. Maude traipsed behind, not sure what she was supposed to do or say next.

"How are you doing?" she asked, trying to make conversation.

Mrs. Williamson said that she was feeling much better, although she still did not have all of her strength back since the surgery.

"And how is Kathy?" Maude was very much aware that Todd considered his sibling an annoyance.

Mrs. Williamson responded, "Katherine is such a popular girl in school. Tonight, she is out on a date with the president of the Future Farmers of America." For a lad to be in this position was one of the school's highest honors.

Supper was soon on the table. Maude was hungry. So also was her daughter. When Emma Lou started fretting and nuzzling at her mother's chest, Ethel's disapproval was not hard to interpret. "Isn't that child weaned by now?" she snapped.

Maude lied and said that she was, but that Emma Lou had not gotten used to the idea yet. Under the guise of trying to avoid a scene, the mother picked up the little girl and took her to the bedroom. Behind the closed door, she quickly unbuttoned her blouse.

The young mother knew the little girl needed to be weaned, but she had just not been able to bring herself to do it. Nursing her baby was the most gratifying thing in her life. During those precious moments, no words could describe the closeness she felt to the little one who came from her womb. They emerged a short time later with Emma Lou her bubbly self, now ready to eat some solid food with the family.

Nothing else was said about the incident at the table. As they prepared for bed that night, Ethel murmured, "She didn't fool me one bit. That little girl is not weaned." As J. P. turned out the light, she uttered four more words. "I don't like it."

He reached over to console her, but she had already turned her back to him. As he put his head on the pillow, John Paul wondered how many times he had heard his wife say those words during the twenty-four years they had been married.

The young mother did not sleep too well at the home of her in-laws. Emma Lou was also restless. Maude heard Kathy when she came in from her date, even though the girl tried to be quiet. Maybe Todd's sister would get to see Emma Lou before they went on to the Kings' house.

Morning finally came. Maude was awakened by the sound of the rooster doing his own version of the reveille. That was something she missed staying in Jacksonville. She missed lots of things.

Maude could not decide which parents she dreaded facing most with her news. Emma Louise was the first and only grandchild on both sides of the family. Neither Todd's parents nor hers were excited when the not quite eighteen-year-old bride conceived so quickly after she and Todd eloped. She thought grandparents were supposed to be happy with the prospects of grandchildren.

Just as when she wrote to tell Todd about the baby news, Maude was struggling to find the right words. No matter how many ways she tried to phrase it, nothing sounded right. Ready or not, she soon had to tell her husband's parents, and her own, that another grandbaby was on the way. It was what she could not tell them that made her chore so difficult.

Maude opened the bedroom door to the smell of coffee brewing and bacon frying on the wood stove. The young woman never developed a taste for coffee. That was something grown folks drank. Maybe Emma Lou would sleep a while longer, since she had already made her first visit to her mother's bosom.

"How long are you going to stay with us?" Mrs. Williamson asked, as they sat down to breakfast. Maude told her she guessed that she had better get on over to see her folks sometime later that morning. A big frown came across her mother-in-law's brow.

Maude knew that John Paul would be headed to the gardens right after breakfast. She must not delay. As much as she dreaded what she had to do, she knew that any day now Todd's parents would receive a letter from their son overseas. There was no turning back.

When Ethel stirred to start clearing the table, Maude stopped her in her tracks. "I have some wonderful news to share with you. You are going to be grandparents again." Ethel dropped the saucer and the coffee cup in her hands. The fragile china shattered all over the floor.

"How could you do this?" she railed at Maude. "When Todd gets home, he will have no prospects of a job. And now he will have another mouth to feed?"

There was a clamor to clean up the broken glass. But there was no way to mend the mess that Maude was in.

After the announcement, Ethel Williamson made no further attempt to keep Maude and Emma Lou with them any longer. She told J. P. to come back to the house in about half an hour, and then to take them on over to the Kings'. This would give him time to get everything watered and fed before moving on to the plowing. Aunt Kathy slept through the whole thing.

Maude had one more item of business to attend to before she went on her way. She put it off, too, as long as she could. She addressed her mother-in-law very politely. "Could I please have the money from Todd's paycheck?"

"Do you need it?" Mrs. Williamson shot back. "You are staying down there with your aunt and that well off doctor. Are they not taking care of you?"

"I want to pay my own way. And besides, that money belongs to Todd and me," Maude answered politely.

Ethel gave out a big sigh. She then went back into her bedroom. When she came out, she handed Maude $12.00 all wadded up. She then walked away muttering, "I really do think Todd wants me to keep up with his money for him."

As they put the tattered old suitcase in the backseat, Maude insisted that she could walk the half mile. Her father-in-law would have nothing of it. He said he was just grateful that he had enough gas in the '36 Chevrolet to get there and back. If they were lucky, no tire would blow out.

When they pulled into the yard, Old Blue, the blue tick hound, was not negligent in his watchdog duties. His sonorous yelps startled Emma Lou. George King was sitting on the front porch puffing on a cigar.

"Looks like your Pa is already celebrating," Mr. Williamson said. That was indeed a half-truth. Maude's father was indeed savoring the significance of the few days ahead of him. The cigar had nothing to do, though, with him going to be a grandpa again.

J. P. gave Emma Lou a big hug. He then handed the girl to her mother. He leaned over to Maude and said that he hoped everything would be fine. He shook hands with George, and then quietly drove away.

"Where's Mama?" Maude asked her father, with Emma Lou hanging on tightly while keeping an eye on the dog.

George broke into a big grin. "You mean you did not get the letter she sent you earlier this week? She decided it was time for her to check up on both of her children. Ruby got on the State Line Motor Coach yesterday afternoon headed to Jacksonville. She was then going on to Chattanooga today to catch the Southeastern Motor Lines bus to Adamsonville. Did you just get in last evening? You must have met her somewhere down the line."

It was strange how Ruby could be so un-motherly. Then all of a sudden, it was as if her maternal juices shifted into overdrive for a spell. She had to make up for lost time.

"What have you heard from Earl?" Maude wanted to know.

"Oh, I think his tractor business is doing fine," her daddy replied. "But your mother is all in a tizzy because the boy is now past his mid-twenties, and he has yet to find a wife. She said that it was bad enough for her children to have to grow up with a peculiar aunt. And now she does not want your kids to grow up with a funny uncle."

"Kids" he had said – plural. Something about her father always puzzled Maude. He seemed to know what was going to happen before it actually did. She wanted to be more like that. While she was certainly not slow in school, Maude always wished she could grasp things faster.

Emma Lou's grandpa put out his cigar. He would have to make it last as long as he could. He then turned on the charm and started flirting with his granddaughter. She knew how to be coy. She was after all a female. They enjoyed their little game of cat and mouse until he grabbed her and tossed her over his head. The girl giggled with delight.

"I'm sorry your mother is not here," George King lied to his daughter. He was actually glad to have his big girl and her little girl all to himself. "She left several things cooked for me, but if we run out, I'm sure that you will not let us go hungry." Maude's daddy actually knew his way around the kitchen rather well. When Ruby took to her bed for days at the time, he was able to take care of himself.

Before retiring for the night, Maude decided it was time to share her baby news. She had not rehearsed anything, but the words just came out. It was so much easier to talk to her father than with anyone else.

"Daddy, one of the reasons I came for a visit was so that I could pick up my maternity clothes that are packed away here." She watched for a reaction. She did not have to wait long.

"You are not going to need them again anytime soon are you? Are you going to lend them to someone else?"

"Yes, and no," Maude responded to his questions. It took just a few seconds for this to all sink in.

"Are you telling me that I am going to be a grandpa again?" he quizzed her, with a sly twinkle in his eye.

"Yes, Daddy, that is what I am saying. I have written Todd a letter, but I have not had time to hear back from him."

"Well, I do declare," George sighed. "I'm kind of glad your mother is not here. This would have put her down for days." He then thought to himself, "That's strange. I wonder why Maude waited until now to tell me about this."

The War Baby

Lucille was not surprised to see her sister standing at the door. The mailman was running late on Friday, and Ruby's letter came right after Maude and Emma Lou got on the bus. She was thankful for the warning. She was also glad that Ruby only stayed one night. The physician's assistant had looked forward to some privacy while her other guests were gone.

This untimely visit also put Lucille in a real pickle. Ruby did not know about the baby news. Maude's aunt certainly did not think that she was the one to tell her. She just humored her sister, and then made sure that she was on the bus the next morning headed to Adamsonville.

As John Paul and Ethel Williamson prepared for bed the night after Maude's visit, he was very much aware that nothing else had been said regarding their overnight visitors. It was best to leave his wife alone when she was stewing about something.

When he reached up and pulled the string to the overhead light, darkness enveloped the room. Simultaneously, a pall engulfed the two of them. Ethel started muttering something. J. P. was not sure whether she was speaking to him or not.

"Something is not right about all of this and I don't like it. I just don't like it at all." While he would not give his wife the satisfaction of knowing that he agreed with her, Todd's father did not like it very much either.

At the supper table on Sunday evening, Ethel Williamson was ready to talk. Kathy was off with a church group. "I don't like it," she began. "I don't know how Todd is going to manage when he gets back. How on earth can he support this kind of family? Maude will certainly be no help. It's obvious the only thing she knows how to do."

"Now, Ethel, don't be so hard on the girl," J. P. cautioned.

"Don't be so hard on her? What else can I do? I still have not figured out how that little wench tricked Todd into marrying her. She must have surely raised her skirt. If he had just told me what was going on, I could have talked some sense into his head."

"But Ethel . . ."

"Don't be too hard on her, you say? The least that vamp could have done was keep her legs together until Todd got on the bus so this would not happen."

John Paul really felt sorry for his wife. In her eyes, Maude and Maude alone was responsible for anything and everything.

When she left Jacksonville, Maude did not know how long she was going to stay in Mason. That all depended on how things went. With her mother gone, she might stay for a few days. While he did not always approve of some things she did, Maude knew the one person who accepted her without reservation was her father. If she ever got in trouble over her head, George King might have his say, but he would then do everything in his power to make things work out for the best.

This also gave Maude an opportunity to visit Millie. She missed her friends. When they were coming of age, The Three Musketeers were inseparable. Right now, they needed each other more than ever.

In their youthful virtuousness, none of the girls could imagine the disruptions that this war would bring. They all assumed that they would get married, settle down, and raise their families as generations had done before them. Nothing had prepared them for these difficult and trying times.

When the war broke out, Millie and her new boyfriend, Roy Hancock, sat down and talked things over. The severity of the situation made their feelings more intense. This was the first time that either of them had been in love.

Ministers and justices of the peace were doing a booming business. Numerous couples were tying the knot just before soldier boys went off to war. Their services would not be needed in this case, however. Millie and Roy decided to wait until he came home to see if they wanted to get married.

Roy said there was no guarantee that he would get back. In that event, he did not want to saddle Millie with the burden of widowhood. She promised to wait. He pledged to be true.

When he finished his basic training, Roy became a communications technician. He learned quickly that shortwave radio was the most important tool the military had in sending and receiving messages over long distances.

This medium also had another potential use that the government was investigating. Radio could transmit propaganda into enemy homelands. Roy received additional specialized training in this emerging technology.

Hancock did not know it at the time, but he was to be part of a new chapter in audio transmission. The Voice of America was soon beaming messages in German aimed at the civilian population.

A new transmitter was built in California in 1941. Millie's boyfriend was a production engineer when the inaugural Asian broadcasts went out from this station.

Hancock was later sent to Hawaii when a transmitter was established that could send Voice of America programs throughout the Far East. He eventually moved to the Philippines, after those islands were recaptured 1945, where he helped launch radio signals into Japan. Roy was stationed in Manila until he was discharged when the war was over.

Maggie, one of the most popular girls in the community, had been out with several boys. Yet, everyone assumed that she and Donald Vaughn would get married. They certainly lit up the dance floor when they waltzed (or rather jitterbugged and foxtrotted) to the center stage. They always seemed to slip out quietly, though, before the last dance was announced.

Donald was a year ahead of Maggie in school. He joined the army soon after he graduated. He signed up without even talking it over with her, and she was most unhappy with him.

"You are going to be a what?" she stormed.

"A paratrooper," Donald said again.

They had a big fuss and broke up. Only later did Maggie learn what the word meant. Her now ex-boyfriend would be jumping out of airplanes.

On the rebound, Maggie went out with Everett Hogan a time or two when he was home on leave from the navy. He was two years her senior. He could not believe what good fortune had fallen into his lap. He had been in love with Maggie since she was in the seventh grade. There was nothing flashy about Everett. He was solid and steady.

Believing that the Unites States' involvement in the trouble overseas was inevitable, Hogan joined the navy in 1939, hoping to get his tour of duty over beforehand. On a lark, he and Maggie eloped on June 23, 1941, the next month after she graduated from high school. Two weeks later, the groom shipped out to serve with the Pacific fleet. Everett felt that he was the luckiest man alive to have a wife like Maggie. He wanted it to stay that way.

Hogan was at Pearl Harbor on December 7, 1941 in a control tower watching helplessly as Japanese planes swarmed the island. When a shell rattled the building, he and the others had to evacuate. None of them was injured.

He was then reassigned to the naval base in Norfolk, Virginia where he was headquartered from March 1942 until the end of the war. Maggie joined him there. They lived in a little apartment just off the base. In October 1943, Hogan became a crew chief on a newly commissioned submarine headed for the coast of Europe. Maggie moved back in with her parents in Mason.

Maude married Todd Williamson. That was the big bombshell. Neither Millie nor Maggie yet understood how they got past George King. She had now beaten both of them to the punch, as she was the first to become a mother.

The Three Musketeers hardly ever had a chance to be together anymore. Millie still lived with her parents and worked as a bank secretary. She mailed Roy a letter at least once a week.

In the spring of 1944, Maggie relocated to Taylortown, about thirty-five miles from Mason. The navy wife was supporting the war effort working in a factory that made materials for parachutes.

"How long have you known that you are pregnant?" George King asked his daughter the next day.

"I just found out for sure about a month ago," Maude responded.

Her daddy then conjectured. "Well, I guess it is a good thing you are staying in Jacksonville. Old Doc Elliott can look after you."

Maude was really struck by her father's use of the word pregnant. Other than Miss Barnes, her home economics and health teacher, she had never heard anyone else say that word aloud until just a few weeks earlier. Those kinds of things were just not discussed. First, Maggie had shocked both Maude and Millie when she uttered it, and now her father had just used it.

"Daddy, tonight I want to go over to Dixon and see the Mitchells for a while. Do you think you can drive Emma Lou and me out that way? Millie can bring us back in her father's car."

It had not been that long since Millie, Maggie, and Maude had last seen each other. Even so, if any of them could spend some time together, they never wanted to miss a chance. They had so much to talk about with their men overseas in the war. With the unexpected circumstances that materialized so rapidly, Maude really needed a friend right now.

The old school chums had been together twice within the past couple of months. Maggie sent the other two a letter, explaining that she really did need to talk. Millie and Maude took the bus to Taylortown. Two weeks later, they met again in Jacksonville. That was when they took another Three Musketeer vow. This time they entered into a secret agreement that would bond them together forever.

Grandpa King had a few things to see about down at the barn while Emma Lou took her nap. When he got back, they warmed up more of the leftovers that Ruby had cooked up ahead of time. Maude wondered if she would ever be as good a cook as her mother.

After supper, they took the short ride to the Mitchells' house. Emma Lou worked her shy routine, and then she took to Millie's dad. That girl could charm any man on earth. He took her for a walk to see the pigs, and the cows, and the mules. Mrs. Mitchell followed along.

When the two old schoolmates were alone, the emotional dam broke. Maude burst into tears. It had been building up inside her all afternoon.

"What have I gotten myself into?" she pleaded. "I did not even have time to get used to being a wife before Emma Lou came along. I love her dearly, but that child is a handful. And then Todd got drafted, and he's gone, and I don't have a home, and I don't know what I am going to do."

Millie tried to console her, but she did not know what to say.

"What have I gotten myself into?" Maude repeated again.

Both of them knew what she meant, but neither of them had an answer to the question. Millie told Maude how much she admired her for what she was doing, but that she could still get out from under it if she wanted to.

"No," replied Maude. "It's too late. I will just have to reap what I have sown."

Maude's daddy told her that she could stay as long as she wanted to, but he had to deliver a pair of mules to a farmer up in Tennessee on Monday. She stayed through Sunday, and they went to church together. Everyone was glad to see her, but especially Emma Lou. The folks made a big fuss over the little girl, saying how much she had changed in just the short time she had been away.

Todd's parents were there too, and they sat in their usual place. After the services, John Paul came over, took his granddaughter, and showed her off. Ethel never even so much as acknowledged Maude's presence.

The bus came through Mason four times a day, stopping twice going in each direction. On Monday morning, Maude and Emma Lou took the earlier one going west. The young mother had an extra parcel to lug along, a paper sack with the few outfits that her mother made for her when she was expecting Emma Lou. She looked at the watch Todd had given her, and she knew it was time to get going. Her daddy had already left, so she and Emma Lou walked to the bus stop.

The little girl went up and down the aisle a couple of times, and then settled in beside her mother as the motor coach pulled out. It was only a short walk to the old Jackson mansion from where the bus stopped at the general store. When Maude knocked to announce their arrival, she heard no response. She opened the door and started gathering up her belongings.

About that time, Aunt Lucy came from her bedroom with a somewhat puzzled look on her face. "Back already?" she asked. Maude did not even notice that her aunt looked a bit disheveled. Neither did she see someone else slip out the door when she took her parcels back to her room.

Two letters were lying on the dresser, the one from her mother, and another from Todd. They would have to wait a few minutes. Aunt Lucy wanted to hear all about how it went in Mason. Maude said that although nobody seemed excited, things went about as well as she could have expected them to. "Daddy didn't bat an eye, but I am a little concerned about Todd's mother," she added.

"Maybe Ethel was just being her usual self and did not suspect a thing," Aunt Lucy tried to reassure her.

Todd's letter was unusually long. He generally did not have much to say, but this time he went into some detail about his activities. He even told Maude about a few soldiers in his unit, where they were from, and some of the things they were doing together. This made her feel a little better about her husband. The army wife had worried about him not making friends. Todd had obviously not gotten her letter about the baby news when he wrote this one.

On the Friday that Maude left for Mason, Doc Elliott went to Atlanta to restock his pill cabinets. He could order his pharmaceuticals by mail, but he could not get his booze that way. About once a month, he made a trip in his sleek black Packard. Since doctors had to make house calls, they were granted special privileges when it came to gas rationing and purchasing tires.

The country doctor routinely drove out into the backwoods to take care of patients. Without much money, these kindly folks often tried to repay him in kind. About all some of them had to offer was a quart of moonshine. No matter how many times he tried it, Doc Elliott just could not develop a taste for corn liquor. He much preferred bonded whiskey, now legally available again since the repeal of Prohibition.

He knew that he was drinking too much. Life had just not turned out the way he planned. To drown his sorrows, he was turning more and more to the bottle.

All Ross Elliott ever wanted was to be a family physician. Both his father and grandfather before him were morticians. Growing up in and around the funeral home in Chattanooga, young Ross was convinced that too many people were being buried prematurely. Simple basic medical care would have prevented some of their deaths. He dreamed of the time when he could save lives.

While his folks were not wealthy, they did have the means to send Ross to medical school. He was not a dumb kid, but he had never been up against this kind of competition before. Twice, he almost dropped out of school, knowing that he could always continue in the family business. Dr. Elliott persisted. He was not sure of the official ranking of his graduating class, but he never doubted that he was near the bottom.

Getting his practice established in Jacksonville was like a dream come true. While Doc Elliott anticipated that he would have good standing in the community, he was not prepared for just how much he would be held in high esteem. When he married Mary Kate McWhorter, things could not have worked out any better.

She was an ideal wife and mother. Her physician/husband was free to devote his time to taking care of the sick. Much advancement was being made in the field of medicine. In his spare time, the young doctor tried to keep up.

Then, the unthinkable happened. Dr. Ross Elliott lost his beloved wife during childbirth. This was just the kind of unnecessary death that had initially driven the young man to become a doctor. Yet, he was unable to save his beautiful wife. Nightmares haunted him when he went to bed.

The physician knew that he was not much of a parent. Malcolm grew up taking advantage of his father's status in the community to bully his way around. He did not just run with the wrong crowd. He was the ringleader.

Over the years, Doc Elliott put up considerable sums of money to keep his son out of trouble. He was helpless, however, after the accident. Malcolm and his friends had been out partying and drinking. When the car was brought into town, the tangled steel hardly resembled an automobile.

Miraculously, all of the boys survived the crash except the one in the front seat beside Malcolm. The driver was charged with vehicular homicide and sent to prison. The distraught father wept bitterly and openly.

Then, there was Baby Jane. The doctor always wondered if she suffered from oxygen deprivation during her difficult birth. Without a mother to nurture her, the infant was slow in her development. She seemed listless and unmotivated, staying mostly to herself. This was in such stark contrast to her vivacious late mother and her rambunctious older brother.

When Jane was a teenager, rumors circulated around Jacksonville that the girl was just not right. She never finished high school. Jane began cloistering herself within the old Jackson mansion, unconcerned about her personal appearance. For days, she never left the house.

Doc Elliott was still not sure how Jane met Lucille Moore. He never asked. He did know that the two of them had been corresponding for some time. When his daughter suggested that Lucille come and live with them and be his assistant, the struggling physician thought it a good idea. There was no doubt that he needed some help.

Soon, more rumors stirred along the grapevine. Some thought Doc Elliott had moved a mistress into his backyard. The more wary were talking in whispers about something else.

Driving back to Jacksonville, Doc Elliot saw little traffic. Not that many people had the wherewithal to be out on the road. He had lots of time to think. Then again, the reason he kept pouring himself first one drink, and another, and then another each evening was so that he did not have to. What distressed him most was what his beloved late wife and the mother of his children would think about him now.

On one long stretch in the road, the troubled man pushed the accelerator down hard. The Packard responded. The driver never looked at the speedometer. He really did not care how fast he was going. At one point, he considered just veering off into the woods, letting the impact take him out of his misery. He then thought about Jane. What would become of his daughter?

Maude knew it was going to happen. She just did not know exactly what day. The day was Thursday. When she heard the knock at the door, she knew who was on the other side. After being on the bus most of the day, her mother appeared rather haggard. Ruby could have taken the train from Adamsonville to Chattanooga, but it would have cost a dollar more. That was wasted money.

Emma Lou came running to see what was going on. Brushing past Maude, the woman said to the child, "Well, aren't you going to give your grandma a hug?" The girl grabbed her mother's skirt and would not let go.

Aunt Lucy was next door. She had been over in Doc Elliott's office most of the afternoon reorganizing and restocking the pill cabinets. She would be back soon.

They had talked it over ahead of time. Maude offered to sleep in the big house so that her mother could have her room. Aunt Lucy would have nothing of it. She would spend the night in one of the guest rooms, and let her sister have hers.

"Well, I've got news," Ruby blurted out. "But it will have to wait until Lucille gets here so I don't have to tell it twice." Maude had some news of her own. It, too, would have to wait.

"Did you get to see your daddy?" her mother wanted to know. "How are the Williamsons getting along?" she asked before Maude had time to answer.

"I couldn't believe it when I got here, and you were on the bus going in the other direction. A bus was just leaving Saxon's Cross Roads as we were pulling in. I guess you and Emma Lou were on it."

Maude filled her mother in with the barest of details. "Let's walk over to the office and see if Aunt Lucy is about finished," she then suggested, needing her aunt's presence for reassurance.

They were too late. Lucille came walking in the door. "Well, hello again," she said to her sister. "How is Earl getting along?" Before she gave Ruby a chance to respond, she asked, "Are you hungry? I'll bet you haven't had a bite to eat since you left Adamsonville."

Without anything else being said, Aunt Lucy and Maude started putting the leftovers on the table. They had cooked on Wednesday, knowing that Ruby would arrive any day.

Emma Lou had nursed about an hour before her grandma got there. She sat in her highchair like a big girl. The toddler ate a few bites of mashed potatoes and butter beans after her mother crushed them for her. She then turned her nose up at the cup of milk.

"Are you ever going to get that baby weaned?" Ruby scolded Maude.

After the food was put away, it was soon Emma Lou's bedtime. She would want her mother's milk again to put her to sleep. When Maude returned to the sitting room, Ruby was chomping at the bit to tell what she knew. Earl was engaged to be married. She was able to meet his future wife and her parents. Ruby was tickled pink.

So were Maude and Aunt Lucy when Grandma announced that she would only be staying the one night. Ruby had to get back to take care of George. She wondered aloud how that poor man had managed that long without her.

Maude decided to wait until the next morning to share her baby news. She would tell her mother on the way out the door, and then let her daddy handle it from there.

"She was dumbfounded, speechless," Aunt Lucy took some delight in saying, after she returned from walking her sister to the bus. "But I assured her you are in good hands, and that Doc Elliott will be taking good care of you." If Ruby had any idea what was indeed going on, the cat really would have gotten her tongue.

Ruby King left Mason to go check on her two children. Before she got back home, this mother had learned that she was going to have both a new daughter-in-law and a new grandbaby.

Larry G. Johnson

One for All – All for One

When that letter came from Maggie in April 1944 inviting Maude and Millie to come for a visit, both recipients recognized a sense of urgency. If one of the Musketeers was in need, the other two had to reach out.

Millie caught the bus in Mason. Maude and Emma Lou got on in Jacksonville. Millie had brought along a nursery rhyme book to read to the little girl. The mother was glad to have some relief. Neither woman said anything about what they thought might be awaiting them down the road.

Maggie's apartment was sparsely furnished. She had to borrow a chair from a neighbor for all of them to have a place to sit. Emma Lou was about ready for a nap. She was soon asleep after gaining access to her mother's breast. Maude put her down on the bed.

Maggie wished that she had some Cokes to serve her friends, but all she had to offer was a Three Musketeers candy bar and a glass of water. She confessed that she had been craving chocolate.

After they nibbled and took a few sips, the room grew more and more restive. Maude and Millie knew that this was not just a social call. They waited for Maggie to take the lead. They did not have to wait much longer. Just like that, she blurted it out.

"I'm pregnant."

The other two noticed that she used the big grown up word.

Maggie got exactly the kind of initial response that she was anticipating. Both Millie and Maude jumped up and started hugging her. Tears were streaming down the cheeks of all three of them. There were no trite words like congratulations. Their actions said it all.

Then, reality began to set in. "Maggie, you don't look all that pregnant," Millie mused aloud, making a point also to use the "p" word. "Everett has been gone, what, six months now?"

"The baby is not his," Maggie responded, dropping her head.

"Maggie Hogan, what have you done?"

The tears really started flowing. Maude finally took her turn to speak. "Maggie, we're The Three Musketeers. Whatever is going on, we will stand by you all the way."

Millie nodded in agreement.

"Oh, I am so glad to hear you say that. I was afraid that you would get up, and walk out, and never want to see me again," she said, sounding very relieved.

"Maggie, you know better than that," the other two said in unison.

"If you really want us to know, we're all ears," Millie volunteered.

"Are you sure you won't hate me?" Maggie pleaded for reassurance.

Her friends scoffed at the idea.

"Well, make yourselves comfortable. This may take a while."

"We've got until the bus comes back by at three-thirty," Maude said, supportively.

Maggie did not know where to begin. She finally found a starting point. "Everett Hogan is such a good man. I would never want to hurt him for the world. You know he is the one Mama and Daddy wanted me to marry. Everett is so sure and steady. He is the kind of husband no woman could ever doubt. I do love him. I swear I do."

She looked down at her lap. Now came the hard part. She bit her lip.

"But Donald Vaughn is the bad boy who lights my fire. I never forgave myself for breaking up with him the way I did. I found out later that I broke his heart."

Maggie paused again. This was not getting any easier.

"When Donald joined the army, he did not think he would have to go overseas. He was promised that by the recruiter who signed him up. If the United States was drawn into the war, those with seniority would have the option of staying stateside to train those who would deploy. It seems that old Uncle Sam forgot his promise. Or, maybe it was just that Donald wanted to be in the thick of things."

She took a deep breath before continuing. She bit her lip again.

"He came home around the first of February on a weekend pass just before he was to ship out. I heard that Donald was at his parents' house. I wanted to see him so bad so I could apologize to him. I could not bear the thought of something happening to him, never knowing how horribly I felt for what I did."

Again, Maggie hesitated. The other two sat motionless and spellbound, each cradling one of the distraught woman's hands with both of their own.

"There was a dance that Saturday night at the gym. I know I should not have gone. Millie, I am sorry, but I told my daddy that I was going over to your house.

"I could not believe my eyes when I walked in. There was Donald all dressed up in that starched and pressed military uniform. His jet-black hair was all slicked down. So tall and so handsome, he was leaning up against the wall talking to some girls.

"I thought I was going to faint. I knew he saw me come in. I wanted to go over and drag him to the dance floor, and to cut the rug like we had done so many times before. But I knew I was a married woman."

Maggie released her grip. She nibbled nervously on the candy bar and then took a sip of water. She then reached back for the hands of her loyal friends.

"I walked around the gym and spoke to a few people. Then I decided that I had better get out of there. Millie, I swear I was going to come on over to your house. When I got to Daddy's car, Donald was leaning against the driver's side door with that cocksure look on his face. 'Get in' was all I had to say."

Maggie took a deep breath and then continued. "Donald opened the door and crawled in. I got in on the other side and pitched him the keys. 'Where are we going?' he wanted to know. I just said, 'I don't know. You're driving'."

Maggie got up and walked to the door. The other two did not know whether to go to her or not. She just stood there for a couple of minutes looking outside. She then returned to her chair.

"What am I going to do?"

Neither Millie nor Maude responded, other than with a shrug and a grimace.

"I suspected the worst when I was late for my next period," she continued. "That is when I started trying to figure out what to do next. My daddy will kill me if he finds out."

Maggie started sobbing openly, but she knew she had to go on. "I saw a poster in the post office that the factory here in Taylortown was looking for workers. Many of the men around here were drafted, and the mill was short of help. I knew the only way that I could ever convince my daddy to let me move away was if I were in some way assisting the boys in uniform. He was not happy with the idea at first, but Mama told me later that he was bragging all over town about what I was doing."

"You do know what I am doing, don't you?" Maggie asked. The other two had some vague notion, but they had not connected the dots. "I'm making materials that are used in parachutes. Every day I wonder if Donald will ever jump from an airplane holding on to a cord that my own hands helped to strand."

All of this was so overwhelming that the other Musketeers simply did not know what to say. They commiserated as best they could. The three of them looked at various options, and there simply was not a good one in the bunch. Neither of them had the foggiest idea how Maggie was going to get herself out of this.

It was soon time to go. Maggie asked if they could meet again in two weeks. Maude invited them to Jacksonville, since it was right in the middle for the other two. She would figure out how to have some privacy when the time came.

The three of them embraced once again. They recalled what they had pledged to each other the night before their graduation. One for all! And all for one!

The Three Musketeers were in this together. They would not abandon their friend who was now in trouble.

Maude and Millie were both very quiet on the bus ride back home. Emma Lou slept most of the way.

Todd's mother did not go to the grocery store very often. The Williamsons grew most of what they ate on their scrappy little farm. Ethel did have to buy flour and sugar. She had to purchase other staples, too, like baking powder and baking soda. She also had to get laundry powder, starch, and Octagon Soap, the latter being the only kind of shampoo her family had ever known. Of course, Mrs. Williamson had to keep plenty of coffee on hand. J. P. loved his morning cup of coffee.

The nearest A & P was actually in Morris Creek, Tennessee. They only went to Mountain Home, the county seat of Townsend County, Georgia when J. P. had some business to take care of. Either way, Ethel did not want her husband tagging along when she bought her Tube Rose Snuff. If he did not have anything else to do, he just sat in the car.

Ruby King, on the other hand, always wanted George with her when she went to the store. A little short in stature, she needed his long arms to reach things. Besides that, Ruby was not nearly as independent minded as Ethel was.

About a week after Maude's visit to Mason, Ethel ran into the Kings in Morris Creek. The two families had always been nothing more than casual acquaintances. For the womenfolk, not much changed in that regard after the Williamsons' son married the Kings' daughter.

"How's Earl?" Ethel asked just being polite. For the next five minutes, she heard all about his thriving tractor business and his new love interest.

Ethel responded rather unemotionally. "J. P. is going to need a little old tractor of some kind one of these days if he keeps doing what he is doing. Maybe Earl can help him out."

As she was about to pull her cart away, George blocked her path. Then he said, "I hear you're gonna be a grandma again." The sly man fully anticipated the scowl he got in return.

"I don't like it. I just don't like it." Ethel snorted. "I don't know how my boy is going to feed so many mouths." George moved his buggy so that she could get by.

"What's wrong, child?" Aunt Lucy wished to know. "Ever since you got back from Taylortown, you've been moping around like a cat that's lost her kittens. I thought getting together with your friends was supposed to cheer you up."

"I just can't talk about it, Aunt Lucy," Maude replied, trying to turn her away.

"Now, girl, you know you can tell me anything. My tongue doesn't wag out of both sides of my mouth." Maude knew that was the truth.

"I can't help you unless I know what's going on," her aunt continued.

Then, just like that, all the sordid details about Maggie's situation started spilling out. Maude had not intended to breathe a word of this to anybody. Without actually thinking it through, though, she was turning to the one person who might see the larger picture.

"Just what is Maggie going to do?" Maude asked.

"What does she want to do?" Aunt Lucy inquired back.

"She does not know. She just does not know," was all Maude could say.

"Does she want to get rid of the baby? Maybe Doc Elliott could help her abort the fetus." Using such words as those, Aunt Lucy sounded like Miss Barnes back in health class.

"No, we talked about that. Maggie said she believes that God could forgive her for bringing a life into this world, but he would never forgive her if she killed an innocent baby."

"Maybe she could have the baby, and then put it up for adoption," Aunt Lucy suggested.

Maude countered. "Maggie does not like that idea at all. For one thing, she said somebody told her that with so many people still going through hard times, and with the war going on and all, most unwanted babies are put in orphanages. For those who can afford to adopt, there are too many kids to go around. Maggie said that she would never let her child be raised in an institution like that."

"What other options does she have?" Aunt Lucy inquired next.

Maude continued getting it out. "Millie advised her to come clean, to face the music so to speak. She encouraged her to write a letter to her husband, and explain to him what is going on. If he is half the man everybody thinks he is, then he will forgive her, and they will go on with their lives when he comes home. Then, they can raise the child together."

"What does Maggie think about that idea?" Aunt Lucy wanted to know.

Maude tried to explain. "Maggie is terrified that Everett will go berserk and try to harm Donald. Even worse, he might contact her parents, and then divorce her. She said that she would not blame him one bit if he did."

Maude paused, and then she continued. "Maggie says that there is no way she can raise this child alone in times like these."

"Maybe her parents would take her back in and help her raise the child," Maude's aunt suggested.

"Maggie thinks they would disown her," Maude answered.

"What about the baby's father?" Aunt Lucy asked next.

"Maggie does not want Donald to know anything about it," Maude replied. "She refuses to do anything that might trap him into doing something that he might regret the rest of his life."

"I see," Aunt Lucy reflected. Several moments passed.

The aunt looked over at her niece. She then said rather impassively, "There *is* one option that none of you mentioned."

"What could that possibly be?" Maude asked curiously. "What else could Maggie do?"

Just like that, Aunt Lucy made a proposal that sent Maude's head spinning. The woman was right about one thing. None of them had come up with this possible solution.

It really had slipped up on her. With everything else going on, Maggie had totally forgotten about Little Ray's upcoming birthday. He would be sixteen, and that was one of those big ones. The note in the mail from her mom snapped her out of it.

On the upcoming Saturday, the extended family would be gathering at the McDonalds' house to celebrate this rite of passage. Maggie's mother was hoping that her daughter would be there. Her daddy had already purchased a Remington bolt action .22 rifle from George King for Little Ray's birthday present.

That was the same Saturday Maggie was going to meet Millie at Maude's in Jacksonville. She must do whatever it took to ride the bus on to Mason with Millie after their meeting. She really did need to go back home one more time before she began to show more dramatically. She sent a brief note back to her mother saying that she would be there.

Maude tried not to think about the conversation with Aunt Lucy. It sounded like some kind of business transaction. She thought back to the time of slavery. She wondered if this was what it was like when babies were moved around for the convenience of the owners, with little regard for the feelings of anybody else.

Aunt Lucy did not seem to understand things like this. Then again, she was not a mother. Saturday was fast approaching.

Maggie got on the bus in Taylortown going one direction at almost the same time Millie took her seat on a motor coach in Mason coming from the opposite. It was a little closer to Jacksonville from Mason so Millie got there first. She made a big fuss over Emma Lou. Neither Musketeer mentioned Maggie's thorny dilemma.

Both of them were surprised when Maggie showed up carrying a piece of the Samsonite luggage that she got for graduation. "Did you come to stay?" Maude jokingly asked her. Maggie then told them about the letter that she had gotten from her mother.

Aunt Lucy offered to take Emma Lou for a walk while the women visited. The little girl was at first a bit fussy about going with her, afraid that she might miss something.

Should Maude come forward with the proposal they discussed, Aunt Lucy insisted that her name be left out. It would be all Maude's idea.

If she never brought up the suggestion, it was highly unlikely that either of the other two would think of it. Once Aunt Lucy's words reached Maude's ears, though, she had to deal with them. There was no way to un-ring that bell.

A sense of uneasiness cloaked the room after Aunt Lucy left with Emma Lou. No one knew exactly how or where to start the conversation. They all seemed to be tiptoeing around the inescapable.

Millie finally broke the silence. She asked Maggie if she were having any trouble with morning sickness. The pregnant woman frowned. She nodded her head in the affirmative. She was concerned about having a bout the next morning at her mother's house.

Maggie then burst into tears. "Oh, what have I gotten myself into? What am I going to do? Sometimes I just want to die. I know I could kill myself, but then I think about that little life growing inside me. I would rot in Hell for sure if I did anything to harm that precious, innocent little baby."

Maude was not prepared to see how distressed Maggie really was. She had seen her become overly dramatic many times in the past when she was upset about something, or miffed with somebody. This was different. Maggie was not just blowing off steam. She was terrified.

Simultaneously, Maude and Millie reached for her. All three of them were now welling up. Their tear ducts were about to get another major workout. Wiping their eyes as they eventually released their embrace, the women were back to square one.

Maude had by no means decided what she was going to do. More than likely, she would just do what she always did – nothing. Uneasiness hung over them like a cloud of doom.

All of a sudden, the person in the room least likely to was the one who spoke. "Maggie, maybe there is a solution."

Maggie's head shot toward Maude with a look of incredulity that said, "Are you out of your mind? There is no solution to this problem."

"What are you talking about?" Millie asked, with doubt written all over her face, too.

The Three Musketeers had vowed always to be there for each other. Aunt Lucy had pointed out how one of them could fulfill the promise that she had made.

Maude hesitated. She could back up. She could say something like, "Never mind. I do not know what I was thinking. That would never work."

Then, just as if somebody flipped the "on" switch to some windup toy, Aunt Lucy's words started flowing from Maude's mouth.

"Maggie, I could pretend that I am pregnant. I can then take your baby and raise it as my own."

What was she saying? Did she mean this? Maggie's mind began shutting down. In shock, she sat motionlessly. A blank stare came across her face.

Millie was thinking, "No, Maude! No, Maude! You can't do this."

(What happened next is what literary critics might refer to as a pregnant pause.)

"Maggie, Maggie, are you all right?" She could hear what Millie was saying, but it was as though the words were coming from deep down in a well. Millie reached over and shook her gently. She snapped to, as if coming out of a hypnotic state.

Millie turned to Maude. "Do you know what you just said? Have you thought about this earlier, or did it just come up and come out?"

Maude tried to be convincing. She said that she had been thinking about it ever since she left Taylortown two weeks earlier.

The heads of the other two turned to face her. Their expressions were changing from amazement to admiration. Maggie reached out for Maude and said as she embraced her, "That is the most wonderful thing anyone has ever said to me in my whole life. I will never forget you for making that offer. I can't believe that you would even think about something like that."

"But I meant it," Maude injected.

"You did?" Maggie responded, still not believing what she was hearing.

"Okay, let's talk about this," Millie interrupted, convinced that the notion would fly apart when subjected to some harsh reality checks. "Do you honestly think that you could get away with faking a pregnancy?"

Maude, now in the unfamiliar position of actually having taken a stand on something, was feeling rather good about herself. It was almost as if somebody else had taken over her body. She started answering the questions, sounding amazingly like Aunt Lucy would have.

"I already have some maternity clothes. I can take some of my aunt's padding and fit it under them," she conveyed with a measure of confidence.

"But will she miss it and suspect something?" asked Millie.

How could Maude respond knowing that Aunt Lucy would actually be helping her with the adjustments? "Then, I can purchase some stuffing of my own," she volunteered.

"What if the baby does not look like you or Todd?" Millie asked, now acting like an attorney cross-examining a witness.

Maude countered. "You know how much alike Maggie and I are. Everywhere we go people think we are sisters." Millie could not refute that.

"Are you sure about the dates? Were you and Todd intimate about the time Maggie conceived?" Millie continued.

Maude turned to Maggie for confirmation. "Didn't you say that Donald was home the first weekend in February?"

Maggie nodded in the affirmative.

"Todd did not leave until February 22. There would be no reason for him to think that the baby is not his."

Maude, trying to convince herself as much as anyone, assured them that there was nothing to worry about. There was that problem of her having a period just before Todd left, but predicting exactly how long a mother would carry a baby before it decided to come out was far from an exact science in those days.

Without waiting for further interrogation, Maude went into overdrive. She said that she could keep mostly out of sight in Jacksonville while she was pretending to be pregnant. Maggie would stay in Taylortown. Doc Elliott could take care of her, and then when the time came, he could deliver the baby.

It was now Millie's time to hone in. "Doc Elliott? Why on earth would he go along with something like this?"

Maude was now on shaky ground. Regarding this piece of the puzzle, there was no way she could convey the certainty that Aunt Lucy had. When she asked her aunt that same question, the doctor's assistant responded assuredly, "Don't you fret now, and worry yourself silly over something like that, child. I can take care of old Doc Elliott."

After a few seconds to recover, Maude got back on track. "He is a very compassionate man. He has devoted his life to taking care of others. I think he will be willing to help us."

The other two took a moment, still trying to fathom what was now before them.

"He is in his office this morning. I guess we can just go over and ask him," Maude then advanced, validating her resolve for everyone to see.

Millie was not quite ready to go there, yet. "There is one more thing, Maude. Do you know what you are doing? Are you sure about this? Do you honestly think that you can raise Maggie's baby as if it is your own? Are you really convinced that Todd will never suspect a thing?"

After being as convincing as she could, Maude then reminded the girls that they were The Three Musketeers. This was something she could do for one of her sisters. She added that she had no doubt the two of them would do the same for her. Millie had run into a dead end.

The skeptical one then turned to Maggie. "You have been very quiet.

What do you think about all of this? Can you give your baby up? Can you live with yourself if the two of you accept this arrangement? Are you strong enough not to interfere in Maude and Todd's life?"

Millie could not believe that she was asking these questions. She was beginning to sound like she actually thought this might happen.

Maggie did not answer each question directly. Instead, she turned to Maude and repeated something she had said earlier. "I cannot believe that you would offer to do this for me."

With desperation punctuating her every expression, Maggie then began to lament. "What else can I do? I came here today hopeless. I was ready to give up. There simply was no answer, no way that I could figure out to deal with this. Maude has become my angel. If she is really willing to take on this responsibility, I pledge to her, to all of us, that I will do everything in my power to make it work. All I want is what's best for my baby."

First, Do No Harm

"First, do no harm." Doc Elliott had been repeating those words to himself all morning. When Lucille talked with him about Maude's friend and the mess she was in, the physician first thought that she was going to ask him to get rid of the baby. He would have drawn the line there. A botched abortion might well end his medical career.

Like any small town, rural physician, Doc Elliott occasionally found himself in some rather delicate situations. He was about to be put into another one. Although his assistant had filled him in on the details, if the three women came into his office, he would pretend to be totally in the dark.

The clock was ticking. Both Maggie and Millie had a bus to catch by mid-afternoon. They sent Maude to determine if the doctor could see them. She returned, saying that he was available. The three of them agreed that Millie would be their spokesperson.

"First, do no harm." He said those words to himself again, as the womenfolk took their seats.

With the skill of a polished debater, Millie laid out the facts of the matter. Doc Elliott stopped her a few times, asking for clarification. This was not so much because he did not understand, but to make sure Millie was articulating accurately what they were asking of him.

When she finished, he leaned forward over his desk. "Mrs. Hogan, let me express my deepest sympathies to you for the predicament that you are in. As Miss Mitchell has so eloquently put it, your options are very limited."

He then turned facing Maude. "Let me commend you for your loyalty to Maggie, and for your courage to make this most generous and self-sacrificing offer to her. I cannot at this moment think of anybody else I know who would come forward like this. But these are difficult and challenging times. It brings out the worst in some people. In your case, it has brought out the best."

Doc Elliott looked down at his desk as though studying something. Then, he continued. "What you are asking of me is most irregular. Should I agree to this, and I am at some point called into question regarding this matter, I would have to swear under oath that I did indeed deliver this baby straight from your womb, Maude. Is that understood?"

They all nodded in agreement.

The presiding physician then went over the fine details of the arrangement. The bottom line was that he would sign the child's birth certificate, listing Maude and Todd Williamson as its parents.

"Now, before we go any further, I will have to have an unswerving and unremitting pledge from each of you. You must swear that what we have agreed to today will stay right here in this room. We must vow that all four of us will take this with us to our graves without ever breaching or betraying the covenant that we are about to enter into with anyone, least of all to the yet unborn child whose heart is already beating in its mother's womb."

Doc Elliot was neither a lawyer nor a judge. Nevertheless, in barrister-like presumption, the physician took the Bible from the corner of his desk. He then asked the three young women to step forward. All three of them raised their right hands. With their left hands planted squarely on the Good Book, overlapping each other's, he administered the solemn oath, with God Almighty as the acknowledged but unseen witness.

This Doc Elliott did with the full awareness that two of the people in the room were very much aware that at least one other person was already privy to this clandestine operation. He could only hope and pray that the hemorrhaging would stop there.

As the other three somberly left the room, Doc made his way back into the pharmacy.

Maggie and Millie sat mostly in stunned silence during the bus ride to Mason. The motor coach was crowded so they had little privacy. It was probably just as well since neither of them knew what to say. Millie's father was waiting for her at the bus stop. He offered to drive Maggie out to the McDonald place.

Aunt Lucy could hardly wait for the other two to leave so she could get a full report. She was pleased. Maude's aunt pledged total support to her niece.

Meanwhile, Maude was riding a roller coaster of emotions. One side of her was bouncing off the walls. For once in her life, she had let go of her hesitancy. She had actually stood up and been counted. She had agreed to make a great personal sacrifice for the sake of a dear and devoted friend. That made her feel good inside.

Right in the midst of celebrating her noble deed, though, doubts were already beginning to creep in. Was this really going to happen? Would nobody suspect a thing? Was she in way over her head? Had she just gotten herself caught up in yet another whirlwind?

It was now time for Emma Lou's nap. The girl's mother could hardly wait to lie down on the bed with the child, and to open her blouse to her. The intimacy of these minutes was just the solace Maude needed to take her mind off what had happened earlier.

All of a sudden, a shiver went all through her body that caused Emma Lou to whimper. What would she do about nursing Maggie's baby?

Todd eventually heard from his mother after Maude's visit. She told him that something did not feel right about his wife being in the family way again. Then again, nothing felt right when it involved her son. He would get off a letter to her and one to Maude.

May 15, 1944

Dear Maude,

I hope you had a Happy Mother's Day. I thought of you when I sent my own mother greetings. I realized that one day when our children are older, they will be wishing you a Happy Mother's Day.

I am still getting used to the idea of saying children. While I always assumed that we would have more, I am nevertheless still in shock that another child is already on the way. I trust you are doing well.

I need to warn you that getting communication to you might be difficult for a while. I cannot discuss the details, but something big seems to be going on. If we are forced to be on the move, mail may not catch up with us for weeks. It might be difficult to send any at all. If I have only a limited ability to get a message out, I will send it to my parents, and assume that they will then share the information with everyone else.

Your husband,
Todd

Maude thought back to the day that she mailed the letter to Todd, telling him that he was going to be a daddy again. It was shortly after the meeting in Doc Elliot's office. When she went back to Mason a few days later to share the baby news, not one family member expressed joy. Todd now made it unanimous.

At least, he did not express great displeasure. Neither did he mention her living arrangements. For that, she was grateful.

Maggie had heard the expression "I was beside myself" many times. She had just never given it much thought until she was back at home to celebrate her brother's birthday. She was there, but she was not there. She found herself just going through the motions. Would anybody notice that she was not her usual bubbly self? Fortunately, the spotlight was on somebody else.

Martha McDonald outdid herself with the birthday supper. Uncles, aunts, cousins, and grandparents filled the house, along with a couple of Little Ray's friends. The folks found whatever spot they could to sit and eat, since not everyone could get around the table. The big chocolate cake was just about gone after several of the guys had a second piece.

The preacher and his wife were also invited, and he was called on to ask the blessing. Not only did the minister pray a special prayer for Little Ray, but also he was not remiss in remembering Everett and all the boys off fighting for freedom. Maggie's eyes began to well up.

As he continued in his prayer, the preacher petitioned the Almighty to intervene in the horrific slaughter. He asked that wisdom be imparted to the world leaders so they might somehow end this war before Little Ray reached the age when he would be drafted.

That part of the prayer really got to Maggie. It had never occurred to her that her little brother might one day go off to war. In just two years, he would have to register for the draft, and he was still such a child.

It was nearly ten before all of the guests finally went home. Maggie was beyond exhaustion. It felt good, but a little strange back in her old bed. Her thoughts went to Everett buried deep under the sea in that submarine. Even with her husband's descriptive letters, she could not fathom what it must be like living under such strange conditions. She prayed for his safety.

Her mind then shifted to Donald. He was going to be a daddy, but he would never know it. Maggie tried to imagine what it would be like for her and Donald to be together, and to raise this child as a family. She laughed, and simultaneously a tear rolled down her cheek when she thought about the baby. That child was going to be something else with parents like the two of them.

Maggie wondered if she would ever get to raise a child of her own. She pondered whether Donald would ever know the joys of fatherhood. Would either Everett or Donald make it back alive?

As these uncertainties kept sweeping over her soul, the one thing Maggie wanted more than anything else was incubating right there inside of her. She would be able to feel it move, she would be able to hold it briefly, but now she would never be able to claim it as her own.

The distraught young wife turned cynical. "Why do we have to have wars?" she wondered. "Why do people hate so much that they want to kill each other?" she contemplated next. "It's just not fair. None of this would have happened if not for that dreadful war."

Maggie started praying.

> Oh Lord, please be with Maude. If you had a hand in guiding her in what she is doing, I want to thank you from the bottom of my heart. Again, I ask you, God, please forgive me for what I have done. Oh Lord, I beg of you, don't let this baby growing inside of me have to suffer because of my mistake.

She finally drifted off into a restless sleep.

Just as Maggie feared, the next morning queasiness overtook her right after breakfast. She slipped out and headed toward the outhouse but it was occupied. She wandered out in the orchard, thinking that the smell in the outdoor toilet would not be very conducive after all. Behind a big apple tree, she lost her breakfast. She just stood there for a while, trying to let everything settle back down. A light breeze was blowing that helped steady her.

When she finally went back in the kitchen, her mother noticed that she was a little green around the gills. Martha asked her daughter if everything was all right. Maggie told her that she must have eaten too much of her mother's good cooking. The rich food most likely upset her stomach.

"I do hope you will be feeling better before church time," her mother responded, obviously oblivious to what was really going on. Whew. "We are looking forward to you sitting with the family today. Even Little Ray has agreed to sit with us. The preacher will certainly mention something about your brother's big birthday."

Maybe that was exactly where Maggie needed to be – in church – pleading for God's mercy.

The edgy expectant mother caught the late afternoon bus back to Taylortown. When it slowed pulling into Jacksonville for a stop, Maggie saw Maude and Emma Lou sitting in the swing. She waved, but did not think they saw her.

Finally back in her apartment, Maggie collapsed in a heap. She had only been gone overnight, but it seemed like forever.

When she walked out the door on Saturday morning, the woman in trouble was overwhelmed with hopelessness and despair. Within hours, a workable solution to her enigmatic problem presented itself so unexpectedly. Why did the miraculous reprieve now seem like such a death warrant?

May 29, 1944

Dear Maude,

I'll bet you were surprised to get an envelope with your name typed on it. Did you pay close attention to the return address? It said Pfc. Todd Williamson. Yep, I finally got a promotion.

(Maude knew that would mean a little increase in pay, but she did not know how much. She was not likely to either since she still did not know what his regular check had been.)

> I have been playing around with one of the
> typewriters in the office. They sure did put
> the letters in funny places. With two fingers,
> I am now able to fill out some of the forms
> using it.

(Maude stopped reading. She went over the keyboard in her head, wondering if her fingers still knew how to find them.)

> I cannot tell you exactly where we are right
> now. I can only say that we will not be in
> England much longer. I do not know when I
> will be able to write to you again.

(This was the last time Maude would hear from Todd for the next six weeks.)

> I hope you and little Emma Lou are doing well,

> Todd

(No mention was made of the baby on the way.)

Earl King's draft number did come back up, just as the discharge sergeant predicted it would. Casualties were beginning to mount, and the war on both fronts was coming to a critical stage. Earl was twenty-eight, but the military was reaching back for as many able-bodied men as it could find.

Local draft boards met all over the country to go over the lists of those who were eligible. They had the authority to say who was called up and who would receive an exemption. Generally, the patriotic men placed on these boards only made exceptions under the rarest of circumstances. It was always interesting, though, how some influential people's sons were able to avoid military service.

Earl's business partner and future father-in-law Marvin Prince was a member of the draft board in Chappell County. When Chairman J. K. Barrow was looking over Earl's paperwork, he suggested that Marvin recuse himself.

Marvin indicated that he had already decided to abstain from voting, but he did ask permission to speak regarding the matter. Chairman Barrow, a bit reluctant, did relent and allow Prince to have his say.

"Mr. Chairman and members of this board, I want to ask you to give Earl King an exemption from further service in the military. But let me make this perfectly clear. Mr. King is 100 percent behind this country. He volunteered for the army the day after he graduated from high school. He then proudly wore the uniform of the United States of America until he was honorably discharged. What I want to suggest to you today, however, is that Mr. King can make a greater contribution to this war effort as a civilian than he can if he is called back to active duty."

"How so, Mr. Prince?" Chairman Barrow quizzed Marvin, with a somewhat bewildered look on his face. The others around the table also looked puzzled.

Marvin then proceeded to lay out his case. "You see, it is like this. The military is dependent on the farmers and the factory workers to provide supplies for the men in uniform. Food is grown, canned, and shipped overseas. Cotton farmers are struggling to keep up with the demand placed on them to provide enough material to make uniforms and other necessities like sheets and towels.

"Now this is where Earl comes in. Every time he sells a new tractor in this county, that farm's production ability goes up significantly. Men, this is the leading cotton-producing county in the State of Georgia. We need every acre in cotton we can get. Our farmers are already stretching themselves thin with so many of them having sent their sons off to war. But with a tractor, these patriotic citizens can grow more than they ever could with a pair of old mules."

"I see your point, Mr. Prince," responded the chairman. The others nodded in agreement. "But I have a question. With this war going on, do you honestly believe Mr. King is going to sell that many tractors?"

Earl's future father-in-law responded without batting an eye. "That boy can do it if anybody can. I think we need to give him every chance to help his country doing what he does best. Besides that, Mr. Barrow, if it were my son about to marry your daughter, I would feel exactly the same way."

The others nodded vigorously in agreement. Chairman Barrow responded rather cynically, "Yes, Mr. Prince, I'm sure you would."

Earl King was relieved from further military duty based on community service. His file indicated that the vote was three to one, with one abstention.

"It's happening! It's happening!" Aunt Lucy exclaimed as she came storming through the door. "Doc Elliott has had the radio on all morning. He just told me the news is still sketchy, but that during the night and early morning, the Allies have launched a major offensive against the Nazis. He said they are calling this operation D-Day, or something like that."

"So this is what Todd was alluding to," Maude murmured aloud. She wondered where he was at that moment, just hoping that Emma Lou's father was still alive.

Todd had reassured his parents and his wife that his outfit would not be involved in direct combat. They were part of a vast support network always trailing the front lines. These vital companies would be far enough back to be as safe as possible, but close enough to keep the supplies flowing. While this was somewhat comforting, anything was possible in the mayhem of war. Maude closed her eyes, sat back, and took a deep breath.

"The Wad"

Since the meeting in Doc Elliott's office, Maude went about her daily routines as though nothing out of the ordinary had happened. Taking care of her daughter and her concerns for her husband's well-being overweighed everything else. With every passing day, the promise she had made seemed more like something out of a foggy dream. Little by little, reality was about to set in.

Aunt Lucy suggested one morning during breakfast that it was time to start making the padding Maude would wear during the time of her surreptitious "expectancy." After going over to the office and helping Doc Elliott with an early patient who had a sick child, she had some spare time later that day.

The aunt and her niece were jovial as they started taking measurements. Thank goodness, Emma Lou was too young to understand what was going on. They made the strange looking garment from the thickest material Aunt Lucy had. Even so, it had to be doubled for strength and texture. Working without a pattern, the talented seamstress put tucks in, shaping it like a woman's bulging belly. The thingamajig had sashes that tied in the back. It was designed so Aunt Lucy could rip the seam, let it out just enough, and then stuff some more cotton tightly into the contraption when it became necessary.

As it was taking shape, Maude tried it on several times. This was the first, and conceivably the last time they would ever construct a contrivance like this. The two of them were eventually satisfied that the padding was ready for the first stage.

"It is not always going to be comfortable," Aunt Lucy cautioned. Then she added, "But not nearly as uncomfortable if a baby was really inside." They both laughed.

"My problem is going to be remembering to put it on before I go out," Maude said, thinking out loud.

"As you get farther along, you are going to need to wear it all the time except when you are sleeping," Aunt Lucy warned. "If you are not careful, just when you least expect it, somebody will catch you off guard."

Still in a playful mood, Maude suggested that the undergarment be given a name. After Emma Lou was born, the new mother remembered the wad of baby fat that she had trouble getting rid of. Since neither woman was overly creative, they settled on simply calling their apparatus, "the wad."

Doc Elliott gave the women daily updates on the war. He listened to news reports on the radio. He also subscribed to the county's only newspaper, which he read meticulously. A stickler for facts and figures, he informed Lucille and Maude that around 24,000 paratroopers dropped from the skies into coastal France on June 6, 1944, the night of the invasion. The next morning the largest amphibious landing in history took place at Normandy. Some 160,000 Allied soldiers stormed the beaches. Almost 5,000 ships were involved. Countless other military personnel came ashore during the following days, trailing the advancing front line as the Allies pushed their way toward Paris.

What Doc Elliott did not share with his tenants was the remorse in his heart regarding his own son. While he wished no harm upon his offspring, he much preferred that Malcolm was fighting for freedom, rather than sitting and rotting away in a jail cell, his own having been taken away.

So far, three families in Townsend County had gotten the dreaded knock on the door. Maude did not know any of them personally. If something were to happen to Todd, she presumed that his parents would be the ones informed. The war bride wondered how long it would be before she even found out.

Aunt Lucy came through the door with a disturbed look on her face. She had some unsettling news. A poster had been placed behind the counter at the store where the bus stopped. It said that service would be suspended indefinitely after July 15, 1944. The management of the State Line Bus Service regretted having to inform its customers of this inconvenience. They were unable to get any new tires, and they could not put their riders in danger.

At first, Maude shared with Aunt Lucy in her disappointment regarding this unanticipated development. She then realized that this might not be such a bad thing after all. It would now be much easier for both her and Maggie to stay out of sight, as they came down the home stretch.

"Down the home stretch . . ." Maude chuckled at her accidental humor. Once the big decision was made, she had amazed herself at how well she was handling all this.

As she pondered the bus situation, she decided that maybe she needed to make one more trip to Mason. The "expectant" mother was supposed to be more than five months along by now. It was important for her folks and Todd's to see her "in the family way." She did not look forward to the visit, but she found it necessary.

Maude needed to get Emma Lou's baby clothes that were left behind. This would also be her last chance to pick up part of Todd's paycheck. The very thought of that encounter made her shudder.

She decided to wait past Independence Day to make the trip. With the war going on, the twin towns would be celebrating with a parade, picnic, and fireworks that she would be expected to take in. It would be easier after that was all over. She thought about sending a little note ahead informing her parents of her impending visit. Then, she decided just to show up.

On a hot muggy Friday in July, with "the wad" carefully attached to Maude's mid-section, mother and child boarded the bus in Jacksonville. The young woman squirmed a bit, trying to get used to the discomfort of the contrivance.

The windows were open. Emma Lou loved standing in the breeze letting her long curls blow. The girl's mother sat admiring her daughter's beautiful dark brown hair. She had only trimmed it a couple of times to give it shape. Remembering the only movie that she and Todd had ever seen together, the proud mom thought to herself, "She looks like Shirley Temple."

While Emma Lou was sometimes a bit fidgety when her mother was putting the curls in her tresses, the little girl loved to look in the mirror afterward. Maude feared that all the curly locks would be blown out by the time they got to Mason, especially if the hair got tangles in it that had to be brushed.

For now, the young mother just let her daughter be. Emma Lou was so beautiful in the new dress Maude had made for her, with Aunt Lucy's supervision of course. At least she could look forward to showing off her handiwork.

Emma Lou was such a good child. Maude wondered how she could be so lucky. It would be nice to have the little girl's grandparents closer by to help with her care. She knew, nonetheless, that her daughter was much easier to manage the way it was. Aunt Lucy was firm with the toddler. With her daughter's father now so far away, this gave Maude the backup discipline she needed.

"Anybody home?" Maude hollered as she opened the front door.

Ruby came scampering into the living room with her apron flying.

"Why, look who's here," she exclaimed, grabbing Emma Lou up in her arms. Maude had prepared her daughter as best she could on the bus, going over names with her that she might have forgotten.

Nothing had prepared her for this, however. The startled little girl began to cry. "Oh, you are a mama's baby," her grandma lamented, handing her back.

With the sudden intrusion, Maude felt "the wad" shift underneath her dress. She carefully straightened it, hoping that her mother did not notice. She would try to get it tighter the next time she put it on.

Seconds later, Ruby turned to her daughter and said, "Now, let me look at you. I still cannot believe that you are going to have another baby. Why, Earl was eight before I had you." Why was her mother the standard against which everything else was measured?

Trying to deflect attention, Maude asked her mother if she liked Emma Lou's dress. "I made it myself," she added. Relaxed a tad, the now almost nineteen-month-old little girl strutted a bit for her grandma to examine the garment.

If Maude had any illusions of getting her mother's approval, she should have known better. Ruby had to put in her two cents' worth. "The material is kind of plain. This girl would look better in something brighter and cheerier."

"But Mother, there's a war going on. All I had to work with was a scrap that Aunt Lucy had left over from a dress that she made for one of her customers. I could not afford to go out and buy anything I wanted."

The woman continued her criticism. "This seam over here is not straight. And I think the stitch was set a little too tight on Lucille's sewing machine."

Thankfully, the conversation was interrupted with a commotion at the back door. From down in the mule barn, Grandpa King got a glimpse of his daughter and granddaughter coming up the drive. Emma Lou's countenance changed instantly when he came into the house. She started sashaying for her grandpa.

"Why, look at you, so pretty and such a big girl now," the jolly man said to her. She ran and jumped into his waiting arms.

This was the first time Maude had to wear the padding for such long periods at the time. Back in Jacksonville, she was prone to go about her morning routines with it off. She could remove it after supper, assured that no one would see her.

The "expectant" mother was understandably very self-conscious. Fortunately, the maternity clothes were free flowing. "The wad" did not show much until she sat down. Aunt Lucy had also taken a brassier and padded it so that Maude's bosom stood out more.

The next day Maude decided to go ahead and get the visit to the Williamsons out of the way. She was very careful getting "the wad" on straight and tight. Her daddy offered to drive them, but she said that she needed the walk. Emma Lou was old enough now that she did not have to be carried.

Maude was hoping that J. P. would be in the house when they got there. Disappointedly, she could see him down in the creek bottoms plowing corn. She knocked on the front screen door and heard Ethel moving about inside. The woman soon made her appearance. She said rather sardonically, "Well, this is sure a surprise."

No matter how hard Maude tried to prepare herself, she was always uncomfortable when given the once over by her mother-in-law. Emma Lou sensed the uneasiness of the situation. She reached for her mother's dress tail, pulling it tight against "the wad." When Maude bent down and picked up the little girl, Ethel said, "You don't need to be toting that child around in the condition you are in."

"Isn't she a big girl now?" Maude responded, ignoring the criticism. "She walked all the way here from Mama's house all by herself."

"Well, don't just stand out there on the porch. Come on in. J. P. will be coming in soon for dinner. You will stay and have lunch with us, won't you?"

"Yes, that would be nice," Maude said, respectfully. At least Emma Lou was now weaned. She did not have to worry about that fiasco again.

"Oh look, Emma Louise," her mother said. "See Daddy's picture?"

"Daddy," the little girl responded with a smile. Maude thought that she could almost see a tiny glimmer of approval on her mother-in-law's face.

John Paul was all hot and sweaty when he came in from the cornfield. He tried to turn Emma Lou away, but she would have none of it. She ran and wrapped her arms around his legs so tightly that he could not move. Granddaddy Williamson could resist no longer. "You'll just have to give this little girl another bath when you get back to your mama's," he said.

Around the table, Maude brought up the subject of Todd's promotion. His mother again almost managed a smile. "A lot of good it is going to do him, though, if he gets himself killed," she said, as her face returned to a grimace.

"That woman can take anything, no matter how good it is, and turn it into something negative," Maude thought to herself.

"Have you heard anything from him lately?" she asked his parents.

"Not one word since D-Day, and I am getting a little concerned," Todd's mother answered before his father had a chance to say anything.

J. P. did have his say, though, before he went back to his work. "Ethel, I'm sure Maude needs some money. She might be too timid to ask, but don't forget to give her the cash from Todd's last paycheck."

"Timid my foot," Ethel snarled just under her breath.

Ruby was boiling a hen for Sunday dinner when Maude and Emma Lou got back. The weather was a little too hot for that kind of meal, but she would also make dressing since George loved it so much. Maude offered to help in the kitchen, but her mother said that she knew they both must be exhausted after the walk and the visit. Ruby insisted that her daughter and granddaughter take a nap.

Only then did Maude realize just how tired she really was. She could only imagine how she would feel if she were carrying a real baby.

She had deliberately chosen the weekend for the visit. Actually, that was Aunt Lucy's idea. She said Maude and Emma Lou needed to go to church on Sunday so that as many people as possible could see her "in the family way."

On Monday, it was time to head back to Jacksonville. Emma Lou held on tightly to her Grandpa's neck and refused to let go. He finally pried her free and handed her to Grandma. George reached for Maude. She just brushed right past him gathering up her things.

A few nights after Maude and Emma Lou's visit, George told Ruby that he had to deliver a pair of mules the next day to a farmer in the Hardy Community in northern Chappell County. She announced unexpectedly that she thought she would ride with him. "Will we have time to go by and see Earl?" she wanted to know.

George was not anticipating that reaction. He told her that he barely had enough gas to go straight there and back. He would not have enough to go on to Adamsonville. Ruby soured for a moment, and then said she guessed that she would just let him go alone since the truck would be so hot. George did not mention that it was not far out of the way to come back through Jacksonville.

It was a little unusual to get an order this time of year. The crops were already laid by. This particular man thought that he could make it one more season with his old mules. Then, one of them up and died on him during the summer heat. He needed a pair to haul the cotton in from the fields, and then take it to the gin. The farmer decided to go ahead and purchase some young mules, and to get them broken in before next spring.

George had taken an old GMC ¾-ton truck and converted it so that he could haul the big work animals. The original bed was removed and replaced with a wider oak floor. The truck bodies around the side were then built high enough that the mules could not get out. Two full-grown mules weighed enough to put the truck right at its limit. George also added helper springs and six-ply tires so that he had a time or two hauled four mules for short distances.

It occurred to him as he was going down the road that he and Earl were actually in competition. If that farmer had not been low of cash since his crops were not yet harvested, he might just as well have gone ahead and bought a new tractor. Mr. King also knew that it was only a matter of time until he needed to find a different way to make a little money. With his kids grown and on their own, it would not take much for him and Ruby to get by.

George got the mules delivered. He scribbled out a promissory note saying the farmer would mail him a check just as soon as he had his fourth bale of cotton ginned. The mule trader had no doubt that this was a good loan. George King had an uncanny ability to read people.

The kindly man had something else on his mind. He made a left turn in Mountain Home and came back through Jacksonville. George stopped his truck in front of a vacant lot a couple of doors down from the old Jackson mansion. With the smell coming from the mule manure, it would not be neighborly to park it in front of a doctor's office.

It was still not even lunchtime. The mule trader liked to get an early start, trying to beat some of the heat. Nobody inside the big house noticed as he made his way to the apartment in the back.

Lucille was assisting the physician in updating his record book. Doc Elliott often took payments from his patients when he was out in the community, both in money and in kind, and he sometimes forgot to post them.

When Maude heard the gentle knock, she froze. "Who is it?" she timidly inquired.

"Why, it's your old pappy," George replied from the other side of the door.

Maude had not put on the padding. "Just a minute, Daddy, I'm not decent," she responded. She hurriedly tried to get "the wad" on and adjusted. It seemed like it was taking far too long.

Finally, she opened the door to her father's outstretched arms. The whole time that she was in Mason, she had managed to avoid being hugged. Emma Lou was useful to keep between her and others. Now, sensing her mother's anxiety, the child was hiding in the bedroom until she felt it safe to come out.

There was no way to escape. George gave his only daughter a big bear hug. Maude was as rigid as her mother was when Ruby had on her corset, and it was laced up too tight.

Her daddy then came on in. He explained what he had been doing all morning. He added that he could not pass up an opportunity to come by and see two of his very favorite ladies. Emma Lou was now sitting proudly in his lap.

George did not stay long. He said that he would speak to Lucille on his way out. Maude's daddy then lamented that the buses were no longer running and gas was in short supply. He said that he did not know when they would see each other again. He told his daughter to take good care of herself and of Emma Lou. He then said to let him know if he could ever help her in any way.

Maude thought that she should go with her daddy next door. Yet, she just did not want to prolong her time with him. She was not sure what his reaction had been to holding her body close to his. Grandpa King reached down and kissed his daughter on the cheek. He then gave Emma Lou her own little bear hug.

When he walked in the doctor's office, Lucille looked up and said, "Why, George King, what are you doing here?" Before he had time to answer, she told Doc Elliott that this was Maude's father. The two of them shook hands.

George explained where he had been. He then said that he came back through Jacksonville to check on his daughter, and that he had just come from next door after paying her a little visit. Lucille froze. She wondered how Maude handled the unexpected visitor.

"I'm glad I caught you here, Doc." Mr. King continued. "I need to discuss something with you. Maude tells me that you are taking good care of her, but she has said nothing about what it is going to cost to get this baby here. With her husband off in service and all, her mother and I are going to take care of the bill, whatever it is. But I do not want either of you to mention this to Maude."

"That's mighty generous of you, Mr. King, but there will be no charges for my services. We think of Maude and Emma Lou as family. Besides that, Maude is very helpful around here. And she will not take any pay for the chores she does."

"Well then, that's mighty generous of you," George returned the compliment. "We don't have a phone, but there is one down at the store. Maude and Lucille both know the number. Should you ever need us for anything, we do enough business with the Morgans that they will be happy to get us the message."

An Humble Request

George said that he needed to be on his way soon, but he wondered if Lucille could help him with something. He said he had a cousin buried in the church cemetery just up the street, but he had never been able to find her grave. Maybe Lucille's eyes could help him, since she was more familiar with the graveyard than he was.

His sister-in-law hesitated, obviously uncomfortable with that request. Doc Elliott thinking that it was only because she was reluctant to leave her post, told her to go ahead. They could finish what they were doing later.

"George, I didn't know you had a cousin buried over here," Lucille said, as they were walking up the street. Ignoring her, he told her to hold her nose as they went by his truck.

"What name are we looking for?" she asked as they entered the cemetery.

With that, George turned and faced the woman. "Let's you and I keep walking around looking at headstones. Those going by will think nothing of it. In the meantime, we are going to have a little talk. Lucille, there is something funny going on. I'm sure you know all about it. Now I want you to tell me what it is."

Standing right there in that graveyard, Lucille Moore looked like she had just seen a ghost.

"Funny about what, George?" she asked timidly, trying not to look too spooked.

"You know what I am talking about; funny about Maude being with child."

"George, I don't know what you are talking about."

"Oh, yes you do, Lucille, and you're going to tell me what this is all about."

"George, it is not proper for a married man and a single woman to speak about such things," she said, hoping to throw him off balance.

"Lucille, I know all about propriety. You know me to be a discreet man and honorable. But we are going to dispense with decorum for the moment," George said as they kept walking.

"Lucille, I am Maude's father. Her husband is no help to her whatsoever right now. I'm afraid the time is coming when she is going to need me. When it does, I want us to be able to skip the preliminaries and get right down to brass tacks."

Lucille did know George King to be a reputable man. She also knew that he was the person the preacher came to get and go with him if he had to go into a difficult situation. George had worked behind the scenes on several occasions to help people when they had gotten themselves in a mess.

Her brother-in-law could be right about what he was saying. Maude might really need him down the road. Miss Moore knew if there was one man in the county that she could count on, it was the one standing right there in the cemetery with her.

They lingered a long time at the same grave. George moved on. Lucille remained back for a few moments, still trying to figure out the best thing to do. She surmised that he was not going to take no for an answer. It also occurred to her that if he did not get the satisfaction he needed from her, he might go to Doc Elliott next.

"George, why do you think there is a problem?" she asked, still feeling her way through the situation.

"I knew something was wrong when Maude first came home with the news. Lucille, when a woman conceives, there is a natural glow about her. You know that just as well as I do. Maude had no such look about her. Then, the way she nonchalantly told me that I was going to be a grandpa again let me know right then and there that something was fishy."

He continued. "I watched her while she was home this last time. No joy was in her soul about a baby inside her. Just this morning, it took her a long time before she came to the door. When she finally opened it, I gave her a big hug before she had time to turn away from me, as she did when she was leaving the other day. Something was not right. Maude did not have the feel of a woman in the family way."

Lucille had played her hand as far as she could. "I'll have to hand it to you, George King. You saw what apparently nobody else has been able to see. If I tell you what is really going on, you have to promise me that you will not say a word to Ruby."

"Lucille, I hope you know me well enough to know that is the last thing I would do."

Standing right there in front of the Jackson family plot, Lucille then proceeded to tell George her version of the story. As she told it, the whole thing about the baby transfer was Maude's idea. Lucille said that she tried to talk her niece out of doing it. When she insisted on going through with it anyway, Aunt Lucy had offered to stand by her any way she could.

"Who is the other woman, the one who is going to have the baby?" George wanted to know.

"She is one of Maude's friends. I would rather not call her name, please. It might be easier for you not to know who she is." George finally granted his first concession, since he already had a good idea who she was.

Lucille then told George about the vows the women had taken in Doc Elliott's office. She failed to mention that there were actually three friends in the room that day whose names all started with the letter "M."

She then told him about her talk with Doc Elliott. "Since Maude is living under my roof, he understood that I had to know what was going on."

"No one else knows," she added. "All of us who do must take this with us to our graves."

Maude's father gave his implied consent, but made no such promise. Lucille felt relieved that she had an ally. George could be counted on to do what was right. There were few men on earth like George King.

On the walk back to the house, Lucille told George that he should really be proud of his daughter. "What she is undertaking is one of the grandest gestures I have ever known anybody to make," she added.

"I just hope she can do it," he responded. "That which she has promised might be a noble thing as you suggest, but I just pray that she has what it takes to pull it off. I can only imagine what might happen if that husband of hers ever finds out."

Lucille knew George had reason to be concerned.

When she walked back into Doc Elliot's office, he asked if Mr. King had found his relative's grave. She told him that the two of them had looked the cemetery over, and they had not found it. George said that he must be mistaken regarding where his cousin was buried.

The tires on the truck were pumped up to carry the extra load. On the way back up the road, the vehicle was now serving notice of every bump and washboard. Maude's daddy had so much on his mind that he did not even think about stopping and letting some air out.

The driver's eyes were open wide, but this unassuming man was praying more earnestly than ever before in his whole life.

> Please Dear God, let my daughter find the
> wherewithal that she is going to need to
> raise some other woman's child.

(Bleary eyed, he reached for the big red bandana in the right hip pocket of his overalls. He rubbed it across his sweaty brow. He then wiped the tears running down both cheeks.)

> And one more thing, Lord; you know that I
> do not bother You too much. I understand
> that You have a lot to take care of with this
> war going on and all. My wants and needs
> are so insignificant considering everything
> else that is happening in this old sinful
> world. But I do have one more humble
> request, if it will not impose on You too

much. Could You please make this little war
baby into something really special?

Amen.

Emma Lou had a new best friend. Jane Elliott came by to play with
her for a while almost every day. "Aunt Yanie" enjoyed reading to her, and
they often took walks together. Their favorite activity, though, was sitting in
the big front porch swing counting the occasional cars that went by.

Doc Elliott noticed a change in his frail daughter after she took an
interest in the child. He said that it was almost as if she had a pet to care for.

Aunt Lucy told Maude that Jane's unscheduled visits were good
discipline for the "expectant" mother. As uncomfortable as "the wad" was,
she really needed to wear it all the time now except when she was sleeping.
She could not risk letting anyone see her without it. It had already been
adjusted twice, and it was about time to put in more stuffing.

Aunt Lucy also suggested that as many people as possible needed to
see Maude "in the family way" right there in Jacksonville. If suspicions were
ever to arise and somebody came snooping around, the town folks needed to
be able to say without any hesitation that they saw Maude very much with
child.

The three of them started attending church. Emma Lou sat between
her mother and Aunt Lucy. They took turns entertaining her when she got
fidgety.

The women tried to get Doc Elliott to join them, but he was not much
of a churchgoer anymore. The first time that he ever laid eyes on Mary Kate,
she was sitting on the little round stool at the old pump organ. They were
married standing before the altar. Just feet from that spot, her body lay in
state at her funeral. The widower still had not come to terms with the painful
memories going into that sanctuary brought back to him.

Aunt Lucy was also making a sacrifice in going. She dropped out of
church years earlier when she decided that the preacher just preached about
everybody else's sins, carefully sidestepping his own. For now, condemning
the evil Nazis would be the minister's major concern. Everyone could agree
on that.

Lucille had really taken to being Dr. Ross Elliott's assistant. She had
learned most of his patients by name. It was her duty to answer the phone, but
it hardly ever rang. No one out in the country had a telephone, although more

and more people in town were getting one. Most sick folks just showed up.

Miss Moore served as the receptionist. She also did most of the bookwork, including writing the checks for Doc to sign when bills had to be paid.

The doctor taught her how to question patients about their symptoms, how to measure prescriptions, and how to change bandages. Of course, she already knew how to take a person's temperature. She was not yet ready to learn how to give a shot, though.

Doc Elliott found his assistant the most helpful when he had to go out and deliver a baby. While he was attending the mother, Lucille took charge elsewhere. She had a calming effect on the men waiting outside, and she gave good instructions to the women inside. She was, furthermore, quite adept in handing him just what he needed when she was by his side during the delivery.

Occasionally, Maude let her mind drift to Maggie as she put on "the wad." She tried to imagine what the real expectant mother looked like by then. The Three Musketeers had not been back together since that fateful day in Doc Elliott's office. She worried about how her lifelong friend was doing. She wondered if it would be better if Maggie was closer by, and they could go through this together.

Toward the end of August 1944, Doc Elliott discussed with Maude the need to pay Maggie a visit to make sure that she was not having any problems. He suggested that she ride along with him. Maude wrote Maggie a brief note, telling her to expect them on the first Saturday in September.

Aunt Woosie and Aunt Yanie were delighted to keep Emma Lou. This was the first time that Maude had ever been that far away from her daughter, or separated for that long.

During the drive down, the physician had an open and frank discussion with her about her own state. He was amazed at how well she was handling everything. At the same time, he was worried that the realities of the situation had not yet fully weighed in on her.

The doctor asked her what she was going to do if Maggie changed her mind about giving up the baby. While Maude had not even considered that possibility, she said in that case, everyone could just be told that her baby was born dead.

"What about a funeral?" he asked. "Will the family expect you to bury the baby?" She said that she had not thought about that, but she would.

Maggie laughed out loud when she saw "the wad." She had to admit that Maude really did look like she was carrying a baby. As the two old friends embraced, their arms were hardly long enough to go around each other. This brought out a nervous little laugh. Each woman then reached out and patted the tummy of the other. Simultaneously, tears made their way down their cheeks. Neither could find just the right words to say.

Maude went outside when Doc did a little physical examination of his patient. He reported that everything seemed to be progressing normally, and the baby's heartbeat was strong. In a rare display of humor, the physician playfully put the stethoscope to "the wad" when Maude came back inside.

The conversation then turned to what plans they needed to make leading up to the time of the birth. Maggie said that she wanted to work as long as she could. The doctor told her that whenever she was ready, he would come get her. She could stay in a guest room in his house the last couple of weeks.

The physician was then emphatic about a couple of things. He told Maggie that she must retain her apartment in Taylortown. He also wanted to make sure she understood that he would be returning her to it just as soon as she was able to ride.

Doc then asked her what she was planning to tell her coworkers when she came back without a baby. Maggie said she would have to tell them that she lost the baby. There was certainly an element of truth in that.

Maggie then said she had two requests. One was that she wanted to hold the newborn before she handed it over to Maude. Doc Elliott said he would agree to that, but only briefly for the sake of everyone involved.

Second, she asked permission to name the baby, at least its given name. This really caught Maude off guard. She had already been thinking about names. She and Todd had an agreement that if their next child were a boy, it would be named after him. She was struggling with that since the baby was not Todd's. She had a few ideas about a girl's name, but nothing that she was set on.

Maggie begged Maude to honor her request. She said that it might sound strange, but if the child turned out to be a boy, she wished to name him Walter. She then explained why. She said that on the day she was born, Walter Johnson, the great pitcher for the Washington Senators, pitched a no hitter. Johnson was her father's favorite ballplayer. If she had been a boy, she would have been named Walter. So would Maude please name him Walter? Maude agreed to think about it.

"What if the baby is a girl?" Doc Elliott asked.

"Then, I want her named Marcia Leigh. I want to carry on the 'M' tradition, but you can call her Leigh if you wish. That is a very special name."

The medical doctor had one more important question for Maggie. "Are you going to be able to stay out of sight until this is all over?"

"All over," he had said. A sharp pain shot right through Maggie's soul when she heard those words.

Maude also took note and thought, "This will never be all over."

To the family physician, those words simply referred to the time when his immediate services were no longer required.

It took Maggie a moment to right herself. She then tried to answer the question. "Daddy's car is broke down, and he does not have the money to get it fixed. With the bus not running, I don't think any of them will be down this way."

"Good," the doctor responded.

As the physician made his way to the car, Maude and Maggie faced each other. Their eyes locked, but words were again in short supply. Maggie burst into tears. She grabbed Maude and did not want to let go. Through her sobs, she finally managed to say, "Thank you, Maude. I love you so much."

Both the driver and the passenger were mostly quiet on the way back to Jacksonville. Right in the middle of trying to wrap her mind around everything that had just happened, Maude realized how much she missed Emma Lou.

Maude and Maggie eventually heard from their husbands. On D-Day, Everett Hogan was in a partially submerged submarine just off the coast of France. The sailors in the sub were focusing on the skies taking aim at any Luftwaffe warplanes that might be in the area.

Maggie did not know it at the time, but as the massive invasion was beginning, Donald Vaughn dropped out of a plane right after midnight. He was among those who helped clear the way for the infantry to come ashore. He, too, was safe and in France.

Todd crossed the English Channel the next day after the big surge. His unit trailed the advancing troops, keeping supplies moving toward the front lines.

Maude did not get her next message from him until five weeks after the landing. She sent Todd several letters in the meantime. They eventually caught up with him, but not necessarily in the order that she mailed them. This would become a pattern over the next few months.

Meanwhile, Millie's fellow, Roy Hancock, continued serving in the Pacific Theater. She did not understand why the term theater was used. Was this supposed to be like some drama with a producer and director? Mild-mannered Millie thought if people would just sit down and talk, they could work out their differences.

Mail between Roy and his gal might be a little faster than it was to and from Europe. Even so, sometimes a letter took up to a month to get to its destination.

Maude tried not to think about it all the time. It was not going to be very long before she would have another child to raise. She felt so blessed with Emma Louise. No mother could ask for a more darling little daughter. The girl was getting more precocious by the day.

Would Maggie's baby be a boy or a girl? In some ways, Maude was hoping for a girl. The name thing would certainly be less complicated. Furthermore, she already had little girl clothes.

What if the two girls were strikingly dissimilar in appearance and temperament, though? Would anyone think them not sisters? A son would draw fewer comparisons. But what if the boy did not have any of Todd's distinctive features?

What was really beginning to worry Maude was in some ways what every parent wonders when another child is on the way. After loving the firstborn with all one's heart, would there be any love left over for the next one? In Maude's situation, it was far more complicated than that.

Did not parents love their adopted children as their own? Would not her loyalty to Maggie and The Three Musketeers override her concerns? Anyway, Maude kept telling herself that Emma Lou just came along. The new bride had no idea that she would conceive so quickly into her hasty marriage. This next one was going to be her chosen child. That would make everything all right. Wouldn't it?

Doc Elliott decided to make another trip to Taylortown in mid-September. This time he went alone. He found Maggie to be doing quite well. From all appearances, she was going to have a big baby. Its heartbeat was strong, and it was very active in its temporary home. The textile mill where Maggie worked had asked her to stop at the end of the month.

Since her due date was sometime in early November, the two of them decided that the physician would come and get her on Sunday, October 15. If she needed his services earlier, they went over how she could get a call through to him.

Doc Elliott told Maggie he realized that she and Maude had been close friends for many years. However, he wanted the two of them to have minimal contact while she was in Jacksonville.

The doctor had delivered several babies that were put up for adoption. He knew how hard it was on the birth mother. He was trying as best he could to minimize the awkwardness that Maggie would now always feel when she was around Maude.

The Jaded Toad

Publisher and Editor Hiram Harwell of *The Townsend Times* went over wire service reports routinely as he followed the progress of the war. His eyes were especially tuned to see any news involving north Georgia service members. Regrettably, he had published some obituaries of casualties from his county.

One day as he was perusing the Associated Press wire, Harwell saw something that caught his eye. While stationed in France, a soldier from Mason, Georgia had made a startling discovery. An old estate, abandoned by its owners when Germany invaded the country, was taken over by the private's company for its temporary headquarters.

The headline read, "Pfc. Todd 'Toad' Williamson of Mason, Georgia discovers secret cache." The article went on to describe how the company clerk was rambling around in the old mansion looking for more storage space when he inadvertently found a hidden compartment. Before the family left, they tried as best they could to hide from the enemy the family treasures that they could not take with them. The supply clerk stumbled upon their stash.

What the report did not say was that Todd made the astounding discovery three days before anyone else knew about it. He was up in the secret hideaway looking through the items again when intruders startled him. Another GI had brought a French girl back with him, and they were looking for a place for a private tryst. The two of them surprised the unsuspecting private.

The soldier boy was now busted. He had been trying to figure out what to do with the treasures, but had not come up with any workable ideas. All of a sudden, he was the center of attention.

The locals hailed Pfc. Williamson a hero. The collection he uncovered contained some irreplaceable art, several unique pieces of handcrafted jewelry, and some family heirlooms accumulated over several generations.

A newspaper in Paris noticed the report, and it was now making its way around the world via the wire services. It was just the kind of human-interest story that helped divert attention away from the horrors of the war.

The reporter who wrote the article interviewed some of the other men in Todd's outfit. One of them shared the "Toad" part of the tale, which the writer added to the lore.

Harwell was not personally acquainted with the Williamsons. He had no way of knowing that the folks around Mason were unaware that one of their own was called "Toad" by his comrades. The editor published the AP report on the front page, just as it came off the wire.

The day the paper came out, Maude and Emma Lou walked over to the doctor's office about mid-morning. Doc Elliott asked Maude if she knew that her husband was now a big celebrity. Understandably, she had no idea what he meant. When he handed her the paper, she was astounded when she read the account.

Todd had written to Maude about the indignity he felt regarding the "Toad" nickname when he was on board the ship going over. He had made her promise not to mention it to anyone back home. Now it was front-page news.

Maude was saddened that people all over the county now knew about Todd's moniker. She felt sorry for her father-in-law, and she even had a moment of compassion for her husband's mother.

The army wife went to bed that night still pondering the situation. All of a sudden, a big smile came across her face. The news story had just provided a resolution for one predicament that had really been bothering her. Several other dilemmas would still have to be dealt with in due time.

The Williamsons were also subscribers to the local newspaper. When J. P. pulled it out of the box, he usually read the headlines and looked over the front page before he got to the house. On the morning the "Toad" story appeared, he stood in the driveway longer than usual. The humble man felt so terrible for his son.

John Paul realized that he was in a sticky situation. Did this newspaper just need to disappear? Occasionally, the paper did not come. Since others in town would surely see the front-page story, however, it was best to just take it on in the house and give it directly to Ethel.

Her response after reading the article did not surprise him at all. "I don't like it," she said. "I can't believe Todd's commanding officers allow this foolishness to go on about my son's name."

Neither did it catch J. P. off guard when he saw the red flag up on the mailbox the next morning. He went by and peeped inside just to confirm what he already suspected. Two letters were awaiting the mailman. One of them was addressed to Pfc. Todd Williamson, and the other to President Franklin D. Roosevelt.

August 22, 1944

Dear Maude,

How are you and little Emma Lou doing?
Has it been a hot summer in north Georgia?
Can you feel the baby moving yet?

There has been some excitement around here. I'm sure you have heard about some of it by now. Mama wrote and told me about the article that was in the Times. When I stumbled upon that secret hiding place, and saw all the valuables that were stored there, I had no idea it would generate so much attention. My picture was in two Paris newspapers. I will save them and send them to you later.

Now, there is more to the story. The owners of the mansion where we are headquartered are Pierre and Margo Hirsch. They escaped France just in time, and had gone to stay with some of their Jewish relatives in New York. Would you believe they read about what I had uncovered in *The New York Times*?

Mr. Hirsch sent a telegram to the American Embassy in Paris thanking everyone involved for preserving their treasures until they can get home. It seems they were intrigued by my nickname. I was sick when the wire service report included "Toad" in its headlines. But it paid off in a way that I could never have imagined.

Mr. and Mrs. Hirsch instructed the officials to look in the hidden closet, now under lock and key, and to find a jade frog with emerald eyes, diamond toenails, and a Chinese coin in its mouth for good luck. It was handed over to my commanding officer, who then presented it to me on their behalf as a thank you gift. This was done in a special ceremony, with flashbulbs going off in my eyes.

Maybe being called "Toad" is not so bad after all. Whenever I can find something to wrap the frog in and a little box, I will send it to you since it is too valuable for me to carry around over here. We can put it on the mantel of our house when I get home and we find a place to live. By the way, we were told that we would be leaving Paris before too long.

Your husband,
"Toad"

He really did not want to go, but the fellows said that he had no choice. Todd was informed they were going to a local nightclub, and that he was the guest of honor. Tex said that his comrades wanted to raise a toast to their friend who had made headlines around the world. Todd was not much of a drinker, but he was beginning to feel for the first time that he was being accepted among his ranks.

One toast to "Toad" turned into another, and then another. Todd started thinking that his pals were just using his newfound notoriety as an excuse to get drunk.

He looked up just in time to see the bartender pointing someone in his direction. He knew the face looked familiar, but he could not immediately put a name with it.

"Hello, Todd, or is it 'Toad'?" the soldier approaching him bellowed, obviously in a jovial mood himself. "Do you remember me, or have you become so high and mighty that you have forgotten your old friends from back home?"

At that point, Todd recognized Donald Vaughn. Maude was in the feed and seed store one day when he came in while home on leave. She introduced the two of them. After he left, she told him that Donald was one of Maggie's old boyfriends.

"I heard the commotion, and then I realized what was going on," Donald added. "I just had to come by and shake hands with the man who put Mason, Georgia on the map."

"It's nice to see you again, Donald," Todd responded. They chatted for a couple of minutes, and then Sgt. Vaughn was ready to move on. "Maybe next time we see each other it will be under more peaceful circumstances," Todd said as they shook hands again.

September 25, 1944

Dear Maude,

You will never guess who I ran into the other night. Some of the men decided to take me to a club to celebrate the good will that my finding those treasures had brought to our company. None other than Donald Vaughn should be in the place that same night. He asked about you and Emma Lou, but he had not gotten the news that you are expecting again.

Do you ever get to see Maggie and Millie? I think I remember you telling me that Millie is working in the bank, but I have no idea what Maggie is up to. Didn't she get married?

I hope the parcel has arrived by now with the jade frog inside. Isn't it a beauty?

I wanted to get this letter off as soon as possible, because we are going to be on the move again. There is talk of another big push in the works. Even if I knew the details, I could not share them with you. Everything is top secret.

Anyway, if you do not hear from me for a while, that will be the reason.

Your devoted husband,
Todd

Maude's heart suddenly went to her throat when she read the part about Todd's encounter with Donald. Furthermore, why was her husband all of a sudden so interested in her two old girl friends? Was he suspicious of something? Did he know more than he was saying? Was Todd picking her for information?

Maude remembered how Todd had said some disparaging things about her friends. He let it be known that he did not care much for either of them. She had the notion that her husband did not want to share her with anyone else. Before the end of their first year of marriage, she was beginning to feel like she was his personal property.

So why was he asking these questions about Maggie and Millie now? Was he just trying to find out what she was doing behind his back? Even worse, did he suspect anything? Was his mother wary, and had she put ideas in his head?

Yes, she had gotten the package from Todd. When Maude took it out of the box, she thought to herself, "This thing is hideous." Then she said, "No, it is grotesque."

She would never forget that word. She missed it in a spelling bee. Since she was not familiar with the term, she assumed that it had to do with growing something. She therefore inserted a "w." As expected, Millie got it right and won the bee.

The jade frog did not look like anything that would ever belong in the kind of house Maude knew she would always live in. The figurine might be right at home in that Paris mansion, but it would look "grotesque" in her house. If that stupid frog was something that Todd treasured, then she guessed she would just have to go along and pretend that she liked it too.

One more thing struck Maude. Why did he close his letter, "Your devoted husband?" Todd had never used those words before. Was he feeling guilty about something?

All of this had given Maude a massive headache. That little episode of nagging doubts triggered by Todd's letter was but a foreshadowing of things to come. Maude Williamson was learning that people are never free of fears, qualms, uncertainties, and especially stress when they are trying to keep hidden a big secret. Even the slightest slipup could blow things wide open.

Hatched in the Pumpkin Patch

Ruby King made it plain that she fully anticipated being on hand when the baby arrived. When Maude discussed this with Doc Elliott, they hatched up a little plan.

Grandpa and Grandma King would be told the best estimate was that the baby was due around the second week of November. When the time came, the doctor would take Maude to the new clinic in Mountain Home for the delivery so that Dr. Worth could assist should any problems arise. Since Mason and Jacksonville were about the same distance away from the county seat town, the physician would call the general store as they were leaving, sending a message to the Kings.

Instead, the baby arrived ahead of schedule. Doc Elliott had to go ahead and deliver it at his office. Her parents would then be called as soon as either he or Aunt Lucy could get around to it.

Maude was hoping not to see her parents again until after the baby was born. Then, they showed up unexpectedly. She and her mother corresponded by mail every week or so. George and Ruby decided to go check on things one more time.

Grandpa made a big fuss over Emma Lou who enjoyed the attention every bit as much as he did. Grandma, on the other hand, was all business. She had carefully rehearsed each question that she wished to ask her daughter. She did not forget even one of them.

By now, Maude was getting somewhat accustomed to the subterfuge. She was more or less able to give a straight answer to each query. George kept his ear tuned to the discussion, while not actually joining in. He was impressed with the way his daughter was handling the situation.

Fortunately, they did not stay too long. On their way out, Maude's parents went by the doctor's office to go over the prearrangement with him again. Doc Elliott confirmed exactly what Maude had told them. George King was certain that the baby would not be born in Mountain Home.

As planned, Doc Elliott went to get Maggie on Sunday, October 15. While the others were at church, he got her settled in at the big house.

Aunt Lucy kept Emma Lou while Maude went to pay Maggie a visit late that afternoon. Neither of them could find just the right words to say. Maggie was already consumed with the anguish of having to give up her baby. Maude was also feeling overwhelmed with the prospects of what lay ahead. They mostly just sat and held each other's hands. Doc Elliott came and got Maude after about fifteen minutes.

Jane was the wild card in all of this. As far as Doc knew, his daughter was not in on what was going on. He had certainly not discussed any of it with her, and he presumed that neither Maude nor Lucille had either. If she had any suspicions, she had not voiced them to him. Then again, Jane kept mostly to herself. She rarely discussed anything of relevance with him.

He had mentioned to his daughter that another patient would be staying with them for a few days. He told her the woman was having some complications, and that she lived some ways away.

If she asked any questions, Jane would be led to believe that the two expectant mothers delivered their babies on the same night. She would then be told that Maggie's was stillborn.

There was also Miss Liza to think about. She would not ask any questions, however. Doc's maid most likely already had everything figured out anyway, but nobody had to worry about Miss Liza.

Everything seemed to be in slow motion. Everybody was jumpy. This was the critical juncture when the slightest slipup could cause the whole charade to fly apart. Maude would see Maggie only one more time before the birth of the baby. On October 26, Maggie sent for her when she knew the time was getting close. When Maude entered the room, she was lying on the bed crying.

Maggie soon began pouring her heart out. It did not all come at once, but in little spurts between sobs. "Maude . . . I'm so sorry for what I have gotten you into . . . You are such a brave and wonderful person . . . I will always love you for what you are doing for me . . . I promise that I will not interfere in your life . . . You will take this baby and raise it as your own . . . I know that . . . But I want you to please understand . . . that I will also love it, too . . . but from afar . . . I will be sending you strength . . . I will pray for you . . . and for this child every day the rest of my life . . . Oh, Maude, will you ever forgive me for what I have done?"

That question caught Maude off guard. She had never thought in terms of forgiving her friend. She did not know what to say. Maggie took note of the hesitancy, and presumed it to mean that Maude might indeed have ill will toward her. The distraught woman could not constrain her tears.

Knowing that she had to say something, Maude finally responded. "Oh Maggie, there is nothing to forgive. We all get caught in difficult circumstances, and we just have to do the best we can. If I heard the preacher right, he said that God is still in the forgiving business."

"You always know the right thing to say," Maggie replied.

Oh how Maude wished that were true.

Doc Elliott advised them to keep the visit short. It was time to say goodbye for now. This was the last time Maude would see Maggie for almost thirteen years. On that occasion, The Three Musketeers would reunite for a funeral.

On October 28, 1944, Maggie appeared to be going into labor. It was a false alarm. Doc Elliott decided to have one more talk with her. "Maggie, you can still change your mind," he advised her. "Maude's baby can be born dead for the official record, and she can walk away from all this with no harm done. Are you sure you are doing the right thing?"

"Yes."

"No."

"I don't know."

"Did Maude put you up to this? Is she trying to back out?" Maggie asked.

"No, Maggie, Maude has not said a word. She seems as determined as ever to carry out the original plan. I'm asking you. Are you absolutely certain that you still want to go through with this?"

Maggie let out a long sigh, followed by several moments of silence. She finally spoke, as he waited patiently.

"I want this baby more than life itself. I would gladly give my life for this baby. That is exactly what I have to do. For the sake of my child, I have to let it go. I have no other choice. By myself, I cannot give it the life it deserves. A part of me is going to die. If I die during childbirth, as your wife did, that is all I deserve. All I want right now is what is best for my baby. My own life doesn't matter anymore."

Maude lay in bed that night unable to sleep. "This really is going to happen," she thought to herself. "Within a day or so, I will be throwing away 'the wad,' and I will be handed a real baby that will be mine to raise." The bottles were ready. Emma Lou's old diapers were washed and folded.

Since she was weaned, Emma Lou was sleeping in the baby bed that had been Malcolm's and then Jane's. Now the bassinet that had cradled Doc Elliott's infants was about to be used again for the first time in many years.

Maude's thoughts returned to a still big unknown. She had decided that she really did want the baby to be a girl. That would be less complicated. She would honor Maggie's request and name the baby Marcia Leigh. She closed her eyes and tried to imagine holding little Leigh. Maude last heard the clock strike two before she finally drifted off to sleep.

Two more days went by, and there was no news from Maggie's bedroom. Doc Elliott said that she was resting, but not very comfortably. They would just have to keep waiting.

A little after ten the next evening, the beleaguered physician quietly unlatched the door to the residence in the back of his house. He knocked gently on Lucille's bedroom door. When she opened it slightly, he told her that her services were needed. Within minutes, she was by his side.

Maude was asleep, but she roused when she heard what was going on. She would certainly not go back to sleep now. She got up and turned on a lamp. Was this more false labor? Was this it? Either way, there was now no turning back.

For the next couple of agonizing hours, Maude waited. She would go lie back down for a while, and then she would get up and pace around the living room. How she longed for a progress report. She even imagined what it must be like for a father when he is kept in the dark while his wife is trying to deliver his baby.

Ready or not, about fifteen minutes before midnight on Halloween, 1944, Walter Othell Williamson came forth to claim his rightful, or perhaps not so rightful, place in this world.

A few minutes past 1:00 a.m. on All Saints Day, Aunt Lucy came through the door with a little bundle of joy. She handed the newborn to Maude who took him awkwardly. The doctor's assistant said that the baby needed to sense her presence, to feel her heartbeat, and to experience her touch.

Maude wanted to get a good look at the infant. Aunt Lucy opened the blanket slowly and carefully. The adoptive mother was spellbound. Regardless of the circumstances, being a witness to the miracle of a new life has its own mystery unparalleled in anything else.

Maude let out a gasp when she saw the head full of black hair. Once she caught her breath, she gingerly counted ten fingers and ten toes.

After the bonding session had gone on for a few minutes, Aunt Lucy said that it was time to put the baby down. After all, it had been a rough night for the little fellow. She took Baby Walt from Maude, and she placed him in the bassinet. Emma Lou slept through the whole thing.

The place was abuzz the next morning. Emma Lou woke up and discovered that she had a new baby brother. Not quite two, she had already picked up a number of words that she could say. Baby was one of them. Brother was now added to her vocabulary.

There were bottles to warm and soon diapers to change. Maude remembered how everyone else had to do the initial chores when Emma Lou was born. This time she was right in the mix. Aunt Lucy hardly left her side, though, keeping a close watch on how things were going.

Next door, Maggie was a mess. Because the baby was so big, the delivery was especially difficult. After Doc Elliott finally got the newborn safely in his hands and the umbilical cord cut, he worked feverishly to get the baby breathing regularly. He then continued with the delicate task of cleaning him up. Lucille went back and forth between assisting the physician and trying to console the distraught mother.

As promised, the infant was then handed to Maggie. For a few brief moments, she lost all awareness of the physical pain that was wreaking her body. She cradled her baby, rocking him back and forth in her arms.

Doc Elliott then nodded to Lucille. When she tried to take the newborn, Maggie let out a shriek. The physician had to restrain her as his assistant struggled to wrest the baby from her hands. "Walter, Walter, I want my baby!" she screamed as she saw the woman going out the door.

Maggie then had difficulty getting rid of the afterbirth. The doctor was up almost all night with her. She was finally resting in bed, if you could call what she was doing resting. The new mother's hormones were raging out of control. Her emotions were on the brink of bringing her to the breaking point. She lived in a deep dread of the next few days. As far as she was concerned, her life was over.

Doc Elliott had hoped to take Maggie back to Taylortown by noon. She was not ready yet for that ride. Furthermore, he needed some rest himself before the journey. For the sake of all concerned, he was determined, nonetheless, that she would not spend another night in his house.

The grandparents also had to be notified. Everyone knew that after they got the message, the Kings would arrive within an hour. None of them was looking forward to this visit. About mid-morning, the doctor placed the call to the general store. Lester Morgan said that he would send his wife to both the Kings' residence and to the Williamsons' with the news.

Ruby King flew into something. George did not know whether it was a rage or just a fit. "I knew something like this was going to happen," she railed out.

George did too, but he did not say anything. He started trying to calm his wife, telling her that they had to get ready to go see their new grandson. On the way to Jacksonville, Ruby sat all drawn up in her seat like she was pouting. Her husband had the wisdom to let her be.

The reaction at the Williamson house was very different. J. P. was down in the patch gathering corn. After Mrs. Morgan shared with her what she knew, Ethel thanked the woman and closed the door. She made no effort to get the news to her husband until he came in for dinner. She then said without emotion, "Maude had her baby last night."

"How did you find out?" J. P. wanted to know. He then asked if the baby was a boy or a girl.

"It's a little boy," Ethel said to him. "Mrs. Morgan did not know much. I guess the Kings are on their way down there now. Maybe we can find out more from them later."

Doc Elliott greeted Maude's parents when they drove up. He then ushered them into his office. The weary physician assured them that everything had gone well during the delivery. He then congratulated George and Ruby for being grandparents to a big healthy baby boy. The country doctor said that he knew Maude wanted to see them, but they could not stay very long. Since all of this happened during the wee hours, everyone needed to get some rest. Ruby was not running the show this time.

George looked down on the desk, and he asked Doc Elliott if this was the child's birth certificate. The physician said it was. He had just finished filling it out before they arrived. The fact of the matter was that he planned to tear it up and start over.

He had gone to Maude to confirm the baby's middle name one more time. When he came to the place to enter the newborn's weight, without thinking he filled it in accurately. The infant weighed in at ten pounds and six ounces. Remembering that the baby was supposed to be a little early, Doc had intended to doctor that figure a bit.

It was too late. George King reached for the document. He started looking it over. The man wanted to see for himself who was listed as parents. "He's a big boy, I see!" the grandpa exclaimed when he came to that part.

George's eyes then went to the top of the certificate. He looked at the baby's name for the first time. Walter Othell Williamson. The proud man's eyes then began to well up. His grandson's initials were W.O.W.

"Wow!" he said aloud. He then lifted his head toward the heavens and said softly, "Thank you, Lord."

The Corn Patch Prayer Meeting

The visit with mother and child went better than anyone expected. By now, Ruby was over her conniption. Everywhere she turned, though, Lucille pulled rank on her. Maude lay on the bed, drawn up under the covers. Aunt Lucy had worked hard to make her look all bedraggled. The doctor's assistant even swished around some disinfectant to make the room smell antiseptic. Attention was then directed away from the mother in bed, and toward the little baby in the bassinet.

"Look at that head full of black hair," Ruby exclaimed. "He must have gotten that from his Grandma King," she added, now feeling much better about the situation.

Emma Lou did not know what to think about it all. She kept hiding in the closet. This was the first time in her life that she was not the center of attention.

George watched all of this playing out right in front of him. He thought to himself, "It is so amazing what people don't see, when they are not looking for it."

As her parents were about to leave, Maude asked if they would get word to Millie. Aunt Lucy walked them to the car, reassuring Ruby that her daughter and grandson would be fine.

The Kings paid a little courtesy visit to the Williamsons when they got back to Mason. J. P. had just come in from the corn patch to get a drink of water and a sweet tater for an afternoon snack. Todd's parents were told what a handsome new grandson they had.

"Has she named the boy yet?" Ethel wanted to know.

"Yes," responded Ruby. "Maude said they gave him his middle name after your father."

Looking now very perplexed, Ethel asked what his first name is.

"Walter," Ruby replied. "But I think they are going to call him Walt."

Mrs. Williamson did not say anything aloud, but J. P. could read her thoughts.

"Has anyone tried to get word to Todd?" Ethel asked next.

George assured her that Doc Elliott had called the Red Cross, and they sent him a telegram. No one was sure how long it would take the wire to catch up with the soldier, thought to be on the move.

George looked back over his shoulder as they were going down the front steps. "J. P., I want to come over tomorrow and talk about a tractor. Ethel mentioned in the grocery store a while back that you might be interested in one. Maybe Earl should be on the lookout for a good used one for you."

"Come on by anytime, George, but I can tell you right now I cannot afford a tractor," Mr. Williamson answered. "I will most likely be scrapping up the rest of the nubbins. That's where I'm headed right now."

"I might come down tomorrow and give you a hand," George replied.

After the Kings left, Ethel registered surprise that the boy was not named after Todd. She said again that something just did not seem right about the situation. It never had. John Paul then turned and looked out the window so that she could not see his lips moving in sync with hers.

"I don't like it. I just don't like it at all."

Since the bank closed on Wednesdays at noon, Millie was already at home when she got the news. In anticipation of this blessed event, her daddy had been saving up as much gasoline as he could. There was just enough in the tank for her to go to Jacksonville and back.

After a brief visit with Maude and the baby, Aunt Lucy took her to Maggie. While nothing could console the frenetic woman, having a friend in her corner was, nonetheless, something that she needed very badly.

It was getting well on into the early evening when Doc Elliott asked Lucille if the birth mother was ready to go. Millie rode in the backseat with Maggie who was sobbing off and on all of the way. Her avowed friend tried to comfort her as best she could.

As Millie caressed Maggie, rubbing her brow and stroking her hair, she thought back to the day just a few months earlier when The Three Musketeers entered into the pact. Now, it seemed like it was in another lifetime. While things had gone without any major complications thus far, there was no way any of them could have fully prepared themselves for what was now unfolding.

It was hard to know what to say when they took Maggie's things in. Millie asked if she needed to tell any of her neighbors about losing the baby. Her old friend said it was nice of her to offer, but that she could take care of it.

The woman next door saw them arrive, and she came over about that time. She was given the bad news. The concerned lady promised that she would look in on Maggie.

Doc Elliott gave his patient the best instructions he could about how to take care of herself. He said that he would be back in a couple of days. There was nothing else left to say, so the doctor and Millie left. Few words were spoken, either, on the way back to where the little war baby was spending his first day with his new family.

Maude never knew when they left to take Maggie back to Taylortown. Millie did not come inside once she and Doc Elliott arrived back to Jacksonville. She got in the car and started home. The weary physician went straight to his bedroom.

Frost was on the pumpkin the next morning in Mason, Georgia. With the chill in the air, Mr. King knew that Mr. Williamson would not be getting an early start. He, therefore, waited until about mid-morning before he walked over. From the road, he could see John Paul down in the bottoms pulling corn.

"Morning, J. P.," he said, not wanting to startle his neighbor.

"Well, howdy yourself," Mr. Williamson answered back.

What was left in the patch was really nothing but a bunch of nubbins. The larger ears had been pulled in roasting ear stage, many of them sold at the fruit stand. Others had been canned for home use. These nubbins were needed, nonetheless, to feed the mules and the milk cow during the winter.

George started pulling corn alongside John Paul.

"A bit chilly this morning," J. P. continued the conversation. "But it is the first of November."

He then addressed the tractor situation. "George, I appreciate your concern and helpfulness, but I think old Dolly and old Claude are in pretty good shape. They might go several more years."

"I thought that was the case, but one of these days you really do need to start thinking about getting one of those little John Deere L Model cub tractors. You know you are not getting any younger," Mr. King chided him.

"All right, George. Just because I now have two grandchildren does not mean that I am getting old," J. P. fired back. They both laughed.

The expression on George's face changed. "Well, a tractor is not really what I came over to talk to you about, J. P. You remember the conversation we had the day after our young'uns got married, don't you?"

"Of course I remember," John Paul answered, as both of them stopped working.

Mr. Williamson looked at Mr. King pensively as George went on. "We agreed if we ever needed to speak to each other about something, that we would not be negligent in doing so. You came to me on that first occasion. Now, it's my turn to come to you."

"George, what's on your mind?"

"J. P., there's something I need to tell you about our grandson. But before I do, you have to assure me that you will keep this just between the two of us. Ruby does not know, and she is not to know. I do believe that it would not be best for Ethel to ever hear what I am about to say."

"You can count on that, George. There's a lot the women don't tell us," John Paul answered.

"That's for sure," George agreed with him.

"I don't know what you are about to tell me," J. P. injected, "but Ethel has said from the very beginning that something suspicious was going on. Lord knows I don't always see eye to eye with that woman, but this time I've had a notion that she might be right."

George King then proceeded to give John Paul Williamson the details surrounding their grandson's birthright. He said Maude did not know that he suspected a thing, and that he did not want her to know. He did not reveal the source of his information, and J. P. did not ask.

Maude's daddy told Todd's father that he had considered bringing this to him earlier, but he decided to wait. If the mother had not been able to carry the baby full term, there would have been no need to pursue the matter any further. Now that the baby was here, he thought the boy's other grandfather needed to know what was going on, for the sake of the child if nothing else.

"I really don't know how Maude is going to handle this," George added. "You know how it is when a cow dies delivering a calf. It is almost impossible to get another cow to take the orphan."

"You're right," J. P. nodded in agreement.

"With Ethel's suspicions, which I'm positive she will pass on to Todd if she has not done so already, I honestly do not know how my boy is going to deal with this either," John Paul added.

"There's a lot we do not know, but regardless of what happens, it is not the baby boy's fault. He had nothing to do with who his mama and his daddy are," George added.

"That's for sure," Mr. Williamson agreed, nodding his head in the affirmative.

"J. P., I want you to enter into an agreement with me that we will both always keep a close eye on the situation. And that you and I will do all in our power to be good grandfathers to that boy."

"George, you have my word on it."

The two men shook hands and then confirmed that this was something that each must take with him to his grave.

At that moment with tears flowing liberally, both men simultaneously fell to their knees in the corn patch. John Paul Williamson commenced praying out loud:

Loving Heavenly Father,

Once again, you have seen fit to bring a new life into this old troubled world. This precious little baby boy will never know how he came about. His earthly parents will be denied the joys of looking into his eyes and seeing parts of themselves looking back. Now it befalls the lot of my son and Mr. King's daughter to raise him as their child.

Dear God, for the sake of this innocent baby, I beg of you to bestow upon both of them a double portion of wisdom. Help them be up to this enormous task. Give them patience and much understanding with each other.

I pray especially for Maude who must carry so much of this burden alone. Endow her with strength. May she be richly blessed for the selfless task she has so graciously agreed to.

I pray for my boy off in the war serving his country, unaware of the circumstances regarding his new son. Dear Lord, I have lifted my concerns for him up to you so many times. Now, they have multiplied. If you can find it in your will, bring him back safely. If anything good can come out of this war, may Todd come home a changed man, mindful of the Almighty, and ready to face his family obligations.

I thank you God for George King, a man of character and true virtue. We now invite you to join with us in the covenant we have entered into. As this boy's grandfathers, we pray that with your leadership we will be examples for him to follow, and that the two of us will be in a position to offer him guidance and direction. We would be remiss, Heavenly Father, if we did not ask you to find your way into the heart of that little fellow. He is going to need more help than any of us can give him.

Finally, I implore you to be merciful to those who recklessly conceived and bore this child.

Amen.

"Amen," George added, as the two men rose slowly to their feet, wiping their brows with their bandanas.

"Okay, let's get this corn pulled," Mr. King said next, ready to move on.

"I appreciate your help, George, but I can get it done by myself," J. P. responded. His neighbor kept right on pulling corn.

No noise other than the sound of the shucks separating from the stalks was perceptible in that cornfield for the next while. An hour or so later, they heard Ethel ringing the dinner bell. The two men walked up to the road in silence. They shook hands again. George then turned and started toward his own house.

Todd still did not know all the particulars, but he was correct in his assessment that he would be on the move indefinitely. After Paris was liberated, the Allies were involved in numerous skirmishes with the retreating Germans. Pfc. Williamson's mobile company was keeping pace with the infantrymen. He had not received any news from home in over a month, and he was so busy that he did not have time to write.

The telegram regarding Walt's birth eventually caught up with him ten days after it was sent. What neither Maude nor his mother knew was that it gave few specifics. The wire only indicated that the baby had arrived on October 31, 1944. For the next two weeks, Todd did not know whether he had a son or another daughter.

November 6, 1944

My dearest husband,

(Maude did not want to get too sentimental, but she decided that she needed to show some warmth.)

> The baby is doing fine. Emma Lou is adjusting to not being an only child anymore. She thinks that she has another doll to play with. I am almost back on my feet. This delivery was a little easier than my first.

("Actually, it was a whole lot easier," thought Maude.)

> I hope you are okay with the baby not being named Todd Junior. I sent you a letter a few weeks ago in which I mentioned several possibilities of names for both a girl and a

boy. I never heard back from you. When the little guy decided to get here a couple of weeks early, I just had to go on and name him.

(Maude had deliberately waited to send the letter, knowing that Todd would not have time to respond before the baby was born.)

I know how much you want a son named after you. But after that article came out in the paper, and everybody around here learned of your awful nickname, I just could not bear the thought of people calling our son "Little Toad." I hope you understand.

Maybe later we can have another son. You will be around while he is growing inside me, and you will be here when he is born. By then, maybe most folks will have forgotten about "Toad," and we can name the next one after you.

Anyway, I just like the name Walter. I think it sounds so distinguished. I remember studying about Sir Walter Scott and Sir Walter Raleigh in school. There is also the great baseball player named Walter Johnson. My daddy and yours, too, think he was the greatest pitcher of all time. I remember you mentioning once that you could see our son being a famous ballplayer.

Then, I thought about our own Senator Walter F. George who is in the news almost every day. I considered naming our son Walter George Williamson. I know my father would have loved that. Instead, I gave him your grandfather's name for his middle name. I hope your mother is pleased with Othell. As I recall, even her name is derived from her father's.

By the way, I have never asked you who

you were named after. I know about your
middle name. But do you know why you
were named Todd? I don't remember
anyone else in your family with that name.

With love from Maude, Emma Lou, and Baby Walt

When this letter finally caught up with Todd three days after
Thanksgiving, almost all of it was news to him. He had gotten the letter
about the names, but it came the same day as the telegram. He saw no need
in responding, because he knew by then it was a moot point. As for his given
name, he had never questioned it.

Todd was yet to hear from his mother at all since the baby was born.
He had long ago given up his mail delivery duties, but he wondered if the
clerk now in charge was up to his old tricks. He knew his mother had written
to him several times by now. Eventually, the letters did begin to catch up
with him, but not necessarily in the order that they were sent. Todd was
getting used to that, too.

Ethel Williamson made a decision not to trouble her son further with
her concerns. He had enough on his mind as it was. She would just keep her
eyes open and her ear to the ground. If something turned up, there would be
plenty of time to fill him in after the war was over.

This did not keep Todd from wondering, though. Some things just did
not add up, but he would have to wait until he got back home to sort things
out.

Part II: The Ugly Duckling

"Being born in a duck yard does not matter, if only
you are hatched from a swan's egg."
Hans Christian Andersen

"You may not control all the events that happen to
you, but you can decide not to be reduced by them."
Maya Angelou

Baby Walt

Walt was a cute little fellow. He took to the bottle right away. Except
for an occasional whimper when he had needs, others would hardly know he
was around. Maude continued to feel a bit awkward handling him.

Aunt Lucy, on the other hand, felt a special closeness with the baby. It
was not long before she did most of the feeding and diaper changing. Emma
Lou was intrigued by her baby brother, but she in no way felt neglected. Her
mother kept right on doing all the things with her that she had always done
before.

Perhaps not nursing Baby Walt had the biggest impact on Maude not
bonding with him. Giving a bottle was just not the same. The surrogate
mother felt more like a nanny than anything else. She would see to it, though,
that the infant received good care. She owed that to Maggie.

Maude had to believe that when Todd got home, everything would be
all right. She imagined the father taking to the boy as he had Emma Lou,
especially since he wanted a son so badly. She would work hard not to show
any difference between the children. Already, she could see that was not
going to be easy. The holidays were looming, and the young mother had no
idea what to expect.

The Kings got a big surprise when they found out that Earl was
bringing Mary Beth home with him for Thanksgiving. Ruby hardly let her
apron touch her dress for two days trying to get everything ready.

Meanwhile, George had a notion of his own. His son and future
daughter-in-law could come through Jacksonville on the way up, and bring
along Maude and the children. The family could celebrate together. Ruby was
not too excited about that idea, fearing that the new mother was not yet back
on her feet enough to make such a trip. George knew that she would be fine.

Maude was proud that she had just finished the dress she had been working on, with Aunt Lucy's help of course. It was free flowing so that it did not reveal her slim figure underneath.

Aunt Lucy could also come along for the ride if she wanted to. With somebody holding the baby, there was just barely enough room for the four of them in the back seat of Earl's 1940 Ford Deluxe Coupe.

Maude tried to explain to Emma Lou who her uncle was. The little girl was a bit shy at first, but then she started warming up to those in the front seat. As a teacher, Mary Beth was especially impressed with the not yet two-year-old tyke's vocabulary. Aunt Lucy lifted Emma Lou across the seat, and she was soon chatting away.

It was only about a half-hour drive, but Maude handed little Walt off to Aunt Lucy about halfway. George took note of who was holding the baby when they arrived. Maude's attention was focused on Emma Lou, while Aunt Lucy showed off Walt.

Thanksgiving dinner began with a long prayer by Grandpa. He was not negligent in remembering his son-in-law and all the other boys off in service. He gave thanks to the Lord for a good year, in spite of the horrors of war. He asked God to bless the future plans of Earl and Mary Beth. The devout man then said a special prayer for the family's newest arrival.

The Kings invited the Williamsons to come over for a visit during the afternoon. Aunt Kathy had not seen Emma Lou in quite a while. This would be the first time for any of them to see little Walt.

Emma Lou jumped in her Granddaddy Williamson's arms. She started telling him all about her baby brother. Baby Walt was sleeping back in Maude's old bedroom, but they all tiptoed in to take a peep. Aunt Kathy was just dying to get her hands on the infant.

Ethel let out a vocal sigh when she saw Walt's hair. The commotion caused the little fellow to stir and stretch out his long arms. He then began to whimper a bit. Aunt Lucy went into motion. She said that it was time for the baby's bottle. She rushed to the kitchen to warm the milk. Maude asked Kathy if she wanted to give him his bottle when it was ready. The teenager was thrilled.

It was not so with Ethel, however. "Why are you not nursing that baby?" she asked gruffly. Maude knew ahead of time that this moment would come at some point. She might as well go ahead and get it over. She took a deep breath and then began reciting the little speech that Doc Elliott had gone over with her.

Maude began by saying that for some reason she had little milk this time. What she had was not agreeing with the baby. She then tried to explain what the doctor had told her.

He said that this sometimes happened with a second child. While the medical profession still did not have everything figured out, it had something to do with antibodies that build up in a mother's system. Specialists believe that it is related to compatibility problems between the mother's and the father's blood. Maude admitted that she certainly did not understand it all. She was just grateful that Walt had taken to the bottle so well.

No one said much after Maude's little speech. She was not sure how well she had done. Aunt Lucy flashed a smile, signaling that she had done okay. The other person in the room who understood fully was her father. Lucille and George made eye contact, but neither of them showed any reaction.

As the Williamsons were leaving, Maude's father-in-law handed her an envelope with some money in it. She thanked him and hugged his neck.

As J. P. and Ethel Williamson were preparing for bed that night, he wondered what was coming this time. "I don't like it," Ethel said as she sat down on the side of the bed. "And to think, that girl is trying to blame not having any good milk for that baby on Todd's blood."

Pfc. Todd Williamson spent Thanksgiving 1944 near the France-Switzerland border. The Alps were in view. The majestic peaks had already received a good blanket of snow. It was a cold, raw, windy day, spitting a little frozen precipitation in the lowlands. The army tried as best it could to provide some semblance of a Thanksgiving dinner for the troops. It would have to do.

Todd let his mind wander back to Thanksgivings past. His mother had to be one of the world's best cooks. "Maybe next year," he thought, "I will be home, and I can put my feet under her table again."

First, there was work that had to be done. The Allied soldiers were bracing themselves for what was almost certainly going to be the decisive battle of the war. They would not have to wait long.

The next month zipped by back in north Georgia. On the first Saturday in December, Maude had an unexpected visitor. The buses were running again and Millie knocked on the door about mid-morning. She was just itching to get her hands on Baby Walt. While she was giving him a bottle, she was surprised when Emma Lou called her Aunt Millie.

The two old chums soon picked up where they had left off. Maude told Millie all about Thanksgiving, and how she managed to get through her first visit home with the baby without incident. No mention was made of Maggie.

The time passed quickly and Millie had to leave to catch the bus. What she had not told Maude was that she stashed a little overnight bag at the station. Instead of getting on the coach back to Mason, she was going to board the one pulling in fifteen minutes later headed toward Taylortown.

Maggie was just as surprised when she saw Millie was standing at her door. This reunion was much more emotional. Maggie yelped with delight when she saw that her friend had come to spend the night.

For the next several minutes, a man would have been totally lost if he had tried to keep up with the conversation. Eventually, both women began to wind down. As each took a deep breath, Maggie asked, "Have you seen my baby?"

Millie had not decided ahead of time whether she was going to mention stopping in Jacksonville. She decided to go ahead and be forthright.

"Is he a good baby?" Maggie wanted to know. "What does he look like?" she asked next. "Does he still have that head full of black hair like Donald?"

Millie answered her questions as kindly and gently as she could. Maggie did not ask about Maude.

Maude was looking forward to Christmas, while dreading it at the same time. She knew that she would have to stay overnight when she went home this time.

She tried to think of something to send Todd for Christmas. She finally decided on a box of teacakes, using her Grandmother Moore's special recipe. She also included some pictures of herself and the children. They would be the first Todd would see of Walt. She worried a bit about Todd's reaction when he saw Walt's hair so she put a little cap on his head.

Doc Elliott had a Kodak box camera that she used. It took about a week for the pictures to come back after she mailed the film off. The parcel was sent about two weeks before Christmas. Maude hoped that it got to Todd on time.

She did not know what to do about other Christmas presents. Aunt Lucy suggested that nobody would really be expecting anything. Rather, her family was more concerned about doing a little something for her and the grandchildren.

On Christmas Eve, George showed up in his old rusty Dodge to take the little family home for Christmas. Aunt Lucy decided to stay in Jacksonville this time so that Doc Elliott and Jane would not be alone. Maude said that she was not sure she could manage without her, but her aunt reassured her that she would have plenty of help.

The mother sat in the front seat holding Walt. Emma Lou had the big backseat all to herself. That did not stop her from talking to her Grandpa, though. She stood on the hump in the middle of the floorboard, and bent his ear all the way to Mason. Walt slept most of the way.

It was an ordeal getting everything moved into Maude's old bedroom. The baby bed was set up in the corner for Emma Lou. Walt would sleep with his mother. Ruby was flittering around in the kitchen, but she took time out to help them settle in.

Santa Claus came sometime during the night. Maude's mother had been busy sewing. Emma Lou got three new dresses. The baby got a couple of outfits and a hand-embroidered blanket. Maude was not left out either. Her mother had made her a new dress. It would no doubt have to be adjusted since her daughter was not present to try it on as it was being pieced together.

Emma Lou followed her Grandpa around everywhere he went. Her mother sensed how much the little girl must miss her daddy. She tried to keep his memory alive by talking to Todd's picture with the girl every day.

Almost everything on the Christmas dinner table was grown right on the Kings' little plot. They always had a big garden, and the summers were spent canning vegetables for the rest of the year. George raised a hog or two on slop and corn.

Ruby fried slices of a sugar cured ham. They were served with hot biscuits and red eye gravy. Also on the big dining room table was a bowl of potato salad, a pot of green beans, a bowl of corn, a sweet potato soufflé, and a pone of cornbread.

Family members had their choice of sweet milk or buttermilk. Ruby wanted to have ice tea, but the store was out the last time she went shopping. There was also pumpkin pie for dessert. Emma Lou ate a little bit of everything, but she was not too sure about the pie.

Walt was mostly left alone in the baby bed. When he was hungry, Grandma gave him his bottle and burped him. If she did not go lay him down afterward, Maude said that he was not used to being held much. It would make him sore if he was jostled around too much. Ruby could not believe that the baby did not have to be rocked to sleep.

After he finished his first bottle, Grandma held Walt out at arms' length so that she could get a better look at him. Then she said, "I have always thought Emma Lou is the spitting image of her daddy. But I think this baby favors his mother." While none of them responded in any way to what Ruby had just said, two other people in the room agreed with her.

After naps, George drove Maude and the children over to the Williamsons' house. Emma Lou went straight to her granddaddy. Aunt Kathy reached for Baby Walt. They did not stay too long. Ethel had knitted some booties for the baby and a sweater for Emma Lou.

When Maude and her brood got back to her parents' house, Earl and

Mary Beth had shown up. They stayed for supper, and then said that they had better be getting back since it was more than a two-hour drive. Maude had planned to spend one more night, but she suggested that Earl could drop them off, and save her daddy the expense of a trip the next day.

"There's no way I'm letting you leave tonight," Ruby said emphatically to her daughter. "Tomorrow is Emma Lou's second birthday, and I'm going to bake a fresh coconut cake for her. That's why we only had pie today. Isn't that right, George?" she turned to her husband for support.

"Your mother's right, Maude. It's hard to get coconuts, but A & P got a crate in just before Christmas. Yesterday, I took a nail and drove it through the eye to drain the milk. Remember how you used to help me with that? That was one tough nut to crack. I think it might be the hardest one to get the shell off that I've ever tried. But I finally got it done. We then ground up the meat in the sausage grinder. All your mother has to do now is bake the cake."

"And besides that," Ruby said, "We have to make the adjustments to your dress."

"Earl, why don't you and Mary Beth stay overnight, too?" George added, "We can find a nail somewhere to hang you on."

"I wish we could," Mary Beth responded. "I would love to have more time to play with these children. We have to get back, though. I promised my daddy we would not be out too late. And you don't want him mad at Earl."

Maude offered no further resistance. She was proud that her daughter was going to have an enjoyable birthday where she would be the center of attention. Emma Lou's mother certainly did not have anything planned for her back in Jacksonville.

Meanwhile, a family tradition was started. On every December 26 thereafter, Emma Lou wanted a fresh coconut cake for her birthday. Even if it were baked ahead of time, it could not be served on Christmas Day. The little girl's birthday would not be thrown in with the other holiday.

After the cake was out of the oven to cool, Ruby brought out the dress that she had been working on for her daughter. When Maude tried it on, her mother realized immediately that she had made it too loose around the waist. She exclaimed with a little surprise that Maude was really doing a good job getting rid of her baby fat.

Maude was quick on her feet. "Yes, I've worked hard on it. When Todd gets home, I want to look the same way I did when he left. So I decided to get rid of the 'wad,' just as quickly as I could."

"We'll just have to take the dress up some before you can wear it home tomorrow," Ruby replied, unmindful to the little hidden message.

As she thought back over the exchange, Maude was right proud of herself. She was learning. Now if she could just keep it up, she might eventually start believing all of it herself.

The War Baby

Maggie had five days off for Christmas. Since giving birth to the baby, she was having difficulty getting her weight back to normal. She had not seen any family members during the interval. On the bus home to Mason, she worried all the way about her appearance. Would anyone notice the changes in her body?

What concerned her just as much was her own disposition. Maggie had always been the one who knew how to celebrate. This year, however, she had nothing about which to be joyous. Her thoughts were ever on her baby, longing to spend little Walter's first Christmas with him. She let her folks think that she just had the holiday blues because she missed her husband so much.

Since mid-December, the news was full of accounts describing a major offensive being launched by the Germans. They were calling it the Battle of the Bulge. Commentators believed that the outcome of the war would be determined by who came out victorious. The Americans, along with their crippled allies, were giving it everything they had. Casualties were heavy on both sides.

It was bitterly cold, and snowed heavily on Christmas Day where Todd was holed up. Not only did the soldiers have to fight off the torrential assaults of the enemy, but they also had to do battle with Mother Nature. The little camp stoves barely kept the makeshift barracks above freezing.

Knowing that communications were often intercepted by those on opposing sides, the Americans sent a decoded message suggesting a ceasefire on Christmas Day. At first, the Germans thought it was a ploy. Perhaps the enemy was trying to lull them into a trap.

A day or so later, another message came back down the line. The Germans had accepted the offer. There was an uneasy truce all day long, each side wondering if the other was going to violate the tacit agreement. Astonishingly, the guns remained silent throughout the day.

At the crack of dawn on December 26, 1944, the fury was unleashed once more. Todd remembered that it was his little girl's second birthday.

Even though Todd was behind the front lines, Maude could not help but worry about him. She could not bear the thought of having to raise these two children without her husband.

The young mother was comfortable living with Aunt Lucy who was a big help to her. Even so, this war bride looked forward to having her man back in her life again. While she had some justifiable anxiety about what was ahead, Maude needed to move on and start making her own home. For now, she had to put aside her nesting urges and just make do.

The next weeks passed quickly. Maude wrote to Todd at least once a week. She hardly ever heard back from him, though. When she did, he could not tell her where he was, but only that the war was really heating up. He hoped that this big thrust would bring it to a halt. Maude did, too. She needed her husband home with her.

By the end of January 1945, it appeared that the German surrender might be imminent. The enemy was pushed back decisively. Hope rang out all over the country that this brutal war might be coming to an end. Agonizingly, an armistice was still months away.

V-E Day & V-J Day

Winter eventually released its tight grip, and soon the songbirds signaled the arrival of spring as though nothing else on earth mattered. Passover and Easter came and went with the renewal of hope in human hearts far and wide. The Allied forces were about to enter Berlin. This long overdue good news was heralded in newspaper headlines around the world.

On May 8, 1945, the World War II Allies officially accepted Germany's surrender. The day was proclaimed V-E Day (Victory in Europe). Celebrations broke out all over the country. There was dancing in the streets.

In a letter to Maude, Todd advised her that he would still not be coming home immediately. Many ground troops had to stay to secure the peace. Even when some foot soldiers started receiving orders to return home, those in his outfit would remain behind a while longer. The occupying armies still had to be supplied.

Todd said that he hoped to be home by Emma Lou's third birthday. Maude noticed that he had not set Walt's earlier first birthday as his target date. At least she felt much better about her husband's safety. The fighting was over in Europe. Her man would be coming home from the war.

The optimism on the western front was offset with much pessimism regarding the war in the Pacific. The Americans were simply not able to break the defiant spirit of the Japanese. There was even talk that some of the soldiers leaving Europe might be redeployed to the eastern theater.

Doc Elliott was all excited when Maude and the children wandered into his office on August 6, 1945. The United States had dropped an atomic bomb on the city of Hiroshima, Japan. Surely, this would break the stubborn will of the enemy.

Three days later, another such explosive was detonated over Nagasaki. On August 14, the United States accepted an unconditional surrender from Japan, declaring V-J Day (Victory in Japan). World War II was officially over. The Three Musketeers all had high hopes of their men coming home from the war, sooner now than later.

Maude was changing Walt's diaper one day when he was about ten months old. She was aware of how much he watched her. When she finished the chore, he just lay on his back gazing up at her. She looked right back into his dark brown eyes and thought, "Who are you?" What she had no way of knowing was, using whatever concepts already formed in his growing little mind, Walt was wondering the same thing about her.

Summer 1945, was long, hot, and dry. The Williamsons were barely able to keep up with the demands at their fruit and vegetable stand. With little rain, the corn stalks produced mostly nubbins. The sorghum cane would have very little juice unless the rains came in late summer. At least the dry weather would make it rich in flavor.

Despite the drawbacks and the setbacks, the air was filled with hopefulness and optimism. The Williamsons' son and the Kings' son-in-law would soon be home from the war.

Over at the Kings' household, George realized more and more that he was going to have to find something else to do. Fewer and fewer families could make a living off the farm any longer. The demand for mules was about gone. Returning soldiers would be looking for jobs with incomes that were more dependable.

George noticed something else, too. The women employed to help support the war effort had gotten used to seeing paychecks with their names on them. Many of them would no longer be content just being a housewife.

Over in Jacksonville, Maude felt increasingly that she was wearing out her welcome. There was certainly no pressure on her to move out. She really did not have anywhere else to go, other than to move back in with her folks. At the same time, she resented Aunt Lucy's constant involvement in her life.

Maude's aunt was beginning to seem like another mother. Aunt Lucy always had rank on her. She always knew what was best to do. Maude really did appreciate the woman's assistance with the children, but the young mother felt that she was being treated in a condescending way herself. More than anything else, though, Maude needed a man to depend on.

Meanwhile, Maude just had to carry on. After he outgrew his little nightshirts, Walt needed a new wardrobe. As he grew, Aunt Lucy kept altering the one set of patterns she had for a baby boy's clothes. He was so patient when trying on his new garments. Walt was a good baby. Maude thanked her lucky stars for that.

As the leaves began to turn and then start to fall, word from Todd came more frequently. He was hopeful of being home by the end of the year. The anticipation for Maude was at times almost overwhelming. All she wanted for Christmas was her man in her arms.

When Maggie Hogan arrived at work on October 1, 1945, her supervisor made an announcement. With the war over, the textile mill was shutting down on the 26th to start retooling for domestic products. It would be closed for at least two months.

Maggie had been planning to turn in her notice anyway. Everett thought he might be home by Thanksgiving. It was time for her to move back to Mason, and be waiting for him when he arrived. She sent a letter to her daddy and asked if he could come get her and help her move her things home. He wrote back and said that he would be there on the last day of the month.

Maggie said goodbye to the friends she had made. She was glad that this episode in her life was about over. Her fingers ached constantly, and she hoped that she had not done any permanent damage to them working on the stranding machines.

The war bride was really looking forward to her husband coming home so the two of them could get on with their lives. As she packed up her things, her heart was simultaneously heavy, however, because of something that had nothing to do with Everett.

Raymond McDonald was up early that Wednesday. He got to Taylortown by the middle of the morning. Within half an hour, the car was loaded. Maggie barely had room in the front seat.

As they approached Jacksonville, she became very quiet. When they went by Doc Elliott's office, Maggie was struggling to control her emotions. She closed her eyes and her daddy thought she was sleeping.

One year ago that very night, she gave birth to her precious son Walter in that house. She had no idea if Maude and the children were still staying with her Aunt Lucy.

How she envied Walter's other mother for being able to celebrate his first birthday with him. Maggie wondered what kind of cake she baked, and what presents he would receive.

He must surely be walking by now. Maggie tried to imagine the look on her little boy's face taking his first steps toward her. When a smile came across her own, Raymond thought that his daughter was having a sweet dream.

Her expression soon dissolved. The Three Musketeers had vowed always to be there for one another. Now, she felt like "The Scarlet Woman." Maggie understood that she had promised to stay out of Maude's life, but she never imagined that her devoted friends would turn their backs on her. She had seen Millie only once since the day Walter was born, and she had heard nothing whatsoever from Maude.

Walt's first birthday came and went. As Maude turned the calendar, it momentarily rattled her when she realized that she had not even remembered the significance of the last day in October.

Walt's birthday was not the only thing that was overlooked, either. No one could pinpoint exactly when the little boy started walking. By the time he was ten months old, he was pulling himself up and going around the walls.

One day, he was standing in front of a chair rocking it back and forth. Maude thought she smelled something, and she asked the tot if he needed a change. Walt turned loose of the chair and he walked over to her.

As she was putting the second pin in the clean diaper, Maude was pondering what had just happened. "Walt must have known exactly what I was asking him," she thought to herself. Then, it hit her. He walked, not crawled to her. Were those his first steps? She could not say for sure.

When Maude and her brood went home for Thanksgiving, Walt's walking skills certainly did not go unnoticed. Both his Grandpa King and his Granddaddy Williamson took much delight in their grandson's ambulatory abilities. The little boy just took it all in good stride.

Earl and Mary Beth had planned to have a late summer wedding before school started. She was about to begin her second year teaching fourth grade in Adamsonville. Even with the war officially over, they feared that distant kin might not be able to get to the church on time, if at all.

Mary Beth was an only child. With no nieces and nephews, she wanted Emma Lou to be the flower girl, if the little girl was big enough to handle such an awesome chore.

Besides that, Earl was planning a big honeymoon surprise that would involve a considerable amount of travel. Gasoline supplies were still tight. Earl King had waited twenty-nine years to get married. He could wait a little longer.

As things in the country began to stabilize and settle down, Earl and Mary Beth decided on a Christmas wedding. The schoolteacher bride could use her holiday vacation for their honeymoon. Invitations went out, and this time there was no backing out.

On the Saturday afternoon of December 22, 1945, everybody who was anybody in and around Adamsonville, Georgia was at the First Methodist Church for the nuptials of George Earl King and Mary Elizabeth Prince. Todd missed the festivities. He was aboard a ship steaming across the Atlantic.

George and Ruby King had to get an early start. Their granddaughter, the groom's niece, was going to be the flower girl. Mary Beth had mailed the material and a pattern for Emma Lou's dress. Ruby took charge of getting it made. The little girl thoroughly enjoyed trying it on, and then looking at herself in the mirror.

Aunt Kathy offered to keep Walt, since it was going to be a long day. After the ceremony and the reception, the Mason folks would not get back until well after dark. Maude was thrilled. She would be able to devote all of her attention to her daughter.

Emma Lou stole the show. There were whispers all through the audience as the little girl held her basket so properly while dropping flower petals down the aisle. "She looks just like Shirley Temple," Maude heard one person mumble. The proud mother had always thought the same thing.

When the flower girl got to the front of the church, she did not turn around and go sit with her mother as she was instructed. Rather, Emma Lou bolted up the steps. She took her stand beside her Grandpa, who was Earl's best man.

Nobody had to be able to read lips as the gentle man leaned over and whispered into his granddaughter's ear. They did not have to be fluent in sign language when she shook her head no. Neither did they have to be mind readers when the minister looked over with a stern and disapproving look. Even so, Emma Lou remained by her Grandpa's side throughout the ceremony. During the proceedings, as many eyes were on her as were on what was taking place elsewhere on the podium.

Uncle Earl teased Emma Lou at the reception about upstaging the bride. She seemed to glow in her notoriety. Mary Beth reassured the flower girl that she was so proud of her for being a perfect little angel.

The newlyweds drove off for their wedding night in Chattanooga to the rattling of tin cans tied to Earl's snazzy black Ford Coupe. With the dapper groom at the wheel and his elegant bride by his side, the souped up flathead V-8 flat outran the others in the wedding party trying to keep pace.

It did not hurt that Police Chief "Red" Allen, the bride's uncle, was sitting at the first stop sign. He waved the newlyweds through. He then made sure that no one else broke the law in an effort to keep up. The couple would be off the next day for the only place that Earl ever considered taking Mary Beth on their honeymoon – Niagara Falls.

While Aunt Kathy was the one who volunteered to keep Walt, his Granddaddy Williamson devoted most of the day to the boy. The two walked down State Street amid busy Christmas shoppers. Some folks stopped to chat as the jubilant granddaddy showed off his precocious little grandson.

Walt took a long nap during the afternoon. Aunt Kathy commented more than once how little trouble he was. When the Kings stopped to pick him up, he was already asleep. J. P. suggested that he just spend the night. "That's a mighty fine boy you have there," he said to Maude.

Ethel again raised her concerns that something was wrong with the situation as they prepared for bed. "He doesn't favor Todd at all like Emma Louise does," she began.

Mr. Williamson decided not to remain silent. He reminded Ethel of what a good boy Walt was. He told her he certainly hoped she was not implying that Maude had in any way been improper before Todd left for New York. He said that if their son suspected anything amiss, he would have most assuredly confided it in her. He added that Walt was born just a little more than eight months after Todd left.

J. P. concluded by telling his wife that she needed to dismiss her concerns. Then he said, "Mark my word. One day that little war baby is going to make us all proud."

Ethel turned aside, thinking to herself, "I still think something is wrong. And I just don't like it."

The Homecoming

On December 18, 1945, Pfc. Todd Williamson packed up his gear one last time on the European continent. He carried his duffel bags onto the big ship headed for the port of New York. If it arrived on schedule, he would disembark in five days. That would give him two days to get to Mason and be home for Christmas. But, things do not always go according to design. Todd of all people should have known that.

When the ship docked, the trains leaving Grand Central Station were packed. He waited eight agonizing hours before he finally got a seat. The exhausted soldier eventually chugged into Atlanta late in the afternoon of Christmas Eve.

Before he could leave the army base, Pfc. Williamson had to get his official discharge papers. The lines were long and seemed to be moving ever so slowly. The weary GIs were assured that the offices would not close until everyone was processed. At 11:45 p.m. on Christmas Eve, Todd was once again a civilian. He wandered into the almost empty barracks to find a place to sleep.

On Christmas Day, he could not find a train or bus running toward Chattanooga. His only choice was to set out hitchhiking. Not much traffic was on the road, but a couple with a small child eventually picked him up. The driver was one of the discharge sergeants back at the base. Because of the late influx of returnees, the little family was delayed from starting home for the holiday. They were only going as far as Dalton, Georgia.

Todd had given little thought about what he would eat. He reluctantly accepted the invitation to join their family for Christmas dinner. The wife's parents were welcoming. Todd did not realize how hungry he really was, and he tried not to make a pig of himself.

The folks offered him a place to stay overnight, concerned the chances were slim that he would be able to catch a ride on to Mason. The temperature was going down into the low 20s overnight. Again, Todd unenthusiastically relented.

Meanwhile, Maude and the children had moved back in with her parents a few days before the wedding. The air was filled with excitement, knowing any minute that her husband might come walking through the door. Because of the holiday, it was impossible for Todd to get a message through as to his whereabouts.

Maude tried as best she could to prepare Emma Lou for the return of her father. She assumed Walt was too young to understand, but she had no idea what was going on in his little mind.

The anxious wife did not want to go to bed. Her father assured her if Todd got there during the night that he would wake them up. Christmas morning came and he had not yet arrived. Neither did he get home anytime throughout the day. Maude prepared herself for another restless night.

Todd had to be convinced to stay for breakfast the next morning. He was ready to get on the road. His host asked him what he was going to do after the war. The army veteran said that he had been giving it some thought, but he had no idea what opportunities were available. He was certain that he could not make a living for a wife and two children on a rocky farm in the hills of north Georgia.

The man told him that he worked for the post office. He asked Todd if he had ever considered being a rural mail carrier. Nothing like that had crossed his mind. The official then said he believed that the longtime mailman in Mason was about ready to retire. If he was interested in the position, the man offered to put in a good word for Todd. The gracious host then wrote his name and phone number on an old envelope.

Traffic was still very slow the day after Christmas. Fortunately, those on the move were eager to give a lift to a man in uniform. Todd loaded and unloaded his gear four times before he finally got out of a pickup truck on State Street in Mason, Georgia. He stood tall, he stood straight, and then he took a deep breath of fresh mountain air. Todd Williamson was home from the war.

He picked up his bags and headed to his parents' house. He did not know where Maude and the children were. After an emotional reunion with his mother, and a tearful embrace with his father, Todd turned to his not so little sister. Kathy had become a young lady while he was gone.

J. P. then said, "You can take the car, son. I know you want to get on over to the Kings'. We'll have lots of time to catch up on everything over the next few days." It felt strange sitting behind the wheel. Todd had not driven a vehicle since he left to go overseas.

Maude heard it first. A jalopy was coming up the long drive. She ran out on the porch. Her man was home from the war. It was about mid-afternoon of their daughter's third birthday.

George held Emma Lou who watched cautiously as her mother and father enjoyed their emotional embrace, and then a kiss. Ruby stood by relishing the moment. The little girl did not know what to make of the situation. She really did not remember her daddy, only images in her mind from photographs.

Todd let go of his wife, and he held out his arms for his daughter. She clung to her Grandpa. Maude reached for Emma Lou, took her, and held her close. Cheek to cheek, she then started reminding her of all the things they had talked about. It took a few seconds, but then it all began to click.

Maude said to her gently, "I think your daddy has something to say to you," hoping Todd remembered what day it was. He came over and embraced both of them at the same time. Emma Lou put forth her hand and touched his face. She then went to him, and she gave her father a big hug. He held her out and started singing, "Happy birthday to you; happy birthday to you; happy birthday Emma Lou; happy birthday to you."

The others joined in.

No one noticed that Walt had walked out on the porch. Down for his nap, he was awakened by the commotion. The inquisitive little fellow went to investigate. When he tugged on his Grandpa's britches leg, George said, "Well, look who else has come out to join the party."

Looking down at Emma Lou in his arms, Todd asked, "Who is this?"

His daughter said, "Daddy, this is Walt, my little brother. Don't you know who he is?" The man did not answer.

By this time, Grandpa had picked up the toddler. Walt fastened his eyes on the strange man standing on the porch holding his sister. Todd looked over at the boy, and then he turned away. That stare was unsettling to him.

The edgy man did not know what to do next. Should he put Emma Lou down and try to take his son? Would the boy cry and have nothing to do with him?

Maude sensed his uneasiness. She took the little girl and stood her on her feet. She then went and gathered Walt in her arms. Slowly, she walked toward Todd. Walt never took his eyes off the man as they approached him.

Todd reached out and then took the little fellow from his mother. The man held the boy up and out, looking him over from head to toe. Maude held her breath. Walt showed no emotion. Todd made no comment.

As Walt settled back into the man's arms, Todd made eye contact with the child once more. Again, the man looked away. What was this all about? Why was he letting a thirteen-month-old boy's piercing dark brown eyes intimidate him?

About that time, Grandma broke the spell. "There's a big fresh coconut birthday cake just waiting to be cut," she joyfully cried out. "And it has three candles on it." They all went inside, realizing for the first time how cold it was on the porch.

Todd was still carrying Walt. The boy made no attempt to get the man to put him down. The uncertain man looked around. Nobody was making any effort to rescue him.

Inside the house, Maude finally came to Todd's defense. "Let Walt show you how he can walk," she instructed. Her husband could now save face. Once on his feet, the boy went scampering away to the applause of his grandparents.

With a little prompting from her mother, Emma Lou went and crawled up in her daddy's lap as the birthday cake was being served. Just like that, after being separated for twenty-two months, a father and his daughter were reunited. Reconnecting with his wife, and bonding with his son would prove to be much more troublesome.

The mood was jovial, but a bit strained as the family proceeded with the birthday celebration. As they were getting up from the table, Todd took Maude by the hand and led her outside. Beyond the earshot of the others, he addressed his wife in a firm and stern manner. He said he was very disappointed that she and the children were not at his parents' house when he arrived. He then told her to get the children. He was ready to go.

Maude tried to reassure him that they were perfectly welcome to stay with her folks. Todd shot back that this was not something they were going to argue about. He added that he knew how much her father disliked him, and that he would not feel comfortable staying at his place.

"That's not true," Maude tried to get in edgewise, but he ignored her. He then went on to say they would be making his parents' house their headquarters until they were resettled. And it was going to start right then.

It mattered not to him that his wife felt equally uncomfortable at the Williamsons' house. The real issue was that Daddy King overruled Todd when he took Maude and Emma Lou to stay with Aunt Lucy while he was overseas. He was not about to spend a night under that man's roof.

Maude felt that she was between the proverbial rock and a hard place. For weeks, she had been hearing warnings from the media that no man ever comes back from war the same person. Military wives were being cautioned to be patient with their battle scared spouses. Even so, she was not prepared for the tone in which Todd addressed her.

George was watching all of this from behind a curtain. He intercepted his daughter as she came into the house fighting back tears. He asked her if everything was all right. Maude lied and said that it was. She straightened up her face, and then she said that Todd wanted to go to the Williamsons'.

"Then let's start gathering up your things," her daddy whispered.

Todd stayed outside while Maude and her father brought out her belongings. He loaded them into J. P.'s old car. He nodded, but said nothing, when George told them to come back soon. Ruby stood on the porch waving, but nobody saw her. On the short ride, Maude held Walt and Emma Lou stood between her parents on the front seat. Nobody said a word. Walt was the only passenger not keeping his eyes on the road.

"Come in," Granddaddy Williamson said cheerfully. "And Happy Birthday to my granddaughter," he added, as the little girl ran to him. The man picked up Emma Lou, and they pranced around the living room. Kathy ran out of her room to see what was going on.

The greeting from Mrs. Williamson was not as jolly. She announced impassively that Todd's bedroom was made up and ready for them. Pallets were on the floor for the children. J. P. put Emma Lou down much to her dislike, and he started helping Todd unload the car. Maude put Walt down, and he went traipsing through the house.

The leftovers on the table for supper were not the only things cold that evening. A noticeable chill was in Todd's demeanor. His father was full of questions, but his son kept saying, "Not now, Daddy."

While he had ached for the moment that he would again be sitting at his mother's table, Todd was unable to relax and enjoy the meal. Maude ate quietly, and she fed Walt who was sitting in her lap.

Emma Lou was the only one who seemed unmindful of anything out of the ordinary. She and her Granddaddy Williamson had their own little thing going. Ethel kept passing dishes around, making sure that no one would leave the table hungry.

When they gathered in the living room, Todd took a seat on the sofa beside an end table. He was caught totally off guard when Walt walked over to him. "He wants to sit in your lap," Maude said to her husband. The man reached down and picked up the toddler.

All eyes were on Todd. He did not know what to say. Then, Walt's eyes caught everyone's attention. He looked up at his father's face, and then he looked at the picture of the man on the table. To everyone's amazement, the little boy took his finger and pointed at the photograph. He then turned his head again, looked into the eyes of the man holding him, and pointed to his face. Todd looked away. His eyes turned toward his mother's. Hers were wide open, as was also her mouth.

Aunt Kathy asked if she could give the little boy his bottle before he was put down for the night. Maude handed him off, and he went right to work. He was not yet asleep when his mother took him to the bedroom. He seemed happy to be away from everyone else. He lay on his pallet for a while looking around.

When Maude checked on him a few minutes later, he was sound asleep. "That's a mighty fine boy you have there," J. P. said to his son. "Just look at the way he took to you. Most babies would be terrified of a man suddenly showing up like that."

Todd just nodded, in apparent agreement.

Emma Lou protested when she was told that it was her bedtime. Todd shot his wife a look when she asked their daughter if she wanted her daddy to put her to bed. He was relieved when the girl said, "No, Mommy, I want you to. But will you rock me first?" Maude picked her up, glad to escape the others. The little girl was asleep for some time before her mother finally put her on the makeshift bed.

Maude would not have stayed in the bedroom nearly as long if Kathy had not been in the room with the others. She knew nothing would be said behind her back as long as the girl was present. She almost tripped on her own feet when she came back into the living room and discovered that the teenager had left to go to her room. Maude went and took her place on the tattered old sofa beside her husband, wondering what was said in her absence.

While she was rocking her daughter, she contemplated what was going to happen when it came time for her and Todd to go to bed. She did not have to wait long. Shortly after she rejoined the others, Ethel announced that it had been a long day and she was going to retire. John Paul got up and followed her out of the room.

The couple was left alone sitting on the couch. Neither of them seemed to know what to do next. Todd sat up straight and stiff. Maude wanted so much for her husband to take her in his arms and just hold her.

Without saying a word, he got up and went outside. She checked on the children and then put on her nightgown. As she crawled under the covers, she had an uncomfortable feeling that a total stranger was about to get in the bed with her. If Maude had not been the lawfully wedded wife of Todd Williamson, what happened next would be considered rape.

On the Sunday after Christmas, Maude wanted Todd to go to church with her and the children. She asked him to wear his uniform, and to let the people of the community welcome him home. He had no such desire.

J. P. went alone, while Ethel remained at home to cook Sunday dinner for her family. Todd went outside. He was gone for almost an hour. Maude offered to help in the kitchen, but her mother-in-law said that she had everything under control.

Ruby King also stayed home that morning. All of the excitement had gotten to her, and she had taken to her bed. After the worship service was over, John Paul and George shook hands on the church steps. They then retired to the parking lot where they talked for several minutes before each went his separate way.

The next few days were hectic. Todd's father eventually gave up on getting his son to talk about his wartime experiences. J. P. spent most of the daylight hours working in his woodshop. Ethel busied herself cooking and doing other household chores. Maude tended to the children, trying to stay out of everybody else's way. Todd was understandably restless. Emma Lou made herself right at home. Walt was mostly invisible.

Publisher/Editor Hiram Harwell at *The Townsend Times* did his best to keep the citizens of the area informed about returning veterans. There was no official agency of the government from which to get this information. He, therefore, had to rely on local sources. The newspaper's correspondents who wrote community news were commissioned to send in accounts as they came across them.

Already the paper had made note of the return of Roy Hancock. He was saluted for his work with Voice of America. A month later, the picture of his bride-to-be, Millie Mitchell, appeared on the Society Page, announcing the couple's engagement.

In early December 1945, *The Times* did a story about Everett Hogan and his service to his country. It mentioned that the seaman was considering reenlisting.

The editor was also keeping a watchful eye for one particular name. It finally came across his desk right after Christmas. In the newspaper's last edition of the year, a front-page story chronicled the homecoming of Pfc. Todd "Toad" Williamson. The article recounted the episode in which the soldier had uncovered the treasures of a refugee family that had fled Paris. It told how the private came about his nickname, and how the family rewarded the GI with the gift of a jade frog.

On page two of that same paper, the citizens were informed that paratrooper Donald Vaughn, also of the Mason area, had made it home. At the time of publication, Vaughn's plans were uncertain.

After he got home from the war, Everett Hogan took some leave time. He talked it over with Maggie, and he then signed up for another tour of duty. He was given a choice of returning to Norfolk, Virginia, or being stationed in San Diego, California. Maggie encouraged him to take the latter option. She thought it might be easier for everyone concerned if she were all the way across the country.

During the two months that Maggie was in Mason, Millie came to see her once, but she did not cross paths with Maude. Millie told her that Todd was home. Walter's birth mother wished so much for a report on how things went.

Amidst celebrating Everett's return from the sea, Maggie's heart yearned to be with her baby during Christmas. She wanted to send some presents to both Emma Lou and Walter, but Millie did not think that was a good idea. She tried to envision her little boy stumbling out of bed on Christmas morning to go see what Santa Claus had brought him.

The couple had no car and few possessions. They packed some things up and shipped them. Then, right after the first of the year in 1946, Maggie and Everett took the train across the country to their new home in California. As the Hogans renewed their life together, Walter's birth mother presumed that she would never see her baby again.

She must now concentrate on her marriage and just hope for the best. Meanwhile, Maggie honored persistently a promise that she had made. Not one single day passed without her uttering a prayer for Maude and little Walter.

Roy Hancock came home to a waiting Millie. The two of them began planning for a modest church wedding. Maude was the matron of honor, but Maggie did not get to attend. She had already moved away.

With his military training as a communications officer, Roy decided to get into the radio business. He took a job at the local station in Mountain Home as a news announcer. He quickly figured out that he preferred being behind the scenes. When an assistant general manager position opened at a big station in Atlanta, Hancock took the job. Five years later, he became the general manager. Five years after that, he bought the station.

Donald Vaughn went from jumping out of airplanes to flying them. With many of the military pilots leaving the service to take jobs with the fledgling commercial airline industry, Uncle Sam was in need of pilots for his new branch of the service, the United States Air Force.

Donald could not get enough of flying. His biggest regret was that he did not get to sit in the cockpit during the war. The tall angular pilot just barely had room to fit in the tight space. He was coming along just in time to be part of a completely new way of moving a plane through the air. Donald Vaughn would be on the cutting edge of jet engine propulsion. As the technology continuously stretched its wings, the aviator had the right stuff to become one of the country's celebrated test pilots.

Stymied

While the war was going on, Maude's father bought a little farm just at the edge of town. An elderly couple put it up for sale when they moved to Mountain Home to be near their children. The old farmhouse was in need of some repair, but Mr. King offered it to his daughter's family to live in. He made Todd the promise that he could buy the place if he wished, once he got on his feet.

This created a real dilemma for Todd. He was ready to be the man of his own house. At the same time, he was not exactly thrilled at being beholden to his father-in-law. Naturally, Maude was all for it.

Todd wondered if he would ever be able to get out from under the shadow of Daddy King. "That man doesn't think I have a pot to piss in," he mused to himself. The fact of the matter was he barely did.

Anyway, there was one good thing about the arrangement. It was only a hop, skip, and a jump from where Todd's mother lived. It was also located about the same distance from Maude's folks. Like points of a triangle, each residence was about a half mile apart.

The house had not been painted in years. It was on a dirt road with not much traffic. The yards had not been swept in some time and weeds were beginning to take over. One of the first things Maude wanted to do was to cut some dogwood saplings and make a brush broom.

The barn was in rather good shape. It opened up to several acres of pasture, but the fences were in disrepair. The large garden area was all grown up.

The house had twin gables facing the front, with a chimney sticking out of each. It had porches front and back. A driveway went to the rear of the house where the family routinely went in and out.

Emma Lou was thrilled to have her own bedroom. Walt was put in the room next to her. Nothing much seemed to faze the little boy. He mostly just stayed out of everybody's way. With nobody else paying him much attention, he learned to amuse himself. Walt Williamson never lacked for good entertainment.

Maude was not sure what Ethel had told Todd. She was surprised that he asked so few questions about Walt. She was likewise disappointed that her husband was showing no special fondness for his son. She was hoping that Todd would bond with the boy, and take over much of the responsibility for his raising. Her husband rather focused most of his attention on Emma Lou.

Todd wandered into town one day soon after the first of the year. His first stop was Lipham's Feed and Seed Store. "Come in 'Toad'," Luther called out. Todd thought he might be able to get his old job back, but there was not much business during the winter. Before he left the store, though, he made it very plain to his old boss that he would not be addressed by his inglorious nickname.

Word soon spread around town that the returning veteran was a little sensitive about his moniker. Some of the townspeople backed off, but others who remembered him well were insistent on rubbing his nose in it.

Todd also stopped by the post office while he was out. It was indeed true that the aging mail carrier was about to retire. He learned that priority would be given to a returning veteran. He filled out an application while he was there.

Todd Williamson was offered the job a week later. He told Maude that listing his Christmas Day host as a reference made the difference. What he did not know was that he got the position only after George King paid his old friend the postmaster a little visit. Todd passed the Civil Service Exam, and he was named the new Mason, Georgia rural route mailman beginning February 1, 1946.

This meant that he had to purchase a car. Maude was not sure where he found the money, but her husband came driving up in a tan 1937 Plymouth. Todd rode with the retiring mail carrier several days to learn the route before taking it over himself.

The young homemaker now had a place of her own. Todd was receiving a paycheck. Little by little, the Williamsons added to their meager furnishings. Maude stayed busy taking care of her family. Just as her husband had speculated, that gaudy little "grotesque" frog stared at her every day from its perch on the mantel in the living room.

Gradually, the husband and wife began to adjust to their lives. For the first time in their marriage, they had some measure of stability. Todd had mood swings that Maude had to work around, but she kept telling herself that as he put more distance between himself and the war, things would get better.

As the days passed, she breathed a little easier about the situation pertaining to Walt. Todd had shown no particular curiosity about the boy's beginnings. That was all about to change.

On the second Sunday in February, George and Ruby asked if the grandchildren could go home with them after church. Maude was thrilled at the prospects of an afternoon without her brood under her feet. Todd was hesitant, but he eventually agreed.

Soon after the young couple finished their lunch, he removed any notion that Maude might have had in her mind that the two of them would have a relaxing and pleasurable afternoon. Her husband said some questions were nagging at him, and that he wanted to go over them with her. The time Maude had been dreading was upon her.

It did not go well. Todd got no satisfactory answers. Maude's stomach was once more tied up in knots.

Questions concerning Walt kept replaying over and over again in Todd's mind. Some things just did not add up. Maude conceived, and then she had another period, or she got pregnant a day or two after she went off the rag. Both of those possibilities seemed highly improbable to him.

His wife told him that sometimes a woman has a false period the first month after she conceived. She said her flow was very light, and that Doc Elliott confirmed that was most likely what happened. Todd's mother said that she had never heard of such a thing.

When he left to go overseas, Maude was still nursing Emma Lou. Ethel did not think that it was possible for a woman to conceive with another child not yet weaned.

There was also Walt's birth weight. The boy certainly did not come early, even though Maude specifically said that he did in one of her letters. His weight seemed to rule out conception the night before Todd left. That was only eight and a half months before his birthday.

There was also the problem with Maude's milk. Todd's mother stopped Dr. Worth on the street one day, and she asked him if a second time mother ever had trouble with her milk the way Maude had explained it. The physician told her that there were indeed times when there was no problem with the first child, but later offspring got jaundice from their mother's milk. That did not help clear up the picture.

Todd always thought the explanation for the name given the baby was lame. He was forced to admit that Maude had a point regarding the "Toad" dilemma, but he felt there was more to it than that. Why did she wait so long to bring up the name issue, and then send a letter that he did not have time to respond to before the baby was born?

Something else bothered Todd continuously after he got the May Day letter. Maude never seemed excited about having a new baby on the way. All of her reports were void of sentiment. Even after Walt was born, his wife's correspondence did not convey any particular sense of joy.

Added to his consternation was the fact that Maude was not particularly devoted to the boy. That really puzzled Todd. When Emma Lou was born, his wife took to motherhood as though it were the fulfillment of her female destiny. With Walt, Maude was somewhat detached, and at times even inattentive.

Neither could Todd dismiss his mother's suspicions. She felt from the very beginning that something was not right. Ethel had simply not been able to figure out what was going on, either.

He just could not make all the pieces fit. There was no way that he could imagine Maude being unfaithful to him. That was just not her nature. Furthermore, he could not put together any circumstances when she had opportunity.

Then, there was the boy himself. He did not look to his father for endorsement as Emma Lou did. It seemed that Todd's estimation of Walt mattered not to the kid one way or the other.

The most significant thing of all, though, was the fact that not one thing about the toddler made Todd feel that he was bone of his bone and flesh of his flesh. Nothing about the shape of the little boy's head and the color of his hair made him look like a Williamson.

Maude reminded him that her mother's folks all had black hair. She said just because Emma Lou was his carbon copy did not mean that he could expect Walt to get his traits from his father's side of the family, too. She added that he ought to be proud that one of their children bore his likeness. Neither of them took after her.

Besides all of that, however, he could not get used to the way the lad looked at him. Why did that still unnerve him so?

For the moment, Todd was stymied. He would just keep pushing and prodding, and eventually something would shake loose.

The couple's fourth wedding anniversary was fast approaching. Maude did not know what to expect. She wanted to celebrate the occasion, but she did not know how or where to begin. True to her nature, she held back to see if Todd would take the lead.

Much to her delight, he did have something in mind. Valentine's Day was actually on a Thursday in 1946, but he suggested that they go out on Saturday night. The International Barbershop Quartet Convention was meeting in Chattanooga. Since there would be no mail route the next day, it would not matter if they got home late. He said that he had already talked with his mother about the children staying over with her.

Maude was amazed that he remembered where they had gone on their second date. She wanted everything to be just perfect. Todd got up early on Saturday morning so that he would get back from the mail route as soon as possible. She had everything ready when he got home. J. P. had already come for Emma Lou and Walt.

No more than five miles up the road, she reached over and took her husband's hand. She noticed he was a little stiff, but she knew that he had to pay attention to the road. He then abruptly let go. Looking straight ahead, and with both hands on the wheel, Todd picked up where he left off on Sunday regarding his questions about Walt.

"Todd, let's not talk about this today," she said to him.

"Oh, so you are admitting, then, that there is something to talk about, just not now," he fired back.

"No, that is not what I meant," she countered. "There is nothing more I can say. Todd, we are celebrating our anniversary. Let's not have anything unpleasant." That did not satisfy him.

By the time they got to the convention center, Maude really did not even want to go in. Her insides were churning during the performance. When it was finally over, she told Todd that she just wanted to go home. He tried to make conversation a couple of times, but she pretended to be asleep.

Maude later read an article in an undeliverable periodical that Todd brought home. The writer tried to explain how some people use what should be a happy time to badger and browbeat others. The piece went on to describe how, when there is something to celebrate, these aggressors presume others are vulnerable. Their victim might let the guard down to avoid a scene and give them what they want.

Todd Williamson used this ploy repeatedly during his marriage. He was no fool, either. If it did not sometimes produce the results he sought, he would not have been so unrelenting in the use of this strategy. In the one area where he wanted most for Maude to cave, however, she never budged.

Maude stayed in touch with her Aunt Lucy by mail. In one letter that she dropped off at the post office so Todd would not see it, she told her aunt to anticipate a visit from her husband at some point. She also reminded her never to mention anything sensitive in her letters for fear that he might intercept them.

On a Monday afternoon in early March, Todd finished his route a little early. Just as Maude had predicted, he headed the Plymouth toward Jacksonville.

He was not sure which approach he was going to take. If he beat around the bush, he would likely get nowhere. If he were direct, this might put Lucille on the defensive. He would just have to play it by ear. He was convinced something was amiss, and that this woman was right in the middle of it.

Nothing was uncertain about Todd's disdain for Lucille Moore, though. He did not know whether the rumors about her were true or not.

What mattered to him was that she was a willing participant in his wife's defiance of his authority over her.

Lucille was at the reception desk when he came walking in the door. No patients were in the office at the time. They exchanged pleasantries, and she told him how glad she was to see him.

Before Todd could get on with his business, Aunt Lucy wanted a report on the children. She told him how much she missed them, and how wonderful it was to have them stay with her while he was gone. It was very noticeable that Todd said nothing in appreciation for all that Maude's aunt had done for his wife and children.

He began feeling rather awkward about why he was there. He could be wrong. Perhaps nothing out of the ordinary happened. He almost backed down, but then he had driven all the way out there. He had to try to get some answers.

Todd decided to get right to the point. There was no need to pussyfoot around. He asked her if she was aware of anything out of the ordinary regarding Walt's lineage.

Lucille glared back at him in disbelief. "What are you implying, Todd? Are you accusing your wife of something inappropriate? Now you listen to me, Todd Williamson. You know how proper I am. Do you think for one minute that I would shield somebody who had done something like that? I cannot even begin to tell you how disappointed I am in you."

Lucille then became emphatic. "Young man, don't you ever talk to me like that again. I won't stand for it. Do you hear me?"

Todd had not been dressed down like that even while he was in the military. He apologized for his abruptness.

As he got up to go, he asked to speak with Doc Elliott. Todd said that he wished to thank the doctor for taking care of his wife, and to see if he owed him anything. Lucille said that she would see if the physician was available.

Doc Elliott came out of his office with his hand extended. He seemed genuinely pleased to meet Todd, and he invited him to come in and take a seat. The physician then took charge of the conversation. He told Todd what a privilege it was to have Maude and Emma Lou stay with them while he was away. He conveyed to him how much he came to adore his daughter.

Then he said, "I wish you could have seen her. When folks came around, I would whisper to them to ask her where her daddy was. Emma Lou would tell them that her daddy was in the army. As she got older, she added phrases. She started explaining that he was off fighting bad people. She then learned to say that her father was fighting for our freedom. I know how proud you must be of that girl."

Before Todd could get a word in, Doc Elliott continued. "And then that little boy of yours came along. Mr. Williamson, I am so sorry that you could not be here when the time came for his arrival. I'm sure Maude has told you that everything went very well. Except about the nursing difficulty, that is. But the boy took to the bottle right away. We were so glad you finally got to come home, but we really do miss having your wife and children around. Do please bring them to see us soon."

Todd was disarmed. What could he say? This generous physician had obviously been good to his family. How could he even suggest that the kindly old doctor was in on something that might involve malpractice when he had no proof of anything?

The neutralized visitor stood up to leave. He thanked Doc Elliott for all that he had done. He then politely asked him if he owed him anything for his services. The doctor shook his head vigorously in the negative. "Come by anytime," the physician said. "But next time, don't come alone."

On the way back up the road, Todd considered for the first time that he could be imagining things. Nothing at all seemed out of the ordinary in Jacksonville. There might not be anything whatsoever to his qualms.

Todd's thoughts then turned to his mother. She was around when everything was going on, and she had strong suspicions that something was not right. He could not easily dismiss that.

Furthermore, if Lucille and Doc Elliott were in on something, they would have responded exactly as they did. Maude likely even tipped them off about his concerns.

The more he reflected back on the conversation with Maude's Aunt Lucy, the madder he became. How dare that vile woman lecture Todd Williamson!

By the time Walt's second birthday rolled around, his sister had discovered Halloween. Granddaddy Williamson brought over a big pumpkin from his patch. Emma Lou helped her mother carve a jack-o'-lantern. After putting a candle inside, they put it on the porch. From a smaller pumpkin, mother and daughter made a couple of pies.

Trick or Treat was still not that big a deal in small towns and rural areas. Even so, Maude made Emma Lou a little princess costume. She then arranged ahead of time for a few friends and relatives to expect a visitor. Walt stayed home with Todd. He was put to bed early. Nothing was mentioned about it being the boy's birthday.

Todd enjoyed his work, but six days a week on the mail route was confining. Maude sometimes went along when the kids were at their grandparents' house. One day after he came down with a nasty cold, she offered to drive. Todd was very reluctant at first. He did not know if there were any regulations prohibiting this. Yet, he was feeling so miserable that he finally relented.

Maude had driven some, but she soon realized that she was not an experienced driver. It took some practice pulling up to the boxes, especially those on the right side of the car. Todd sat in the passenger seat guiding her as best he could.

As she was gaining her confidence, she just blurted out that maybe they could take turns delivering the mail. Todd was immediately opposed to the idea. They finished the route, and nothing more was said about her proposal.

The more he thought about it, though, the better he liked it. He could have some days off now and then. The two of them went and talked with the postmaster about the proposition. He saw nothing wrong with it. He said that this would take the burden off him to be the substitute carrier when Todd was out sick or taking his leave time. Maude took the Civil Service Exam, and she became a certified mail carrier. The checks, however, were always made out to Todd, regardless of who ran the route.

Hog killing day was a big annual event at the home of George and Ruby King. Weather forecasts were not very accurate. The fresh meat needed a night right at the freezing point to cure, but not cold enough to freeze. George tried to give everyone who would be involved as much notice as he could.

Since his son-in-law had come home from the service, Mr. King raised an extra pig or two. While Todd was appreciative of the hams, sausage, roasts, lard, and cracklings, he always made sure that he was on the mail route the day of the killing. He came over when he got home, after most of the work was done.

Maude's Uncle Jim and Aunt Josie always came to help during the first part of the process. After a hog was put down and the hair scraped off, the carcass was strung from a strong limb with pulleys. Uncle Jim gathered up the entrails in a big washtub. He and Aunt Josie then went off to the edge of the field where they cleaned them. The next night everyone was invited to eat chitlins at their house.

As Maude was getting her children ready to go to their grandparents' on a frosty morning in November 1947, she stopped to take a little extra time with Emma Lou. The little girl had been practicing tying her shoelaces for some time, but she had not yet gotten it quite right. Her mother reminded her that she was going to start to school the next year, and that she would not want to be the only girl in first grade who did not know how to tie her shoes.

After about the fifth try, Emma Lou's knots were tight enough to meet Maude's approval. Neither of them noticed that Walt was paying attention. When his mother turned to him to make sure he was ready, she said, "Why, Walt, when did you learn to tie your shoes?" The little boy just stood there smiling back at her.

Since Todd had the car, Maude and her children walked the half-mile or so to her parents' house. Little Walt led the way. As the three of them came into the backyard where the fire was already heating the water in the wash pots, Uncle Jim was puffing away on his pipe.

"Hello, little man," he said to the boy. Emma Lou was not too sure about her great-uncle, but Walt found him fascinating. The old man had a long gray beard and a twinkle in his eye.

As the other two brushed past, Uncle Jim bent down to continue his conversation with Walt. "What do you have to say for yourself, boy?" he asked, somewhat mischievously.

Walt was not to be outdone. "I tied my shoes all by myself," he boasted.

"Well, that's not bad at all for a war baby," Uncle Jim said, picking at him.

A little while up in the morning, Walt was helping his Grandpa put more wood on the fire. The man was a giant in his grandson's eyes. "What's a war baby?" he asked Grandpa King.

"Why would you ask me that, son?" the man inquired in return.

"When I told Uncle Jim that I tied my shoes all by myself this morning, he said that was not bad for a war baby. I don't know what he meant," the boy answered.

Walt's Grandpa explained to him that babies born while their fathers were off fighting the war were being called war babies. The inquisitive lad who had just turned three was still puzzled.

Realizing that his grandson was not sure how to put his questions into words, Grandpa King knelt down beside him. He said something that Walt would never forget. "Being a war baby makes you something really important. You were born at a time when people were fighting. As a war baby, when you grow up, you will be a peacemaker and help make the world a better place."

Walt nodded, with an air of confidence. Grandpa reached and brought the boy into his bosom. Apparently, the heat from the fire caused a tear to go streaking down his cheek, and the man did not want his grandson to see it.

George was out bright and early the next morning. He dropped by the Williamsons' with a little mess of fresh sausage. Ethel met him at the door, and she thanked him for his generosity. John Paul was down at the barn milking the cow. George went by to say hello.

"That's a mighty fine grandson we have," Maude's daddy said, as Todd's father kept right on milking. He told J. P. about the war baby conversation that he had with Walt.

With a look of pride in his eye, Mr. King continued, "And he has already learned how to tie his shoes."

Mr. Williamson then lamented that he wished his son would show more interest in the lad.

Before he got up from the milking stool, J. P. squirted some milk into the open mouth of the tomcat, waiting patiently for this morning ritual. He then said, "Let's go to the house and get you a quarter pound of butter to take to Ruby. Ethel just churned it yesterday afternoon."

Licking His Wounds

Sometimes he went several days without thinking about it. Then, something would trigger it, bringing it all right back to the surface again. Todd was convinced Maude knew something that she was not telling him. When they argued about it, his wife always came to the same point. She tried to explain to him there was nothing more she could clarify that she had not already been over at least a dozen times. If he continued to badger her, Maude would just clam up. This infuriated him. He had not yet been able to break her, but he had only pushed so far.

Something was not right about the situation. Neither he nor his mother could put their finger on exactly what it was. His trip to Jacksonville proved futile. It was baffling that no one else seemed the least bit concerned about what happened while he was abroad.

Todd wondered about Maude's parents. Surely, they would know what was going on. The Kings were carrying on as if everything was normal and proper. He could not even imagine what his father-in-law's reaction would be if he suspected that his daughter had compromised her marriage and besmirched her family's reputation. He would not, however, be paying Daddy King a visit to discuss the matter with him.

One thing that still confused Todd was the way Maude handled the little boy. While overseas, he feared that he would return home and find a wife who was so wrapped up in her son that little if anything was left over for him. That simply was not the case. Maude seemed to be as devoted as ever to Emma Lou, but she paid little attention to Walt.

More than anything, though, Todd wrestled with his own feelings. When he looked into the eyes of his son, he saw nothing looking back at him that formed a connection. Instead, the boy's gaze made him turn away. Emma Lou had always been his mirror image. He just could not see anything in Walt that made him feel like the boy was made out of his stuff.

Was he just imagining all this? Was he looking for something that simply was not there? Could it be that he was just gone the first year of the boy's life? Was that it?

Todd Williamson did not know what it would take, but one thing he knew for sure. He was never going to rest until he figured this all out. Increasingly, he was beginning to resent the lad as an unwanted intrusion in his life.

Walt's two best friends were his dogs. When his Granddaddy Williamson's dog Trixie had puppies, the boy asked him if he could have one. "Why not two, so they will have each other to play with?" the grand man suggested.

First, they must convince Walt's parents. J. P. was smart enough to broach the subject from a different angle. He mentioned to Todd that it might be nice for him to have a watchdog or two around his house. Since they were not raising any hogs at their place, they would have enough table scraps to feed a couple.

Almost all country folks had dogs. Todd agreed with the condition that both puppies be male. Walt's name was never mentioned.

The boy took instant ownership of the pooches. He started calling one of them Spot, for obvious reasons, and the other more adventuresome one, Scout. Nobody had to remind him to feed the puppies. As the table was being cleared, he was gathering up the scraps. He tried always to give them a little cornbread and buttermilk, too.

If Walt went missing, the place to start looking for him was outside playing with the dogs. Grandpa King had given Earl's old red wagon to his grandson. The boy would put the puppies in the wagon, and then ride them all over the yard. Before long, they could jump in all by themselves. As he pulled them around, they scratched on the floor and barked.

Walt noticed one day that the two now almost grown dogs were trying to get their teeth on the tongue of the wagon so they could pull it themselves. They were growling and shaking their heads, but making little progress moving it.

The boy had an idea. He went and found a small piece of rope in the barn and tied it to the wagon tongue. The dogs could now grasp the rope. Before long, they were snarling at each other for the right to pull the wagon.

Walt had still another notion. He put Spot in the wagon, and Scout started pulling him around. The passenger scratched and barked during the ride. The dogs would do this for hours at the time. Like their master, they had learned how to amuse and entertain themselves.

The boy and his dogs then took it to the next level. Walt sat in the wagon one day to see what would happen. Without any instruction, Spot and Scout both took hold of the rope. In no time, they were pulling him around the yard.

Daddy's little helper – that is what he would be. Emma Lou was off in first grade, and Walt's mother was doing the mail route. It was a cold wintry day with the wind blowing out of the east. Todd, nonetheless, decided that was the time to prune the fruit trees in the orchard. Whichever way he turned, it seemed to the man that the boy was under his feet.

Even though the child was just four-years-old, he and his daddy already had dramatic differences in the way they approached a task. Serious-minded Todd could take play and turn it into work. Inventive Walt, on the other hand, could make play out of just about anything.

The boy was given the assignment of gathering up the pruned branches, and putting them in piles to be dragged off. He was told specifically to be alert, and to stay out from under the tree where something might fall on him.

As several boughs began to accumulate in one spot, Walt looked up to see that his father had just begun to cut through a rather large limb. He ran in quickly, grabbed a handful, and retreated, well before the branch fell. The boy took a deep breath proud of his prowess.

Todd, however, saw it differently. This was a rebellious defiance of his authority. He came down the rickety old wooden stepladder so fast that it almost fell over. He yanked his son up, and he started giving the boy a licking with the pruning saw. Walt protested vigorously. He said that he was being careful, and that he was not hit by anything.

This incensed Todd even more. He would not tolerate backtalk from his insolent son.

Children usually have a keen sense of justice, and Walt's might be a little sharper than most. He had a profound feeling that the punishment did not fit the crime. In fact, he did not believe there was any delinquency on his part to begin with.

The boy's loud protestations sent out an alarm. Walt's dogs came running to his rescue. When Spot and Scout saw what was going on, they growled at Todd, showing their teeth.

The enraged man released his son. He then turned on them. Walt thought that he was going to kill both dogs. At that point, the boy went to the defense of his defenders. He whistled and the dogs came over to him. The lad then took his stance between his father and his loyal canines.

The stanch scorn on Walt's face communicated to the man that he had to go through him to get to the dogs. They were now standing protectively, one on each side of him with their tongues hanging out. The angry and frustrated man almost lost control of himself, but he managed to walk away, slamming the saw to the ground in disgust.

After it was all over, the injuries to the dogs were not too severe. The bruises on Walt's buttocks would soon heal. The one who was really licking his wounds was Todd Williamson. This army veteran had been out flanked, out manned, out maneuvered, and out gunned by a pair of mongrels, and a boy who had not even started to school.

The three of them were now out in the yard playing with that dreadful wagon as though nothing had happened. There was only one reason that the little red wagon would still be in the yard the next morning. That was because of the one who put it there.

Walt always looked back to the orchard incident with the genuine satisfaction that even his dogs knew he was not the one in the wrong. He was the one being wronged. That was a defining moment in the little fellow's life. He would never acquiesce when he knew he was right.

The beating with the pruning saw was by no means the first time that Walt had been "disciplined" by his father. While the boy was not prone to disobedience, Todd's growing dislike for his son was becoming more and more apparent.

When Todd started to rant and rave, he was particularly annoyed that Walt did not immediately capitulate. It was as though the kid did not recognize his rank over him. The boy usually did what he was told, but it was mostly because he understood that he was powerless to do otherwise. Todd saw him as mechanically going through the motions of obeying him, without any reverential regard for him.

That day in the orchard was likewise a pivotal turning point for Todd. He became resolute in his determination to gain the boy's deference, no matter what it took.

The proverbial old irresistible force was now on a collision course with an equally obstinate immovable object.

The "Grand" Son

Walt came to understand and accept his lesser role in the family. He actually thrived playing in the background. He seemed not at all jealous of his older sister who got most of the attention. That was just the way it was. Unlike Emma Lou, he did not need a lot of praise and recognition.

While the little boy was moving about more or less invisibly, he was nonetheless observing what was going on around him. Just like when he learned to tie his shoes. While no one was looking, Walt often mimicked Emma Lou's instructions. That is how he taught himself to read.

By the time his sister started to school, he already knew his ABCs. He learned them from a blackboard that she sometimes did not put back in her room when she finished scribbling on it. He just did not know how to rearrange letters so that they spelled out words.

Emma Lou brought her books home every day. She then made a big production of going over her reading lessons with one or both parents. They praised their daughter for the progress that she was making, especially since she was the youngest member of her class. If their daughter had been born just six days later, she would have waited another year before starting school.

Walt listened, and he learned from the shadows. When no one was watching, he took the "Dick and Jane" reader over into one of his little hiding places. This four-year-old boy was keeping pace with his sister who was almost two years older.

For several months, Walt confined himself only to Emma Lou's schoolbooks. Then one day, he decided to take his reading skills to another level. He picked up a storybook that he had seen his mother read to his sister. It was filled with fables and fairy tales.

The first story in the book was entitled "The Ugly Duckling," by Hans Christian Andersen. Walt started trying to read it. Numerous words were unfamiliar to him. Nevertheless, from the context, the pictures, and the ones that he did know, he could follow the narrative.

As he turned the pages, the boy became increasingly distressed for the misfit little duck. Then, he had to put the book down because his mother called him to supper. That night, Walt lay wide-awake thinking about what he had read. He tried to imagine all the bad things that might happen to the little outcast duck.

The next morning, the boy could hardly wait to pick up where he left off. After breakfast while his mother was busy getting Emma Lou ready for the bus, he took the book to one of his favorite cubbyholes. He read back over the first part, sounding out words and recognizing more and more of them. The same feelings of dread came over him for what was next. A part of him wanted to know, but another was fearful of reading the rest of the sad story. Walt took a deep breath.

No one saw him, but all of a sudden, the boy burst into a big smile. A thrill went through his insides when he found out that the duckling was really a baby swan. The words seemed to get bigger and harder, but the young reader could follow the story. He was so happy for the swan when it found its real family.

That fable touched something deep inside Walter Othell Williamson. Only years later would he understand just to what extent.

Maude noticed that her son liked to sit and turn the pages of books. She did not mind at all because this kept the boy occupied. His mother thought he was just looking at the pictures. She had no idea that he was actually reading the words.

The time had finally come for George King to find another way to put a little money in his pocket. He was looking for something that would still give him the freedom to do some bartering and trading. An opportunity fell right in his lap, so to speak.

The J. R. Watkins dealer drove up at the Kings' residence one day just as George was about to have an afternoon snack. The door-to-door peddler soon had his own feet under Ruby's table. The two men were enjoying some fresh cobbler. On its way to his mouth, a slice of apple fell from George's spoon.

As Mr. King was wiping at the spot on his shirt with his handkerchief, the salesman told him to wait a minute. The man soon returned with a bottle of stain remover. George protested using it, saying that he just had on his old work clothes. The Watkins man was persistent. He wanted to show off the newest product in his line of wares.

When only a wet spot remained, the man said to George, "You know Mr. King, you could sell these items. I am about ready to give up my route after thirty-five years. And I will be happy to hand it over to you."

The man went on to say that he had many loyal customers who would be disappointed if somebody did not continue bringing these preferred products to their houses. "Mr. King, I think you could sell a block of ice to an Eskimo," he added, as a vote of sincere confidence.

The idea intrigued George. The man came by a week later and they struck a deal. The first thing George had to do was purchase another car. Ruby had been nagging him for some time about having to go to church, to weddings, and to funerals in the old rusted out Dodge.

Earl found his daddy a 1939 gray Buick Roadmaster with less than 20,000 miles on it. The car had belonged to an old maid schoolteacher. George was now a confirmed Buick man, and Ruby was ready to ride.

A month later, he was on the road about four days a week selling home remedies, health care items, vitamins, herbs, spices, black pepper, vanilla extract, and soap so pure that you could eat it. Ruby never knew what he would come home with next, since many of the transactions were conducted through simple bartering. Her husband would always be a trader.

Grandpa King drove up one morning right after Emma Lou got on the bus. He blew the horn, and Maude went out to see what he wanted. Her daddy rolled down the window. "I came by to see if Walt could ride with me today. I will be doing a short route, and I can have him home by the time Emma Lou gets out of school."

"I don't know," she answered. "I'm not sure what his daddy would think."

"Oh, let the boy come with me," her father persisted. "Your mother fixed an extra sandwich for our lunch." Walt was standing on the porch listening to the conversation, not wanting to appear too overeager.

"Well, I guess it will be okay," she finally agreed. Maude always felt a little safer making a decision when her daddy was involved. Todd might have his say to her, but he was not foolish enough to go toe to toe with George King.

Walt got to ride in the front seat. The boy sat up tall and straight so that he could see out. He was also holding his head high because he was spending the day with his Grandpa.

When they got to the first stop, the Watkins man raised the trunk lid. He started gathering up some items that he thought the residents might need. He told Walt to open the back door of the car and get him a can of black pepper. The boy did so without hesitation. "Hmm," his grandpa thought.

At the next stop, he asked for a bottle of vanilla extract. He watched Walt as he went from carton to carton until he reached in and came out with one. The rest of the day George continued to test his grandson. He was amazed that the boy never once made a mistake. Did Walt know how to read? Or, did he recognize all of these products by sight, just from observing them in his mother's kitchen?

Todd and Maude were welcome to visit the gardens of both their parents the first couple of summers after he was home from the war. Most of the picking, processing, and canning took place while he was out on his mail route. Depending on how early he got started, he was usually back by mid-afternoon. Maude did not know how often it happened, but she was certain that her husband sometimes stopped by his mother's house before he came home.

Eventually, Todd decided that he wanted his own garden. He knew that he could borrow one of his daddy's mules. Maude was in full support of the idea. She much preferred working alone than with either her mother or his.

The summer before Walt started to school, Todd was leaving his mother's house one afternoon. He mentioned to his daddy that he needed to borrow a mule the next morning to plow his garden. Maude was going to carry the mail. J. P. said that he would walk Claude over after breakfast.

As Todd hitched the mule to the plow, Walt stood beside his Granddaddy Williamson. The boy had already detected that his own daddy was not happy about something that morning, and he tried his best to stay out of the man's way.

The mule was feeling his oats, so to speak, and he could do nothing right. Walt felt for Claude, because he had been in that position so many times himself. The mule was obviously nervous, sensing the mood of the one behind the plow.

Todd began swearing at the beast of burden, and cracking the plow lines against its torso. All the mule knew to do was walk faster. Soon, Todd was almost in a trot trying to keep pace. At the end of each row, Claude turned around and headed back in the opposite direction so fast that Todd had trouble setting the plow.

"Whoa," he commanded, right in the middle of a row. Claude stopped in his tracks. Walt's daddy went to the mule's face, and he started shouting at him. He then returned to his position behind the plow stock. "Gidd'y up," he commanded. The mule refused to budge. "Gidd'y up," Todd shouted out again. He got the same response.

Todd unhitched Claude, took him out to the edge of the woods, and tied him to a tree. He then took a trace chain and began beating the animal. The mule reared up several times as it cried out in pain. Walt frowned and looked away, afraid a hoof was going to hit his father in the head.

Granddaddy Williamson reached down and took the boy's little hand. Tears were running liberally down both their faces. Walt's granddaddy said something to the boy that day that he would never forget.

"Son," he said. "Always be on guard around somebody who mistreats animals, little children, or old people."

Mr. Williamson went over and said to Todd, "Son, let me give you a hand." Like a dog tucking its tail and running, Todd disappeared into the barn. John Paul took the reins, hitched Claude back up, and finished plowing the garden. Walt watched all of this with so much admiration in his eyes for his granddaddy.

As J. P. was about to leave, he sought out his son. He asked him if Walt could walk home with him. The boy knew what the answer would be. Both of his parents instantly said no to anything he wished to do. He also knew that they sometimes changed their minds.

In the words of his Grandpa King, they did not want to "cut off their nose to spite their face." While they were impulsive in their negative responses, on second thought, the request was often in their own best interest.

On this particular morning, Todd immediately turned down his father's request. "Well, think about it a minute," his father responded. "I could use a little help with something, and I believe this little boy can do just what I need," he added.

When he realized that Walt would be out of his hair for a few hours, Todd followed the familiar pattern. He then scolded the boy, "Now, you behave yourself, you hear?"

His granddaddy answered for him. "Why, son, I have never seen this boy misbehave."

"Daddy, you just don't know what I have to put up with," Todd retorted.

Once out of sight of the house, Walt's granddaddy asked him if he would like to lead the mule. Wow! He had never been trusted to do anything like that before.

The boy took the reins like a little man. Even though several paces separated them, he could hear every hoof beat. He kept looking over his shoulder to make sure Claude was not about to click at his heels.

Once they got to the barn, J. P. led the mule to a stall, and he took the bridle off. He then gave his grandson an ear of corn to feed Claude through the hole to the trough. His granddaddy told him to hold on to the corn until the mule reached for it. Walt grimaced when he felt the gritty tongue licking on his fingers. Grandfather and grandson then stood in the hall of the barn grinning at each other from ear to ear.

"What do you want me to help you with?" Walt asked his granddaddy, not forgetting why he was allowed to go home with him.

"It's out here in the shop, son," the man replied.

Twice, his granddaddy had called him "son" that day. He liked that. His Grandpa King also called him "son." As far back as he could remember, his own father had never addressed him that way. He just called him by his given name most of the time. When he was especially condescending, he would refer to him as "boy." If Todd was really upset about something, it was "Walter Othell Williamson!"

Grandfather and grandson walked to the shop side by side. It took Walt about two steps for every one of his granddaddy's for the lad to keep pace.

The furniture maker had already cut out a picture frame. The pieces were ready to nail together. Walt was given the job of holding two sides at a right angle, while keeping his head out of the way, so his granddaddy could hammer in a nail.

On the third blow, the boy let the wood pieces slip. The man saw his grandson flinch, and then recoil. "That's all right, son, let's try again," he gently said.

Walt braced himself, pretending that his hands and arms were stronger than they were. This time he held the pieces together until the nail was driven into place.

After all four corners were joined, the gentle man held the frame up for the two of them to inspect. "I like working with you, Granddaddy," Walt said, with a look of satisfaction in his eyes.

"We do good work together, don't we, son?" Mr. Williamson responded, with an equally proud look on his face.

School Daze

On September 5, 1950, the day after Labor Day, Walter Williamson started to school. His mother had made him a new pair of overalls and a shirt cut out of a flour sack. Maude went with both children on the first day. Emma Lou was going in a new classroom, and her mother wanted to be with her when she met her new teacher. Walt tagged along with his hands in his pockets.

Finally, they headed off to Miss Nell's room. Miss Nell taught both first and second grades. She had been Emma Lou's teacher for the past two years.

"So this is Emma Lou's little brother," the teacher said, as they came through the door. "I do hope you are going to be as good of a student as she was," the woman added.

Walt just sort of puckered his lips and did not reply. He did not think of himself as anybody's brother. Emma Lou hardly ever acknowledged his existence unless she wanted to pester him about something.

Lately, she had learned just how much fun it was to get him in trouble. No matter how ridiculous something was that she made up, their parents always believed her tale. Walt then was punished. On the other hand, if he told on her when she really had done something, his complaint was just dismissed. He was then reprimanded for being a tattletale.

Maude left Walt's little lunch sack with him, and she went on her way. Miss Nell made out the seating arrangement alphabetically. Walt's desk was in the back corner. That suited the little fellow just fine.

When the two students got off the bus that afternoon and started up the drive, Emma Lou said rather haughtily to her brother, "Well, smarty pants, did you learn how to read today?"

"I already know how to read," Walt answered her.

"No, you don't."

"Yes, I do."

As they came in the back door Emma Lou called out, "Mother, Walt says he knows how to read and I say he doesn't. Which one of us is right?"

"You are, dear. Today was just his first day of school," Maude answered, coming toward them from the kitchen. While Emma Lou began telling her mother all about her first day in third grade, Walt shrugged his shoulders, put his books in his room, and went out to play with his dogs.

On Saturday, after completing his first four days of school, Walt asked his mother if he could walk over to his Granddaddy Williamson's house. She said only if he made his dogs stay at home. More and more cars were on the recently paved highway. Spot and Scout were not happy, but they obeyed the boy.

Walt found his granddaddy at the fruit stand. The apples were now ripe, and on weekends, business was usually good. "Well, come on in," Mr. Williamson said to the boy as he walked up. "I was wondering if I was going to have any help this morning."

Walt listened to the customers. He fetched things when he could. Some of them handed him the money. He took it to his granddaddy, and then returned with their change.

When they were not busy, the boy asked his granddaddy to explain how the money worked. Just like that, the first grader had a real life arithmetic lesson. Throughout his schooling, the most important lessons Walt learned were usually outside the classroom.

Mr. Williamson asked his grandson about school. Walt told him that it was fine, and that he really liked his teacher. "Always do well in school," his granddaddy encouraged him. The boy had a serious look on his face as he nodded in agreement.

About that time, Walt's other grandpa drove up. "I see you have some good help today," he said to J. P.

"He's the best hand in the whole family," Mr. Williamson responded.

"Did Walt tell you about going with me on my route the other day?" George asked. The boy just stood there grinning, shifting from one foot to another. The expression on his face lilted back and forth, in accord with the rest of his body.

Walt was an enigma to Miss Nell. Like many of his classmates not used to confinement and structure, she was certain that he was not always paying attention. He was often scribbling when she was giving instructions. The teacher would get up and walk around the room, but when she got near him, he put away what he was writing.

Whenever Miss Nell called on Walt to read, he stopped what he was doing, stood by his desk, and hardly ever missed a word. Occasionally, she asked him if his mother or father helped him with his homework. He would always shake his head no.

Arithmetic was a breeze for Walt. He rarely missed a problem, although his teacher kept encouraging him to improve his penmanship in forming the numbers. Walt knew what the figures were, and that was what was most important to him.

On the playground, the first grader stayed mostly to himself. He never bolted out the door at recess to grab a swing, but he sometimes took his turn after others moved on to something else. He would ride the merry-go-round occasionally, but what he enjoyed most was pushing it for his classmates. The other students did not dislike Walt, but he often seemed to be in his own little world.

As Walt brought his report cards home, his mother looked them over without comment. For the most part, his grades were always the best he could get. Conduct and Writing were two areas that sometimes indicated room for improvement, however. In her comments, Miss Nell said that Walt did not always pay attention in class. Subsequent teachers often voiced the same concerns.

Walt's father said nothing about his superior grades. On the other hand, he would rebuke his son for his deficiencies. The boy learned to stand with his head down, and promise to do better. Once when there was no blemish of any kind, the man said, "Well, I can see you still have your teacher fooled."

Todd tried to make Walt feel that he was not sure the report card was deserving of his signature. Then, he reluctantly signed the back of it. The boy came to expect this routine.

Christmas was not a particularly exciting time for the Williamsons. Walt knew not to get his hopes up about anything. After being told that he would likely get a bag of switches or a lump of coal, Santa Claus usually brought him an orange, and perhaps a stick of peppermint candy. As he got older, he got clothes that he needed anyway.

When Walt was in first grade, though, he got a truly unexpected gift. Uncle Earl and Aunt Mary Beth came to Mason on the day after Christmas. They were not only able to celebrate the holiday a day late with Earl's family, but they were also there for Emma Lou's eighth birthday.

Late in the afternoon as they were getting ready to leave, Uncle Earl said to Walt, "Go home with us. We'll find a pallet for you to sleep on." Of course, the boy thought he was teasing.

Grandpa King then chimed in, "I think that is a great idea. I will come get you before school starts back after the first of the year."

Walt stood in stunned silence as the adults in the room discussed the situation. After the usual negative reaction from his parents, he could not believe his ears. In a matter of just a few minutes, he was sitting between his uncle and his aunt as they headed down the road. "Don't forget to feed my dogs," he said as he got in the car.

Aunt Mary Beth wanted to know all about school. Walt knew that she was a teacher, and she knew just the right questions to ask. The little boy was walking in tall cotton.

Not long into the trip, his aunt told him that she and Earl had been talking about something. Since she had no nieces and nephews, she was not used to being called Aunt Mary Beth. She preferred that Walt just address her by her first name. To make it simpler, he could also refer to his uncle as Earl.

The boy was not too sure about that. He was taught to respect his elders. If they said it was okay, then he would go along with it. He did slip a few times over the next few days, but he was always gently corrected.

This was the first time Walt had ever been away from home, other than to stay overnight at his grandparents' houses. He relished every moment of it. He did not have to stay in the background, as he was so accustomed. Earl and Mary Beth treated Walt as if he were important. He just about talked their ears off.

Mary Beth let him read to her. She was astonished. She told her husband that Walt could read better than some of her fourth graders.

His aunt took him downtown one morning. During the after Christmas sale at Carter's Department Store, she bought the lad some new clothes. This was the first time that Walt had ever put on anything that was not homemade.

The highlight of the trip, however, was when he got to ride on a tractor. Earl let the boy go back to work with him a couple of times after lunch. His uncle took him out to an older tractor that had to be started with a crank. After a couple of spins, the motor went "putt-putt-putt-putt-putt . . ." Walt was enthralled.

Next, he put the boy in the driver's seat of a brand new John Deere. Earl then told Walt how to engage the electric starter. The boy was most impressed as the engine responded to his pull on the lever. With his uncle sitting behind him, they drove the tractor up the drive.

The fun was not over yet. Earl put the tractor in first gear, and he handed it over to Walt. Turning the steering wheel and feeling the tractor respond was exciting. The man slid off the back. The boy was driving the John Deere all by himself. He could not reach the pedals, so after his nephew took it around the yard several times, his uncle climbed back aboard to stop it.

On the ride back home, Grandpa and Grandma King heard all about Walt's adventures. When he went in the house, his mother asked him how his trip was. "It was good," he said.

"Fine," she responded. "I'm glad you had a good time. Now it is time for bed. You've got to get up in the morning and go to school." First, Walt had to go check on his dogs.

Whuppin's

Navigating around in his own little world, Walt started mocking his daddy. When he would knock something over, or accidentally break something, or trip on his own feet, the boy would say, "Walter Othell Williamson, do you need a whuppin'?" He had gotten quite good at mimicking the man.

Walt really did not know much about his great-grandfather from whence he had gotten his middle name. He had seen a picture of him with a long gray beard standing beside his wife. The boy did remember going to the old man's funeral one cold rainy day. The road was so muddy that his Granddaddy Williamson had to turn the car around and back it up one hill to get to the Primitive Baptist Church way out in the country.

That was the first funeral Walt could remember attending. He wanted to go up and look at the dead man, but his mother stayed with him while the rest of the family went. He, nevertheless, sat soaking it all in.

Walt did not remember exactly what prompted it. Not long after the funeral, he started addressing himself as Othell when he was talking to himself.

When he was trying to figure something out, he started saying things like, "Othell, what do you think about that?" Or, "Othell, what should I do?" Having a conversation with himself helped to clarify his thoughts.

If something pleased Walt, he would say something like, "Wow! Othell! Can you believe that?" Of course, anything that went wrong was always Othell's fault.

Along the way, Walt started having fun with the rhymes he could connect with his middle name. He would say such things as, "Do tell, Othell, now that's just swell." And, "Oh well, Othell, better luck next time."

The whuppin's became more frequent as Walt got older. He gave up on pleasing his dad. When he did something right, Todd never gave him credit. Contrarily, the man could usually find some fault with anything he did.

There was absolutely no way to anticipate what would set his father off. Walt knew it could be anything, or nothing at all. The boy avoided Todd as much as he could, especially on weekends. On Sundays after church, he went home with either Alex Oldham or Julian Huffman if he could get permission. His friends never wanted to come to his house, though.

Often without warning, the enraged man would come charging through the door or around the corner with his belt in his hand. He would then spit out something about what the boy's mother told him, or what Emma Lou reported, or what he had asked Walt to do that did not meet his standards, or any kind of excuse that would justify, in his mind, what he was about to do.

Walt knew the routine well. First, was the tongue-lashing. The boy was berated for about five minutes because of his stupidity and ineptitude. He would then be reminded of what a disappointment he was to his parents. He was told that the only hope his father had was to try to beat some sense into him. Todd would then proceed to give it his best shot.

Walt varied his strategy. Sometimes the boy just gritted his teeth and took the licks as if feeling no pain. That infuriated the man. His daddy would then say, "Oh you like it, do you? Well here is some more where that came from."

At others, Walt wailed and screamed as though his father was killing him. The louder he hollered, however, the more the man seemed to enjoy what he was doing.

At no time, did Walt's mother ever intervene on his behalf, or even indicate that she was in any way aware of what was going on. That was just the way it was, and the boy was powerless to do anything about it.

After one particularly brutal session, Walt retreated into his room still grimacing from the pain. "Othell," he said. "What are the chances of a man whose middle name is Allgood, having a son who is all bad?"

For as long as Walt could remember, he had chores to do. It was his responsibility to give the laying hens fresh feed and water in the mornings. In the afternoons, he went back and gathered the eggs. He learned not to put his hand over in a nest without looking first. One day he reached in and a chicken snake was in the nest sucking eggs.

In the winter, Walt stacked firewood on the back porch. As he got older, he chopped kindling. The boy actually looked forward to his chores. He enjoyed doing things and figuring out how stuff works. He knew if he did a good job whether anyone else noticed or not.

Another task was getting the water ready when his mother needed to wash clothes. Walt had to tote hot water from the bathtub and fill up the old ringer washing machine on the back porch. He then had to haul cold water from a faucet beside the house, and fill a pair of No. 3 washtubs for rinse water.

He never understood why a hose could not be run from the spigot to the back porch, but his daddy always tried to make things as difficult for him as he could. After his mother finished with the washing, Walt then had to empty all of the dirty water out in the yard.

Getting apparel dirty was inevitable. Country folks out where Walt lived were prone to say, "You might not have the nicest clothes in the world, but they can at least be clean." Just about everyone believed "cleanliness is next to godliness" is in the Bible, although no one was sure exactly where it was.

Fortunately, not nearly as many clothes had to be washed in those days. Children only had one type of clothing – school clothes. Sunday duds were the newer school clothes. Work clothes were worn out school clothes.

One of Walt's earliest memories was handing clothes pins to his mother when she was hanging wet laundry on the line. Her washday did not end when the clean, dry clothes were taken down either. Some garments then had to be starched and ironed.

One day, Maude sent Walt out to the clothesline to see if his daddy's shirts were almost dry. If they were still a little damp, she could iron them without having to sprinkle them down.

The solar powered clothes dryer was strung between two walnut trees. He went to the row of shirts, hanging by their shirttails. He proceeded to reach for the first thing he came to and check for dryness. After squeezing the collar of one shirt, he was not sure whether it was dry enough yet. Wanting to please his mother, he went to the next, and the next, all down the line just to make sure.

Walt then made the call. The shirts were just right for her to take down right then and iron them. He was quite proud of his judgment.

Moments later, the boy was summoned back to the clothesline. An unmistakable dirty handprint was on the collar of each shirt. Walt had already emptied the wash water. He had to go back and fill the machine and the tubs again. "Just wait until your father gets home," his mother scolded as the boy poured in the last bucket.

The whuppin' Walt got afterward really did not teach him much of anything. It was not as though he did not learn something from this experience on his own, however. The boy figured out that before a meal is not the only time hands should be washed. Besides that, sometimes a sample really is ample.

The sky turned dark and menacing. Soon, the wind started howling. Lightning lit the sky, and the thunder made the windows rattle. Then, it began to hail. The lights flickered a time or two and went out. The family huddled in the hallway, not sure what was going to happen next. After a few harrowing minutes, the storm passed.

Grandma King had invited the family over for some of her famous fried chicken, served with hot biscuits and gravy, and with some seasoned vegetables on the side. After the early spring storm blew through, tree limbs were down in the yard. Todd suggested that they stay home. Maude knew her mother would have everything ready, so she insisted that they go on.

As the family was getting out of the car, George greeted them on his way to town. The power was out everywhere. Mr. King had been meaning to replace the broken kerosene lamp globe, and he had just not gotten around to it. It was getting dark. Grandpa invited Walt to go with him. The boy did not even look toward his parents for permission.

The businesses on State Street were all dark except for the faint glow of candlelight coming from the hardware store. George pulled over to the curb and they went inside. Walt was so proud to be by his Grandpa's side. The proprietor indicated that he would have already gone home, except for staying open to take care of customers who needed supplies because of the nasty weather.

When the man checked his back stock, he said that he only had two lamp globes left. Grandpa paid for one of them, and the man wrapped it in hardware paper, taped at the ends. Walt offered to carry it. "Be careful," Grandpa warned, as he handed the fragile parcel to his grandson.

Walt's brogans were probably about two sizes too big. He rarely had duds that fit him. His parents said that he had to have plenty of growing room. His clothes were usually worn out by the time he grew into them.

On the cold dark wet sidewalk, the boy tripped on something, most likely his own feet. Everything was in slow motion as he tried in vain to regain his balance. Walt was on a collision course with the pavement. With all of his might, he held the globe up, trying to cushion the fall with his knees and elbows. His best efforts fell short. The flimsy glass was shattered into a million pieces.

Something strange then happened. The boy's grandpa rushed to his side, concerned only with whether or not his grandson had been cut by the broken glass. Fortunately, it was all still contained within the wrapping paper.

The man did not shout at Walt. He did not lecture him. He did not scold him, or berate him. Absolutely nothing was said about punishment, and no mention was made of telling on him when they got back to the house.

Grandpa took the damaged goods, and they headed back to the hardware store. Without making any explanation, he said to the clerk, "I guess you better wrap up that last one for me, too."

After he paid for it, something even more remarkable happened. Grandpa King handed the precious merchandise to Walt. As the boy reached for it, he looked up into the man's eyes with so much admiration. He then measured every step, picking his feet up to about the level of his knees before carefully planting them again. Once in his seat, he held the globe as though it were a crown jewel.

Immediately upon arriving back at the house, the lamp was lit. Grandpa placed the globe on it carefully, and then he set it in the middle of the dining room table. The family feasted on the supper Grandma had already prepared before the storm. From the flickering lamplight, Walt could make out the faces of the others.

Near the end of the meal, Grandpa said that they arrived at the store just in the nick of time. He then declared that he had purchased the last two globes in the store.

"Two?" Grandma asked. "Did you buy an extra one?"

The gentle giant never answered her question. Instead, bending his head slightly to see around the lamp, he looked across the table at his grandson. With a sly grin, he gave the boy a wink. Walt winked back. The boy wondered if he would ever be as big a man as his Grandpa.

School was sometimes a challenge for Walt. For one thing, he had trouble following instructions. This trait was one of the few things upon which the boy and his daddy could agree. All of his life, Walt had been more or less left alone to figure things out for himself. He did not always understand why stuff had to be done the way somebody else said. This was especially true if he thought he knew a better way. The teachers learned to work around it, but this character attribute continuously exasperated Todd.

Spelling was Walt's biggest obstacle. He taught himself to read largely by determining what words meant from their setting. How a word was strung together was not nearly as important as knowing its meaning. He did not have to know all the terms to get the gist of what he was reading, either. He put things in context and always tried to see the larger picture rather than focus on a single piece of the puzzle.

Walt worked hard just before a spelling test to memorize the words on the list. This did not mean, though, that he would remember how to spell those same words the next time he tried to write them.

In spite of this deficiency, Walt made excellent grades without half trying. Even so, he did not always understand what grades were for. The lad learned at home that his parents were not good evaluators of what he did. His father routinely judged Walt wrong, when the boy knew he was right. Consequently, he did not always trust his teachers to evaluate his work, either. He knew he often got a good grade when he did not deserve it.

Walt was still more or less a mystery to Miss Nell when she handed him off to Mrs. Jacobs, his third and fourth grade teacher. Miss Nell knew that he was a smart kid, but she was not sure that she had helped him much at all.

Mrs. Jacobs had a warm place in her heart for the students with limited opportunities. She tried to give them the love and nurture they might have missed at home. Walt operated right under her radar screen. He tried not to do anything that called attention to himself.

About the time Old Man Winter decided to give it a rest during Walt's fourth school year, the boy came down with a good old case of spring fever. He wished to be outside with his dogs every afternoon until he was called in for supper. One night, he simply forgot to do his lessons.

The next day, Mrs. Jacobs asked a classmate across the room to take up the homework papers. "Homework, did she say homework?" Walt froze. What would he do?

His devious little mind went right to work, and he quickly devised a plan. His classroom had a water fountain near the door. The teacher did not mind if her pupils went to get a drink so long as they did not disturb anyone. Walt nonchalantly cleaned off his desk to make it look like the student who sat there was absent that day. Then, he went to the fountain.

He drank and drank, keeping an eye on his classmate as he went up one aisle and down the other. Mrs. Jacobs told the boy to put the papers on her desk. Walt then returned to his seat. No one even noticed what happened.

Had he pulled it off?

Trepidation began to set in, though. His teacher knew he was at school that day. What would Mrs. Jacobs do when she discovered that his paper was missing when she graded them? Would he be in less trouble just to go to her, and to tell her that he forgot to do his homework? He decided to just wait and see what would happen.

Walt dreaded going to school the next day, but it passed without any mention of his missing homework. He was sure the following day would be the day of reckoning, but it too passed without incident. He was feeling rather smug when report cards went out on Friday, and there was nothing to indicate that his ploy had been detected.

A week or so later, Walt got his books out and started to do his assignment. He did not see any value in what he was asked to do. After running it through his crafty little mind a couple of times, he decided to try the old water fountain trick again. Once again, he did not get caught.

On the last day of school, Mrs. Jacobs told her pupils that they had learned some important lessons during the year that would go with them the rest of their lives. Walt looked at his teacher with a straight face. On the inside, however, he was smirking. He knew he had figured out some stuff that Mrs. Jacobs knew nothing about.

Walt Williamson discovered in fourth grade that teachers do not always grade homework. He also learned an important health lesson. A growing boy needs to drink lots of water.

Maude never knew from one day to the next who would be running the mail route. No matter what was agreed upon ahead of time, Todd was subject to changing his mind at the last minute. Sometimes he would take to his bed for several days at the time. Maude thought in this regard that he was like her mother. When she left him at home, she really had no idea what he did during the day.

Maude enjoyed carrying the mail. She became acquainted with many people out on the route. They would let her know when they were expecting a package, and she would blow the horn the day it came. She also kept a supply of stamps with her. Some folks would leave some money in the box, with a note explaining how many they needed. Oftentimes, a letter had coins taped to it instead of a stamp.

The mother was usually home when the kids got out of school. This gave her plenty of time to cook supper, and to get her other household chores done before bedtime. Sometimes, she wished Todd would get another job and let her be the full time mail carrier. How nice it would be to have a paycheck with her own name on it.

One day when Maude got home, a strange vehicle was in the yard. She assumed that they must have company. She found out instead that Todd had bought a new car. He took her out and showed her the black 1951 Chevrolet, with a Power Glide transmission.

Todd explained how much easier it would be delivering the mail without having to change gears. Besides that, the old Plymouth was about worn out. They would keep it, nonetheless, so the one at home had a way to get around.

Walt took notice of the development. "Do tell, Othell. We are now a two car family."

Where Walt grew up in the rural south, family, church, and community were very important. Some relatives lived in distant places, but most grandparents, uncles and aunts, and cousins were usually close by. Holidays were occasions for special family gatherings. Most kinfolk also had annual family reunions. The adults would embarrass the children by telling them how much they had grown during the past year.

Bringing and keeping the community together was one of the major functions of the church. The month of May was the traditional time for homecomings and memorial days. To keep in touch with the living and to pay their respects to the dead, those who had moved away made annual pilgrimages back to connect with their roots.

August was the conventional month for revival meetings. This precedent was established in rural areas because it corresponded with "laying by" time on the farms. There was a brief window when farmers got a little break between cultivating their crops and the time of harvest. Each church had a particular week set aside for its annual meeting, as it was sometimes called. A minister from another church was customarily invited to preach the revival. Many churches got the majority of their new members during this time.

Some churches also had annual all-day singings during the summer. These events had a very loyal following who went from church to church singing out of the "new books," published every year. To those accustomed to hymns, this gospel music sounded a bit strange.

Dinner on the grounds was one of the most anticipated aspects of these annual events. The ladies spread a feast, a veritable smorgasbord, although not one woman in the bunch was familiar with that word. The picnic tables were laden with homegrown fresh vegetables seasoned to perfection. Meats raised on the farms, and prepared in the womenfolk's own gifted styles, were served with pride. The women competed to see who could bring the dessert that received the most attention, and was the first to be eaten up.

Walt's paternal grandparents went to one all-day singing every year at the Mt. Pisgah Primitive Baptist Church. He knew the story about how his grandparents met at one of those singings. His grandmother was the one who was insistent that they go back each summer.

One year, Walt was inquisitive about what went on. His Granddaddy Williamson asked him if he wanted to go along to see for himself. Getting Todd's permission to do something was easier if his grandparents were involved.

Walt was not too impressed with the music, but he did make note of how much those in the church were enjoying themselves. He was furthermore very fascinated with what was on the tables when the group finally broke for dinner.

After the food was all cleared, the boy and his granddaddy did not go back inside. While his grandmother took a walk through the cemetery, they stood under a shade tree with a group of men talking about the weather and their gardens. An announcement was made inside that one of the elders would be passing the hat for a free will offering to help defray the cost of buying the new songbooks.

The man came outside. He gave the ones milling around an opportunity to contribute. Walt watched as a man sitting in a black Chevrolet coupe at the edge of the crowd reached out the window and dropped in a quarter. Only he missed the hat. The coin fell to the ground. The boy thought he was the only one who noticed.

Finders, keepers, Othell.

After several anxious moments of watching that quarter, he casually went over and picked it up. Walt's conscience did not let him just put it in his pocket. The lad strolled over to where his grandfather was standing. "Look what I found on the ground," he said, hoping of course that his granddaddy would just tell him it was his to keep.

"Oh," Mr. Williamson exclaimed, "I'm sure whoever lost that quarter would want it put in the special offering taken up today." Walt's grandfather then had him march down the aisle, and put that coveted coin in the hat now on the communion table.

Granddaddy Williamson saw the quarter miss the hat, too. He was about to go pick it up when he observed the look on Walt's face. He stood back and watched to see what his grandson would do.

The lad learned that day what it feels like to be a hypocrite. As he traipsed down the aisle, the approving audience watched him adoringly. They were thinking how sweet it was that he wished to make his own little offering. Secretly, he desired the coin for himself. Walt did not like that queasy feeling in the pit of his stomach.

Losers, weepers.

Lordy Mercy, Boy

The community was abuzz about the new preacher at the Mason Baptist Church. The Reverend Jerry Patterson was fresh out of the seminary. He told the congregation that God led him to this north Georgia community because it was poised for growth.

As the fear of Communism was gripping the nation, church attendance was up all over the country. With more people having jobs during the post war boom, people were also able to put a little more in the offering plate.

Walt heard his Grandpa King say that he was all for calling the Reverend Patterson, but the parson would not be there long. George said that the single preacher was only using the church as a steppingstone, before he moved on to bigger and better things.

The enthusiasm of the young minister was contagious. Within a year, the church was making plans to build new Sunday School rooms, and to install a baptistry in the sanctuary behind the choir loft. Some in the congregation, however, were not that pleased. They preferred assembling at the swimming hole in Tumbling Creek and baptizing in running water.

Meanwhile, Preacher Patterson was making some moves of his own. The pretty and personable daughter of J. P. and Ethel Williamson had caught his eye. The devout Mr. Williamson said that he would be honored to have a preacher as his son-in-law.

The church was filled to overflowing for the wedding. Walt's friends decided to sit in the back where they usually did, but he wanted to be where he could get a better look. He went and sat with his Grandmother Williamson. After his granddaddy walked Aunt Kathy down the aisle, he came over and took his seat with them. The ceremony did not impress young Walt very much, but he was fascinated with the word honeymoon.

Preacher Patterson was disappointed that the new baptismal pool had not been filled for two months after it was completed. That soon changed. One Sunday morning after the sermon, Emma Lou walked down the aisle and talked to the minister. He announced to the congregation that she had trusted Jesus as her Lord and Savior, and that she wanted to be baptized. An "Amen" chorus rang out all over the sanctuary.

The next Sunday was like a holiday. The women planned a covered dish luncheon to commemorate the momentous occasion. At the conclusion of the worship service, Walt watched as the preacher and Emma Lou went through the door behind the pulpit. The organist played soft music as the congregation waited.

After a few minutes, the curtain then opened and a light came on in the baptistry. Preacher Patterson came into sight. Walt could hear the sound of water. The minister made a little speech about how nice it was now that the church could baptize its new converts all year long instead of having to wait for warm weather.

Next, the parson offered up a prayer, dedicating the new modern convenience. After he said "Amen," the pastor reached out his hand and led Emma Lou into the water. She was wearing a white robe. Walt heard the woman behind him say, "She looks just like an angel."

The minister explained that he did not normally approve of such, but since this was such a significant occasion in the life of the church, he had made an exception. He asked a photographer to take a picture or two for the record. After three or four flashbulbs went off, Preacher Patterson dunked Walt's sister under the water.

At the luncheon afterward, Emma Lou stood beside her proud parents and grandparents with her hair still wet. Folks just kept coming by to congratulate her. Meanwhile, Walt went to get some more banana pudding before it was all gone.

"What-cha-doing, Granddaddy?" Walt asked as he came into the woodworking shop. "I'm sharpening these chisels, son," the man replied as the bench grinder was slowly winding down. "I'm getting them ready for my new job."

Mr. Williamson decided to close the fruit and vegetable stand since business had dropped off steadily. Besides, with Aunt Kathy married off, there was one less mouth to feed. After considerable persuasion, Walt's granddaddy had agreed to be the cabinetmaker for the Hickory Hollow Construction Company.

"I have to be careful when sharpening steel not to get it too hot," Granddaddy Williamson added. "That's something my father taught me in the blacksmith shop. If steel gets too hot, it loses its temper. Did you know that, son?"

Walt's granddaddy went on to explain to him how temper is what gives the metal its strength. "If the steel is heated too much, it becomes soft and brittle," he clarified. While the boy did not totally understand the process, he had a pretty good idea what his granddaddy was talking about.

"And you know what?" the grand man continued. "People are just like that too. Temper is not a bad thing. It gives a person grit and determination. But if a man gets hot and loses his temper, he is showing his weakness, not his strength."

Both of Walt's grandfathers took time to explain things to him. He never stopped marveling at what all they knew.

After the object lesson about temper, Walt wondered just how much his granddaddy knew about what went on at his house. Things seemed to get a little better for a while after Emma Lou joined the church. Her brother actually said to himself, "Othell, I wish that girl had gotten saved a long time ago." It did not last very long, though.

If Grandpa King said something, you had better listen. That man generally knew what he was talking about. He was not wrong, either, about his prediction regarding the Reverend Jerry Patterson. Just a little more than two years after he came to Mason, God had spoken to him again. This time He was calling the preacher to the First Baptist Church in Adamsonville, Georgia. Walt's Uncle Earl and his Aunt Kathy were going to be living in the same town.

Spending a couple of weeks every summer at Earl and Mary Beth's house was something that Walt looked forward to every year. With both sides of his family having a member living in Adamsonville, the boy was usually able to catch a ride with someone from one branch going in one direction, and with the other coming back.

With no children of their own, Walt's uncle and aunt more or less adopted him. Earl played ball with him and took him fishing. Walt caught his first fish, a speckled cat, in the Coosapoosa River.

One Christmas, they gave him a baseball, a glove, and a bat. The next, he got his own rod and reel. During his summer visits, Walt spent a lot of time at the tractor place. Mary Beth cooked his favorite foods, and she talked to him about girls and such.

Earl and Mary Beth were members of the First Methodist Church, but Walt liked to go to First Baptist at least once while he was in Adamsonville. He usually spent that Saturday night with Aunt Kathy and Uncle Jerry. He then sat with her in church the next day. He did not particularly like the fuss the members made over him, but he had to admit that sometimes getting a little attention was not so bad.

Walt was not prepared for a conversation Uncle Jerry had with him one night right before bedtime. The Reverend Patterson told his nephew how proud he was of Emma Lou. He then said that it was about time for Walt to think about giving his heart to the Lord, also.

He said some other stuff, but the lad was not halfway listening. What he did hear was that when the time was right, he would feel a tugging at his heart like nothing he had ever felt before. "Don't fight it," his preacher uncle told him.

The next morning, Walt tried to listen to the sermon, but his mind kept wandering. Then, during the invitational hymn, something got hold of him. He did have a strange sensation unlike anything he had ever experienced. Was this what Uncle Jerry meant?

About that time, the pastor said, "I think there is someone here today that God is dealing with. I believe there is someone who needs to walk down this aisle, to give his heart to Jesus, and join those who are awaiting baptism."

Aunt Kathy sensed that Walt was fidgety. She looked down at him and nodded. He stepped out.

It just so happened that the church was planning a baptismal service that night. Uncle Jerry explained to Walt that he should be baptized with the group, and then he could transfer his membership back to Mason if he wished. Walt did not understand everything that meant. Before he decided what to do, he wanted to talk it over with Earl and Mary Beth.

Earl thought it was better for him to wait, and to be baptized back in Mason. Walt said Uncle Jerry told him that it was important for him to go ahead that night. The boy did not want to make God mad.

That afternoon he made his decision. He thought it would be neat for Aunt Kathy's husband to baptize him, too, just like he had dunked his sister. Earl confided in Mary Beth that it seemed to him the preacher was more concerned with padding his record of baptisms, than with what was best for their nephew.

When Granddaddy Williamson came to pick Walt up a week later, Earl mentioned to him that the boy had something important to share. Rather awkwardly, Walt told his granddaddy about joining the church. Mr. Williamson shook his hand, man to man. He then told him how proud he was of him.

On the way back home, Walt asked his granddaddy several questions about his new faith. The man the boy loved and respected so much told him that more than anything else, he would now always want to do the right thing. Then he added, "But when you slip up and make mistakes, God will forgive you."

It was dark when Mr. Williamson delivered Walt back to his parents. J. P. went inside and told them what happened to Walt while he was in Adamsonville. Neither of them said much.

After his father left, Todd said, "It's about time you got your heart right with the Lord, boy. I will expect better out of you now."

When Walt slid under the covers, he reflected back over what had happened. He thought about all the commotion when Emma Lou was baptized. He mused to himself, "Othell, I don't think your parents would care one way or the other if you just went straight to Hell."

Then he said. "Hell, Othell, you've hardly been a Christian a week. Now you've started cussin'. Oh well, I guess God will just have to forgive you. Lordy mercy, boy."

Dousing the Flames of Passion

Girls actually discovered Walt, before he discovered girls. What they seemed to be more interested in, though, was copying his homework. They also tried to position themselves so they could see his answers during an exam. He still had not figured out why he was the one who was punished, and not the girl, when she was caught copying his test paper. The teacher said that he did not try hard enough to conceal his work.

In sixth grade when Valentine's Day rolled around, Walt and Cheryl were sweethearts. Maude bought Emma Lou a big packet of valentines. One was for the teacher, and a few others were designed for specific persons. After she picked through them and got what she wanted, she gave the three or four left over to Walt. He was only interested in one. Eventually, he decided on the best valentine from the bunch to give his girl.

During recess, he lured his beloved behind the coat rack. Cheryl took one look at the envelope, and without even opening it said, "Walt Williamson, I've a good mind to slap you."

Well, she just had, only she had not used her hand. Walt stammered and stuttered. He could not come up with anything that made any sense.

"You call me your girlfriend, and you treat me like this?" she said, to break his spell.

Actually, spell was the whole problem. Walt's ubiquitous spelling woes had gotten him in trouble with his sweetheart. He had scribbled "Shirl" on her valentine.

"Now you are going to have to kiss me, to make this all right," Cheryl said condescendingly.

At that point, he still did not know what he had done wrong. How could he make it right? At least his girl gave him a hint, although he had no clue what that would fix.

Walt leaned over and gave his valentine a peck on the cheek. At that precise moment, the teacher came around the corner to see what was going on. Cheryl was told to go to her desk. Walt was sent to the office.

Report cards went out the following Friday. Walt grimaced when he opened his. He knew what was coming. He just did not know how bad it was going to be. It could have been worse.

When he handed the report card to Todd, the boy knew the routine well. His father went over the grades painstakingly trying to find anything worthy of censure. Then, the man's whole body constricted when he saw the conduct grade.

"How do you account for this B in Deportment?" Todd quizzed him sternly.

"Just got lucky, I guess," Walt answered, trying not to let a smirk show on his face.

Whatever good fortune he might have gained with a grade less punitive than he anticipated, Walt's luck had just run out.

Walter Othell Williamson undoubtedly improved his intellect from the subjects he studied during his sixth year in school. He also learned two very important life lessons. One was that life sure seemed less complicated before he got saved. About the time his adolescent juices started kicking in, the young whippersnapper also figured out that being a romantic is risky business.

Todd Williamson was falling deeper and deeper into despair, fighting his demons. After more than a decade, he had not been able to shake anything out of Maude. Every avenue he and his mother had explored trying to get to the truth about Walt had turned into a dead end. Maude long ago just clammed up if he brought up the subject. While she never came right out and said so, whenever he did try to pry something out of her, his husbandly privileges dried up for a while.

Todd grew up during the Great Depression. He knew all about hard times. He longed for prosperity to return during his lifetime. Now, he had a good paying job with benefits. As they came on the market, he and his wife were able to purchase many of the laborsaving devices. He was providing opportunities for his children denied those of his own generation. Yet, "Toad" Williamson was a miserable man.

Pundits were calling the times, "The Age of Anxiety." The Russians and the Americans were in a sprint to see who could amass more atomic weapons. People all over the country were building bomb shelters in the event of a nuclear attack. The superpowers were also in a race to see who could control outer space.

On many mornings, he did not want to get out of bed. He felt like a wretched failure. How could he look himself in the mirror, married to a woman he suspected had a secret that she would not share with him? He needed to be in control, but this made him subservient to her. Agonizingly, there appeared to be nothing he could do about it.

Then, there was the boy. Even though he despised Walt, Todd knew in his heart that he was a good kid. He was the kind of son of which any father should be proud. Nevertheless, nothing in that boy's demeanor indicated any connection between the two of them. Walt was an intruder, an imposter, who was ruining his life.

It troubled Todd that he could not get a handle on how to deal with the little twerp. It sometimes frightened him when he went into a rage. He did not know the extent of his capabilities. Something kept telling him that it was wrong to keep beating the boy. But it was like an addiction. He could not stop himself from taking his wrath out on Walt.

In his self-loathing, the anxious man turned to religion. He actively sought jobs in the church. To the outside world, Todd Williamson painted himself as a righteous man. He had the respect and admiration of people throughout the community. Inwardly, however, he could not escape the anguish and the agony that dogged him persistently, like a foxhound on a never-ending hunt.

Walt had never given much thought to sports. When he saw how the girls swooned over jocks that could play ball, though, he decided he had better look into it. He was amazed at how quickly he went from being one of the last players chosen, to one of the first. The young athlete did not have great skills. What he lacked in brawn, he made up for with brains. It tickled him when he could outsmart, or rattle, a much better player.

Sunday afternoons were usually spent shooting hoops with the other kids in the neighborhood. During the summer, if enough of them could get together, they played baseball over in his Sunday School teacher, E. C. Chambers' cow pasture.

One Sunday about the time school let out following seventh grade, Walt went home with Julian after church. His father told him to be home by five. None of the boys had a watch, and the time slipped up on him. When he went to check, it was already a quarter past five.

Walt knew he was in trouble. He got home as fast as he could in hopes of slipping in unnoticed. No such luck; Todd was waiting for him.

The twelve-year-old followed the man to the back bedroom. First, the boy was given the obligatory speech, reminding him that he was a worthless piece of human flesh. After the tirade, Walt was supposed to feel like the scum of the earth. He didn't, and it showed. There was no turning back.

After Todd laced the belt across the boy's backside about a dozen times, he stopped and stood him up. He then said something that Walt had heard numerous times before. "You know this hurts me as much as it hurts you."

This time the boy went ahead and said aloud what he had thought so many times in the past. "If this is hurting you so much, and it is hurting me so much, why do we keep doing it?"

Todd exploded. For the next few minutes, Walt kept repeating to himself things he had also said over and over, time and time again. "You can have my body, but I will not surrender my soul to you. You can beat me to a pulp, but you will never break my spirit."

They had no way of knowing it then, but this was the last time that Todd Williamson would ever lay a hand on Walt.

Walt loved his Grandmother Williamson's fried pies, but his Grandma King made the best applesauce. There were a few old mountain apple trees down in the pasture. Some people called them horse apples. The fruit was knotty and wormy, but the sauce came out looking like thick crimson colored soup. It was so rich in flavor.

Through a government program, many schools added canning plants to their agricultural shops. These facilities were then made available for citizens to use for putting up their fruits and vegetables. All the patrons had to do was pay for the cans. The only canning plant in Townsend County was at the Mountain Home High School.

One year when there was a bountiful crop of horse apples, Grandpa decided that the Kings would avail themselves of this service. Walt came over late one afternoon and helped gather two washtubs full. Grandpa wanted to get an early start the next morning to get ahead of the crowd. His grandson just spent the night so he would be ready.

It took more than an hour to quarter the apples, and to cut out the rotten spots. The fruit was partially cooked in a large vat, and then run through a sieve to remove the seeds and peelings. It was next spooned into cans, which then went through a sealing process. The applesauce was next pressure-cooked for a few minutes.

Several other families were also working on their own produce. On the closest big stainless steel table, the folks were canning tomatoes. The womenfolk exchanged pleasantries, and the men talked some.

Walt and the girl with them made eyes a couple of times. He thought she was flirting with him, but he could not be sure. He kept hoping that they would all introduce themselves so he could find out her name. Instead, the work just continued.

While the cans were cooling, it was time to wash out the big vat. The water hose had a leak in it, and it had to be turned off when not in use. Grandpa handed it to Walt, while he went to turn on the faucet.

As the boy stood waiting, he was enchanted by the beauty of his new beloved before him. He was mesmerized by her blue eyes and long curly blond hair. He imagined himself a knight in shining armor riding in on a steed. He reached down, swooping her up as she swooned.

Walt was so deep into his fantasy that he did not feel the little twitch in the hose. Neither did he have any awareness that the nozzle was pointing in the same direction as his wistful gaze. A surge of water went flying. It was too late. It hit his princess right smack in the face.

The silence between them was about to be broken.

"I am so sorry," Walt yelled above the din of the canning plant.

"Oh-no-you're-not!" the girl retorted, with fire in her eyes. "You did that deliberately to humiliate me," she snorted, as she ran from the building, with more than just her spirits dampened.

Walt just could not seem to get it right. Once again, he managed to douse the flame of passion, this time by literally pouring cold water on it.

Walt was not much of a sportsman. He did go deer hunting once or twice a year with his Granddaddy Williamson, but he never managed to bag a buck. Just being in the great outdoors with the man he idolized was satisfaction enough.

The boy was a little better at fishing. He would sometimes grab his rod and reel and head for the creek just to get away from things. One day, he happened up at this granddaddy's house just as the grand man was about to wet a hook. Walt went along to see if he could pick up a few pointers on how to hang a trout.

They stopped at a wash hole just below an old bridge. Mr. Williamson explained to the lad that this was the home of Old Gus. The big brown trout had been holding court there for a few years.

"Old Gus will make you cuss," the man added. He told Walt about hooking the fish several times, only to have him get away. The boy tried to picture those encounters, although he could not imagine any foul language escaping his granddaddy's lips. If Old Gus was hanging out in the hole that day, he was not hungry.

A week or so later, Walt dug a few worms. As he trotted toward the creek bottoms, he was drawn to that spot near the bridge. The small fry nibbled at the worms, and soon the young angler only had a lone fat one left. He carefully threaded it on the hook, and he sent it flying.

All of a sudden, there was a huge explosion on the water. Walt could hardly believe his luck. He carefully worked Old Gus, trying to wear him down before he broke the line.

Walt's heart was racing. He began to imagine walking with a bit of swagger on his way to show off the big brown trophy on his stringer. His grandfather would be proud of him, even if his grandson had upstaged him.

Like a skilled angler, Walt kept the line tight. He gave Old Gus no opportunity to get to brush where he could become entangled. With little fight left in the fish, he began to reel him slowly toward a smooth spot on the bank where he would slide him up on the gravel.

With one last burst, Old Gus rose about three feet out of the water. He spit the hook out, sending it sailing right past Walt's ear.

Reflexively, "What the #W@!*#&!-*$X#%Z?" spewed from Walt's mouth.

Granddaddy Williamson was right about Old Gus. Walt was not sure he could ever remember that man being wrong about anything.

D-V Day

In the summer of 1957, Walt Williamson was hitting his stride. He was the starting first baseman on the Mason-Dixon Babe Ruth Baseball team. Incredibly, they had real uniforms. Even the high school team that went to the state play-offs earlier in the spring played in their school clothes.

The coach of the team was the father of Alex Oldham, his best friend. Alex played shortstop. Mr. Oldham solicited various businesses in the area for their support. Each jersey had the name of the company that paid for a uniform stitched right above the number on the back. Walt advertised for Robinson's Texaco Station, and he wore the number seven.

Babe Ruth Baseball was for boys ages thirteen through fifteen. Walt would not be thirteen until the end of October. However, the rules stated that any player whose birthday fell within the calendar year, was considered the age he would be on his birthday.

Walt was the youngest player on the team. Even so, he beat out a fifteen-year-old for first base, one of the skill positions on the team. Lean and lanky, he was now the tallest member of his family, except for his Grandpa. About the only way to get a ball past Walt, was to throw it over his head. The other infielders appreciated him. He saved them from getting errors on errant throws.

The first game of the season was an away game. Walt got to ride with the coach in his turquoise and white 1955 Ford. On the way to Hope Junction, Alex's little sister Frances entertained the boys in the back seat with her singing. She had learned the lyrics to Pat Boone's hit song "Love Letters in the Sand." Walt would never forget just how sweet she was when she sang, "On a day like today, we pass the time away, writing love letters in the sand . . ."

Frances was in some ways like a little sister to him. He remembered well when she was born. A few months before that blessed event, he went home with Alex one Sunday after church. That afternoon, Walt's friend said that he had something he wanted to tell him. This was something really important. The boys went around to the front of the house, and they crawled behind the shrubbery under the living room double windows. Walt was sworn to total secrecy.

Alex, with a glimmer in his eyes, confided in his buddy that he was soon going to have either a new baby brother or a new baby sister. Walt was to tell no one. He gave his best friend his word.

A few weeks later, Walt was caught totally off guard when his mother asked him at the breakfast table one morning how Alex felt about the anticipated new addition to his family. The boy froze. How did his mother know this? Would Alex now and forevermore think that he was a snitch? For the next day or so, he could not face his friend.

Walt eventually went back to his mother. "How did you find out that Alex was going to have a new brother or sister?" he wanted to know. Maude laughed at him. She said that Alex's mother was "showing," whatever that meant, and that everybody knew. Little sister was now five-years-old.

The starting first baseman was a big baseball fan. His favorite team was the Milwaukee Braves. He hated the New York Yankees. Walt felt certain this was the year that the Braves were going to win the World Series. First baseman Joe Adcock was his favorite player. He also liked Hank Aaron.

Mr. Oldham did not reveal the batting order ahead of time. He waited until after the team had taken both batting and fielding practice. Walt's heart skipped a beat when the coach said, "Williamson, you will be leading off."

Rumors were circulating that the opposing pitcher had not only hurled for his high school team, but also that pro scouts were already taking a look at him. The overgrown lad was warming up on the mound. The catcher's mitt thundered a resounding pop with every pitch. As Walt watched the hurler heave the ball home, he wondered if he would even be able to see it. He did not even want to think about being hit by a pitch.

The opposing pitcher had a huge wad of chewing tobacco bulging from his right cheek. Walt learned quickly that he did not care to chew. He kept a supply of raisins in his pocket, and he could spit with the best of them without anyone knowing his secret.

The umpire hollered, "Play ball!" Mr. Oldham took his place in the third base coach's box. Before stepping up to the plate, Walt nonchalantly trotted down to Coach Oldham. Positioning himself so that his opponents could not hear him, he said, "You see how deep the third baseman is playing? I think I'll try to lay down a bunt."

The coach gave him the green light. Walt was taking his role as leadoff batter seriously. He knew that he needed to find a way to get on base.

He took the first pitch just to make sure he could see it. The umpire bellowed, "Strike one!" Walt stepped out of the batter's box and took a deep breath. He knew all eyes were on him. He could not afford to take another strike. If the batter tried to bunt with two strikes on him, and he fouled the ball off, it was a strikeout. He figured that he had little chance of making contact swinging at the ball.

Walt stepped back up to the plate, determined to keep the bat high above his shoulders so as not to tip off the third baseman, still playing deep. As the pitcher wound up, the leadoff batter squared his stance. He made a feeble attempt to put the wood in the path of the speeding horsehide.

Miraculously, Walt felt contact. Instead of going toward third base as planned, however, the ball was spinning toward first. Walt had bunted it right off the end of the bat.

Suddenly, everything was in motion. The ball was spiraling toward first just inside the base line. Walt was running about the same speed, trying not to kick the baseball. The pitcher, the first baseman, the ball, and the batter all converged at one point, with the runner having to thread a needle to get through.

The pitcher thought the ball was going to twist foul, so he hesitated for a moment. Too late, he picked it up and made a quick toss to the second baseman covering first.

"Safe!" yelled the umpire, as Walt crossed the bag only a split second ahead of the throw. Whew!

While the next batter was trying to size up the pitcher, Walt was taking his lead off first. All of a sudden, there was a blur of motion from the direction of the mound. The pitcher was throwing to first, trying to pick the runner off base.

Walt's body seemed frozen. He desperately lunged back toward the bag. The umpire again shouted, "Safe!"

"Whoa, Othell, that was really close." He was not even sure the umpire got the call right.

About that time, Mr. Oldham cupped his hands to his face. He shouted across the diamond. "Hey, Williamson . . . Get in the game!"

"What do you mean 'get in the game'?" Walt said to himself defensively. "I'm batting a thousand. I got the first hit of the season. I am the potential winning run."

Nevertheless, Walt knew the coach was right. Those words reverberated in his head all season. He never forgot them. Walt Williamson would always be in the game.

His team went on to finish as the runner up in the league. The first baseman ended the season with a cool .333 batting average, and he made only two errors. Walt even managed to jack one pitch over the fence. Young Williamson fell just short, though, of making the all-star team.

It did not bother Walt at all that neither his father nor his mother showed up at any of the games. The way he figured it, when his friends' parents hollered from the stands, it just put extra pressure on his teammates.

He was excited about the rest of the year. Rumor had it that the Big Three automakers were all coming out with new models in the fall of '57. Those who seemed to know about these things said that they were going to be trendsetters for years to come.

Walt would be entering the eighth grade over in the high school building. Now that he enjoyed sporting with females, he actually looked forward to getting back into the classroom. During this school year, he would finally become a teenager.

Monday, August 26, 1957, began like any other late summer morning. It was just a few days before the start of school. Walt was up early, soon out the door to finish his chores. He loved this time of day. The dew always had things freshened up. The rooster was crowing and the birds were singing. He did not understand how Emma Lou could stay in bed so late.

The lad stopped to play with his loyal canines for a couple of minutes. Those boys were getting old. Walt had to start thinking about the time when Spot and Scout would no longer be around.

He then looked over at the black sedan that his father left for him to clean up. He would wash it later in the morning. It was hard to get the dull black paint clean without leaving spots and streaks. He would do the best he could, but expect the worst when the man inspected the job.

Not long after breakfast, Walt went to his room. He turned on the radio that Earl and Mary Beth had given him for Christmas. He wanted to be familiar with the latest rock 'n roll tunes. When the music stopped for the news on the hour, he was only halfheartedly listening. Something then grabbed his attention.

The announcer said that a Mason, Georgia native was killed in a tragic accident in Utah. The commentator went on to explain that Donald Vaughn was one of the air force's top test pilots. He was flying a new prototype jet fighter when it exploded over the desert sands. The pilot was killed instantly.

Walt went toward the kitchen to tell his mother what he just heard. He found her standing near the sink crying. It was then that the boy noticed the radio on the counter playing in the background. She had obviously heard the same bad news.

He went to his mother, and he tried to comfort her. He had never seen her this way before. Her body was convulsing with each sob. Not realizing that her son had been listening to the same newscast, Maude told him that one of her old school friends had been killed. She said he was a year ahead of her, but that they were close.

This was the first time in Walt's life that tragedy had hit so close to home. He was about to find out just how close. Without any premeditation on her part, or warning to her unsuspecting son, Maude Williamson blurted out, "He may have been your father."

Walt released his grip in stunned silence. Freed from his embrace, his mother bolted and ran to her bedroom, closing and locking the door behind her. He was left standing in the kitchen replaying those words through his mind. "Othell, what the hell . . . ?"

Walt then went outside and let out a whistle. Spot and Scout came running. For the next several minutes, the boy embraced the dogs. He wrestled with them, and they licked the occasional tear that ran down his troubled face.

Todd Williamson came home from his mail route in a foul mood. Nothing had gone right all day. He needed to vent his frustrations. When he tried to talk to Maude, she acted like a zombie. There were times when the man wanted her undivided attention. This was one of them. His wife's mind was a million miles away.

Todd gave up and went outside. Where was that boy? Todd had driven the old Plymouth, leaving the Chevy for Walt to wash. There it sat in the yard, still covered with grime.

He called the boy's name. Walt came running from behind the barn. Still trying to get some kind of a handle on what his mother told him earlier, the confused kid had much more important things on his mind than washing a car. He simply forgot to do it.

Seeing Todd standing beside the dirty vehicle was a memory refresher. He lied and said that he was right then on his way to start the job. It was too late. This was just the excuse the fuming man was looking for. He yanked off his belt and told the boy to bend over the fender. There was nothing to discuss.

Todd had no way of knowing it, but something had changed between the two of them during the day. As the enraged man raised his right arm to deliver the first lash, Walt stood up and lifted his own left forearm to block the blow. He then looked Todd squarely in the eye and said, "We're not going to do this anymore."

The startled man started sniveling, and his lips began to quiver. He put his belt back on and walked toward the house. Walt calmly picked up the water hose and began washing the car.

All day long, Walt kept thinking that his mother would seek him out, and explain to him what she had said. Instead, she stayed to herself. What did she mean by "he may have been your father?" Does she not know for sure? If he was my father, who else knows? Did the man who was killed in the exploding aircraft even know?

After supper, Todd went into the living room and turned on the television as he usually did. Walt watched from a distance. Donald Vaughn's death was the headline story on Huntley-Brinkley. They showed a picture of the famous pilot, and a photograph of the Mason-Dixon School where he graduated. The commentator said that this accident would most likely move the military forward in the development of ejection seats for fighter planes.

After the news cut to a commercial, Todd called to Maude, still cleaning up the kitchen. "Isn't this Donald Vaughn the same man I met in Paris, the one who used to date your friend Maggie?"

"Yes, it is," she answered back. "It is so sad. I have been blue all day since I first heard it on the news this morning."

"Why didn't you tell me when I got home?" Todd asked her.

Maude started rattling dishes and pretended not to hear him.

Walt did not want to go to bed that night. He needed to keep an eye on things. How would Todd react to all of this? Never again would he think of that man as his father. Todd obviously hated him. Did he know the boy might not be his own kid? Did he know about Donald? Was he jealous of him? Would his mother and Todd have a big fight tonight?

Actually, nothing out of the ordinary happened at all. Walt's mom went to bed early. Emma Lou went to her room right after supper oblivious to anything. Todd stayed up late watching TV, but he seemed to be over his little snit from earlier in the afternoon.

As Walt finally crawled between the sheets he said to himself, "Othell, who are you? Are you a Williamson? Or, are you a Vaughn?" He lay there with his eyes wide open for a long time. He then turned over and said, "You know what, Othell? You are the same person you were when you got up this morning." Within a few minutes, he was fast asleep.

Walt Williamson got up on Tuesday morning feeling that he had bridged some kind of indefinable span. While it was still a couple months shy of his thirteenth birthday, he certainly no longer felt like a child. Since he always more or less had to figure things out for himself, it never occurred to him that he might need to talk with someone about the big revelation of the day before.

While there was certainly no love lost between them, Walt actually felt a little sorry for Todd. Even though the man pulled rank, he had never prevailed.

Walt wondered if Todd would back off, lick his wounds, and come at him again. The lad honestly did not know how he would react if this were to happen. He undoubtedly had a new weapon, but he would have to be very careful how he used it. They might continue living under the same roof, but the playing field had been leveled considerably the day before. The rules had all changed.

Something else puzzled Walt. His feelings for his mother had not changed much at all. The two of them had never been close. He marveled at how some of his friends' moms seemed so wrapped up in their boys. He always considered that to be somewhat of a burden for both mother and son.

On the other hand, he sometimes wished that he and Maude could have shared more things together. She seemed rather to always be focused on her husband and her daughter.

Now, what was he to think? Was he a bastard, a son of a bitch? Was his mother a whore? While Walt could not overlook the fact that Todd might not be the only man she had slept with, something did not feel right thinking of her in that way.

He did see his mother as weak. For her own sake, he wished that she had more backbone. He wondered how she must feel about herself, letting others make the important decisions.

Walt hoped that he and his mother could continue the conversation she started in the kitchen the day before. It was not to be on this day. She left early to do the mail route. He was left to figure out what he was going to do. He had no desire to hang around the house if Todd was going to be there.

Not long after breakfast, Walt decided to go over to Alex's house. He did not ask Todd's permission. Rather, he told Todd where he was going. The man just glared at him, and did not respond.

Over the next couple of days, Walt learned that a memorial service was being planned for the man who "may" be his father. It would be held on Saturday morning in the high school gymnasium/auditorium, since that facility had the largest seating capacity of any place in town. Nothing was said at home, at least in his presence, about the upcoming event. His mother was carrying on as though nothing had happened, and Todd stayed out of his way.

About an hour before the time of the gathering, Walt slipped out unnoticed. He wanted to take in everything. He got to the school in time to help finish setting up chairs on the gym floor. It was a muggy late August day, and it was already warm inside the gym. The service was scheduled for 10:00 a.m., before the day got any hotter.

As folks started to assemble, Walt took a seat up in the bleachers near the stage where he could see what was going on. On the floor below, a large area was roped off for family and other dignitaries. Another section was designated for Donald's schoolmates.

As the auditorium started filling up, Walt was continuously panning the crowd. He saw his mother come in with two other women he did not recognize. They took their seats in the reserved area. Each had on a hat with a veil. At one point, he was sure all three were looking up at him.

Just before the memorial service began, he saw his Grandpa come in. Right behind him was his Granddaddy Williamson. They found seats near the back. It occurred to Walt how few times he had ever seen his two grandfathers together.

The funeral processional was quite impressive. The deceased aviator's immediate family members took their places. Walt had read the obituary in the paper, and he learned that Donald Vaughn never married. Men in all kinds of military uniforms laden with colorful ribbons and lots of brass were seated on the stage.

Walt listened as one speaker after another hailed the virtues of Donald Vaughn. He was portrayed as a person of conviction, courage, and valor. The man who "may" be his father was saluted for his services to his country. The citizens of Mason-Dixon were told how proud they should be of their native son, who was indeed an American hero.

Reporters came from all over the country to cover the story. Flashbulbs kept going off from all directions.

As the proceedings were coming to a halt, one of the women sitting with Maude looked up toward the bleachers one more time through bleary eyes from behind her veil. Walt was gone.

After she heard the news of Donald's sudden death, Maude did not know what to expect from Maggie. They had not seen each other since a couple of days before Walt was born. Millie called and said that Walt's birth mother was flying in from San Diego. She would be staying with her in Atlanta, and the two of them were driving up for the funeral.

The reunion of The Three Musketeers at the school where they had been such close friends was unlike anything any of them could have ever imagined. Walt's two mothers embraced awkwardly, neither knowing what to say. Once as close as sisters, they were now strangers.

Millie sat between Maude and Maggie during the memorial service. The women on each side of her were in their separate worlds. One could not keep her eyes off Walt. The other was hoping he did not know that she was there.

When the service was over, they said polite goodbyes. As Maggie gave Maude a little obligatory hug, she pressed a small envelope into her hand.

The Three Musketeers would not see each other again until they reassembled in that auditorium in about five years. They would not sit together on that occasion. After that brush, they would not all be in each other's presence for another fifteen years. That reunion would be only a few weeks before another funeral.

Maude made her way home after the memorial service. Once again, she had let someone talk her into something that she did not want to do. She had no desire to see Maggie, but Millie insisted that they all sit together.

A part of her wanted to strike a match to the note without even opening it. Then, she let her curiosity get the best of her. A check fell out, made out to Maude for $1000.

"How dare that woman? Does she think she can buy her way out of this?"

For a brief moment, Maude considered cashing the check and splurging. She realized immediately, though, that there was no way she could get away with that. Todd would come charging at her for an explanation.

Just looking at the fancy folded note made her furious. The expensive stationery was engraved.

"I understand why Everett reenlisted in the navy. He can spend months at the time out to sea, just to get away from you," the peeved woman took some satisfaction in thinking.

"Thank you," the little missive from Maggie began.

"Right," she said to herself cynically. "Thank you, Maude, for carrying my load so I can play and party."

Maude then vented more of the venom building inside her. "She's out there in sunny California living the Life of Riley, while I'm stuck here in Podunk Hollow."

She further fretted, "If that woman had any guts, she would have gone to Walt, told him why she came to Donald's funeral, and then taken him back with her to San Diego."

Ahhhhhhhhhhh!

On the drive back to Atlanta, Maggie and Millie experienced their own kind of awkwardness. Millie was mostly detached as she discussed the details of what had happened. Maggie, on the other hand, was overwrought with a wide range of competing emotions.

For one thing, she had just buried the love of her life. Donald was her fantasy. Her thoughts always turned to him when she had the blues, or when she had something to celebrate. Now, he was gone.

At the same time, Maggie was trying to come back down to earth after seeing her Walter for the first time since the night he was born. What a handsome lad he was. His father would have been so proud of him.

Donald was dead. Their son was very much alive. Maggie just existed from one day to the next.

The flight back to San Diego was a bit bumpy going across the plains. The troubled woman eventually got a chance to go to the restroom when the pilot finally turned the seatbelt light off. As she looked into the tiny mirror, she asked aloud, "Maggie, who are you?"

When she returned to her seat, the soul searching continued. She revisited her carefree childhood. The girl never questioned the love of her parents. She grew up with self-confidence, easily making friends and always turning boys' heads. She was the apple of her daddy's eye. She was the cat's meow and the belle of the ball. How could everything that seemed so right turn out so wrong?

Maggie was married to a man she loved and admired, but was not in love with. After they were settled into their new home in California, she wanted to go back to school and have a career. Everett was opposed. He could provide amply for his wife, and he wanted her available when he came home from the sea.

Maggie's social calendar was always full. She had many friends, but not one single confidant that she could pour out her heart to.

As the couple began to accrue a little nest egg, Maggie handled the finances. She made wise investments and their little estate began to grow. Someone looking in from the outside might think she had everything a woman could want. How many girls who grew up in Townsend County, Georgia during the Great Depression could write a check for $1000, and not have to explain it?

"I'm living a lie," Maggie admitted to herself. Nothing about her seemed authentic or genuine. What could she do about it, though? Too many people would be burned so badly if she followed her heart. The last person on earth she wanted to hurt was her Walter. Her greatest fear was that he would hate her for abandoning him if he found out the truth. That would only make matters worse.

For now, Maggie would sit tight until the plane landed. She would take a cab home. Then, she would just keep right on going through the motions of living. What else could she do?

Not much changed after D-V (Donald Vaughn) Day. That is what Walt called the day of the kitchen encounter. Then again, everything had changed.

His folks kept right on pretending to be a family. His mom would act as if she could not do enough for him. Then, she became distant again. He just did not feel like it was his place to unburden her. If she had anything else to say, he would certainly listen.

His mother and Todd were not fussing as much as they used to. That did not make any difference to Walt one way or the other. Emma Lou went around with her nose in a joint, in the air, or stuck in a book. There was certainly nothing new about that.

The big difference was what was happening inside Walt. He finally had Todd off his back, both literally and figuratively. The boy was a little surprised that the forceful and controlling man backed down so meekly. Perhaps his army buddies got it right. Maybe a "Toad" was all he ever was to begin with.

He still did not trust him, though. Unpredictably, Todd might come charging at him again. If he was in a rage, Walt was not too confident of his abilities to handle the man. He was very sure, nonetheless, that he could out run him if he had to.

Walt had already learned the importance of having a backup plan. If Todd decided that these two bulls could no longer live in the same pasture, then he would hitchhike to Adamsonville. He had not one, but two sets of uncles and aunts who would take him in under those circumstances.

The word empowered was likely not in Walt's vocabulary yet. Nevertheless, he had a clear understanding of its concept. He had some leverage in this situation. He did not ask for it. It was thrust upon him.

Control and freak were likewise words that Walt had never heard used together in the same sentence. He was nonetheless living with one. He was ever mindful of Todd's obsession with having everything under his sway. Nobody had to explain to the boy why his refusal to knuckle under just about drove the man crazy.

Walt could not help it that Todd's opinion of him hardly mattered at all. From the time the man showed up in his life when he was barely a year old, it never had. Neither could he do much about the man's relentless crusade to whip him in line. That had all changed on D-V Day.

The War Baby

Maude did not know how much longer she could hold her breath. A month had passed since Donald's death. In the thirteen years since she was so unfairly pressured and coerced into taking somebody else's baby, this was the first time that she had ever slipped up. As far as she could tell, until that unfortunate moment in the kitchen, the five people in on the big secret from the beginning were the only ones who knew.

Since her misstep, Maude's insides had been churning day and night. She fully expected Walt to confront her again the day it happened. He did not. Nor did he say anything the next, or the next.

The anxious and apprehensive woman was hoping against hope that the boy did not hear her. Perhaps her emotionally wrought words were imperceptible. With the noise of the radio playing in the background, maybe she spoke so softly that he did not comprehend what she said.

Then, the boy showed up at the memorial service. He sat there soaking up everything being said about the man who was indeed his biological father. Was his presence just natural curiosity? Was he drawn simply because of a sensational event happening in a part of the world where normally even the distant sound of a wailing siren was a rare occurrence?

Added to Maude's woes was something she saw as she was leaving the auditorium. As she was exiting with the group in the reserved section, she was shocked when she looked over and saw her daddy sitting with Todd's father. She knew how close Walt was to his grandfathers. Had he said something to either or both of them? She could not be sure. Why were they there together?

The deeply disturbed woman did have one consolation. She felt confident that Walt was not going to discuss anything with Todd.

Maude tried to put her blunder out of her mind, but it kept replaying like a broken record. What possessed her to blurt out those words to Walt? Was she so tired of carrying the burden that she secretly wished to just lay it down and walk away?

The last few weeks had proven one thing. Todd did not suspect anything involving Donald. If he had, she was certain that her husband would have made his move.

Maude was furthermore surprised at how cooperative Todd was the day of the memorial service. He offered to run the mail route. Normally, he would make something like that difficult for her. Instead, he was civil. He then gave her some space the rest of the day, seeming to respect her need to grieve the loss of a friend. Even this caused her to be uneasy.

Maude still did not know what to do about Walt. It was beginning to look like he was not going to come to her for answers. Just when she would get to the point that maybe she needed to go ahead and approach him about the unfortunate gaffe, she started talking herself out of it. Would she ruin everything if she brought it up, only to find out that he did not hear what she said?

One other possibility intrigued Maude. Maybe she should just go ahead and tell Walt the truth. She still had the check from Maggie. She could use the money to buy the boy a one-way ticket, and send him to his mother.

When Maude did not know what to do, she usually just did nothing. This time would be no different. She just wanted Walt to hurry up, grow up, and get out on his own. Could she keep everything together for that long? She was not sure, especially in light of her blunder.

Walt tried to keep a low profile throughout eighth grade. He was a starter on the junior varsity basketball team, but not much else seemed important to him. The girls in his class had taken a sudden interest in the older high school boys.

Not once did Walt bring a report card home after D-V Day. To his amazement, neither parent seemed to notice. He just signed his mother's name and turned them back in. He knew if he ever got caught, he had some clout if he needed to use it.

"I think she's trying to get your attention," Alex interrupted Walt, as he was messing around with Mary Jo.

"Who?" asked Walt.

"Mrs. Webster," he was told.

The eighth grade homeroom teacher was at the other end of the gymnasium. She pointed straight toward Walt, and then gestured with her right index finger for him to come to her.

"I wonder what this is all about," Walt mumbled. He blew Mary Jo a kiss, and then he told her to hold that thought.

As the student approached his teacher, he did not like the look on her face. Without saying a word, she pointed him to the school office.

"Young man, empty your pockets on the desk," Mrs. Webster instructed him.

"What is going on?" Walt thought to himself.

"Not just your hip pockets, your front pockets, too," she added.

Walt looked down at the collection on the principal's desk. There were a few coins, his wallet, his comb and handkerchief, his Barlow knife, and a couple of rubber bands.

"Walter, why do you find it necessary to carry rubber bands around with you?" she wanted to know.

He shrugged, but gave no answer.

"Do you use them to shoot spit wads?"

"Well, ma'am, I suppose in the past I might have been guilty of that a time or two," Walt answered. "But never in your class," he added quickly.

"Why then are you carrying them around today?" Mrs. Webster inquired next.

"I don't know. They were just with my stuff when I loaded my pockets this morning," the perplexed student answered.

"Have you had either of them out of your pocket since you got to school today?" she asked next.

"I don't think so," Walt lied.

"Then, I suppose Mary Jo was not being truthful when she told me that on the way to the gym, you popped her on her backside with a rubber band?"

"So that is what this is all about, Othell," Walt mused to himself. "How dare Mary Jo tell on me when she knew I was just flirting with her? It could not have hurt that much through her jeans. I didn't tell on her when she jerked the shirttail out of my pants."

"Walter Williamson, bend over the desk," Mrs. Webster further directed as she reached for the principal's paddle. "You are going to think that this whipping is a little too severe for the crime you have committed. Your rear end is going to hurt a lot more than Mary Jo's did when you inflicted the pain upon her. Let me tell you something young man. This paddling is also for all those things that I know you have done, when I was never able to catch you."

Mrs. Webster could not see the smirk that came across Walt's face. It did not stay there long, though, when she started applying the Board of Education to his buttocks to the tune of twenty-five hard licks.

Walt skipped the rest of school that day. The next morning Alex asked him what happened. He said that he went home and helped his granddaddy dig sweet potatoes, which was in fact what he did.

Scout went off one day, and he never came home. Spot missed his companion so much that he soon grieved himself to death. The boy missed his dogs. This loss was just one more unsettling development for the adolescent now entering the awkwardness of puberty.

More and more, he felt like an alien that Buck Rogers must have plucked from some far away planet and dropped off on Earth. He sometimes imagined himself sitting in the catbird seat on a ship of fools, watching everything happening below, while no one was aware that he even existed.

With members of the opposite sex, Walt was still a novice. Would he always be stuck in first gear? Just when he thought that he had some things figured out about females, somebody changed the rules again.

Other than his two grandfathers, and perhaps Earl and Mary Beth, he could not think of anyone else who had any idea who he was. These individuals had only gotten a few glimpses.

When the fall came, Walt was ready for high school. He breezed through the ninth grade, playing whatever games his teachers required.

Oh, Please, Mr. Postman

Todd had not missed a Saturday carrying the mail since about the time of Donald Vaughn's death. He told Maude he understood that she needed to be home then since the kids were out of school. This gave her a chance to do the week's laundry, and to get ready for Sunday. She was not one to question things, and for that, Todd was grateful.

The Haygood place was the last stop on the mail route. It was several miles from town at the end of an unpaved road. Todd had never met the Haygoods, although he turned around in their drive.

Almost a year earlier, he had noticed an increasing volume of greeting cards in their mail. Soon thereafter, extra cars were parked in the yard, sometimes making it difficult to get to the box. One day, vehicles were all up and down the road, and a big white wreath was on the front door. He read Clyde Haygood's obituary in the paper that night.

On a Friday several months later, the mail carrier had a parcel addressed to Helen Haygood which was too big for the mailbox. Todd knocked on the door but no one came. A couple of dogs were milling around. He was concerned about leaving the package at the door for fear they might get into it. He decided to hold it until Saturday when perhaps the woman would be home.

The next afternoon, Helen was working in the yard. Because where she lived was so isolated, the attractive woman was not too concerned with modesty. She was, however, a bit startled when the mailman drove into her yard instead of just stopping at her box. When Todd told her that she had a package, the woman acted even more surprised. She had not ordered anything.

When Mrs. Haygood saw the return address, she laughed out loud. It was from her secret pal. Todd had no idea what that meant so she explained it to him. One of her friends heard about women drawing names and becoming secret pals. She thought it would be good for Helen. The participants did little gestures anonymously on birthdays, anniversaries, and holidays. Sometimes they did something out of the ordinary for no occasion at all.

The woman could not wait to see what was inside. She started ripping the box open right in front of Todd. That was a big mistake. It was a gag gift, of the kind not proper in mixed company.

"What did you say your name is?" she asked.

Actually, he had not told her his name. "It is Todd Williamson," he said, a bit awkwardly.

"Well, Mr. Williamson, I'll bet you do not get an eye full like this every day, do you?"

"You can rest assured, ma'am, that is the truth," he answered.

They both laughed. Helen explained that when the year was over, the women would get together and reveal their secret pals. She would have quite a tale to tell. They laughed some more.

Changing the subject, Todd then told Mrs. Haygood he was sorry to note that she lost her husband a while back.

"Yes, that was tough," she responded. "Clyde was a good man. It was just awful to see him suffer so much."

"You have my sympathy," he conveyed to her.

Helen went on to say that because of the medical bills, she had to go back to work. She was trying to keep the place, but she had so little time on weekends to get everything done. Todd then said that he would be happy to lend a helping hand. She thanked him and he left.

Todd volunteered to take the mail the next Saturday, the day of Donald Vaughn's memorial service. He was disappointed when he did not see anything of Mrs. Haygood. Then on the next, she passed him on the road and waved at him while he was putting mail in another box. When Todd got to her house, Helen was still unloading groceries. He pulled into the yard.

"Oh, I'm so glad you stopped," she called, as he was getting out of his car. "Can you help me change a light bulb in the kitchen? I don't like heights, and I'm afraid I might fall off the ladder."

Noticing the short dress she was wearing, Todd said that he would be glad to steady the ladder for her if she wanted him to.

"Now Mr. Williamson, are you trying to get an eyeful again?" she asked him with a little devilish grin on her face. Todd made sure that Helen saw him as he let his eyes wander.

The old ladder was rickety. He feigned that he was falling off a couple of times. They both laughed. When he got the new bulb screwed in, it did not work either.

"I think there must be a shortage," Todd reasoned. "Do you have a screwdriver and a pair of pliers?"

Helen quickly produced them from her husband's toolbox. He tripped the breaker, found a loose screw, and tightened it. He said it was working for the time being, but the socket needed replacing. It was burned a little from the short.

"Can you fix it?" she wanted to know.

"I'll be glad to pick one up and replace it next Saturday," Todd offered.

"That is mighty nice of you," Helen responded. "I'll be glad to pay you."

"Oh, no trouble at all," he said. All week Todd imagined ways the woman might repay him for his good deed.

It started that way. Saturdays were soon a ritual for the two of them. Before long, Helen Haygood not only had a secret pal. She also had a secret lover.

Todd Williamson was soon a tormented man. His little tryst with the Widow Haygood energized him initially. Somebody actually found him desirable without him having to prove himself. Even that was not entirely true since he had become Helen's handyman.

The euphoria did not last very long. Helen started making demands. Meanwhile, Todd was tortured with his guilt.

Helen Haygood fell head over heels in love with Todd. She did not mean for that to happen. Although she had started giving him up months earlier as he gradually left her while surrendering to Lou Gehrig's disease, Clyde had been dead less than a year.

The mailman confessed to his lover how unhappy he was with his wife. Helen made him happy. The solution was simple to her. He would leave his wife and marry her.

It was more complicated than that for Todd. He had his image to uphold. He was the chairman of the deacons at the Mason Baptist Church. The preacher preached a sermon just as the affair was beginning on the importance of visiting the fatherless and the widows. Righteous Todd initially rationalized his actions as just carrying out his Christian duty.

He kept stalling his illicit lover while trying to sort things out. Once again, he was up against something that he could not discuss with his mother. He wanted the relationship to go on indefinitely as things were. It was not so with Helen. She imposed a deadline on him.

One thing eating at Todd was how he had lost his moral superiority with Maude. He was also growing a little anxious that Helen might just pick up the phone, give his wife a call, and force his hand. The man who had to be in control of everything was in control of nothing.

Maude was so worried about Walt's situation that she more or less lost sight of Todd. For several weeks, her husband just came and went with little concern for much of anything. Best to let sleeping dogs lie. All of that was about to change.

"Where did you go today?" he demanded to know, as he came charging in the door one afternoon.

"How do you know I have been anywhere?" she inquired in return.

"The car is not parked like it was when I left," he snapped back.

"Well, if you have to know, I went to the A & P so you can have food on the table when you get hungry."

Over the next several days, it went downhill from there. Maude watched out the window as Todd checked odometer readings before he left to make sure that she was not running up extra miles.

Why was he so suspicious of her all of a sudden? The last thing on her mind was doing anything to create problems for them. No man anywhere had so much as flirted with her.

Then one day, Todd lit into Maude again about Walt. This time he was finally going to get to the truth. When the infuriated man kept running into the same old dead ends and roadblocks, he became enraged. In his desperation, he crossed a line that he had never crossed before.

Maude lay on the bed in the fetal position afterward, sobbing uncontrollably. What she had no way of knowing was that if her husband had been able to beat the truth out of her, he would have then been justified in leaving her. If she had only known, she would have given him what he wanted.

Emma Lou was blossoming into an attractive young woman. Her hair was much lighter now, almost the color of her father's. Maude showed her daughter one of the few pictures she had from her own youth and suggested to her how much alike they were. Emma Lou said that she did not see any resemblance. She always thought she favored her Grandmother Williamson.

The high school junior was also quite a good musician. She had been taking piano lessons since she was twelve. Emma Lou could play just about anything that anyone requested. She was often asked to play at church on Sunday nights.

Walt's fascination was with the sound of brass. The war baby grew up listening to the big bands so popular about the time he was born. As a kid, he imagined himself one day a famous trumpet player.

Starting before his birthday one year, and continuing right up to Christmas, he kept hinting for a trumpet. He got one all right. Under the tree on Christmas morning, was a shiny new horn still in its box. The plastic child's toy said that it was for ages four through eight. On that sour note, Walt Williamson's musical career fell flat on its face.

Emma Lou always went straight to the piano when she got home from school. Her brother could tell within the first couple of minutes what kind of day she was having by what and how she was playing.

"Othell," he said to himself one day, "Wouldn't it be sad if a person went all the way through life, and never played or sang anything but somebody else's songs?"

As he watched his sister, Walt could not imagine a more model daughter. Unlike him, she had pleasing her parents down to a fine art. "Othell," he said yet again, "One day that girl is going to make some man a fine wife."

Maude wanted to die. How could she live with herself any longer? Her husband obviously despised her. Instead of beating Walt, he was now taking his wrath out on her. He had not made love to her in months.

In the midst of it all, the woman was battling a growing resentment toward Walt that had been building inside her for years. The preacher said that there is a time to love and a time to hate. She was letting her feelings toward the boy turn to spitefulness. He was ruining her life.

Alone in her thoughts, Maude often replayed things in her mind. When Todd came home from the service, she hoped to hand the boy off to him and let him do most of the raising. She knew how much Todd wanted a son. Unfortunately, he just did not take to the boy at all.

She now regretted letting Maggie talk her into naming the baby. If she had just stuck to her guns and insisted that the boy be named after Todd, it might have all turned out so differently.

If not for Walt, their relationship would be so much better. She just knew it. She dreamed of her husband loving her dearly, and of them doing things together. The boy was responsible for Todd's ongoing frustration and anger. There was no doubt about it. Things would never be right between them because of Walt. Maude wanted to crawl in a hole somewhere and die.

Then, there was Emma Lou. Her spring piano recital was coming up in two weeks. Maude had promised to take her daughter shopping to get a new dress. It was time to pick herself up yet again.

Walt was not too excited about going to his sister's recital, but he decided to go anyway. At least he could count on some good-looking girls being there.

The observant lad always tried to take a seat where he could see what was going on around him. As he looked about the auditorium, he was amazed that he knew just about everybody there. There was one glaring exception, however. He did not recognize the pretty woman wearing a sundress who was seated in the back row. She had not taken off her shades when she came in from the sun.

Helen Haygood's deadline came and went. Todd begged for more time. The woman said that her biological clock was ticking. She and Clyde were unable to have children, and she wanted a family while she was still young enough.

All of this added to Todd's dilemma. Maude had not given him a son; at least a son he knew was his. What was it with his wife? She conceived so quickly when they first got married. Then, Walt came along under circumstances that still mystified him.

Now, he had been home from the service more than a dozen years, and she had not conceived again. Time was running out for him, too, to become the father of Todd Allgood Williamson, Jr.

The pressure continued to mount. Todd was like a volcano raging inside a mountain that might erupt at any moment. That moment came the night of Emma Lou's recital.

To the delight of the crowd, the girl performed magnificently. Afterward, she went to a sleepover at a friend's house. Walt came in and went to his room. He turned the radio up a little louder so that he did not have to hear what was going on elsewhere in the house.

All of a sudden, he heard his mother screaming.

"Walt, Walt, he has a gun!"

The boy ran out of his room and down the hall. Todd had a rifle all right, but he was not pointing it at his wife. He was aiming it at himself. Walt could see that the safety was off. He had no way of knowing whether the chamber held a live round.

The lad drew a bead on Todd. He then charged him like a linebacker blitzing a quarterback. The teenager knocked the man to the floor. The two of them struggled for control of the weapon. Maude stood by screaming.

Walt eventually prevailed. He wrestled the rifle away from Todd. He then removed the hollow point bullet. The gun was indeed ready to fire.

Cautiously, the fourteen-year-old boy handed the rifle to his mother. He then asked for a moment alone with her husband. He ordered Todd to stand up. The man obediently gathered himself, came up on one knee, and then pulled himself to his feet.

Walt looked Todd straight in the eye. He spoke to him slowly and deliberately. "If you want to kill yourself, there is no way I can stop you. But if you decide to go through with it, I am begging two things of you. First, please do not do it in front of my mother. And second, try to make it look like an accident. Do you really want Emma Lou to spend the rest of her life with the stigma that her daddy committed suicide?"

Todd Williamson just stood there. He felt humiliated. Once again, Walt had upstaged him. The man did not know which one he detested most at that moment, himself, or the boy.

Walt went outside for some fresh air. He took a deep breath. After the episode was over, he realized what a dangerous situation it had been. In the scuffle, the rifle could have easily gone off. The bullet did not have a conscience. Somebody could have been seriously hurt, or even killed. The Williamsons might well have been on the next night's evening news.

As he stood in the moonlight still reflecting on what had just happened, the grimness in his demeanor changed. He said aloud, "Othell, why the hell did you try to stop him?"

Helen Haygood said something about her mail carrier at work one day. "Oh, you mean 'Toad' Williamson?" her coworker asked. Helen had no idea what that meant. She soon found out. Todd had said nothing to her about his awful nickname.

Where was she? Todd got to the end of his route, and Helen was nowhere to be seen. He had hinted, but she never gave him a key to her house. He did not have to wait long. The woman came whizzing into the yard in a cloud of dust.

The Widow Haygood was about to see a side of Todd Williamson that she had never seen before. She did not like his tone, or his insinuations. She tried to explain to him that Saturday was her only day off, and that she had to take care of some business when she had the chance.

Todd gave her one of his non-apology apologies, the kind that starts with "if." It would have been better for him *if* he had not opened his mouth.

"Oh, please, Mr. Postman," Helen said in derision and disdain.

Todd was about to see a side of this feisty woman that he had not seen before, either. She then said, "Toad Williamson, why don't you just get in your car and go on home to your wife where you obviously want to be?"

Todd regretted later that he did not do just that, instead of trying to reason with her.

Before Helen put her head on her pillow that night, she wondered what she ever saw in the man. Had she been that lonely? Was she that vulnerable?

Then, she really got into a big tizzy when she considered the possibility that the mailman had taken advantage of her while she was still grieving. The widow woman started plotting all kinds of things that she could do to the "Toad" to exact her pound of flesh.

On the road home, Todd never doubted for one minute that it was over with Helen. He knew that she would not listen to anything he had to say. Maybe it was better this way. He wished that they could have found a peaceful way to end the affair. He could only hope and pray that there would be no further repercussions.

He was madder than an old wet setting hen, however, because of Helen calling him "Toad." He was so hopeful that he had lived down that awful nickname. Now, he could not help but wonder how many people were still referring to him that way behind his back.

Todd eventually turned his attention to Maude. He was ashamed of the way he had treated her. He knew that she deserved better. He was not sure that he could ever give her what she needed, though. She was yet to give him the one thing that he had to have.

Fortunately for Todd, Helen Haygood decided to focus on the recovery of her lost dignity, rather than directing her energies toward retribution. Once she started regaining a measure of self-respect, payback became less important to her.

Gradually, she came to see that she was just as guilty as he was. There was no need to hurt innocent people. As for "Toad," Helen had no doubt that he would get his just deserts, with no need of any assistance from her.

Todd continued to take the mail on Saturdays, though. He had no aspiration of seeing the widow woman. He just wanted to make sure that Helen and Maude did not have an encounter. A couple of months later, he was not surprised to see a "For Sale" sign on her property.

Todd was finally able to breathe a sigh of relief that he had apparently gotten away with the tawdry little affair. He then started concentrating more on his home situation. Emma Lou was going to be a high school senior next year. She had already served notice that she was going to the University of Georgia to study to become a teacher. That was going to put a real strain on the family budget.

Todd and Maude gradually worked out a nominal truce. Things settled down again for a while. The ever-watchful Walt called it a stalemate. He just loved the juiciness of that word.

The Rusty Hinge Grill

George King had a way of showing up unannounced. It was as though he had the instincts of a bloodhound. He had come sniffing around several times just when the pot was about to boil over.

The man rarely came empty handed. He usually had some certifiable reason for showing up. One day he drove into the yard looking for Walt. He handed his grandson a beautiful old double barrel 12-gauge shotgun, along with a box of shells. Then he said, "Son, try it out, and see how you like it."

Walt could only imagine what his Grandpa had in mind. Why would he possibly not like it?

Granddaddy Williamson was more the sportsman in the family. He routinely kept the family in fresh trout, and he often brought wild game home for Ethel to cook. He always killed a deer or two each year. Walt went with his granddaddy on a few hunting trips. The youth had gotten quite good at shooting squirrels with a rifle. He was yet to kill his first rabbit, though. Maybe his luck was about to change.

One cold, raw, winter day not long after his Grandpa dropped the gun off, Walt went to borrow his other granddaddy's dogs. The beagles saw the shotgun, and they were ready to go. Across the road near the old Williamson home place, the dogs jumped a rabbit almost immediately.

Walt knew the cottontail was leading the hounds in a wide circle, and that it would eventually bring them right back to where the chase began. All he had to do was wait and be ready.

The boy had already familiarized himself with the weapon. Unlike some older models, this one was hammerless. Once the safety was off, the triggers were ready to pull. With a shell in each chamber, he would cradle the forward-most trigger for the barrel on the right first. If he needed a second shot, his finger would move to the one behind it.

While listening to the forlorn sounds of the beagles, Walt was shivering, thinking that he should have worn a heavier coat. Someone who did not know what was going on might think the dogs were being beaten.

While the rabbit and the hounds were still a good way off, the young hunter noticed some movement in a tree overhead. A squirrel was jumping from limb to limb.

Anxious to shoot the gun, Walt decided to take aim at Mr. Bushy Tail. If he came home with a squirrel and a rabbit, his mother would have enough meat for supper. He had plenty of time to reload.

Walt had shot a 12-gauge several times before, so he braced himself for the inevitable kick. He took the safety off and raised the shotgun carefully.

When the squirrel paused for a second on a limb, he got the shot he wanted. He drew a bead right at the squirrel's nose, aiming to do as little damage to it as possible. He gently squeezed the front trigger. **BOOM!** The blast almost knocked the boy down. The squirrel fell from the tree, decimated.

Somewhat dazed, the youthful hunter realized that the dogs were getting closer. He hurriedly breeched the gun to reload. Smoke was still pouring from the weapon. When he looked closer, Walt discovered that both chambers were spent. No wonder he was still reeling. His shoulder was sore for a week. Jack Rabbit lived to see another chase.

The next time Grandpa King came by he asked, "Son, did you get a chance to try out that old double barrel I left with you?"

"I sure did," Walt answered. He then explained in graphic detail what happened. The man looked on contemplatively, nodding as his grandson laid it all out.

"Well, I guess I'll have to take it back to the gunsmith," Grandpa lamented with a shrewd look on his face. "He must not have gotten the old gun fixed."

George King served notice that this was the last year he would be having a hog killing. He and Ruby had barely enough table scraps for the dog. Feed had gotten so expensive, and Mason now had its own Piggly Wiggly with a fresh meat department. Besides that, the doctors were saying that lard was not good for people.

About a week before Thanksgiving in 1958, the clan gathered one more time. A lot of reminiscing was going on as the work proceeded. Yarns were shared from years gone by. Walt even told the story about the day he learned how to tie his shoes. He and his Grandpa were about to make another memory, though, that both would cherish forever.

Little by little, the butchering progressed. Uncle Jim and Aunt Josie made off with the entrails. Hams and shoulders were separated for curing. Middling was set aside for bacon. Ribs, roasts, and pork chops were carved. The remainder of the meat was divided into fat and lean. The lean was ground into sausage, and the fat was cooked in the wash pots for lard. The bits remaining were preserved for good old crackling cornbread.

By late morning, most of the meat was cut. An old gate from the barnyard had been used for firewood around the pots, now boiling the fat. The huge hinges had burned off, and they were lying in the hot coals.

Walt took a butcher knife and cut off two pieces of tenderloin. Grandpa King watched curiously. The lad went in the kitchen. He salted and peppered the pieces of meat, and then he grabbed a couple of biscuits left over from breakfast. The teenager went to the fire. He placed the loin carefully on one of the sizzling hinges. He put the biscuits on another to warm them.

"What are you doing, son?" his Grandpa asked him.

"I'm frying some tenderloin at The Rusty Hinge Grill," Walt answered, with a big smile on his face.

"Gonna share?" Grandpa asked next.

"Of course," his grandson replied.

While no one else was watching, the two stole off behind the smokehouse. They savored the best tenderloin biscuit either of them would ever put in their mouths.

In the fall of 1959, Walt was a sophomore. This was a big year since he would get his learner's license when his birthday rolled around. He had been driving his granddaddy's old Studebaker truck around the farm since he was able to reach the pedals. Now, he was ready to get on the road.

Nothing much of significance happened in tenth grade. Walt played on the basketball B-team, but he decided that he was not cut out to be an athlete. He was not doing much better in the romance department either. The girls in his class still seemed to be only interested in older boys. He just did not seem to have much in common with any of the gals at school.

Then again, Walt was not exactly Mr. Excitement. He never thought of himself as all that good looking. Because of circumstances at home, he had neither the means, nor the opportunity to be much of a social animal. It did not help that he was one of the youngest members of his class.

Walt was a joiner and a loner at the same time. He participated in church and school activities, occasionally taking leadership positions. When he was sitting on the sidelines, his mind was never idle, endlessly sizing up the situations all around him. Whether in the fray or not, Walt Williamson's head was always in the game.

When Walt was about to turn fifteen, he kept reminding his mother that he needed his birth certificate in order to get his learner's permit. She promised to go by the Health Department the next time she was in Mountain Home. She just kept forgetting it. A week after his birthday, he asked if they could go by and get it on the way to the Georgia State Patrol Station. She said she guessed so.

A parent had to go with applicants, and it had to be his mother. Todd wanted no part of it. Walt filled out the forms, and then he took his birth certificate out of the envelope. He actually wondered if something was on it that his mother did not want him to see. Yet, everything seemed to be in order.

While they were waiting, he decided to push his luck a little. "Mother, tell me about the day I was born."

Maude shrugged. She said that she really did not remember much about it.

"What day of the week was it?" Walt asked.

"I think it was a Saturday. Yes, I am sure it was a Saturday. But remember, you were born just before midnight." The patrol officer interrupted the conversation when he called Walt's name over the intercom.

Later that night, he was looking at a calendar. Not sure what made him do it, he turned to October and started running the months backwards. He knew that the yearly calendar advanced one day forward each day of the week, and two on a Leap Year.

It did not take long at all to see what October 1944 looked like. Halloween was on a Tuesday. Now why did his mother not remember that?

You Win Some, You Lose Some

Walt volunteered to be the chauffeur for both sets of grandparents when they needed to go somewhere. That was about the only driving he got to do. As the all-day singing at Mt. Pisgah was approaching in May 1960, Granddaddy Williamson asked his grandson if he would like to escort them.

Mr. Williamson had just traded cars. Walt got to drive the blue and white 1956 Chevrolet Bel Air for the first time. With an automatic transmission, it was not as much fun as driving a stick shift, but that V-8 would get up and go.

After lunch when his granddaddy went back in the church, Walt stayed outside. He watched his grandmother go to the car, get some flowers out of the trunk, and place them in a fruit jar. She then walked toward the cemetery.

The woman looked back over her shoulder a couple of times, and that caught Walt's attention. He positioned himself where he could see her, but she would not notice him. She went straight to a grave, knelt down, and placed the flowers by the headstone. His grandmother stood at the foot of the grave for several moments before returning to the church.

"Oh Todd, my love," she said aloud. "How could you have been so careless to let that horse throw you?"

Ethel's thoughts then went back to the fifteen-year-old boy's funeral. She recalled vividly the vow she made that day that if she ever had a son, he would be named after her first love. He would be their child.

After his grandmother returned to the church, Walt made his way to the grave. The marker said that the boy buried there was born in 1901 and he died in 1916.

When the singing was over, the youthful driver delivered his grandparents back to their home. As he and his granddaddy started unloading the leftovers from the trunk, the boy asked him a question.

"Granddaddy, who was Todd Laney?"

"I don't think I recognize that name," the man responded. "Why do you ask?"

"I saw his grave in the cemetery today, and I wondered why he died the same age I am now," Walt replied.

"Why don't you ask your grandmother?" his granddaddy suggested. "She knows that community better than I do."

Emma Lou's high school graduation was a grand spectacle. No one ever doubted that she would finish at the top of her class. After she delivered the valedictorian's speech, the principle strolled up beside her. He announced that Emma Louise Williamson had received an academic scholarship to attend the University of Georgia. The audience broke out into applause once more.

Todd explained when they got home that it would not cover all of her expenses, but it would certainly help. The family focus shifted to getting the girl ready to go off to college.

Walt was glad to get on with the summer. The first time anyone was going to Adamsonville, he would hitch a ride.

A couple of weeks after school was out, Aunt Kathy and Uncle Jerry came to Mason to visit her parents. Their daughter, Rachel, was now two and a half years old. Walt had fun playing with her in the backseat.

"Why don't you come over and read to her sometime?" his aunt asked, as they dropped him off at his other uncle and aunt's house.

"I might just do that," he replied.

Walt was hardly settled in when Earl and Mary Beth started quizzing him about his future. He was going to be a rising junior in the fall. They said that it was not too early for him to be thinking about his further education.

He did not have much to offer. The lad told them that with Emma Lou going to Georgia, he was certain that his parents would not have anything left over to send him to college. What he really knew was that it would not have made any difference even if his sister had not gone to college.

Walt was surprised that Earl and Mary Beth were already thinking about what he was going to do after he graduated. They then told him of their plans to build a new house with a full basement. Construction was to begin later that fall so that it would be dried in before the winter rains.

Walt listened with interest, but he was not sure what any of that had to do with him. Then, his ears shot up. Earl said that they were going to finish a portion of the basement. If Walt wanted to come and live with them, he could attend Adamson State College. He could also work part time at the tractor dealership, earning enough to cover the cost of his books and tuition.

Not much caught Walter Othell Williamson off guard, but he never saw this coming. This one time in his life, he was for the moment speechless.

"I love you guys," he finally mumbled.

"We love you, too, Walt," Earl and Mary Beth said in unison.

He lay in bed that night, still a bit in awe of the prospects. He mused aloud, "Othell, that's just swell." He repeated it several times. For the first time in his life, Walt Williamson could see a glimmer of hope for a future beyond the confines of the isolated little community tucked away in the foothills of north Georgia.

Walt had to be on guard not to get a swellhead that summer for another reason, too. He and Judith Muse discovered each other. Walt was fresh meat so to speak. He was the boy from out of town that several of the girls in Adamsonville had been keeping an eye on the past summer or two. Judith was the first one of them to catch his. She went to the First Baptist Church.

Walt never did move his membership to Mason. Somehow, he just could not bring himself to be a member of the church where Todd was a mover and a shaker. He had not been much of a churchgoer for the last couple of years, but in the summer of 1960, he was all involved with the youth activities of his church.

One night when he was staying over with Aunt Kathy and Uncle Jerry after a cookout and volleyball game, his aunt asked Walt if he would read Rachel a bedtime story. He took the girl up in his lap and opened the book. "Here's one I especially like," he said to his toddler cousin.

With lots of inflection and expression, punctuated with some tickling and giggling, he read to her the story of "The Ugly Duckling." He stopped along the way to explain what was happening. Little Rachel's eyes got really big when Walt announced dramatically that the ugly little duck had turned into a beautiful swan.

He then explained the meaning of the story to her. He said that people just have to be who they are, no matter what anybody else thinks about them. The girl looked into his eyes lovingly. He hoped that what he was saying was making an impression. He did not envy Rachel growing up a preacher's kid.

After he handed the little girl back to her mother, Walt took a walk through the streetlight-illuminated downtown. He thought back to the first time he read that story to himself. Then he said, "You know what, Othell? You just got hatched in the wrong nest."

After several feeble attempts, Walt finally got to first base with Judith, but no farther. The summer romance came to a tearful end. He and Judith promised to stay in touch. He said that he would get back down to Adamsonville every chance he could. They exchanged a couple of letters, and then hers stopped coming. He was never sure if he got all of his mail.

Walt found himself in a different kind of situation when school started back in the fall of 1960. He was no longer in the shadows of his sister. He had to admit that being in the same school together seemed to bother Emma Lou a lot more than it did him. Far more people referred to her as Walt Williamson's sister, than they did to him as her little brother.

It was weird how much Walt missed her at home. The house now had an eerie silence about it. He had never given it much thought, but Emma Lou was the spirit that enlivened the place.

He especially missed his sister's piano playing. He vowed to tell her that the first chance he had. True to his word, when Emma Lou came home for Thanksgiving, he did just that.

Walt was most unprepared for his sister's response. She looked at him with a bit of disgust and said, "Okay, what do you want?"

"What do you mean, what do I want?" he asked, perplexed.

"You would not be paying me a compliment like that if you did not want something," Emma Lou responded, in an obviously condescending tone. He tried unsuccessfully to convince his sister that all he had in mind was telling her how much he missed hearing her play the piano.

"Isn't that just swell, Othell?" Walt said as he walked away. "I can't even be nice to the people in this family without them thinking that I am up to something. Oh, well."

During the Christmas holidays, Walt caught a ride to Adamsonville. The first thing on the young man's agenda was looking up Judith Muse. Much to his chagrin, she was now in love with a boy who was both president of the Beta Club, and the drum major for the high school marching band. Apparently, absence did not make the heart grow fonder.

"Oh well, Othell. You win some, you lose some, and some just get rained out."

Pray Tell, Othell

Walt was never a very good history student. He understood the importance of knowing the Egyptians came before the Greeks, and the Greeks came before the Romans. He just saw little need in having to remember that, according to somebody's calendar, Plato lived between 427-347 B.C. If he ever needed to know that, he could go look it up.

He had some appreciation for Lincoln's "Gettysburg Address." It might even be important to know that Gettysburg is in Pennsylvania, since President Eisenhower made his home there. He did not understand, though, why he had to remember that old Honest Abe delivered the speech on Thursday, November 19, 1863.

Walt mostly just went along with the teachers. Then, just before a test, he paid careful attention when they were spoon-feeding the lazy students. He did a little cramming, and he usually came out with one of the top grades in the class.

His eleventh grade U. S. History teacher was also a Baptist minister. While the man was referred to as the Reverend or Preacher Hazelwood in his little church community, he insisted that his students address him as Mr. Hazelwood.

The bi-vocational minister had to be away from school occasionally on church business. The school board understood that when they hired him, and they tried to provide able assistants when he was absent.

Within Walt's class was an element that never missed an opportunity to have a little fun. The substitute teachers, regardless of their qualifications, could never keep order like Mr. Hazelwood did.

One particular sub was not having much success in maintaining decorum. She therefore took a piece of paper and made a list according to the seating arrangement of those who were being disruptive. She could then call down the unruly ones by name.

When the period was over, the woman inadvertently left the list on the teacher's desk. When Mr. Hazelwood found it the next day, he thought she had taken names.

As class began, he picked it up and said rather sternly, "Walt Williamson, did you misbehave yesterday?" How did Walt's name happen to be at the top of the list? Caught totally off guard, he stammered a bit.

The reverend, who could have been a trial lawyer, redirected the question. "Did you do anything that you would not have done if I had been here?"

"Yes, Sir!" Walt responded. The preacher had him dead to rights on that one.

One by one, he called out the other names on the list. They all 'fessed up to the preacher man. Mr. Hazelwood then made an announcement. "Okay boys, let's go to the office." Having already confessed their guilt, the fun loving high school juniors walked solemnly to the front of the school.

"Do tell, Othell. What have you gotten yourself into now?"

The preacher closed the office door with such force that it rattled the windows.

"Boys," he said, "This is serious."

The students were preparing themselves to get the living daylights beaten out of them. The history teacher was also a former all state high school football player.

The man of God then caught them totally off guard when he said, "I think you boys know that I am a praying man. And I do not do anything that is this serious without first praying about it."

The guys looked around at each other wondering what was going to happen next. They did not have to wait long.

"So, we are all going to get down on our knees in a circle, and pray about this matter," the minister then proclaimed to the now mystified miscreants.

The boys meekly obeyed. The preacher nudged the one on his right, and he asked him to begin. They would proceed counterclockwise, with each student offering his own prayer about this ominous state of affairs.

Walt was raised in and out of church. He looked around at his friends on bended knees. He feared that it had been quite a while since some of these lads had darkened the doors of the Lord's House.

The first couple of supplicants uttered some rather sincere words of penitence, much like the kind of sentence prayers they offered in Sunday School. Then, it was Walt's turn. He humbly bowed his head and with the piousness of a parish priest prayed, "Dear Lord, please forgive us Christians for acting like the devil in front of all those sinners."

The snickering stopped only when the preacher loudly cleared his throat.

Next in line was a young man from a holiness background. He started talking to the Lord. Before long, he was "in the spirit" so to speak. According to his entreaties, those in his prayer circle might well be among the vilest sinners on earth. Without repentance and mercy, they could very well expect the wrath of God to descend upon them at any moment. He prayed long, and he prayed loud.

When the student finished his dramatic entreaty to the Almighty, there was a pronounced silence in the room. The student next to him was one of those who seldom, if ever, attended church. With all sincerity, he uttered his brief supplication. "I feel the same way Thomas does."

The prayer meeting was over. In the ensuing pandemonium, the preacher instructed the students to go back to the room. If he had followed them down the hall, they would have all been right back on their knees.

It was a few minutes later before the teacher/preacher returned to the classroom. The boys were still trying to stifle their laughter. Walt could not help but notice that the one at the head of the class was also having trouble keeping a straight face. He kept turning his back to the class. Mr. Hazelwood looked at his watch anxiously as he tried to make the assignment for the next day. Finally, the shrill sound abruptly ended the period.

Walt started gathering up his books to go to his next class. He not so reverently said to himself, "Pray tell, Othell. That old preacher man just got saved by the bell."

Seeing Mr. Hazelwood looking at his watch reminded Walt that he needed to go ahead and get one for himself. He was in the eleventh grade, and he had owned only one watch in his life. When he was in the eighth grade, he asked for one for Christmas. Santa Claus obliged, and brought him a pocket watch ordered from the Sears catalog.

When he expressed obvious disappointment, Todd said that every boy should have a pocket watch. Walt thought to himself that might have been true when there were no wristwatches. However, nobody he knew his age had a pocket watch. Some jeans did still have a watch pocket, and Walt carried it a few times. Then, it stopped working. He told no one because if Todd found out he would accuse him of being careless, or of deliberately breaking it.

Money was not easy to come by. Todd did not believe in allowances. He certainly did not think kids should be paid for what they were supposed to do anyway.

If it were not for Walt's grandfathers, he would have no pocket money at all. Both of them slipped him some change every now and then. When he was in Adamsonville, Earl also paid him for mowing the grass and cleaning up around the tractor place.

Walt had been saving his money for some time. He finally had enough to go to the Five & Dime and buy himself a new Timex. Nobody at home seemed to notice that he was wearing a watch.

Walt did not tell anyone about the conversation with Earl and Mary Beth. When Emma Lou's grades came at the end of the first quarter, Todd did say to him, "Now don't you go getting any ideas in your head about going off to college. Your sister is keeping us in the poor house as it is."

The oft lazy student realized that he needed to start approaching his schoolwork differently. He could no longer just play the teachers' little games in order to make good grades. The high school junior knew that he had to work harder to get himself prepared for college.

When school was out, Walt wanted to get to Adamsonville as quickly as possible. Granddaddy Williamson said that he was about ready to hear his son-in-law preach again. Besides that, his grandmother would love to see her granddaughter. Walt got to drive all the way with his granddaddy sitting in the front seat beside him.

After a brief visit with the Pattersons, John Paul took Walt over to his other uncle and aunt's house. Only this time he had to follow directions to a different part of town.

Wow! Earl and Mary Beth had moved into their new brick home. After touring the upstairs, they took him to the basement. Just as they promised, Walt had his own quarters.

Non-Conformity

Entering his senior year, Walt had already finished all the required courses except for his fourth unit of English. He did need three additional general credits to graduate. Agriculture/shop would be an easy course. Since he loved math, he also enrolled in advanced algebra and trigonometry.

This still left one elective. He was trying to schedule only morning classes, and the only thing left was typing. Thinking it would be of little use to him, he registered for it anyway.

Having his afternoons free, Walt went looking for a part time job. Mr. Grady Robinson at the filing station said that he really did not need any extra help. Walt then mentioned that he advertised for Robinson's Texaco the year he played Babe Ruth Baseball.

"You did?" the station owner replied. "In that case, I'm gonna give you a chance to prove yoreself."

Walt did not disappoint Mr. Robinson either. He got good at pumping gas, cleaning windshields, and adding oil when necessary. Before long, he was hoisting vehicles on the grease rack and giving them a lube job. He even learned how to fix flat tires.

The conscientious employee also gained Mr. Robinson's trust handling money. On more than one occasion, the proprietor took some time off to go trout fishing. Between customers, Walt got his homework done. Earning a dollar an hour, he thought he had found a gold mine.

All the boys at the Mason-Dixon High School took at least two years of agriculture, and they were members of the Future Farmers of America. The shop did not have much in the way of tools, though. That changed during the summer of 1961. Returning students found all new equipment, with an instructor ready to teach the lads some lessons in woodworking.

Each student had to select a project for his final grade. Walt had helped his Granddaddy Williamson on many occasions, but he had never really attempted anything on his own. He poured over the manuals, feeling some pressure. He had a lofty family standard to live up to. The journeyman woodworker finally decided on building a bookcase for his mother.

Walt meticulously measured and cut the pieces according to the specifications. With supervision, he mitered the joints so that the sides and top fit without any gaps. He then joined it together, set the nails, and filled the holes with plastic wood.

The drawing he was following did not call for a back, but he wanted one for the bookcase. He cut a piece of plywood, stained it to match the other wood, and put it in place.

The student then sanded and sanded and sanded. All of the corners and edges were rounded. The beautiful pine was eventually smooth as silk. After three coats of varnish, it was ready for inspection. The teacher found only one slight imperfection. Walt said he doubted that anything he ever did would be perfect.

About a week before graduation, the proud shop student asked to borrow his granddaddy's Studebaker truck. He carefully padded the piece of furniture, as he had learned watching his mentor. On the way home, Walt stopped to show off his work to his granddaddy.

The master craftsman said to his grandson, "Walt, this is the kind of work that would look good in any home. You did a really good job."

The young man stood a little taller, and a lot straighter. That meant more to him than the A he got for his shop class.

Maude watched curiously, as Walt backed the truck up to the front door. When she came out to see what he was doing, he asked for her help. He watched for a reaction as they took the quilts off the cargo. The proud shop student then told her that it was a little late, but the bookcase was her Mother's Day present.

Together, they unloaded it and placed it in the living room. Maude said that it was nice. She thanked him, but offered no particular show of emotion. Walt was naturally a little disappointed, but he had grown accustomed to this kind of treatment.

When the class ranking was posted, Walt was a bit surprised to learn that he finished second in his class. He intended for his graduation to be considerably less dramatic than Emma Lou's was. Her mirror opposite, he shunned the spotlight. It would be fine with him if he just slipped through the cracks. The principal told him, nonetheless, that he had no choice but to give the salutatorian speech.

Walt's English teacher provided him with all kinds of canned material from which to draw. He saw nothing he liked. After a couple of weeks, his homeroom teacher was concerned that he did not yet have his speech written. She sent him to the principal, who likewise pressured the honor graduate to get it ready for approval.

All Walt would tell any of them was that his address was about conformity, one of the buzzwords at the time. A decade later, he might have said peer pressure.

What could they do? He did not want to give the damn speech to begin with.

When they could wait no longer, the programs had to be printed. Beside Walt's name, the title of his speech was simply listed as "Conformity."

When it came his time to speak, he strolled nonchalantly up to the podium with no notes in his hands. There were some furrowed eyebrows throughout the faculty.

The salutatorian decided to dispense with the usual salutations:

"To the ever boring board of education;

To the most unprincipled principal in the state;

To the faculty that has lost many of its faculties;

To parents who have forgone lifesaving medical procedures, so their snotty-nosed kids could go to school;

To the little piss ants, just itching for the day that they will don cap and gown;

And to the fellow graduates in the Class of 1962, the most underachieving ever in the history of the school."

That sort of thing.

But he was tempted.

After looking the crowd over for a couple of seconds, Walt began.

"I am a human being. I am not a human doer. I do the things I do because of who I am. I am not who I am because of the things I do."

That sure got everybody's attention.

Walt then began retelling the story of "The Ugly Duckling" in his own words. More than one head was leaning a bit sideways. Where was he going with this?

He gave no warning when his speech was about over. He lowered his voice and leaned closer to the microphone as his tassel tickled his cheek. Stressing every syllable, he looked straight at his mother and Todd.

"If you are a duck, then just be a good little duck. Quit going around with your head all stuck up in the air trying to act like a swan. But if you are a swan, then for goodness sakes just be a swan. Don't go around trying to quack like a duck."

Walt went back to his seat. Not once had he used the word conformity.

All of the class salutatorian's former teachers started, one by one, coming to their feet. Applause began timidly, and then it broke out into a thunderous roar as the crowd joined the faculty in a standing ovation.

Walt stood back up and took a bow. He then sat down and mused to himself, "Now miss-goody-two-shoes-brown-nosing-boot-licking-ass-kissing-teacher's-pet-valedictorian, you get to follow that."

As the crowd settled back down, Todd leaned over and whispered to Maude, "That little bastard doesn't have a clue who he really is," watching for her reaction.

She just glared back at him thinking, "And neither do you."

Walt knew many of the folks who came through the receiving line after the Recessional. Two couples that he did not recognize were especially congenial. One of the men wore an impressive military uniform. Both of the women gave him a hug. One held on tightly, to the point that it started to make him feel a bit uncomfortable. They said that they had all gone to school with many of the parents of his classmates, including his mother. Walt was not surprised that his own parents did not make an appearance.

The salutatorian's grandparents from both sides got to the reception at about the same time. His Grandmother Williamson shook his hand with the same kind of formality that she displayed with the minister going out the front door of the church on Sundays. His Granddaddy put a hand on both of Walt's shoulders, and he told him how proud of him he was. Their eyes locked.

Ruby King gave the graduate a polite hug, and she simply said, "Congratulations." His Grandpa lifted him off the floor with a big bear hug. With tears in his eyes, nothing more needed to be said.

As the four of them were walking off, John Paul asked George if he would give him a hand the next day. He had to make a delivery of bathroom vanities to a construction site.

The next morning, the two men loaded the fixtures carefully on the truck, padding them so they would not be damaged. They were hardly seated in the cab when Mr. Williamson remarked, "That was some speech Walt gave last night."

"It certainly was," Mr. King agreed.

"Do you think he knows anything?" J. P. continued.

On the way down the road, the two men went back over what Walt had said regarding the fable.

"It's hard to know what that boy's thinking," George surmised. "But it sure seems like to me he must have something figured out."

J. P. nodded, but he did not know what else to say.

"I wonder what his plans are now," the boy's granddaddy pondered.

"Walt hasn't said anything to me about it. But I do know that Earl and Mary Beth have fixed a room for him in their basement if he wants to go to college in Adamsonville," George informed his neighbor.

A big smile came across the face of John Paul Williamson. "That's mighty nice of them," he said. Mr. King made no attempt to hide the pride that he had in his son and his daughter-in-law.

Emma Lou missed Walt's graduation. She said that she was still in her sophomore spring quarter finals at the university. When she did get home a couple of days later, the first words she said to him were, "I hear you tried to upstage me at graduation."

"No, big sister. (She hated it when he called her that.) My graduation had nothing to do with you. It was just about me being me."

The Gall of that Woman

Maude did not know that Maggie and Millie were going to be at Walt's graduation. She had not heard from either of them since Donald's funeral. Only when she turned around and saw the Hogans and Hancocks during the Recessional, did she know that they were there.

All she wanted to do then was get out of there. Todd certainly had no objection, although he had no idea why she was in such a hurry.

How dare Maggie let her carry the burden of raising Walt, and then come back all cheery and smiley for the celebration? The gall of that woman – to show up at a time like this! And how could Millie possibly go along with something like that?

One for all, and all for one – huh!

Margaret "Maggie" Hogan became more than just a typical military officer's wife. After the war, Everett moved up the ranks rapidly. He was now the commander of a nuclear submarine, poised to become one of the youngest admirals in naval history.

She busied herself with all kinds of civic projects and charitable events while he was out to sea. Since the couple had no children, she was the go to person when a job needed to be done.

When her husband was in port, Mrs. Hogan was the consummate hostess. She threw lavish parties for the brass and their cohorts and consorts in the greater San Diego area.

Everett was proud of his wife, and he rarely missed an opportunity to tell her so. He put her up on a pedestal. He wanted to make sure that she never lacked for anything she wanted.

Maggie realized just how fortunate she was. From her humble beginnings, she had come far. The woman now lived in a beautifully decorated house. She wore designer clothes, and she drove a luxury automobile. She was a member of a bridge club, and she played tennis at the country club.

Two things Maggie's loving husband could not provide for her, however. One was another child. After three or four years went by and she had not conceived, Maggie was afraid that it was her fault. She feared that Doc Elliott had botched things delivering Walter.

When she made an appointment with a gynecologist, she lied on the form. She indicated that she had not given birth. Then, she explained to the doctor that she had put a child up for adoption and asked that it be kept off her medical record.

After a thorough examination and some tests, the gynecologist confirmed that everything was in working order. He also indicated that when her child was born, the attending physician most likely saved her life.

A couple of years later when they were still childless, Everett agreed to have some tests run. The results confirmed what the doctor suspected. He was unable to father a child.

Maggie's husband suggested that they adopt. She could not explain to him why she would never consider that possibility.

The other thing that Everett could not give his wife was the one thing that she coveted more than anything else on earth. He was living on the other side of the continent.

It was so thrilling for Maggie to see her son get his high school diploma on the same stage where she had received hers. She had to admit that she did not quite understand where he was coming from in his speech, but she hardly had time to think about that.

Something else was so much more pressing. Maggie was actually able to hold Walter in her arms. That was the first time that she had touched her baby since the night he was born. How she envied Maude for being able to watch him grow into the fine young man that he had become.

At the same time, the strain of putting on a front was sometimes almost more than she could handle. More than once, Maggie considered telling her husband about Walter. In light of the way she had conducted herself, she felt certain that he would be supportive. She had taken a vow in Doc Elliot's office eighteen years earlier, though. She felt duty bound to honor it.

One thing had not changed through the years. More than anything else in the whole world, Maggie still wanted only what was best for her son.

Lucille Moore went to open the doctor's office at the usual time. Lately, Doc Elliott was a little slow getting over to that side of the house. Once or twice, she had to go rush him up a bit when he was not yet in his office and a patient had arrived. When he did not immediately show that morning, she was not overly concerned.

An hour went by and Lucille was starting to get worried. He had an appointment in fifteen minutes. When she knocked on his bedroom door, there was no response. She knocked again. After waiting a couple of minutes to make sure that he was not in the bathroom, his assistant slowly turned the doorknob.

The doctor did not move when Lucille called his name. Two empty bottles were beside the bed. One of them was a Canadian Scotch. The other was labeled barbiturates. Before she picked up the phone, she removed them both.

The combined news story/obituary in *The Townsend Times* reported that the beloved sixty-nine-year-old physician died in his sleep. When Maude read it, she said to herself, "One of them has now taken it with him to his grave." She wondered who would be next.

When Todd saw the article, he said that it probably did not matter. He doubted that Maude told the old quack anything anyway.

By the time he graduated, Walt had saved $400. He decided to wait until he got to Adamsonville to open a checking account. Mr. Robinson hated to see him go, but the young man had to get out of town as soon as possible.

He needed his own wheels now that he would be starting college in the fall. Walt went to the used car lot in town a couple of times, but he could not find anything with any useful service left in it that he could afford. He would have to wait and let Earl help him find something.

Grandpa King offered to give Walt a ride. Everyone understood that the high school graduate would be staying for the entire summer this time. There was therefore nothing unusual about the amount of clothes and gear he loaded into the car. What none of them knew was that Walt Williamson would never again be a resident of Mason, Georgia.

The day before he left, Walt went by and told his other grandparents goodbye. His Granddaddy Williamson was busy making cherry kitchen cabinets for a new house. He stopped his work, and the two of them talked.

Walt filled his granddaddy in on his summer plans. He told him about how his uncle and aunt had made provisions for him to live with them so that he could go to college. Mr. Williamson welled up with pride, making no mention of the fact that he was already privy to that information.

Walt was delighted when his Grandpa King handed him the keys. Maude was on the mail route, and he had no idea where Todd was. Emma Lou was still asleep. So much for tearful goodbyes.

On the way down the road, Walt told his Grandpa about his college plans. He had sent in his application, but he used Earl and Mary Beth's address since he wanted his grades to go there. He was hoping for a letter of acceptance when he got to their house. Mr. King assured his grandson that he would have no trouble getting into any college anywhere. Walt was justifiably not as certain.

That night, Maude and Todd were sitting at the kitchen table. He reminded his wife that as soon as Emma Lou left for summer school, it would be just the two of them again. She was as proud that Walt was gone as her husband was, but she would not let it show.

"I wonder what he is going to do when the summer is over," Maude thought aloud. "Do you think he will come back here?"

"Now that the little bastard has gotten a taste of making money, he will never live under this roof again," Todd answered. He watched for Maude's reaction when he used the "b" word again, but she was as impassive as ever. He was right in his prediction, too, but Walt never spending another night in that house again had nothing to do with either love or money.

Walt was not surprised that Earl had already been thinking about the car situation. He had his friend Leonard Holmes over at the Chevrolet place on the lookout for something. The day after Walt got to Adamsonville, the two of them went by to see if there were any prospects.

"I've got something that just came in that might fit the bill," Leonard said when they came into his office. Walt wondered if that was not always the car dealer's response when a customer came in. This time, maybe he was right.

A beloved country preacher had just retired. The members of the congregations of the churches that he had served in the area got together, and they gave the minister and his wife a new Buick as a retirement gift. His old dark blue and white '54 Chevrolet was used as a trade in.

Walt was somewhat amused that the folks let the devoted servant drive low-end models while he was out ministering to them. He wondered if a little guilt might have prompted the generous gift. At any rate, the Chevy was worth a look.

It had a lot of miles on it, but Mr. Holmes said that it had a motor job about 10,000 miles back. The six-cylinder engine was not using any oil. The body showed no signs of rust, and the inside was clean as a whistle.

Earl's friend then made an offer. He said that he had not really allowed much for the vehicle as a trade in. As a professional favor to a fellow dealer, Mr. Holmes said that Walt could have it for $250.

That would still leave him with a little money for college. The best part about the old car was that it had a standard transmission.

There was one problem, though. The legal age in Georgia was still twenty-one. Walt could not purchase the car and have it in his name. Earl told the dealer to make the tag receipt out to him.

Walt's uncle then made a generous offer to his nephew. He said that he would pay the liability insurance, but that Walt would be expected to keep the car up. It was a three-way handshake deal.

The young man drove the car off the lot. He had just made his first big purchase. He had wheels of his own. Wheeeee!

Walt always had a penchant for naming things. Before he even got to Earl and Mary Beth's house, he was already affectionately calling the vehicle "The Rev." This he did in honor of the one who had run up the miles on it in his work. Whenever the new owner called on the car for a little pep, he would say, "Come on Rev. – rev it up some more."

The King and Prince Implement Company expanded its services through the years. It now had a well-stocked parts department. Rarely did a farmer have to wait for something to be ordered. It also had a shop where just about anything pertaining to a tractor could be repaired. Earl King was now the sole owner, but he had not changed the name.

Walt worked full time during the summer. He was making twice the wages that he did at the service station. Then, he had to cut his work time back considerably after school started. He did come in a couple of hours on some days, and he was available all day on Saturdays if needed. The college freshman was able to pad his checking account, only to see it nosedive when he paid his fees and purchased his textbooks at the beginning of each quarter.

Things were working out amazingly well at his new home. Earl and Mary Beth shared in the domestic duties. Walt learned some things about cooking from both of them. He often made his own breakfast, and then he usually joined the couple for supper. No one objected when he offered to clean up afterward. The cupboard was never bare.

Walt also learned how to run a vacuum cleaner, and he took over that chore. He did his own laundry. At night if he wished to talk, there was always somebody interested in hearing about his day.

The Dean's List

Walt was just as unprepared for college as perhaps college was unprepared for Walt. As he began his postsecondary education, the new college student found that his professors had a different attitude from that of his high school teachers. While he did not always agree with them, Walt always knew the faculty members back in Mason had the best interests of their students at heart.

He did not always find that to be so in this educational setting. The instructors for underclass students made it plain that one of their primary responsibilities was to weed out those who were not college material. It seemed to him that some of them actually enjoyed flunking students.

Walt started noticing a pattern right away. Often, questions on tests were about subject matter not covered in class. He decided this was a way to separate the wheat from the chaff, as his old preacher used to say. Or, was it the sheep from the goats?

The Mason-Dixon High School graduate was somewhere in the middle as far as his academic preparation for higher education was concerned. He found his college algebra courses to be no more difficult than high school algebra. History was still history, and the professors played the same old games wanting lots of memorization.

English Composition was a horse of a different color. Walt found out rather quickly that he did not know much about introductions and conclusions, paragraphing, topic sentences, dangling participles, split infinitives, and run on sentences. Of course, he already knew that he was not much of a speller. He felt fortunate to come out of English 101 with a solid C. More than half of the class got Ds or Fs.

"Come in, Mr. Williamson. How can I help you?" Academic Dean Eugene Rowell greeted the freshman student that he had never met before.

"Thank you for agreeing to meet with me, and I promise not to take up too much of your valuable time," Walt responded, as the dean directed him to have a seat.

"That's what we're here for," Dr. Rowell replied.

Walt pulled out his Blue Book from his midterm history exam. He handed the printed test to the administrator. "Sir, I would like for you to look at the last question on this test."

Professor Nicholson, his history teacher, had explained to the class that three-fourths of the exam would consist of objective questions. Walt knew what that meant. He had to fill in the blanks with times, places, and people. There would be some true or false questions, and somewhere he would have to match things on the left column with their counterpart on the right.

Dr. Nicholson then informed the class that the discussion question at the end would count one fourth toward the grade. Walt wanted the dean to examine that question.

Dean Rowell read it aloud. "Do you think Henry VIII was justified in severing Great Britain from the Roman Catholic Church and forming the Anglican Church of England because the Pope refused to recognize his divorces?"

The dean then addressed the student. "I suppose you are concerned with how your teacher graded you on this question. I could ask for your Blue Book and read your answer, Mr. Williamson, but why don't you tell me in your own words how you addressed this conundrum?"

Walt went right to work. "Well, I began, sir, by saying that I really did not have much of an opinion about this matter one way or the other. Like we say out in the country, 'I don't have a dog in that fight.'

"I then said that it is usually hard to make a choice between the Pontiff and a monarch, because as a general rule neither of them can be trusted. But if I had to come down on one side or the other, I guess I would go with the king this time."

The dean leaned back in his chair, and he looked at the ceiling as Walt continued.

"I wondered why King Henry just stopped with creating the Anglican Church, though, which is little more than warmed over Catholicism in my opinion. If he was going to make a drastic change, I felt that he should have gone ahead and formed the Mormon Church right then and there. That way, he could have as many wives as he pleased."

"I see," said the dean, with a little chuckle. "How much credit did Professor Nicholson give you for that answer?"

"Not much, sir; he knocked off twenty points. That dropped my score two letter grades in one fell swoop."

"Did you talk to him about your disappointment with your grade?" the dean asked.

"I tried to, sir. I went up to him after class. He told me that I had obviously not been paying attention. Dr. Nicholson then opened the textbook, and he started reading to me what the book had to say. He then closed the book, and he walked out while I was trying to tell him what my problem was."

"And what would that be, Mr. Williamson?" Dr. Rowell asked as he sat forward, looking at Walt over the top of his reading glasses.

"Sir, you have the test in your hands. The discussion question does not ask me what Dr. Nicholson thinks about the issue. It does not even ask me what the writers of the history book think. It asks me what I think. Well, sir, I told him what I think fair and square and right down the middle. I answered his question. I do not feel that he has any right to take any points off my grade."

The dean leaned back in his chair again. "I see, Mr. Williamson. Let me talk with Dr. Nicholson about this. Come back by my office tomorrow around three."

The next afternoon Walt was punctual. He was once again ushered into the dean's office. "Have a seat, Mr. Williamson," Dr. Rowell said, as he gestured with his right hand.

"I have spoken with Professor Nicholson about your quandary. He was forced to admit that he saw your point. Dr. Nicholson said that he has been asking the question that way for fifteen years, and you are the first student ever to challenge it. He has assured me that it will be rephrased in the future. But that does not help you out right now, does it?"

"No sir, it doesn't," Walt agreed.

"If you will go back and discuss this matter with Dr. Nicholson again, he might be open to reconsidering your grade. If he restates the question, would you reconsider your answer?"

"Yes sir, I would. Thank you for hearing me out," Walt said. "I hope I do not have to bother you again."

And so it was, by the midterm of his first quarter at Adamson State College, the name Walter O. Williamson had already found a permanent home on the Dean's List. This was not, however, because his grades placed him near the top of his class.

Walt did not make it back to Mason for Thanksgiving. He had too much work yet to complete before his upcoming final exams. He decided to wait and go during the Christmas break after the quarter was over.

While home for the holidays, he decided to stay with his Grandpa and Grandma King. He also wanted to see Emma Lou and to check on his other grandparents.

Aunt Kathy told him that his sister was bringing her boyfriend home with her to meet her folks. Walt did not get to meet him, though. He received no overtures from his parents, or an invitation to any of their Christmas gatherings.

Walt noticed a big change in his Granddaddy Williamson. The man looked like he had aged several years in just the six months it had been since his grandson last saw him. As he was leaving to go back to Adamsonville, his granddaddy followed him out on the back porch.

Walt was suddenly not in such a big hurry. He felt like the man was trying to tell him something, but he did not know how. Ethel came out about that time. She told her husband to get back in the house, because he did not have on his coat and hat.

Walt knew whatever his granddaddy wished to say could not be said in front of his grandmother. He just gave the grand man a big hug and said that he would try to get home again soon.

"You be a man, son," his granddaddy said over his shoulder, as he turned to go back in the house.

"Come in again, Mr. Williamson. I see you are still with us. So, I guess you must have passed some courses last fall," Dean Rowell said to Walt.

"Well, actually, sir, I made an A in algebra, a B in history, and a C in English. I must be trying to reinvent the alphabet."

"And what do I owe for the pleasure of your visit today?" the dean asked, as if he did not already know. Walt produced a paper that he had gotten back with an F across the front of it.

In English 102, students were taught how to document and footnote the sources they used in their compositions. Walt had written one term paper in high school where he had to use footnotes and a bibliography. The problem was that he had mostly forgotten how to do it. On the first paper Walt submitted for this college course, his instructor wrote in bold red letters, "You are neither correct, nor consistent in your incorrectness." That about covered it.

The students had a handbook that they were supposed to follow to the letter of the law. From what Walt could figure, every fact had to have a footnote, telling where the writer got that information. In his mind, concentrating on what others have published leaves very little room for the student's opinion.

"You have to quote your sources," Professor Hendrix kept telling the class. His operative word, however, was scholarship. He was determined to produce a class of topnotch scholars who knew how to research a subject.

Walt was confused. He had a high estimation of scholars. He thought that they were truly intelligent people. If he was hearing Professor Hendrix correctly, though, scholars deal only with the thoughts and ideas of somebody else. Instead of stating their own sentiments, scholars are experts on what others have said and done.

Good scholarship then, as the professor seemed to be saying, is the process of taking scissors and paste, and piecing together a mosaic. Through careful documentation, the scholar must be careful to give credit to every other scholar he has quoted.

Not without a struggle, Walt gained some expertise in the mechanics of documenting his sources. He pulled his average up to a low B.

For the final exam, the students were to select a topic, and then write a thesis style paper documenting every bit of the factual information contained therein. The paper would include a bibliography, alphabetizing all of the sources from which the student had gleaned.

Walt was ready to challenge the system. He was already finding that the year of typing in high school was coming in handy. He never did develop good penmanship, and he wanted this paper to be neat. Mary Beth let him use her Royal Typewriter anytime he wanted to.

When he got his paper back, there were no red marks on the inside. No comments were on the back. There was simply a big F across the front. Professor Hendrix locked his office, and he had left town for the spring holidays. Final grades would not be posted until he got back.

As he handed the paper to Dr. Rowell, the dean asked Walt to give him a brief synopsis of the situation. He said he would read the paper later, and that he would get with Professor Hendrix, if he found it necessary. For now, would the English student just give him an overview of what he would find?

Walt entitled his paper, "A Discourse on the Myth of Scholarship." His opening sentence was, "Scholarship is nothing more than legalized plagiarism." In essence, he then proceeded to debunk the widely held notion that scholars make a significant difference in higher education.

He did not stop there. Walt charged that arrogant scholars seem far more interested in impressing their students with what they know about the subject matter, when they should be concentrating on teaching students to think for themselves. He questioned whether a mere grasp of the opinions of others justifies such a lofty position on a college campus.

Walt then moved in for the kill. He said that scholars are terrified of having an original thought. He indicated that they are comfortable discussing endlessly the minutiae and infinitesimal nuances of somebody else's work. Conversely, they are afraid to sign their name to anything that they might have to defend.

Walt postulated that colleges and universities would be far better off to rid themselves of grandstanding scholars. He recommended replacing them with well-informed teachers who impart wisdom, and with innovative instructors who inspire originality and creativity.

For his grand finale, the brash student speculated that the highest paid scholars are those with the sharpest scissors and the dullest minds. The paper contained not one footnote.

Actually, Dean Rowell already knew what was in the paper. He had a Xerox copy of it on his desk. Professor Hendrix brought it to him on the day that Walt submitted it. Both of them were convinced that the freshman copied it from somewhere, and that he did not document his source.

Asking Walt to describe what was in the paper was a little test of its own. The dean knew generally that those who borrow material from others could not remember five minutes later what they had lifted. Walt, however, repeated back to the dean almost verbatim what was in his paper.

"He's good," the dean mused to himself. "The boy did his homework before he came in here today."

Dean Rowell seemed in a hurry to get out of the office. He said that he would look into the matter, but he could do nothing until Professor Hendrix got back to the campus.

A week later when Walt was ushered into the dean's office, he was asked to take his usual seat. Dean Rowell looked at him over his glasses. "Mr. Williamson, I am going to tell you something that I think you already know. Your paper is brilliant. If you will grant your permission, I would like my secretary to make mimeographed copies to be placed in the mailboxes of every faculty member on this campus. Your name will be left off, of course. We wouldn't want to poison the well for you with our scholarly professors."

Walt did not give an immediate answer, but he said that he would think about it.

The dean paused and looked down. "I must inform you, though, that I can do nothing about your grade. I did discuss the situation with Professor Hendrix. He said that you did not follow the guidelines for the paper. You were instructed to document all of your sources."

Walt could not sit still. "But I did sir. I signed my name to the paper. I am the only source."

"Is that really the case?" the dean countered. "Professor Hendrix pointed out to me that in your very first sentence, there was a glaring omission. You used the word plagiarism, and you did not footnote where you got your definition of that word."

Walt jumped to his defense again. "I accepted the commonly held definition of plagiarism, without quoting a verbatim definition from a dictionary. If I had, then I would have put it in quotation marks, and then footnoted which dictionary I used."

Then he added, "If the professor is going to use that standard, then he has to be consistent with it. Every word in every student's paper would have to be documented to show how he or she came about a definition of each term."

"Well, maybe you do have a point there," the dean reluctantly granted.

"More seriously, though, Mr. Williamson, your instructor told me that he did not think any freshman could have written this on his own. He said he feels certain that you were quoting someone else. He thinks that you were trying to trick him, and to put him on the defensive to locate and prove your source."

Walt was animated. "But sir, I wrote every word of that without referencing anyone else." He was puzzled that anybody would level such a charge at him.

"If you say so, Mr. Williamson; if you say so."

The dean then added. "But we have something around here called academic freedom. Our teachers are free to assign grades without interference from the administration."

"Oh, I get it," said Walt. "The professors have academic freedom, but the students are not allowed to think for themselves. And you call that scholarship?"

Walt paused and waited for a response. When one was not

forthcoming, he knew that he had the old boy back on his heels.

Walt redirected the conversation. "Dr. Rowell, I would be honored for you to reproduce copies of my paper for the faculty on one condition."

"What is that?" the dean inquired, not sure that he wanted to know the answer.

"That the grade on the front of it is included," Walt said.

"Agreed," the relieved dean responded, as he stood up to shake Walt's hand.

"Sure as shootin', Othell," Walt mumbled as he went out the door of the Administration Building. "The fun is just beginning."

When the final grades were posted, Walt breathed a sigh of relief when he saw the C- for English 102. He got out of the class by the skin of his teeth. His extracurricular work for that course, though, was far from over.

The Truth Shall Make You Free

When Walt got to work one Friday afternoon in late March, Earl was waiting for him. He could tell that something was wrong. He braced himself.

"Daddy called a while ago," his uncle said. "I hate to be the one to have to tell you this, but your Granddaddy Williamson died this morning."

Walt began to choke with emotion. Knowing that he would want the details, Earl waited a few moments. As Walt looked back up, he went on.

"Mr. Williamson went out to his workshop about mid-morning. When he did not come in for lunch, your grandmother rang the dinner bell. He still did not come, and she went to check on him. Walt, your granddaddy had taken his Bible with him. Ethel found him sitting on an old church pew in the back of his shop slumped over with the Bible open and still in his lap."

Walt stood in stunned silence. The last moments they spent together flashed back through his mind. His granddaddy was trying to tell him something. Oh, how he wished they had finished that conversation.

"You be a man, son." Those parting words would be an unremitting source of inspiration for Walt. The many other conversations that he and his mentor had through the years would also replay in his memories the rest of his life. Walt's Granddaddy Williamson was one of the finest men he had ever known.

Walt planned to sit with Emma Lou at the funeral, but she was all wrapped up in Andrew Singleton, Jr. He just went and sat with his Grandma and Grandpa King.

This beloved grandson wondered what his granddaddy was reading when he died. After the funeral, he asked his grandmother, but she said that she did not think about it when she closed the Bible. He then asked if he could have his granddaddy's well-worn old Bible. Ethel said she guessed so. She could not think of anybody else who might want it.

On his way back to Adamsonville, several things were running through his mind. No one else made any effort to let him know about the death. If his Grandpa had not heard about it at the store, his granddaddy might have been dead and buried before he even found out.

Something else bothered Walt, too. He was not all that surprised that his Uncle Jerry gave the main eulogy. Yet, he could not help but think that the son-in-law preacher did not even know the man. It sounded more to him as if Jerry Patterson wanted to make sure everybody knew who he was.

Walt would hate to see his Aunt Kathy and little Rachel move away. At the same time, he just did not like the way his pastor was leading the First Baptist Church of Adamsonville.

What struck Walt more than anything, though, was how his granddaddy's immediate family showed so little emotion. He never saw his grandmother, or Todd, shed a tear. Only his Aunt Kathy seemed to be grieving the loss of her father. Did these people not know what a giant of a man had walked among them?

When he got back to his little basement headquarters, Walt opened his granddaddy's Bible where it was marked with the ribbon. A single verse was underlined on one of the pages. It read, "And ye shall know the truth, and the truth shall make you free."

A couple of days after the funeral, Ethel Williamson was going through her late husband's things. John Paul's Last Will and Testament was amidst his insurance policy, deeds, and other important papers. She already knew what the will said. They had drawn it up together.

Gem clipped to the folder was an envelope, sealed and taped shut. It said, "To be opened only by Walt Williamson after my death." Ethel held the envelope in her hand. "What could that old fool possibly have to say to the little twit?" she snarled.

The woman was determined that Walt would never lay eyes on what was inside. Todd and Maude were coming over at any minute to help eat some of the leftover food that had been brought in. Without really thinking through what she was doing, John Paul's widow went to the fireplace, and she tossed the envelope in the fire. Immediately, she regretted what she had done. There was no reason that she could not have read its contents. It was too late.

During the spring quarter of his freshman year, Walt signed up for a psychology course. It satisfied the requirements for a Core Curriculum social studies elective, and it was being taught at a time that fit well into his schedule.

Walt did not know much about psychology. He imagined that it had to do with understanding and treating crazy people.

On the first day, the instructor gave the students an assignment to write a little essay describing who they are. She said this would not only give them a chance to do some "introspection," but that it would also give her an opportunity to get to know each of them better.

That night, Walt sat down to do his project. His high school English teacher had taught him that it is sometimes easier to define something by saying what it is not.

"I am not a child of the Great Depression," he began. He had grown up hearing endless tales of the struggles and difficulties during that austere era. It had shaped that generation's values, right down to the core of their beings.

"I am not a baby boomer," he continued. Walt was hearing a lot about the baby boom after the war. Schools were adding more classrooms to accommodate the swelling enrollments. Those a few years younger than he was, were fast gaining the reputation of being a bit spoiled, and not as respectful as he was taught to be. Walt wanted it understood that he was not part of that age group.

"I am a war baby," he said, steering his thoughts to the positive.

After this opening, he did not know how to proceed. Then, he remembered what he said at his high school graduation. That sounded cool.

"I am a human being. I am not a human doer. I do the things I do because of who I am. I am not who I am because of what I do." That should do it. Walt signed his name followed by his initials, W.O.W., and he turned in his paper the next day. He had gotten in the habit of adding his initials to anything he had to sign.

A couple of days later, Miss Robbins asked Walt to schedule an appointment with her secretary. When he came in for the consultation, his instructor had his paper on her desk. "Mr. Williamson, in my ten years of teaching psychology, I have never had a student turn in anything like this before," she began. "My students usually tell me all about their parents, and their siblings, and where they grew up, and what their aspirations are."

Walt had no idea where this was going. The paper was not for a grade, so he did not have to worry about that. He suspected that she was going to send him back to do it over.

"Have you ever thought about majoring in psychology?" she then asked.

Wow! That caught Walt flatfooted.

"And one more thing, Mr. Williamson," Miss Robbins said. She reached in a file folder and pulled out a mimeographed paper with an F on the cover. "You don't have to answer this question if you don't want to, but did you write this?"

"I'd rather not say," Walt replied a little sheepishly.

"Just as I thought," she said, as she put it back in the binder.

After his last final test paper was turned in, Walt had one more little item of business to take care of before he left the campus for the summer. "I hate to pop in unannounced," he said to the receptionist, who did not have to ask him his name. "But may I have a quick word with Dean Rowell?"

His secretary said he was on the phone, but that she would hand him a note. About five minutes later, the dean came out into the lobby area. He really did not want to take the student with him back into his office.

"Thank you for seeing me on such short notice," Walt said. "I have a question for you. Did anyone ever bring you a copy of what I wrote for my English 102 paper with somebody else's name listed as the author?"

"Mr. Williamson, you know very well the answer to that question. If they had, you would no longer be enrolled at this school. Or in any other institution of higher learning either, for that matter," the dean replied, with a scorn upon his face that confirmed his annoyance.

Walt noticed the day they discussed the paper that Dean Rowell never actually said that he believed the student had written it. He also knew that his paper could be distributed to the other faculty members, with or without his permission.

The dean and the professor were playing a little game of cat and mouse with him. If he refused to grant his consent for it to be reproduced, that would indicate that he had likely borrowed the material and was afraid of being busted. In distributing it, they were hoping that some faculty member might recognize it, and reveal the source. No one had.

"Well, may I request one simple favor?" Walt asked.

The dean reluctantly just nodded his head.

"Since my paper has now gone out all over creation without my name on it, if it does get back to you with someone else taking credit for what I wrote, will you please let me know? I would be interested in seeing who has plagiarized me."

"You have my word," the dean said in a dismissive way.

"Have a good summer, sir, and I will see you in the fall," Walt added, gleefully.

"I'm certain you will, Mr. Williamson," the dean sighed, as he rolled his eyes while turning away to go back in his office. "I'm certain you will."

"Is it possible that the boy really did write that?" Dean Rowell questioned himself as he sat back down at his desk. "Not a chance," he clarified his thoughts. "I will spend the rest of my life keeping my eyes open for that essay. When I eventually find its source, if Walter Williamson has a degree from this, or any other institution of higher education, I will see to it that he hands it back."

The summer after his first year in college, Walt put in many hours working for his uncle. He also kept the grass cut at the house. On trips out in the country to deliver a new tractor or some piece of equipment, he kept thinking that just maybe he would catch the eye of a farmer's pretty daughter. Apparently not. Out on the edge of town where he worked was not a good place for standing on the corner watching all the girls go by, either.

In Mr. Hazelwood's eleventh grade U. S. History class, a television monitor was brought into the room for the students to hear President John F. Kennedy's inaugural speech. Walt would never forget the powerful moment when the youthful president issued a challenge. "Ask not what your country can do for you. Ask what you can do for your country." He also felt the excitement when JFK later announced that the country would put a man on the moon by the end of the decade.

In a U. S. History class at Adamson State College, the professor came into the classroom one day with a distressed look on his face. It was right before Thanksgiving, 1963. The teacher announced to the class that President Kennedy had been shot.

Over the next few days, Walt followed the proceedings as best he could. His youthful idealism and exuberance now had a big hole blown right through the middle of it, too.

During the next few months, he sometimes caught Walter Cronkite, and at others, he watched Huntley-Brinkley. The young man coming of age was increasingly disturbed by what he saw on the news. Racial protests were turning more violent. The conflict in Southeast Asia was escalating. A feeling of deep unrest was slinking its way across the country.

Walt had registered for the draft when he was eighteen, but he was assured of a student deferment as long as he remained in college. Some of his peers were not so fortunate. If notified that they had lost their academic eligibility to register for the next quarter, most of them were more than acceptable to further their education with Uncle Sam.

The college student watched with intensifying interest as university students all over the country became more agitated. He had to admit he agreed with many of the things that they were saying. He was appalled, however, by some of the ways the defiant leaders went about getting attention. Before he would earn his degree, the whole structure of higher education was beginning to shift dramatically.

Society as a whole had also entered a period of remarkable change. Walt was often impatient with so much rebelliousness. He understood the need for authority. At the same time, he had more or less always been his own boss, and he had paid his own way. He considered outrageous behavior just to ruffle feathers as ridiculous.

Try as he might, Walt just could not identify with hard rock. The tenderness and earnestness of folk music, on the other hand, touched something deep inside him.

Walt completed his sophomore year at Adamson State the spring of 1964. Meanwhile, Emma Lou graduated from the University of Georgia with a degree in early childhood education. The big news was that she and Drew Singleton, Jr. were getting married.

Walt thought that he might be asked to be an usher groomsman, but no such invitation was forthcoming. Emma Lou did not know the minister at the Mason Baptist Church who had come while she was away in college. Uncle Jerry performed the ceremony.

Drew's younger brother met Walt at the front door of the church. He was all decked out in a tuxedo, but he looked a little strange in that attire with shoulder length locks and scraggly facial hair. "Friend of the bride, or friend of the groom?" he asked.

"That's okay," Walt responded. "I can find my own seat."

Emma Lou took so much ribbing about her performance as a flower girl at Earl and Mary Beth's wedding that she was afraid some mischief might be staged at her own. She decided that her eight-year-old cousin Rachel was big enough to be a junior bridesmaid.

The June bride was stunning. The perfect father walked his perfect daughter down the aisle. He then went and sat with his perfect wife. Too bad the bride did not have a perfect brother. Else, they could have all lived happily ever after. The lavish nuptials set a standard that future weddings would have a hard time living up to in those parts.

Todd seemed to like his new son-in-law. At least the Singletons got it right. Andrew Senior had himself a Junior.

Drew had just gotten his MBA at the university. The new CPA had joined his father's accounting firm in Etowah, Georgia as a junior partner. Emma Lou got a much-coveted job teaching third grade at the prestigious Woodland Academy. It paid to be well connected.

Walt sat over in the corner by himself during the reception, taking it all in. "You know, Othell," he said to himself. "People have to be who they are. And some folks just do an outstanding job of being who they are."

Then, he chuckled to himself, "Thank God I am one of them."

Never-the-Less – Always

Walt's own love life left a lot to be desired. He had taken a few girls out in The Rev., but he kept finding girls fickle. He really had his eye on one spirited filly in his speech class, but then one day he saw her smoking in the student lounge. That was the end of that.

It was in this speech class that Walt learned one of the most important lessons of his whole college experience. The teacher had a flare for the dramatic. Walt figured out right away that boring presentations would not impress him. Since this student was part ham anyway, he decided to have a little fun. The professor was highly complimentary of his productions.

Toward the end of the quarter, it was rather obvious that he was one of the best students in the class. The only competition for the top spot came from a girl who was obsessed with making nothing less than an A in all her classes. Walt really did need an A to help raise his grade point average.

After giving several speeches during the quarter, each student had to come up with something extra special for the final presentation. Walt did a monologue, mimicking Mark Twain. It was a huge hit.

Members of the class were still required to assemble at the time set aside for the final exam. As they filed in and took their seats, they had no idea what to expect. The speech teacher said that there was only one question to answer. "What grade do you think you deserve for the class?"

Walt was taught that modesty is a virtue, although he certainly did not always practice it. Thinking that a little humility might impress his professor, he wrote B on his paper, and he turned it in.

When the grades were posted, to his shock and dismay, Walt received a B for his final grade. Besides that, several students got an A. He made a beeline straight toward the speech teacher's office.

"Mr. Williamson," the professor said rather earnestly. "I was planning on giving you an A. However, you thought you only deserved a B. I could not with a clear conscience give you a better grade than what you thought you had earned."

At that moment, Walt learned an invaluable lesson. "Othell, don't you ever again sell yourself short. Never-the-less – Always."

The first horde of baby boomers stormed the campuses of colleges and universities all over the country in the fall of 1964. Adamson State entered into a building boom of its own, trying to provide housing facilities and classrooms for the swelling enrollment. Staid old administrators were unprepared. The incoming students, having been raised more permissively, were a little challenged when it came to respect for authority.

Something else went mostly unnoticed by the local media. The school's first black student enrolled without incident. When Walt saw him sitting alone in the student center one day, he went over and introduced himself.

As he entered his junior year, Walt was somewhat over his penchant for making waves. He watched with amazement, though, as the times, they were a 'changing.

Miss Robbins in the Psychology Department had found herself a protégée. Walt had been a psychologist all his life. He just did not know what to call himself. He found the study of human behavior fascinating.

This psychology major could do without animal testing. He figured that how dogs or rats respond to stimuli has little to do with how a person would react under similar circumstances. Walt did not give much credence to psychological tests, or any kind of contrived ways to evaluate performance for that matter. He had no great interest in the treatment of mental illnesses, although he did want to know as much as he could about the various theories.

Walter O. Williamson came along just at the right time to become a part of the human growth and potential movement. This meshed well with his concepts of *being vs. doing*. The way he saw it, most people's problems come about because of some combination of not knowing who they are, on the one hand, and trying to be something they are not, on the other.

Maude switched off the TV. She had heard enough bad news for one day. Newscasts were filled with scenes from race riots, violence on college campuses, and massacres in Vietnam. She poured herself another cup of coffee and sat down for a minute.

Then, the phone rang. Her mother said, "I'm glad I caught you. Lucille's eat up with cancer."

Unable to get another physician to replace Doc Elliott, the folks in Jacksonville let Aunt Lucy and Jane continue living in the house after his death. The facility would be better off occupied. Besides that, no one wanted the job of confronting Lucille, and telling her that she must vacate the premises.

Ruby King had just gotten off the phone with her sister. Maude was already aware that her aunt had been to the doctor, and that she was waiting for test results to get back. The specialist in Mountain Home said that at best she had only a few months to live.

"They say cancer runs in families, and that must be true for mine," Ruby lamented. "I have already lost one sister and one brother to cancer. I suspect that is what killed Mama, too, although she never went to a doctor."

Maude just listened. She did not know what to say. She would go to Jacksonville within the next day or so. Soon, another one was about to take it with her to her grave.

Walt struggled to maintain a 3.0 grade point average. He knew if he had any hopes of going to graduate school that was the magic number. He hardly took a course where he did not have some kind of confrontation with his professor over grades. They were quibblers. He was far more concerned with seeing the broader picture.

When answering one particular question on an exam in a sociology class, he chose his words very carefully. Walt felt some passion for the issue, and he wanted that energy to come across to his professor.

After the papers were graded and handed back to the students, he was really taken back when he found red marks all over his answer. The instructor had struck through a number of the student's words. He then substituted the ones he used the day he lectured on that subject.

After class, Walt stopped the professor on the way out the door. He let him know how unhappy he was with his grade. He said to him, "If I memorize your lectures, and I regurgitate it word for word on the exam, all it proves is that I know how to memorize. But if I restate it to you using my own concepts, then you know that I understand it."

The professor looked back at him as if he did not understand a word that Walt had just said. Dean Rowell had another unexpected visitor that afternoon.

Since Walt's birthday was on Halloween, he had grown accustomed to spending it by himself. He occasionally thought about the contrast between the way Emma Lou's birthday was celebrated and his. She was emphatic that her big day was not to be confused with Christmas. His seemed always to get lost in the shuffle.

He thought nothing of it when Earl mentioned that they were going to have some friends over for a Halloween Party during the fall of Walt's senior year in college. His uncle insisted that he come up and join the festivities when he got in from work.

Walt was left to close up the John Deere dealership. Earl went home early to help Mary Beth get things ready. Before he left, he reminded his nephew that they were expecting him at least to just drop by.

On the way home, Walt almost took off in another direction. He did not want to be rude, though, since Earl and Mary Beth had been so good to him. He would put in a polite appearance, and then slip out unnoticed when he wanted to.

When Walt came upstairs, the place was packed with people all wearing Halloween masks. An eerie silence filled the room. All of a sudden, they broke out into song. What they were singing, however, had nothing to do with ghosts and goblins.

Walt was overridden with emotion. His uncle and aunt remembered that it was his twenty-first birthday. Friends and faculty members were hiding behind those masks.

Earl then came out with a gift, wrapped in orange and black paper. Walt had to open it right away. As he pulled out a stein with W.O.W. engraved on it, the group cheered.

His uncle then said that maybe the guest of honor wished to go ahead and try it out. A couple of fellow students came from the kitchen with a keg of Budweiser. As the group lifted a toast to him on this important milestone in his life, Walt had his first legal drink.

The celebrating was not over, yet. Earl then produced a manila envelope. He looked at Walt mischievously as he handed it to him. Walt had seen that look before. It was the first time that he noticed how much Earl was beginning to resemble Grandpa King.

As he cautiously opened it, Earl exclaimed, "Walt, you are now the proud owner of a 1954 Chevrolet." Earl had signed the title of his own car over to him.

Since he was now coming down the home stretch of his college days, Walt had to start giving some serious thought to his career options. He talked this over with Miss Robbins several times, and it always boiled down to the same thing. With a degree in psychology, there were not many viable options. He could teach, become a social worker, or he could go into counseling.

He gave considerable thought to the teaching possibility. He would relish messing with young minds. Nevertheless, if he became Professor Williamson, he saw endless confrontations with administrators. He anticipated never-ending battles over his non-conventional ways of doing things.

At the same time, he was not too sure about being a social worker. That generally meant being employed by some bureaucratic government agency.

Counseling would give him far more freedom and flexibility. Even so, Walt did not want to become a school counselor. That would keep him all tied up in red tape and paperwork.

If he went into private practice, he would have to jump through some additional hoops. He could then hang out his own shingle. One major hurdle included getting at least a Master's Degree. Even though Adamson State was now offering that program, he knew he had about burned all his bridges at that institution.

"They're going to do what?" Walt asked in disbelief.

"Streak," his classmate responded back.

"You mean they are going to take off all their clothes, and run through the campus?"

"You got it, buddy; right past the Administration Building"

"Males and females?"

"That's what I have been told."

As the crowd gathered, Walt made sure that he got a good spot. For one thing, he had never seen a woman completely naked. He also wanted to position himself so that he could see the look on Dean Rowell's face.

The Saturday of Walt's college graduation was a hot muggy day. He had gone to Dean Rowell, asking for an exemption from going through the ceremony. The dean told him with an air of haughtiness, "Barring an emergency that you will have to footnote and document, you will not get your degree unless you show up." Walt was not sure the school could do that, but he decided not to press it.

The graduates lined up outside the auditorium. They marched in with something less than precision. Some of them actually pretended that they were enjoying the proceedings. All they were really interested in, though, was hearing their names called so they could go across the stage and pick up the fancy piece of paper. Ten years hence, a person would be hard pressed to find a single member of the Class of 1966 who could tell him who the speaker was that day, much less recall anything that he had said.

Following the Recessional, the graduates formed a receiving line. Few of them stayed in it very long.

After Earl and Mary Beth came through, college graduate Walter O. Williamson was about to cut out. He had no need to hang around any longer. As he made his move, he found himself in a not so accidental face-to-face encounter with Dean Rowell.

"Congratulations, Williamson. This place is never going to be the same without you," he said.

"Oh, come on Dean Rowell, there will be at least a dozen of my clones in the incoming freshman class that I have already programmed to pester you," Walt chided him.

"Now that you have paid your dues, and you have your sheepskin in hand, may I ask you one more question?" the administrator tried to bait Walt, yet again.

"This humble alumnus is at your service," he answered, mocking him.

"During your freshman year, did you really write that paper you turned in to Professor Hendrix in English 102?" the dean asked.

"Why, Dr. Rowell, I am disappointed in you. I thought you ran a tighter ship than that, especially when it involves anything coming out of the Psychology Department. The answer to your question is found on page seventeen in this year's 'Psycho-journers'."

With that, Walt was off, as were soon also his cap and gown.

On Monday morning, Dean Rowell was in his office long before his executive secretary reported for duty. He was going over last minute changes to the summer schedule. After he heard her come in, he buzzed her. "Miss Bradshaw, did we get a copy of this year's 'Psycho-journers'?"

He was referring to the Psychology Department's annual literary journal. The dean still could not believe the audacity of the department to use such a name for its publication. "Alfred Hitchcock would be proud," he mumbled to himself.

"Yes we did, Dr. Rowell. I put a copy of it on your desk a couple weeks ago," his efficient secretary told him.

With all that was involved in bringing a school year to the end, the dean had let some things pile up. He reached for the stack on the far right side of his desk. He then turned to page seventeen in "Psycho-journers."

Now copyrighted by one of the college's own publications, Dean Rowell found himself staring at a submission entitled, "A Discourse on the Myth of Scholarship." It was written by Walter O. Williamson, W.O.W.

Walt had only seen his mother and Todd once since Emma Lou's wedding. When he went by the house while home for Christmas during his senior year, he felt like an intruder. There was nothing welcoming or beckoning. Neither asked him about college, nor about anything else going on in his life. After a few minutes of him trying to make conversation, and the two of them just sitting there like he was not in the room, he left.

As he was wrapping up his undergraduate studies, they made no effort to find out about his graduation. He subsequently did not bother letting them know anything.

Aunt Kathy called to congratulate her nephew, and she told him that she had a little present for him. He could drop by at his convenience to pick it up. The afternoon of his graduation, Walt and The Rev. were out and about. He decided to go ahead and stop in before it slipped his mind.

Todd and Maude had pulled in the drive ahead of him and were getting out of their car. They had driven to Adamsonville to see his sister on the day their son was graduating from college. They did not even come to the commencement. He decided to pick up the gift later.

Somewhere about this time, Walt started asking himself questions that would replay over and over again in his mind. "What have I done that caused both of my parents to reject me?" "What is so bad about me that my own family finds me unlovable?" "Why do they just want me out of their lives?"

Walt had some appreciation for the fact that Todd was unable to relate to him. His mother's actions, though, were a complete mystery to him.

Soon after Walt got to work at the John Deere place on Monday, he received a phone call. The man on the other end identified himself as Fred Beckett, President of the Adamsonville State Bank.

"Is there a problem with my account?" Walt asked.

"Oh, not at all," Mr. Beckett assured him. "But I would like for you to drop by the bank at your earliest convenience. I need to have a word with you."

About mid-morning, Walt took a break and made his way downtown. Within five minutes, he was ushered into the bank president's office.

"I'm glad to meet you," the executive said as he extended his hand. "I think congratulations are in order. Do I understand that you got your college degree on Saturday?"

Walt told the man that he was correct in that assumption.

"Mr. Williamson, I see that you have been a good customer for four years. Are you going to stay around here now that you have graduated? We would hate to lose your banking."

Walt had no idea where this was going. He told the man that his future was still uncertain, but that he had no plans to move his checking account anytime soon.

"That's not really why I asked you to come in," Mr. Beckett then told him. "Actually, I am saving you a call. When you receive your next bank statement, I have no doubt that the phone will ring here shortly thereafter. You would think that the bank has made an error."

Walt did not know what to say.

"Mr. Williamson, let me see if I can clear up this little mystery for you. Soon after the bank opened this past Saturday, someone unfamiliar to one of our tellers presented a cashier's check from an out of town bank. This person asked to deposit the draft into your checking account. This individual wanted to remain anonymous.

"This person claimed to know something of your background, and wished to give you a graduation gift as a token of appreciation for all of your hard work in getting your education. Your benefactor was then in a hurry to get to the university to attend your commencement service."

Walt remained speechless.

Mr. Beckett then picked something up from his desk. "Mr. Williamson, here is the deposit slip."

Walt took it but did not immediately examine it. He was still trying to make sure that he had heard what the bank president had just told him.

When he did look, he came up out of his chair. Five thousand dollars had been added to his checking account on the day of his college graduation.

"Good day, Mr. Williamson, and thank you for your promptness in coming by," Mr. Beckett said as he stood, extending his hand again. "If there is anything we can ever do to help you, please let us know."

Walt walked out of the bank more than a bit befuddled. When he got back to work, he told Earl about his experience. His uncle assured him that he knew nothing about it.

Walt had only one clue as to the source of the bequest. The deposit slip indicated that the cashier's check was drawn on a bank based in California.

Walt was especially appreciative of the nice raise Earl gave him. Even with his padded checking account, thanks to an anonymous donor, he was going to need all the savings he could muster to pay his way the next year if he got into graduate school. He was hoping The Rev. would hold together a little while longer.

The raise was not without merit. Earl and Mary Beth decided to take a lot of time off during the summer to do some traveling. They were gone almost a month when they drove to California and back.

After a couple of weeks at home, they took off again, this time to revisit Niagara Falls, and then take a trip through Nova Scotia. Walt was the acting CEO for the King and Prince Implement Company most of the summer. Besides that, he had the run of the house.

Earl and Mary Beth were not Walt's only uncle and aunt in Adamsonville to take a leave of absence that summer. Jerry Patterson met with the deacons. He asked them to pay his expenses to attend a preacher's meeting in Orlando, Florida. The First Baptist Church's pastor said that he would then forgo attending the convention's annual meeting.

When the governing body met to discuss the proposal, one of the deacons said that it sounded to him like the minister was asking the church to fund his family's vacation. "Isn't that what we do when we send him to the convention?" another responded. They all laughed. While it was not a unanimous vote, the measure was approved.

When the Pattersons returned after the two weeks in Florida, the pastor asked for a called deacon's meeting. He then informed them that while he was gone, God told him that the church needed to disband the deacon board. The pastor would then lead the church, with direct authority straight from God.

"Well, this is kind of sudden," responded Chairman Ford Heath. "Let us take this matter under advisement. Please wait for us in your office. We won't be long."

After the Reverend Patterson left the room, the chairman turned to the other deacons. "Have any of you men had a talk with the Lord in the last few days?" he inquired. There were nods all around.

"Has God told any of you that the church needs to get rid of the deacons?" he asked next. This time their heads shook in the other direction. "Well then, what do you propose that we do?"

"Pay him thirty days salary, give the family sixty days to vacate the pastorium if he is not relocated before then, and dismiss him immediately," Deacon Bailey proffered.

"Is that in the form of a motion?" Chairman Heath wanted to know.

"I so move," said Deacon Bailey.

"Is there a second?" the chairman then asked. Not one second, but a chorus of seconds rang out.

"All in favor, raise your right hand." There was no need to ask if there was any opposition.

When Walt heard the news, he went over to see his Aunt Kathy. She said that her husband was not surprised at the church's response. Then she added, "But when he is with a bunch of preachers like those he met up with in Orlando, he gets all kinds of wild ideas in his head." The minister's wife said she thought that Jerry was going to start a church of his own.

As he was getting ready to leave, Walt said something a little unusual for him. He told his Aunt Kathy that he would be praying for her. She knew he meant it.

In another day and time, Walter O. Williamson might have taken a little time off, too, before continuing his education or beginning his career. His student deferment would end immediately, however, if he did not go directly into another program. It was not that Walt was unpatriotic. He believed very much in the ideals of his country. He just could not see them having much of anything to do with what was happening in Southeast Asia. He would be a hypocrite if he applied for conscientious objector status, and he had no desire to move to Canada.

Walt very much enjoyed his time in Adamsonville. He made memories that he would cherish the rest of his life. He would be eternally grateful for all Earl and Mary Beth had done for him. Nevertheless, it was now time for him to move on.

PART III: THE IDENTITY DILEMMA

"Be yourself; everyone else is taken."
Oscar Wilde

"Amid a world of noisy, shallow actors it is noble to
stand aside and say 'I will simply be'."
Henry David Thoreau

Hannah

Walt Williamson missed the mountains. He had been away from the highlands since going off to college, and they were calling him again. That was a priority when he started looking for a school where he could continue his studies. Miss Robbins suggested Ephesus State University, about forty miles from Asheville, North Carolina, set right in the midst of misty mountains.

After he visited the campus and met with Dr. Susan Fitzpatrick, the head of the Guidance and Counseling Program, ESU was the only school that he considered. He was beginning to get a little worried when he had not heard anything regarding his admission status a week after his college graduation.

Then, it finally came. With his acceptance, the university also regretted informing Walt that he had not qualified for any kind of academic fellowship or scholarship.

As was his way of looking at things, Walt tried to see the larger perspective. With no financial assistance from the university, he would not have been able to enroll in the program except for the cryptic graduation gift. Even so, he would still have to be very frugal for the next year.

Since that day in the bank president's office, no further evidence had presented itself to explain the mysterious gesture. It was not Walt's nature to be an ungrateful person. He simply did not know whom to thank.

"Come in and take a seat, Mr. Williamson," Dr. Kenneth Harris, Dean of the Graduate School at Ephesus State said. "It is finally good to meet you, after knowing you only on paper."

"It's nice to be here, sir," Walt replied.

The dean then continued. "Before you begin your graduate studies with us, I called you in to go over a couple of things with you. Mr. Williamson, we take great pride in our students. We are very selective in those we accept into our programs. We follow our students carefully as they progress, and then we make every effort to help them succeed after they leave us."

"That is certainly the reputation of this university," Walt responded. "And those are some of the main reasons I applied here."

Dean Harris went on. "I want to be very frank with you, Mr. Williamson. You were the last person approved for admission by our graduate committee. In fact, that body had already rejected your application. Your credentials are marginal. Your grade point average barely meets our minimum standard, and your Graduate Record Exam scores are a little below what we normally expect.

"Then, one final letter of recommendation came in. You did not put this person on your list of references, so it was a surprise for us to get it. Based on that letter, the committee decided to reopen your file.

"As you know, Mr. Williamson, letters of recommendation are confidential. I am not at liberty to show you the contents of the one I have mentioned. I do not mind telling you, though, that it was from Dean Eugene Rowell at Adamson State College. You must have made quite an impression on the dean there."

"Yes, he and I have quite a history," Walt replied, working hard to control the smile trying to take over his face.

"Mr. Williamson, the school here has decided to take a chance on you. You have been granted full acceptance. We do not have anything like probationary admission. Nevertheless, in a sense, you will be on trial. It is our hope that you will take full advantage of the opportunity now being afforded you."

"Dr. Harris, you do not know how much it means to me for us to have this conversation," Walt responded. "If I run into any problems, may we pick right up where we are leaving off today?" he wanted to know.

"Of course, Mr. Williamson; my door is always open to you."

"Othell, you won't always have to dwell . . . in a basement." A little furnished basement apartment over near the mill village was the most efficient place Walt could find in Ephesus, North Carolina. One day he would be able to look out on the world again from eye level. For the next year, though, he would again "dwell" mostly underground.

At least he was already accustomed to plumbing noises and hearing someone bumping around overhead. The one big disadvantage was that he had to wash his clothes at a Laundromat.

The small house was set on a sloping hillside. A walkway from the street led to a porch with a swing on it. The period residence had asbestos siding and a tin roof. The basement entrance was on the left side of the house, convenient to the driveway. A garage was around back with a little shop/storage area attached to it. An undeveloped wooded area extended beyond the backyard.

His new landlady, Mrs. Pauline Neumann, was a widow. Walt was drawn to her because of her gentle spirit. She was getting on up in years, and time was beginning to make its presence felt. Mrs. Neumann always wore her mostly gray hair in a bun with a comb in it. She stooped a bit when she walked.

The woman's late husband was the son of German immigrants. The widow woman used the rent money to supplement her meager income. Walt sensed that Mrs. Neumann would welcome a little assistance in keeping the place up. He was happy to lend a helping hand. Who knew, there might be a piece of chocolate pie in it for him every now and then.

Dr. Fitzpatrick invited all of the new graduate students in her department over for a-get-to-know-everybody-cookout as the invitation stated. She and her husband lived in an upscale subdivision. The pool and patio were in a nice fenced-in backyard, with sleepy mountains in the distance.

When Walt arrived, a number of his new classmates were already socializing. He was greeted at the front door by Mr. Fitzpatrick, and directed toward the back.

As he came through the sliding glass door, his attention was drawn to a young woman who was chatting with the others at the table where she was seated. As he approached, she looked up and stopped in mid-sentence . . . the moment was frozen in time. Their eyes locked and refused to let go. The words of another person inviting Walt to join them barely resonated in his ears.

For the first time in Walter Othell Williamson's life, somebody ripped open the curtains and peered right into his soul. It knocked his socks off. It bowled him over. It blew him away. He was captivated, and he was mesmerized. Walt struggled to get through the evening making new acquaintances, while he really wished to know only one person at the gathering.

When he got back to his little basement apartment about midnight, he felt fortunate not to have been pulled over for driving under the influence. For sure, he had enjoyed a couple glasses of wine, but he was not impaired by alcohol. Instead, he was intoxicated by the connection he felt with this captivating creature.

The woman said later that what went through her mind was, "This one is going to be trouble." There was a big problem, too. Hannah Parker was wearing a wedding ring.

Walt found a different attitude among the graduate faculty members from that of some former college teachers. Just as Dean Harris had suggested, the professors really were concerned with helping their students be successful. He found out quickly why Miss Robbins recommended this school.

While they taught all the theories of counseling, the bent of this program was "client-centered therapy." Dr. Fitzpatrick had studied under Dr. Carl Rogers, the guru of the new approach.

Walt liked what he had heard so far. Instead of a professional figuring out what was wrong with a client, and then telling him what he had to do to fix things, the counselor was more like a facilitator. The person most likely already had within himself the solutions to his problems.

The counselor simply clarified and mirrored back what the person was discovering as he worked through the pertinent issues. The therapist would then help the individual determine his alternatives, and the consequences that went with each option. The counselee would thus take ownership of his circumstances, and make changes accordingly.

Walt had always been his own counselor, with Othell as his sidekick and sounding board for sure. He very much endorsed the notion that people should utilize the resources within themselves, rather than rely upon somebody else to tell them what to do or not do. He had patterned his life this way from the beginning.

The work seemed easier than when Walt was an undergraduate. When he discussed this with Hannah, she said that he now knew more what to expect. He could process things much faster.

Hannah was a drop dead gorgeous blond with eyes the color of the deep blue sea. Her natural beauty needed little in the way of enhancement.

The woman took a fast track to get through college and graduated in three years. After one year of teaching social studies, she decided to go back to school and get a Master's Degree in Guidance and Counseling.

Hannah's husband was in Vietnam. With what she saved during her first year of teaching, and with his military pay, she could afford to take the year off from her job.

For about two weeks, Walt and Hannah tiptoed around what happened the night of the party. They sat in classes together, often making eye contact. They gravitated toward each other during breaks. They then went their separate ways.

Walt was in "blondage." The love-struck graduate student yearned to run his hands through those golden strands. She was a married woman, though, and her husband was off putting his life in danger every day for his country.

It was magical, nonetheless, as their knees touched under the table. When Walt brought out some of his patented off brand humor, Hannah laughed. She got it. When she started sharing an impression, he knew exactly where she was going with it. He got it.

Could he be imagining all of this? Maybe she was not on the same page with him at all. Was he just some starry-eyed fool, back in seventh grade?

Hannah removed all doubt when she just blurted out one day, "Walt Williamson, I want to make love with you in the worst way. But you know I can't."

"Where have you been all of my life? And why did you not wait for me?" was his immediate response.

One thing did not get lost in translation. Walt got it. He was not going to get it.

Mrs. Neumann was thrilled when her tenant offered to cut the grass. She said that she did not mind doing it, but she had so much trouble cranking the mower. It did not start right up for Walt, either. When he replaced the fouled up spark plug and put in some fresh gas, it ran much better. The carburetor was also a little out of adjustment. That night for his supper, Walt's landlady brought him a plate full of vegetables, along with some meatloaf made from her special recipe.

As he turned off the light still trying to get used to his new surroundings, Walt was contemplating something. "Othell, I wonder what Hannah meant by making love to me in the worst way?"

Once everything was out in the open, Walt and Hannah were now free to set boundaries on their relationship. They both felt less pressure. Hannah suggested that maybe they should try to find a good counselor to help them with their problem. They both laughed.

Ephesus State was on the semester system. This meant the school year was divided into halves rather than three quarters. In the program Walt and Hannah were in, morning classes were repeated again in the evening for the working students. There was also a colloquium after public school hours that everyone had to attend. This meant a gap of almost four hours between the time the morning classes ended and the afternoon session began.

Walt and Hannah figured out rather quickly that they could do their assigned work during this break. Just as rapidly, they discovered that two heads are better than one. He was the visionary, always seeing the larger picture. She was the detail person, piecing it all together.

Initially, the two of them worked jointly only at school. Sometimes they got a little too animated in the library, or in the student center. One day Hannah suggested that they go back to her place. Walt was hesitant, but he trusted her to know what she was doing.

The rented house was nothing elaborate. The first thing he noticed was a picture of Hannah's husband in his military uniform. He also spotted a photo of the two of them at their wedding. This made him very uncomfortable. Hannah, however, got right down to business on the assignment.

As Walt was about to leave, he reached for her. Before she could react, he pulled her close. Hannah stiffened, and he released his grip. He apologized for his forwardness and left abruptly.

Dr. Fitzpatrick remarked to a colleague one day that it was as though Walt and Hannah were having their class, and the rest of the students were having theirs. The two of them fed off each other. One sparked the other. If he was point, she was counterpoint. If she was part, he was counterpart. They were often navigating around in their own world, while others were oblivious to what was going on between them.

Walt was energized. He felt more alive than ever before in his entire life. While some others had gotten a few glimpses, Hannah was the first person who ever really knew him. It was so from the first moment they looked into each other's eyes. He believed that she had known him forever. Amazingly, she felt exactly the same way about him.

The two of them established one ground rule. They would not see each other after the late afternoon class unless it was at some evening school function. That did not keep them from talking on the telephone, however.

Mrs. Neumann had run an extension into the basement. She and Walt worked out an arrangement. If any of his friends wished to call him, they would let the phone ring twice, and then hang up. He would answer when it rang again. If he was on the phone and heard his landlady pick up, he would get off the line within a couple of minutes. Fortunately, Mrs. Neumann hardly ever used her phone except during the morning hours.

Between classes, they started taking turns going from one of their residences to the other. Walt introduced Hannah to Mrs. Neumann. She wanted to know all about this person so important to her tenant.

When Walt got home the afternoon after he cut the grass, a note was on his door. Mrs. Neumann was inviting him to come upstairs and help her eat the leftovers from the meal she had cooked the day before. The two of them were beginning to form their own kind of little bond.

Walt inquired about the late Mr. Neumann. He learned that the childless couple had lived in Ephesus all of their lives. He had been a millworker in the big textile plant, and he died of lung complications. She worked for a time at a small department store.

Walt's landlady knocked on his door one afternoon a few days later. She again invited him upstairs for supper. He told her he hoped that she had not gone to any trouble. Mrs. Neumann laughed and said, "Walter, you are never any trouble."

As they were eating, she said that she wanted to talk with him about something. Mrs. Neumann then extended an ongoing invitation for him to take his evening meals with her. He was flabbergasted. Cooking was never his strong suit, but he had managed to stave off starvation.

"You will have to go up on the rent," Walt offered. "I will need to help you pay for the groceries."

"I would never think of such," she answered right back.

"Walter," she said, "When I lost my husband, one of the hardest adjustments I had to make was not having someone to cook for, and then having to eat alone. This would be my pleasure."

How could he turn down a deal like that? Not only did he get at least one good nutritious meal every day, but he also found in Mrs. Neumann a warm and gentle spirit. He soon came to realize and appreciate just how much these daily sessions meant to the woman who was sharing her home with him. He had to admit that he also looked forward to supper every evening.

The gracious lady then mentioned something else. She said that she would not mind at all doing Walt's laundry. She would just put his clothes in with the few things that she had to wash each week. From then on, the door going to the basement was never locked.

Mrs. Neumann relished hearing Walt talk about his childhood experiences. She told him that he should become a comedian.

He in turn listened to her as she poured out her heart describing her difficult upbringing. She also spoke of the struggles that she and Mr. Neumann had as they eked out a living during hard times. The humble woman conveyed to him how much they wanted children, but they guessed the Good Lord just did not have that in His plans.

Walt's landlady also had a dry sense of humor that he understood and appreciated. He was so happy to be around someone who could see the funny side of life.

When the first semester grades were posted, there were no surprises for Walt or Hannah. They both received an A in all of their classes. Walt went by Dr. Harris' office to make sure the administrator made note. This was the first time in his entire higher educational experience that Walt Williamson's name was on a dean's good list.

Both Walt and Hannah had a decision to make as the second semester began. After the students finished all the required courses, they could either write a thesis, or take additional classes during the summer to complete their degree requirements. Walt decided to write a thesis. Hannah wanted to do the extra course work.

He spent as much time as he could developing his thoughts. He already knew where he was going. He just had to figure out how to get there.

After the break, the two of them picked right up where they left off. Walt tried to get Hannah to talk about her husband, but she would say little. Nevertheless, Phillip Parker was the ever-present elephant in the room.

Walt continued to struggle with his feelings for Hannah. She was so close, yet she was so untouchable. When they were together, he felt like a teenager jockeying for position so that their bodies might accidentally touch.

Hannah occasionally granted him a polite hug as they were parting. His hands, what would he do with his hands? He wanted to run them through her long blond hair, and then ravish her backside as he held her. Once when he let them drift a little too far, Hannah had no difficulty deciding what to do with her own. Walt left red faced, and it was not just from embarrassment.

As he was driving away, the song "Hard-Hearted Hannah" was playing on the radio. He reached up and switched it off.

In the evenings when he was not on the phone with Hannah, Walt began organizing his thoughts for his thesis. He picked up a used electric typewriter at an office supply store. His major professor kept trying to impress upon him that he was not just writing a term paper. He had to state a premise, a thesis, and then defend it. He was getting close to figuring out just how he was going to do that.

Walt kept telling Dr. Fitzpatrick that there would not be many footnotes. It was his thesis, and he would be the one defending it. The student was not relying so much on the opinions of others. His major professor was a bit concerned.

The second semester went by fast. Walt not only had to think about his thesis, but he also must start giving serious consideration to what he was going to do after he finished his degree.

One day when he was talking to Hannah, he remarked that except for the mock therapy sessions in class, he had not ever actually counseled anyone. She responded that except for practice teaching, she had never been a teacher, either, until the first day she went into her classroom.

During the second half of the semester, the program they were in did involve getting some practical counseling experience. The faculty had an ongoing arrangement with local therapists that allowed graduate students to intern with them. Most of the professionals were graduates of the school. Walt was assigned to Dr. Richard Fredrickson, a crusty old character who had been around the block a few times, and the world a couple of times.

Walt was impressed with the rapport and the repartee Dr. Fredrickson had with his clients. The student sat in on several sessions a week, observing this skilled therapist at work. Toward the end of the semester, the graduate student actually did some elementary counseling, with Dr. Fredrickson looking on.

Uncertainty

By the time he finished his class work for the second term, Walt had his thesis statement almost ready. He had refined it several times, with the help of Dr. Fitzpatrick. It now went something like this: "A person's self-concept plays a larger role than does both heredity and the social situation into which an individual is thrust, in determining his or her core values, objectives, and overt behavior."

The thing he liked most about his thesis was that he was the living embodiment of it. He was not trying to prove something that his heart was not really in.

When the semester ended, Walt missed the scheduled time with Hannah. She would now take classes during the summer to complete her requirements, while he worked at home or in the library.

The two of them did manage some rambling together in the mountains on weekends. Hannah grew up in the area, and she knew of nearby trails and waterfalls. On one occasion, they packed a picnic and headed out with no set agenda. Another day they spent a whole afternoon in Scott Meadows, searching for and identifying wildflowers.

Walt yearned for Hannah to let her guard down. He learned the hard way, though, that if anything were ever going to happen between them, she would have to make the first move.

One Sunday afternoon, Walt needed a break from his studies. He needed some fresh air, and he invited Hannah to go trekking with him. She offered to pack a picnic.

He was surprised when she showed up at his place with her hair in a ponytail, wearing short shorts and a halter-top. Walt was not unhappy at all that women were getting liberated in some ways that he found very exciting and enticing.

When they got in The Rev. and headed out of town, he made no mention of her attire. He said nothing as they spread a blanket in a shady, secluded spot on a creek bank. He seemed oblivious as they sat listening to the rippling water's enrapturing sounds. Walt still pretended not to notice as they got the food out of the car. He made no comment as they enjoyed the delicacies Hannah brought.

As she lay back looking up at the clouds, he finally made his move. "Did you burn your bra?" he asked mischievously.

"No, I didn't," she answered. "For one thing it would not have made much of a fire. And for another, I still need it for moral support," she added, not to be outdone by him in the least.

Eventually, Hannah did begin to open up some about her marriage. She and Phillip had grown up together. He was the only boy she ever dated. Everyone in both families just assumed they would get married.

Phillip was one of the top students in their class, but he had no aspirations of going to college. All he ever wanted to do was fool around with cars. He went to the vocational technical school and became a certified mechanic. Hannah's husband then took a job working for a man who had been repairing vehicles for the local folks for almost four decades.

Phillip was able to bring to the shop the latest in the fast developing technology. He envisioned buying the business when his boss decided to retire. Then, he was drafted. Walt noticed that Hannah was careful not to say anything about the nature of her relationship with her husband.

Walt's summer days were now spent mostly at home scribbling on legal pads as he worked to get his concepts on paper. It was cool in the basement, but he did not like having to depend on artificial lighting. He often took his work to the swing on Mrs. Neumann's front porch. When he did go to the campus to discuss his progress with Dr. Fitzpatrick, he always looked for Hannah.

Walt was really not very skilled in typing. He was also a bit concerned that his thesis would have to be turned in without any corrected mistakes. Hannah made him an offer that he could not refuse. She said if he did the first draft, she would type the final copy. He was overwhelmed that somebody actually cared so much for him.

Walt's progress on his thesis came to a screeching halt one day. Something was blocking his path, and he needed to find the underlying cause.

The troubled graduate student went to the city park, but too many people were milling around. He got in The Rev. and started driving up a narrow, twisting, mountainous road. He parked near a stream, and then sat on a rock listening to the rushing clear cold water.

As he was digging deep into himself, he thought back to something that happened during Bible days. King David had his lover Bathsheba's husband reassigned to the forefront so that he would almost certainly be killed in battle. Walt then realized, at least in his mind, that he was every bit as guilty as the Jewish monarch was.

He did not like himself very much, but he was so in love with Hannah.

When Walt came up for supper after he got back to his apartment, Mrs. Neumann had placed a piece of mail beside his plate. It was a questionnaire from the draft board wanting to confirm his current enrollment status. It also inquired as to whether there would be any changes in his situation within the next few months.

Even with his draft situation now weighing heavily on his mind, Walt was still unable to shake his afternoon encounter with himself. For the first time since he met her, Walt felt no urgency to hear Hannah's voice. That changed, though, when he heard the phone ring twice, and then stop.

The graduate student was still trying to come up with a title for his thesis. As things always seemed to, it just popped right up in his head, "I. D. – The Identity Dilemma."

That started him off on a completely new tangent. He decided to go back and revisit Sigmund Freud's concept of the *id*. In his thesis, Walt declared that Freud's *id*, *ego*, and *super ego* were nothing more than fancy ways of describing different aspects of a person's sense of identity.

He was due an appointment with Dr. Fitzpatrick to update her regarding his progress. When he explained this new revelation to his major professor, she asked him, "Walt, have you always been able to take complicated concepts, and simplify them like that?"

Walt had never felt so much uncertainty in all his life. That was just a sign of the times. Would his thesis be approved? What was he going to do next if it was, or if it was not? What about Hannah? Would he get anything else in the mail from the draft board?

The clock was inevitably ticking. Fortunately within short order, he started getting some answers to his questions. Dr. Fredrickson contacted him. The therapist offered him a counseling job in his practice. The veteran counselor said something about Walt fascinated him, and that he wanted them to have a chance to work together. That was an option certainly worthy of consideration.

The much anticipated, and at the same time, dreaded day finally came for Walt to meet with the graduate committee to determine the fate of his thesis. The faculty members categorically did the job they were paid to do. For almost two hours, they grilled Walt about every facet of his submitted work. Then, they asked him to excuse himself.

After pacing back and forth agonizingly for about half an hour, Walt was called back into the conference room. Dr. Fitzpatrick said she was happy to inform him that his thesis had been accepted, and that he would be awarded the Master of Science Degree in Guidance and Counseling.

Dr. Fitzpatrick did have one recommendation, though. She suggested that at some point he delve deeper into the concept of identity, expand his thoughts, and then one day publish them in a book. Each of the faculty members came to Walt, congratulated him, and shook his hand.

In June 1967, Walter O. Williamson once again donned cap and gown. Hannah was four seats across from him. During the commencement ceremony, a continuous amount of life energy was flowing back and forth between the two, although no one else seemed aware of it.

Not wanting to distance himself from Hannah, Walt decided to take the job offer from Dr. Fredrickson. He began looking around for another place to live, but he had not mentioned that yet to Mrs. Neumann. He liked this town, and he might consider making it his home.

Not a month into his apprenticeship, Walt got a notice in the mail from his Uncle Sam. The draft board had taken notice that he had gotten his degree. The military was in desperate need of counselors to help returning Vietnam veterans deal with their debilitating emotional scars. Walt had been drafted. He was to report for duty in two weeks.

The one question still unanswered had to do with Hannah. Would they now go their separate ways, and perhaps never see each other again? Would she come to mean no more to him than Judith Muse did after that summer romance when they were barely teenagers?

Before he left to begin his military service, Walt would not get a chance to discuss any of this with Hannah. She got her own call from the armed forces. Phillip's name had been added to the Vietnam casualty list, and he was being shipped home. She packed some things hurriedly, and left to go meet the plane. Walt had no idea which way she went.

Unlike the horrible fate that he had one time wished upon Sgt. Parker, however, the soldier was not coming home in a body bag. Hannah's husband was dead only from the waist down. He was assigned to Walter Reed Hospital in Washington, D.C.

P.T.S.D

Saying goodbye to Mrs. Neumann was harder than Walt anticipated. In the year that he had lived in her little furnished basement apartment, she had become like a second mother to him.

She mentioned that she was thinking about not renting it again. She might just leave it as it was for Walt to come back to whenever he could. He did promise her that he would return the first chance he had. Of course, Mrs. Neumann knew that he had other business in Ephesus as well.

How could it feel so strange driving into the yard where he lived all his growing up days? The places that had at one time been as familiar to Walt as the back of his hand now seemed foreign. The dogwood trees that he set out along the drive as an FFA project were all grown up. The house looked about the same, except it now had vinyl siding.

Before he was inducted into the military, Walt wanted to go by and see his mother. He had no idea how he would be received. He felt that he had to do his part, regardless of what anyone else did.

He went to the front door. When Walt was a kid, he never imagined that he would ever feel awkward about going to the backdoor that he went in and out of all the time. Now, he stood on the front porch like a stranger, a guest, a visitor.

He saw a doorbell button. That was new. Walt took a deep breath, and he then pressed it. After a few moments of silence, he heard some shuffling inside. Maude opened the door.

She said, "Well, hello," but she did not reach out for him. "I was out on the back porch. Do you want to sit there?" she asked. He nodded in agreement and followed her.

When he stepped inside, what caught Walt's attention next was what he did not see. The bookcase that he had made for his mother was missing from its place in the living room. Without giving any indication of his observation, he looked around to see if it was in another room as they walked through the house. He did not see it anywhere.

He started to inquire of the bookcase's whereabouts, but he decided not to. Walt had picked up on a pattern. He did not get straight answers to his questions. The Mother's Day gift was never again mentioned. He decided later that Todd probably broke it up and used it for kindling.

"How are Emma Lou and the baby?" he asked, as they sat down. Walt had heard that he was an uncle now, but he did not receive a birth announcement.

"They're fine. Have you seen Ben?" his mother responded.

"No ma'am," he answered.

"Drew says Benjamin means 'Son of my right hand'," she added.

Walt had a moment of angst for his own parents. They could never make that claim about him.

"I don't know whether you've heard or not, but I now have my Master's Degree in Guidance and Counseling," he continued.

"Your grandpa did mention something about it," she responded.

"What you may not know is that I got drafted this month. Because of my education, I will be commissioned a second lieutenant. I will be stationed at the Walter Reed Hospital. Imagine that, your little Walter will be working at Walter Reed."

Maude showed no emotion. Nevertheless, he continued to try to make conversation. "I will be working with returning veterans who have been injured. My specialty will be treating those suffering from shell shock and battle fatigue."

His mother seemed to be listening, but she said little. After a few more minutes of awkward conversation, Walt said he needed to go. On the way back through the house, he said he wanted a drink of that good well water before he left. When he went into the kitchen, he noticed something right away that was not there when he was growing up. A picture of a beautiful swan was hanging on the wall.

"Where did you get this?" he asked his mother.

"It was among Aunt Lucy's things," she told him. "Jane said that she did not know where she got it."

Walt took a sip standing in that same kitchen where he heard the words many years ago, "He *may* be your father." That swan prompted him to go ahead and have a discussion with his mother that was long overdue.

He began by asking her if she knew that he taught himself to read. Maude said that she always knew he was smart, but no, she did not know that. He told her about listening in on his sister's reading lessons, and then getting her books when no one was looking.

Walt next told Maude about the first story he ever read to himself. Without any further explanation, he turned and looked up at the swan. "That's me, Mother. I'm the ugly duckling. I just got hatched in the wrong nest."

Maude stood frozen like a deer caught in the headlights. No other words were spoken. Walt left his mother standing in the kitchen as he let himself out.

As he drove out of the yard, he thought back over what just happened. He would confront his mother in a more direct way at some point. For the time being, he would just let the swan fable serve notice to her that he had not forgotten the conversation years ago in that same kitchen.

He then said to himself, "Othell, just think. When Mother goes in the living room, that toad is glaring at her. Then, when she is in the kitchen, a swan is looking over her shoulder. I know the frog is not going anywhere, but I'll bet you that swan will not be still hanging on the wall the next time we are in that house."

As Walt drove away, Maude was panic-stricken. Her worst fears were realized. Walt had just confirmed what she had suspected all along. He did hear what she said the day she blundered. What was she to do? He was gone. She could not call him back to continue the discussion. Because of his military obligation, she had no idea when she would see him again.

Was this the time to go ahead and tell Todd? One side of her wanted to believe that her husband would be relieved. He would reach out to her, admire her for her courage, and appreciate her so much for the load she had been carrying. The other side said that he would go into a rage because he had been deceived and forced to raise another man's son.

Many things had changed during Maude's time on this earth, but one thing remained a constant. When she did not know what to do, she usually did nothing. Handling this crisis would be no different. One thing she was sure of, though. Walt would be back, and he would come looking for some answers. She must now live in fear of that dreaded day.

The greater Baltimore-D.C. area was a jungle compared to anywhere else Walt had ever been. With almost no time to make any adjustment, he moved from the serene mountainous area of North Carolina, to the jaws of madness and mayhem.

His basic training was minimal. He was needed on the job. He was about to be thrown in the mix for some intense on the job training.

Walt's cash reserves were just about used up, but he did not owe anything. He would squeeze a few more miles out of The Rev., and live on the army base until he could afford something of his own.

As the counselor began visiting the rooms of wounded soldiers, he heard stories about jungles on the other side of the earth. His recent concerns about his future seemed so trivial compared to what these young men had been through.

The hospital itself was old, and it had obviously been neglected. Paint was peeling from the drab green rooms. Walt suspected there were nicer private rooms for the higher ups, but the wounded veterans that he was working with were placed in depressing multi bed wards. The equipment looked like something out of a World War II movie. He struggled with the smell of the place. The therapist wondered if the patients felt like injured animals being kept in a holding pen.

Walt thought about his own attitudes toward the Vietnam War. Initially, he was supportive. He trusted his country to know what it was doing. His grandparents' generation had grown up with World War I as a primary marker in their lives. He himself was a World War II baby. He grew up hearing war stories about how the United States rescued the world from tyranny during that conflict.

The nation's leaders then assured its citizens that the task was not yet completed. It had to take a stand to halt the spread of godless Communism wanting to take over the world. At first, Walt could not understand burning draft cards, and going to Canada to avoid military service.

Then, he recalled how surprised he was when Dr. Martin Luther King, Jr. came out in opposition to the Vietnam War. That caused him to stop and think. It started getting personal when he realized that he could not stay in school forever. He was not sure what he would have done if he had been called up as a foot soldier.

It was different, however, being drafted to work with returning veterans as a counselor. He would not let his growing opposition to the war get in the way of serving his country in this constructive way.

One morning during his first week at Walter Reed, Walt did a double take when he saw the name Sgt. Phillip Parker on the chart he held in his hand. Cautiously, he entered the ward. The man was asleep so he decided not to disturb him. "Could it be Hannah's husband?" he wondered. Was this another wounded warrior with the same name? Walt had a hard time recognizing this battered Vietnam veteran as the same innocent young man in the wedding photo that he had seen at the Parkers' house.

Lt. Williamson dropped back by later in the day to find the patient awake. He introduced himself and watched for a reaction. Sgt. Parker registered no response to indicate any recognition of Walt's name. The neophyte therapist struggled as he asked some leading questions. He learned that the soldier was indeed from Ephesus, North Carolina.

Phillip spoke lovingly of his wife Hannah who had been with him for the first week of his hospitalization. He said that he was so proud of her. While he was away in combat, she had gone back to school. She had recently gotten her Master's Degree, and she had now returned home to begin the new school year as a counselor.

Apparently, Hannah had never mentioned Walt to Phillip. Lt. Williamson likewise never told Hannah about this encounter.

The therapist learned a couple of days later that Sgt. Parker was well enough to be transferred to a veteran's hospital in his home state for about a month before being discharged. Walt wondered if Hannah's husband would get the professional help that he might well need. He was not at all concerned, though, about the personal care Phillip Parker was certain to receive once he got home.

The military therapist found little use for the theories of counseling that he had meticulously studied. He had to throw just about all of that out the window and start over. On the other hand, there was one thing Lt. Williamson was sure of now more than ever. A sense of personal identity was the only key that would unlock the enigmatic doors behind which many of these veterans were trapped.

In his master's thesis, Walt had theorized about the significance of a person's "self-concept." Now, he was seeing it exemplified in the real world. As he perceived it, people come to terms with who they are through some combination of how they view themselves and what others think about them.

This "self-concept" gives them grounding and a sense of relevance and purpose. Walt believed that those who get the bulk of their self-worth from within, and not from what others think, are far less likely to let someone else define them. These self-assured and self-confident individuals follow their own paths, rather than let others use them for the furthering of their own agendas.

It did not take Walt long to figure out that the first thing the military did was to take innocent and naïve boys, and strip them of their sense of self in order to make killing machines out of them. It then thrust them into a dangerous world to fight an enemy with whom they had no beef.

Those who were vulnerable to this kind of manipulation of their selfhood were left with identity voids. It was like walking around emotionally naked. To compensate, many of the GIs turned to drugs and alcohol just to help them cope.

Now, those with battered bodies were no longer useful to Uncle Sam. The military wanted them released back into society as quickly and as efficiently as possible. Getting their psychological wounds healed was in many instances more difficult than patching up their bodies.

No one seemed to understand the anguish and despair of these wounded souls. Walt was disturbed by the insensitivity for the plight of these soldiers by many of the military professionals with whom he was working. Some of the older counselors seemed to view the emotionally overwrought veterans as crybabies.

Physicians apparently believed that alleviating physical pain would also diminish emotional distress. Doctors had an increasing supply of medications available to dope up the chronically injured while their bodies healed. They showed little concern that the patients might become increasingly dependent upon those drugs.

As Walt saw it, before these emotionally wounded veterans could assimilate back into society, they had to rediscover their original core values. They needed to get back to their roots. They must regain their bearings. They must stop relying on the opinions of others, and discover all over again who they were from the inside out. Many of them could not do it alone, but they did not know how to ask for help. Even if they did, little assistance was available.

Walt was fighting an endless uphill battle. He never had enough one on one time with those who wanted to talk. Often just before a session, the patient was shot up with pain numbing narcotics.

Lt. Williamson and his counterparts helped redefine what was referred to in previous wars as battle fatigue and shell shock. Thereafter, those having difficulties recovering from the emotional scars of combat would be diagnosed as suffering from post-traumatic stress disorder (P.T.S.D.).

Sitting on his bed one night, Walt was beginning to wonder if his own fragile connection with humanity was in danger of being severed. He thought of Hannah, as he always did when he was contemplating something. Phillip was now home. It seemed such a short time ago when he and Hannah were all enthralled in their studies and wrapped up in each other. Within hardly the blink of an eye, they were now both spending the bulk of their energies tending to wounded war veterans.

During the first two months of his military service, Walt was hardly away from the hospital except for an occasional day off on a weekend. He asked for, and he got a five-day pass. He told his commanding officer that if he could not have a little breathing room, they were going to have to put him in the nuthouse.

The Rev. had been on its last leg for months. It was using oil heavily, and Walt was certain that it had a burned valve. With what little he had saved for a down payment, he was able to get a car loan. He hated borrowing money, but he no longer trusted the old Chevy out on the open road. The dealer promised the man in uniform that he would go straight to the army if he were ever late with a payment.

Walt drove off the lot in a solid maroon 1964 Dodge Coronet 440 two-door hardtop, with a V-8 engine, and whitewall tires. It had an AM-FM radio, power steering, power brakes, and air conditioning. The only thing he did not like about his new vehicle was that it had an automatic transmission.

He was allowed almost nothing for the Chevy as a trade in, but he left it on the lot anyway. Walt laughed when the man offered him $100 for it. He had paid only $250 for the car, and that was more than five years and 50,000 miles ago.

In honor of the minister who put the bulk of the miles on it, Walt said a little benediction over it. The automobile had served them both well. The Rev. was now put out to pasture, as was the parson.

He said goodbye to the faithful old Rev. Then he declared, "Hello, Dolly." Walt's new ride was named after one of his granddaddy's mules.

The weary army therapist was soon on his way down the road headed toward the Shenandoah Valley. The mountains were ablaze with fall color. He was not sure that he had ever seen the leaves more spectacular. Some of them matched the color of Dolly perfectly.

His destination was still farther on down the road, though. Mrs. Neumann was thrilled to see him. His apartment was just the way he left it. Walt asked if he could stay a couple of days. She said supper would be ready in about an hour.

After he unpacked his gear, he picked up the phone. He heard a dial tone and nervously dialed a number. He then took a deep breath.

"Hello."

"Hannah?"

"Walt????"

"Happy Halloween."

"Happy Birthday!"

A whole section was devoted to the addictive personality in Walt's Abnormal Psychology class back in college. At the time, alcoholism was about the only malady that provided case studies. He never forgot coming across the fragment of an entreaty by Reinhold Niebuhr that Alcoholics Anonymous had popularized, known as "The Serenity Prayer."

Walt decided it was time for him to heed the wisdom in that little homily. He might occasionally effect a bit of change in his work with returning wounded veterans. Realistically, though, many other circumstances were beyond his control. It would be a continuous challenge for him to know which was which.

Walt Williamson came to the realization that he was not going to change the world. At best, he might have just a little impact on somebody's world. He would do what he could while working within the system into which he had been thrust. He tried equally hard not to compromise himself in the process.

Could he apply this prayer formula to his own family? That would prove to be an even greater challenge.

I-N-V-A-L-I-D

As the group assembled in the conference room, some of them with much effort, Walt walked up to the blackboard. Without saying a word, he started writing.

I-N-V-A-L-I-D

"Would somebody please tell me what that word is?" he asked his clients.

They started looking at each other, wondering if this was some kind of trick question.

"Come on now, do any of you know how to read?" he inquired.

"Invalid?" one wounded veteran said, timidly.

"Invalid, is that what you are?" Walt then wanted to know.

"Say it all together, 'I am an invalid'."

"Again, 'I am an invalid'."

"Is there another way to pronounce that word?" he then asked.

Once more, there were shrugs.

"In-valid, in-valid," he finally phrased it for them.

"Now say that all together, 'I am in-valid. I am in-valid'."

A serious look then came across the therapist's face. "I have heard each one of you say today, 'I am an invalid.' In addition, I have also heard every one of you say, 'I am in-valid.' Now I don't want to ever hear any of you say those words again."

The cost of living was much higher in the D.C. area. Walt was making his car payments on time. With careful budgeting, he hoped to move into a little flat right after the Christmas holidays. He eventually found something he could afford, and he made a deposit to move in on January 1, 1968.

Most of Walt's colleagues had families. They wanted time off during the holidays, so he volunteered to work. Some people in Ephesus, North Carolina were disappointed, but he told them that he would get some compensatory time after the first of the year.

Working near the nation's capital, Walt became very conscious of what a sheltered life he had lived. He was within striking distance of the nerve center from which decisions were made that affected just about everybody on the earth.

During time off, the lieutenant visited many monuments in the nation's capital, and he learned his way around some of the historical buildings. It was customary to see sleek black limousines pulling up with dignitaries coming or going. He recognized some of them from news reports.

One day he caught a glimpse of Secretary of State Dean Rusk getting out of a limo with Senator Robert Kennedy.

Walt never knew who might show up at Walter Reed. Both supporters and opponents of the Vietnam War used the hospital for photo opportunities. Often, he had to step aside to let an entourage pass. This was after all 1968, a very important election year.

He was in the middle of a group session one Saturday morning when there was a commotion. None other than President Lyndon B. Johnson came strolling through the door. A host of others crammed into the room.

"Good morning, my fellow Americans," the president bellowed. Walt's Commander-in-Chief came over to him, extending his hand. With cameras whirling the president asked, "And how are you doing today?"

The individualist that he was, Walt never batted an eye. "I am a human being, sir. I am not a human doer. I do the things I do because of who I am. I am not who I am because of what I do."

Before the president had any chance to respond, Walt turned the tables. "And who might *you* be, sir?"

"I am the . . . ugh." The president tightened his lips in his patented manner. This young army therapist had thrown him a curve ball. After a moment of reflection, arguably the most powerful man in the world finally spoke again.

"I, too, am a human being. So also are these other men in this room. So are all of their fighting comrades in Vietnam."

The president paused. "Even so are our enemies, the men and women, the boys and girls from the North. We must never lose sight of that."

The next night, Sunday, March 3, 1968, President Johnson called an evening news conference. At the conclusion, he stunned the nation when he announced that he would not be a candidate for reelection.

(On January 22, 1973, former President Lyndon B. Johnson, at the age of 64, died of a massive heart attack on the day before a ceasefire was signed effectively ending the War in Vietnam.)

When Walt got back to his apartment the night after his encounter with the president, a message was on his answering machine. "I saw you on the news tonight. You looked tired."

It was time for Walt to have a talk with his commanding officer about the leave time that he had been promised for working through the Christmas holidays. As they sat down together, Lt. Williamson was informed that a lot of buzz had gone through the hospital regarding his encounter with LBJ. Walt was granted a whole week off beginning on Wednesday, March 13.

When he got to work on Tuesday before he was to begin his leave, a note was in his box. The hospital chief of staff wanted to see him. The army therapist placed a call to the receptionist, and they set up an appointment for 10:00 a.m.

After the usual formalities, Walt took his seat in the executive office. Without any further posturing, the major picked up a parcel and said, "Your boss has something for you."

"Whatever it is, sir, I'm sure I will be appreciative," Walt responded.

"Oh, it is not from me," the chief of staff responded. "It's from your big boss."

Walt took the bag, and he pulled out a box with the seal of the President of the United States of America on it.

"Go ahead and open it," he was instructed.

Inside was a framed photograph of Walt shaking hands with President Johnson. It was inscribed:

"To Lieutenant Walter O. Williamson

My Fellow American

My Fellow Human Being."

It was signed by the president, and dated March 2, 1968.

As he was putting it back in its box, his superior said he thought something else was in the sack, too. Walt reached in and pulled out a first lieutenant bar. He had been given a promotion.

"Do I thank you for this?" he asked the major.

"No," the hospital administrator answered. "It came with that package."

Walt did not understand why he had earned a promotion. Nevertheless, the extra $100 or so a month in pay would certainly come in handy. He hardly ever wore his military uniform anymore. He had convinced some of the staff that they would have better rapport with their clients if they presented themselves as regular people.

Mrs. Neumann had not been feeling very well lately. That was often the case after a cold winter in the mountains. She really perked up, however, when Walt called and said that he was on his way.

He and Hannah met at the Dairy Queen on Friday after she left school. She was now a counselor at the junior high school. In some phone conversations, she had already told Walt a good bit about her work.

Hannah was in a newly created position. Teachers were struggling with overcrowded classrooms. Because of rowdy students and unsupportive parents, administrators were dealing with more and more disciplinary problems. School systems were adding additional counselors to their staffs trying to stem the tide.

Like Walt, Hannah agreed that much of what she had learned in graduate school was useless. "No classes were taught on the impact that television is having on kids," she said. "Some experts think that children are developing short attention spans because they are so accustomed to commercial breaks."

She continued. "One of the biggest problems we are having with junior high students pertains to the pressure that consumer advertising puts on them to all like and do the same things. They get so caught up in conforming that they are losing their individuality."

"What are you laughing at? This is serious," Hannah chided Walt. She had never heard about his high school graduation speech, but she was about to.

Eventually the subject got around to Hannah's husband. Phillip was getting along very well in his wheelchair. He was one of the luckier ones, if there was anything fortunate about never being able to walk again. Only a single sharp piece of shrapnel had penetrated his spine, leaving him paralyzed from the waist down. Many of Phillip's comrades who survived their wounds lost limbs or had severe head injuries.

Hannah was amazed at how well he was adjusting. He joked about his new "hot wheels." They had made their house wheelchair accessible, and he was able to stay at home alone. She was convinced that he would eventually get back to work. Phillip could pull himself up, and then stand leaning against something for short periods. His goal was to tinker around under the hood of a vehicle once again.

Walt asked about psychological issues. Hannah said that he did have some nighttime problems with flashbacks, but they seemed to be lessening.

He then told Hannah about the I-N-V-A-L-I-D routine that is part of every new therapy group. "That's good, Walt. Maybe you need to come over and go through it with Phillip." Walt just rolled his eyes, knowing that would never happen.

"You said that you had something to show me," she said, changing the subject. He reached under his chair and pulled out the box with the picture of him and the president inside. Hannah leaped from her chair and gave him a big hug. "I am so proud of you," she said.

"Oh, this is nothing," he responded. "I just wish I could do something to help shorten this bloody war. Maybe the next president will find a way to bring about peace." He did not even mention the promotion.

"What are you doing tomorrow?" he asked.

"Why?" she wanted to know.

"Want to go on a picnic?"

"Oh Walt, I would love to. But you know right now I can't."

On Saturday, Walt took Mrs. Neumann's old Oldsmobile and had it serviced. He then devoted himself to some things around the house that needed a little attention. For three days, he feasted on home cooking.

Mrs. Neumann had her Sunday lunch all prepared before she went to church. She had never done so before, but she asked Walt if he would like to join her. He had not been in a church in a while. He was honored to sit with his special friend.

With all the turmoil going on throughout the country, Walt did not know what preachers were using for their texts. He was hoping to hear a sermon for something, not just against everything. He was pleasantly surprised. The Lutheran minister's text was the verse where Jesus says that the truth makes people free. Walt remembered this as the same Scripture his Granddaddy Williamson had bookmarked and underlined in his Bible.

After lunch, Walt went downstairs to get the framed photograph of him and President Johnson. Mrs. Neumann beamed with pride when she saw it. The young man who had lived in her basement apartment was shaking hands with the President of the United States.

She then told Walt that she knew he would always have a special place in his office to display it so that anybody coming in could see it.

"No ma'am," he answered. "I want to leave it here with you."

"Oh, Walter," she said. "You are like a son to me."

He loved it when she called him Walter.

Michelle My Belle

Walt's notoriety did not go unnoticed around Walter Reed. Even though celebrities came and went, it was still big news when somebody bent the president's ear. In President Johnson's case, that was a tall order.

That Walt was gone for a few days soon after it happened just added to the mystique. By the time he got back to work, he had been the subject of several copy machine conversations. More than a few young women then tried to catch his eye. Still a bit romance-challenged, he did not even realize that they were flirting with him.

That is until Michelle Bell, a redheaded young nurse got right in his face. "You stubborn old mule," she said. "Am I going to have to get a two-by-four and knock you over the head to get your attention?"

"And just how would you know anything about mules?" Walt curiously wanted to know.

"For your information, Mr. High and Mighty, my granddaddy was a mule trader," Michelle shot right back at him.

"Mine, too," said Walt.

"You've got to be kidding," she responded, thinking he was mocking her.

"Nope," he answered. "I'll bet my Grandpa King sold more Tennessee Mules than anybody else in Georgia."

"And mine sold more than anyone in Alabama," Michelle matched him stride for stride.

"So that's where that cute little accent comes from," Walt said, this time really mocking her.

"Did you say Grandpa King? You don't mean George King, do you?" she asked, with a different look on her face.

"The one and only," he responded.

Michelle went on. "He spent the night at my granddaddy's house one time. I met him. He brought a pair of mules to my granddaddy when he was in a bind. I remember that old GMC truck."

"She knows about trucks," Walt mused to himself.

"After he left, I remember my Granddaddy Bell saying that George King was one of the finest men that he had ever met. He could have gone straight to the farmer. But he respected Granddaddy's territory, and they split the profit."

"So you're the snotty-nose-smart-ass-kid my grandpa came home and told me about," Walt injected, now making it all up. "He said that your Granddaddy Bell was a dirty rotten scoundrel."

"You'd better watch your smart mouth, Williamson. Bama gals kick butt."

Walt had finally been outflanked.

"Want to do something sometime?" she took the lead again, knowing that he would probably just walk away if she did not.

"Sure," Walt answered, not believing his own ears.

"Othell, is Michelle Bell going to be my belle?" he said on his way home that night.

To the redheaded nurse's surprise, Walt actually suggested dinner and a movie. He wanted to see "Dr. Zhivago." She had not seen it either, although it had been out for a few weeks.

The next Saturday on the way to the restaurant, Michelle Bell admitted that she had taken a lot of ribbing about her name since the Beatles' hit song made the charts. She then shared with Walt the rest of the story. Her middle name is Anne. The kids in school had fun with her initials. Michelle said that she went from being MA Bell, to My Belle.

Once they were seated, the waiter asked if they wanted a glass of wine. Walt's date declined without hesitation, so he also shook his head in the negative. She then turned to him and said, "Walt, I will tell you something if you promise not to laugh at me."

He nodded in agreement, not wanting to get off on a bad foot with her.

Michelle continued. "Because of my religious upbringing, I was never around wine. I have only tried it once. About a month ago at a nursing sorority convention, I took a few sips of some Sin Infidel. I really did not like it."

Walt admitted he was not much of a wine connoisseur either, and that he was not familiar with that brand. What did she call it? He was not exactly sure if he heard her correctly, but he decided not to ask for clarification.

Walt and Michelle enjoyed lively conversation throughout dinner. They barely got to the theater on time. He was supposed to be on a date, and being the southern gentleman that he was, Walt was attentive to Michelle. At the same time, he was captivated by the movie.

Boris Pasternak had captured the essence of the identity struggles of the Russian people during the Communist Revolution. Identity – it was all about these people trying to figure out who they were, as their world was so rapidly falling apart all around them.

Walt was particularly intrigued by the orphan girl, Tanya. Perhaps, she was the daughter of the late physician/poet Dr. Zhivago and his mistress Lara. Tanya seemed disinterested in her heritage. She and her boyfriend were concentrating on building a future together, rather than fretting over things they had no control over from the past.

At that moment, a big piece of the identity puzzle fell into place. "Now it's beginning to gel, Othell."

While the credits were running and everybody else was getting up to leave, Walt was thinking, "Regardless of who furnishes the egg, and who supplies the sperm, genes unite in a random configuration to form a fetus. Every individual is unique, and must live out his or her own destiny, regardless of the setting of one's birth and upbringing." Walter Othell Williamson was living proof of that.

Something else about Dr. Zhivago's Greek tragedy-like life tugged at his heart. Was Yuri Zhivago's Lara, his Hannah?

Michelle invited Walt in, but he declined with the promise that they would go out again soon. He was just too deep into his own thoughts to try to keep up with her banter. Besides that, he was ready for a glass of wine.

As Walt uncorked the bottle, he suddenly roared with laughter when he looked at the label. He had just broken the vow he made to Michelle earlier in the evening. He was about to have a glass of Zinfandel. From that moment forward, Sin Infidel would always be his favorite wine, no matter what it said on the bottle.

When Walt got to his apartment on the evening of April 4, 1968, he switched on the news. Parts of him wanted to unplug the TV. Yet, so much was happening that he felt he must try to keep up with what was going on. Suddenly, the regularly scheduled program was interrupted by a special news bulletin.

Almost immediately, his phone rang. "Do you have your television on?" Hannah asked.

"Yes," he responded.

"I was just thinking of you," they both said simultaneously.

"It is so awful, Walt. Dr. King preached nonviolence, and now he has been gunned down."

For the next several moments, the two of them were like symbiotic twins, nestled in the womb of the universe, tethered by a thousand-mile copper umbilical cord.

After their first date, Walt and Michelle had lunch together a time or two in the hospital. He learned that she had been raised on Sand Mountain, in northeastern Alabama. Her parents were both teachers. Her maternal grandfather was a cotton farmer. He also raised sweet potatoes, curing them, and selling them to the public.

While Michelle was in nursing school in Birmingham, she met Grover. They were engaged to be married when he was drafted. He was killed in Vietnam within the first six months of his tour of duty.

When Michelle became an RN, she learned through the placement office of a nursing shortage at Walter Reed. As a tribute to her late fiancé, she decided to go work among the wounded at the military hospital. She had been in this position almost three years now.

Walt and Michelle were sometimes able to coordinate their days off. He had a cohort when he went exploring. Being with Michelle was fun. Her lighthearted spirit helped provide a diversion from the stresses of his job. She enjoyed Walt's spirit of adventure. They were a good match.

Larry G. Johnson

The morning of June 6, 1968, Walt almost overslept. He and Michelle were out late the night before. As a backup, he kept the alarm set on his clock radio, although he rarely had to rely on it. That particular morning he was awakened by continuous news coverage out of Los Angeles. He got up and turned on his television.

He was trying to find out what was going on. Finally, Walter Cronkite, who had been up all night, gave a recap. About the same time Walt crawled into bed the night before, Robert Kennedy was assassinated as he was leaving a hotel after a campaign rally.

Visibly shaken, the ringing phone startled him. "Walt, are you okay?" Hannah asked. "I worry so much about your safety living in Washington, and working among patients who are sometimes mentally unstable."

Walt told Hannah about seeing RFK just a few weeks earlier. Now he, too, had been slain.

A shroud of sorrow enveloped the entire hospital. Even those not enamored by the Kennedys were grieving over what was happening to the country. The times were out of joint. Walt sympathized with his first client who said he wished he had a joint, although one of a different kind.

During crazy and inane times, even those who are trained as professionals sometimes do things that they would have otherwise considered foolish. Walt never imagined that he would live with a woman out of wedlock. Even so, when Michelle's lease was up, she moved in with him. They did the usual rationalizations of how much money they could save. It was nice to have someone to come home to, and a warm body to snuggle with in bed.

Walt's ego was a bit inflated when he first got the assignment to work at Walter Reed. He mistakenly thought that his educational qualifications must have earned him the privilege of jumping ahead of others who received appointments not as prestigious. He found out quickly that he was wrong. Those with rank wanted to be anywhere but at this dilapidated old military hospital.

The therapist was amazed that the least experienced counselors were assigned to work with the most critically wounded soldiers. The more he stayed around the military though, the less things like that surprised him.

After his first year at Walter Reed, Walt was up for a transfer. He and Michelle talked it over, but they had trouble coming to an agreement. One possibility particularly intrigued Walt. He could be reassigned to a veteran's hospital in San Diego. Michelle was emphatic. She said there was no way she would live in California.

The army was also beefing up its counseling staff at Ft. Benning, in Columbus, Georgia. This base was one of the main staging areas for training combat units going to Vietnam. It was also staffed with many career soldiers who had already served tours of duty in Southeast Asia.

Walt and Michelle eventually decided that this was the best option. She would have no difficulty finding a job. Columbus was only a few hours down the road from where each had grown up.

He noticed Michelle growing distant as the time approached for them to move. At the last minute, she decided to stay at Walter Reed. Nevertheless, it was time for him to move on. He was not sure that she had moved on from her first love.

On Labor Day weekend, 1968, Walt rented a small truck and loaded up his meager possessions. Dolly tagged along behind on a dolly.

As he was settling into his new apartment, he hoped that this would be his last move before he finished his three-year obligation. Adamsonville was less than two hours away. Besides that, it was not far out of the way to go through Mason on his way to Ephesus.

In his new assignment, Walt worked out of the office of the base psychiatrist. He and three other licensed counselors did the doctor's flunky work. A receptionist served as the traffic cop. One of the biggest adjustments that Lt. Williamson had to make was wearing his military uniform when he was on duty.

The change of pace was a welcome relief for Walt, however. He was now just biding his time until his release. The one good thing about his job was that he was beefing up his résumé. In the meantime, he missed Michelle.

Sanctuary

"Hello, Dolly," Walt said as he loaded the car. "It's time to put you back where you belong." It felt good to be on the road, headed north up U.S. 27, sitting in Dolly's lap. Walt finished his last appointment at 4:00 p.m., and he was eager to get going. He had a whole week off.

Columbus was just far enough south that the fall colors were not very dramatic. He scheduled this time off so that he could go north and enjoy the annual spectacle.

About an hour or so up the road, Walt noticed a mostly red building with Coca Cola advertised on its side. It looked amazingly like the one in a painting that Michelle had of her grandfather's sweet potato curing house.

A Studebaker was backed up to the door and a farmer was unloading crates of potatoes. The truck was almost identical to his Granddaddy Williamson's that Walt learned to drive when he could barely reach the pedals. He wondered what happened to that old truck.

He had not seen Earl and Mary Beth in almost a year. Before heading on to Mason, he planned to spend the night with them.

As he drove up at King and Prince, he did not know where to look for Earl. His uncle now had a Toyota dealership next to the John Deere place. It did not matter. Earl was in the parking lot just about to get into a Corolla to go home. "See you there," Walt said out the car window.

Around the dinner table, it took a while for them to catch up on everything. After four years as the assistant, Mary Beth was named the principal of the Adamsonville Elementary School. She was the first female in the county to hold such a position.

Earl was now the mayor of Adamsonville. He had also taken his father-in-law's seat on the board of the Adamsonville Savings & Loan Association. He reminded his nephew that he could get him in a new Toyota whenever he was ready.

"How's Grandpa doing?" Walt wanted to know.

"Just as crotchety as ever," the man's son answered. "But Mother is failing some."

Walt had never known his Grandma when she was not "failing some."

He was looking forward to seeing his grandparents. He wondered if he might run into anyone else while in Mason. He might even go by and see his Grandmother Williamson.

"Walt, there is something I need to tell you if no one else has," Earl continued. "Your mother discovered a lump in her breast a couple of weeks ago. She just found out that it is malignant."

Walt grimaced. "What's next?" he asked.

"The doctors are trying to decide whether to just remove the lump, or to do a mastectomy. Walt, I do hope you will go by and see her."

Walt thought seriously about telling Earl and Mary Beth about D-V Day. He had no doubt that they would both keep it in the strictest of confidence. He also knew that they would be very supportive. Once again, he decided not to. As a counselor, he knew it sometimes places an unfair burden on others to share problematical information with them.

"Kill the fatted calf, Grandma. The prodigal grandson has come home." George King embraced Walt and pulled him in the house. "You're just the boy I wanted to see," he added. "I've got a shotgun in yonder, and I want you to try it out for me."

"Fool me once, Grandpa, shame on you. Fool me twice, shame on me." They both broke out into sidesplitting laughter.

"What I came by looking for is a good tenderloin biscuit," Walt countered.

He talked with his grandparents by phone about once a month. They were pleased that he had moved a little closer by, and they were hoping to see him more often. Walt did not know whether to bring up his mother's situation or not. He did not have to. His grandma asked him if Earl told him about her cancer.

He learned a little more about her condition. The doctors said the tumor appeared to be encapsulated, and that they were hopeful it had not spread. They decided to just remove the lump, and then treat the surrounding area with radiation.

The time passed so quickly. When Grandpa started nodding off, Walt knew the man was ready for his nap. It was time to make some other visits before getting on up the road.

He might as well go ahead and get it over with. When his Grandmother Williamson came to the door, she said, "Well, this is a surprise."

"How are you doing, Grandmother?" Walt asked.

"Oh, very well I suppose," she answered.

They went inside and Walt tried to make conversation. After a few minutes of awkwardness, he asked his grandmother if she had done anything with the workshop.

"No, it's just like J. P. left it," she responded.

Walt then told her that he would be back in a few minutes. He wanted walk around some and go out to the shop.

The door creaked as Walt pushed it open. He went and stood in front of the old pew over near the wood stove where his granddaddy breathed his last breath. A tattered cushion was at one end of the bench where his granddaddy must have rested his head. A stack of periodicals was at the other end. They were all covered in dust. For the next several minutes, the weathered church pew became an altar as John Paul Williamson's grandson knelt reverently before it.

Once back on his feet, Walt looked at the heap of reading materials, presuming them to be shop manuals. He picked up the dusty one on top, and he realized that it was a Sunday School quarterly. Curiously, he began examining what was beneath it. He found other religious publications and an old hymn book.

Two books were also in the stack. Walt recognized them immediately. One was *Profiles in Courage*, by John F. Kennedy, and the other was *The Secret of Happiness*, by Billy Graham. He had given both of them to his granddaddy.

All of a sudden, it hit Walt. The day his granddaddy died was not the first time that he had read his Bible in this spot. This place was his sacred sanctuary.

"Have you been to see your parents?" Walt's grandmother asked when he came back in the house.

"No, I'm headed that way next," he answered.

"Todd should be home by now," she added.

Without any warning, Ethel Williamson's demeanor changed. "Walt, I can't believe how you've turned your back on your family. Emma Louise checks on her parents a time or two a week, but they almost never hear from you."

He did not know what to say, so he just waited to see what was next.

"You would think that you would be more grateful for the way you were raised. Your Granddaddy Williamson would turn over in his grave if he knew the way you are acting."

"Grandmother, I'm sorry you feel that way. I promise I will try to do better."

As Walt got in his car to head on over to his parents' house, he paused and took one deep breath, and then another. "Do tell, Othell, can you believe that? It's my fault that my folks don't want to have anything to do with me."

He had to agree with his grandmother about one thing, though. His granddaddy would not be happy at all about the way things were going in the Williamson family.

Soon, Walt found himself again at the front door of the only home he could remember before he went off to college. "Well, look what the dogs drug in . . . that the cats wouldn't have," Todd said when he opened the door. Walt felt certain the man received a phone call between the time that he left his grandmother's house and when he arrived there.

Todd looked up at Walt's six foot two inch frame towering over him. Almost completely bald himself, the man eyed the boy's full head of dark hair.

"To what do we owe the pleasure of your highness' visit?" he added sarcastically. The man made no effort to contain the disdain that he had for the unwelcome person standing on his porch.

"You Toad," Walt almost said aloud. Instead, he just brushed by the man and mumbled, "I'm here to see Mother."

As he went through the living room, the jade toad was still perched in its spot on the mantle. He looked in the kitchen as he went by. There was no sign of a swan anywhere. "Told you, Othell," he muttered to himself.

Maude was on the back porch. She grimaced when Walt came out. This was the first time she had seen him since the swan incident. She braced herself.

A vehicle started up, and Walt knew that Todd left. He asked his mother about her health condition. She filled him in with the barest of details.

Walt asked his mother to keep him informed about the developments. She half-heartedly agreed. He knew that if he found out anything it would be through her parents.

Since they had some privacy, Walt wondered if this would be a good time to bring up D-V Day in a more direct way. He decided that his mother had too much on her mind at that time to broach the subject with her. No one had mentioned it, but everyone was very much aware that cancer ran in his mother's family.

As Walt left, Maude breathed a big sigh of relief. Still, she knew a day of reckoning was yet ahead. She could think of nothing to do in the meantime to prepare herself for it. When she tried to pray, she did not even know what to ask for.

Exile

As Walt pulled out of the yard, he knew that he did not have time to get to Ephesus before dark. Mrs. Neumann promised to leave the light on for him.

As he headed toward North Carolina, he had a lot on his mind. His grandmother confirmed what he had long felt. Somehow, everything was his fault. He thought back to the times Todd beat him on a regular basis. As a boy, he knew he was being punished for something other than the trumped up charges that Todd used to justify the whuppin's. Walt was now the whole family's whipping boy.

On up the road, the colors were almost as brilliant as last year's in the higher elevations. The peak of the leaf season was only about a week away. When the weary driver saw the city limit sign, it was a couple of hours past sundown. Ephesus was still buzzing with witches and goblins, but some candles had already burned out in a few jack-o'-lanterns. Older kids were roaming the neighborhoods now. Walt drove carefully.

He was exhausted when he took his key and unlocked the basement door. Sitting on the little dinette table was a black walnut birthday cake.

The weekend was coming up, and Walt was hoping for some quality time with Hannah. He had planned his trip that way. He really did want to discuss some things with her. He called her at school on Friday and left a message.

Hannah was planning to go to Asheville to do some early Christmas shopping the next day. She invited Walt to go along with her. She picked him up at 9:00 a.m. The first part of the trip was consumed with the two of them filling each other in on what had been going on.

Hannah told Walt how sorry she was that things did not work out with Michelle. He confided in her that he had developed some strong feelings for the nurse, and that he was disappointed when she backed out on making the move to Columbus.

Phillip was still adjusting to his disability, but some of their initial optimism was now waning. Hannah said that her husband wanted to go with her to Asheville, but on his own, he decided that he would hold her back too much.

The school counselor was finally settling into some routines with her work. Meanwhile, what was expected of her was constantly changing, as new rules and regulations were being imposed from the higher ups.

Asheville had recently built its first shopping mall, and they made their way to it. It was small compared to the ones Walt had been to in the D.C. area. He felt strange out in public with Hannah. Sensing that she was afraid she might run into somebody she knew, he offered to do some shopping on his own. They agreed to meet for lunch in the food court.

Over burgers and fries in a crowded mall was not the setting Walt found conducive to the kind of conversation he wished to have with Hannah. They both showed each other their purchases. At three, they met at her car to start the hour or so drive back to Ephesus.

"Fasten your seatbelt, Walt," Hannah instructed, as she backed out of the parking space. Since neither of them had grown up doing this, it was still hard to get used to the little ritual.

"Hannah, can I ask you a question?" Walt asked, as they pulled up to the first red light.

"Walt, you know you can ask me anything . . . well just about anything," she answered.

"How did you come to be who you are?" he phrased it.

After ten years of marriage, Hannah's parents were unable to have children. She was in foster care when they adopted her at six months of age. As it sometimes happens, however, within a year after they got her, her mother was pregnant. Two years later, a baby sister then followed Hannah's little brother.

"I don't know how to answer that, Walt," she responded. "I have just always been who I am."

He was already aware that Hannah knew nothing about her birth parents, and that the records were sealed. "Do you ever wonder about the two people who gave you your genetic makeup?" he asked next.

"Walt, I would be lying if I said I had never thought about that. When I was a little girl, I used to imagine all kinds of things. But I never ever thought that my father abandoned me. Somewhere in my soul, I presumed that he did not know about me.

At one time, I felt certain my mother died giving birth to me. That was just a gut feeling. At other times, I could put her into all kinds of other difficult scenarios."

"How did all of this play out with your adoptive parents?" he inquired next. "And how did you feel about your siblings? Did any of this make any kind of difference?"

"I really love my parents. I never doubted that they wanted me. Sometimes I felt they tried a little too hard, like they had something to prove, though," Hannah answered.

"As far as my brother and sister are concerned, they are my brother and my sister. I could always see traits in them that I do not have. They were, and still are, closer to each other than they are to me. I saw nothing unusual about this."

After a moment of reflection, Hannah continued. "Walt, somewhere back there, I'm not sure where, I just had to be me. I always knew that my parents had my best interests at heart. They just did not always know what was best for me. I did not want to hurt or disappoint them, but I had to be true to myself. Does any of this make sense?"

She already knew the answer to that question.

"As I got older, I kept trying to gain a perspective. When I studied reproduction in a health class, I was fascinated with genetics. Each egg in a female has a different makeup of chromosomes. The thousands of sperms swimming toward that egg have a diverse, almost infinite, combination of genes. So the way I figured it, regardless of what male and which female contributes the DNA, every human is different, and should celebrate his or her uniqueness."

Hannah had just said in her own words what Walt concluded while watching "Dr. Zhivago." She just got to that point a little ahead of him.

He was right on the verge of telling her about D-V Day, but they were coming into Ephesus. Time always seemed to go by so rapidly when the two of them were in their element.

Walt decided to go through Etowah to see his new nephew before he went back to Columbus. He called Emma Lou, and she said that they would take him to the country club for dinner. He protested that he might not have the proper attire, but she said for him to wear what he had. Although many of the men would still have on their business suits from work, other folks would be dressed casually. Andrew would meet them there.

Walt followed the directions his sister gave him. The two-story brick house with fancy landscaping was located in a new subdivision with a guard gate. The Singeltons were obviously doing well.

Before they left for the club, Little Ben slept most of the time. Emma Lou offered her brother a guest room if he wished to spend the night. Something told him not to get his things out of the car just yet.

He mostly listened at dinner as his sister and Drew filled each other in on their days. People were socializing, but Walt noticed that little effort was made to introduce him.

When they got back to the house, Drew took the babysitter home. Walt and Emma Lou had hardly taken their seats when she said she was glad that he came by, because there were some things she wanted to discuss with him. He detected a condescending tone.

To begin with, Emma Lou was very troubled that, as she put it, "You were so ugly to your grandmother the other day."

"What are you talking about?" Walt asked incredulously.

"When you went by to see her when you were in Mason," she added, as though he knew exactly what she meant.

This was baffling to Walt. His grandmother was a little haughty with him, but he treated her with no disrespect. He knew there was no way he could defend himself, though. In his sister's mind, that would only add to his transgressions.

Emma Lou then proceeded to criticize Walt sharply for the way he treated their parents. According to her, he was very insolent with his father.

She accused her brother of trying every way he could to show the man up, and to put him down. His sister said that it was obvious to all of them how much disdain he had for the man.

Again, Emma Lou's mind was made up. Nothing he could say would make any difference. Well, almost nothing, but he was not going there.

Walt's sister registered her greatest contempt for him regarding their mother. She stated, as though it were common knowledge, that Maude's health problems were brought about because of what he had put her through all his life. Her body was weakened by the stress, and thus, she became susceptible to disease. According to Emma Lou, if their mother were unable to make a full recovery, it would all be on his shoulders.

Adding insult to injury, Walt was told that he neglected his mother. He almost never went by to see her, or called and checked on her.

Wow! Walt was not only the family's whipping boy, but he had become the clan's scapegoat as well. His Grandmother Williamson hinted at it. Emma Lou had just put it all in perspective, and rubbed his nose in it.

When he got up to leave, she asked Walt if he was not going to spend the night. He said that he really needed to get on down the road.

"Othell," he said, as Dolly pulled out into the highway. "I do not even know that person my sister was describing. If I did, I'm certain we could never be friends."

Walt Williamson had every right to be insulted by what his sister told him. What he was unable to comprehend at the time, though, was the ring of truth in what Emma Lou said. Maude's life had not been free of tension since the day he was born. It had undoubtedly taken its toll on her health.

Furthermore, he was indeed the reason for much of the rancor and discord in his family. However, it had little to do with anything that he had ever done or said. It was all just because of who he was.

I Took Care of It

The first thing Walt noticed as he entered his apartment was the light blinking on his answering machine. There were five messages. Two were work related. Three were from Michelle.

The first two just said to call her as soon as possible. Walt sensed some anxiety in her voice. Then, the third was more specific. Michelle said to call her, day or night, no matter what the hour, when he found the message. He looked at the clock. It was a little past midnight.

From the shakiness in her voice when she answered, he could not tell if Michelle was asleep when the phone rang, or if she was just distraught about something. He apologized for not calling earlier, and he told her where he had been. He then asked her what was wrong.

"Walt, I am so sorry," she began. He could tell that she was crying.

"I shouldn't have called you," she said between sobs.

"I took care of it, and I shouldn't have bothered you."

"Michelle, would you please tell me what's going on?"

"Walt, I am so ashamed," she continued, now weeping profusely.

"What are you talking about, Michelle?"

"The baby, Walt . . . our baby."

Before Walt had a chance to respond to what Michelle had just told him, she hung up. He dialed her number and got a busy signal. He tried again several times during the next hour with the same result.

He started second-guessing himself. Trying to process what she had said, did he hesitate too long? Were there signs that he missed before he left Washington? Should he have seen this coming and been ready? He wanted to go to D.C. immediately, but he had just used up all of his leave time.

Every day for the next two weeks, Walt left at least one message on Michelle's answering machine. Then, one day he got a recording saying that number was no longer in service.

Walt so much wanted to comfort Michelle. She should not be going through this alone. At the same time, he was angry with her. That was his baby, too. Did he have no say so in this?

Walt asked Emma Lou to keep him informed about their mother's impending surgery. When he heard nothing, he left several messages on her answering machine. None of his calls was returned. He called his parents' house and got no answer.

Grandma King told Walt that the doctors changed their minds. As a precaution, they thought it best to go ahead and remove the breast. The next time he called, Grandpa said that Maude was home from the hospital, and that the prognosis was good. Walt sent his mother a get-well card telling her that he was thinking about her, and that he loved her.

Christmas at Ft. Benning was a lot different from the holiday season at Walter Reed. Much of the army brass abandoned ship to go home for the holidays. Walt was given a ten-day leave. Mrs. Neumann was thrilled when he called. She said that having him home for Christmas was the best present she could remember. For Christmas dinner, she baked a turkey with all the trimmings. She loved it when he helped her in the kitchen.

Walt asked if there was something special that she wished to do while he was there. In her own modest and unassuming way, she did indicate that she would love to go see her ailing sister who lived in the next county. He was honored to drive her.

It felt good to be back in the mountains. Snow was visible in some of the higher elevations. Over the next few days, there was also a good possibility of snowfall in Ephesus. On the Sunday after Christmas, big flakes started falling, and falling, and falling. Before it stopped, almost six inches of the white stuff was on the ground.

Walt built a snow-woman in the yard for Mrs. Neumann. She got her old Kodak out and took pictures of it. She said only Walt would think of making Frosty into a female. She took one photo of him kissing his snow angel.

Dolly was barely able to get through the streets later that afternoon. Only a blizzard would prevent Walt from keeping his date with Hannah, however. They met in the Kroger parking lot where they sat and talked for a while.

What Walt wanted to discuss the most was the one thing that he knew he could not bring up. He was still grieving for his unborn child that he would not ever be able to hold. He would never see its eyes light up on Christmas morning.

Abruptly, Walt started up Dolly. "Where are we going?" Hannah inquired.

"Just for a ride," he answered. "Let's go walking in a winter wonderland." About three miles out of town, the roads were becoming almost impassable. He pulled the car over. With neither saying a word, both front doors flew open and snowballs began to fly.

Well, I'll Be Damned

Walt got along reasonably well with his professional colleagues at Ft. Benning. Then, there was the receptionist, Ms. Coalson. He decided that this woman considered it her patriotic duty to make sure that there was always some kind of hullabaloo to deal with at all times. While the others on the staff were all married, he was still rather naïve regarding the not so weaker sex.

When things got a bit touchy, they introduced Walt to something called PMS. He jokingly told his associates that he thought the abbreviation stood for pre-marital sex.

One staff meeting was particularly contentious. As Ms. Coalson left the room, the others stayed behind.

"I think that woman is a DOB," Walt injected.

"A what?" the others asked in unison.

"A daughter of a bitch," he explained. "If women are so insistent on having equal rights, then it is time that we recognize the female equivalent of SOB," he added.

The others agreed that maybe Walt had a point.

He was not through yet. "I guess that would make a DOB a dastard," he added.

It was time to get back to some serious work. Each of them, nonetheless, had difficulty walking past the receptionist with a straight face.

As Walt reached the halfway point in his military commitment, he realized that he must start considering what he was going to do after his discharge. He thought about going back to school and working on a doctorate. He was just as eligible for the GI Bill as any veteran was.

Once again, though, some graduate school would have to stretch its standards to find a way to fit him in. Perhaps with his Master's Degree, he could teach at the undergraduate level. On the other hand, he could go into private practice as he originally planned. He had certainly beefed up his credentials. The lieutenant would just wait and see what doors opened.

After moving to Columbus, Walt was not much of a social animal. In a military town, there were not nearly enough females to go around for the many footloose foot soldier boys on the prowl. He went out with a secretary down the hall from his office a few times.

On Mother's Day weekend 1969, Walt had the strangest sensation. As he pondered it, he realized that it had nothing to do with his own mother. His thoughts went to Michelle, but the connection he felt was with the child that she had conceived. Walt had no strong feelings about reincarnation. He had never given much thought to when a life actually becomes a being. Yet, he could feel the presence of his baby.

From somewhere deep inside him, he always knew that she was a girl. He tried to imagine himself holding his little daughter. Then, it hit him. He did the math. This would have been just about the time that the baby would have been born.

Walt did not mind winters in Columbus, but the old mountain boy detested the hot humid summers. With some time off in July, he headed north. He thought about bypassing Mason, but somewhere back there he had added something else to his lore. "If you are damned if you do, and damned if you don't, do." Anyway, he needed to check on his Grandpa and Grandma.

Walt wanted the satisfaction of knowing that he had done his part. He could be true to himself, regardless of the actions of others. He figured that it is better to try to get forgiveness for what he did wrong, than it is to try to justify why he did nothing at all.

When he went by to see his mother, he could detect nothing different in her demeanor. He told her how happy he was that things went well after her surgery. She did mention that the chances of a recurrence are much greater for those who have a history of cancer in their families.

Maude mentioned Todd several times, but not once did she refer to him as "your father." Walt noticed that. She disclosed that Todd could retire from the government soon based on his years of service. He was considering giving up the mail route since she was not helping him anymore. She had no idea what he would do then, but she actually confided in Walt that she hoped that her husband would not be around the house all day under her feet.

That was the warmest Walt could remember his mother being with him in several years. He got really close to bringing up D-V Day, but he decided not to at that time. He fully intended to discuss this matter with her at some point, though.

Maude breathed another sigh of relief when he left. She felt proud of herself for taking charge of the conversation and not giving Walt an opening before he had to leave.

When Walt got to Ephesus, he learned that Phillip Parker was in Warm Springs, Georgia, for a month of rehabilitation. That was not far from Columbus where the lieutenant was stationed. Phillip's progress had not only stalled, but it appeared to be regressing. While Walt was not pleased with this news, he was at the same time excited about the possibility that he and Hannah might have some quality time together without her having to make excuses.

On Saturday, July 20, 1969, she came over to his basement apartment. It was a forgone conclusion now that Mrs. Neumann was not going to rent it again.

The little black and white television set did not get much of a picture. The two of them watched all afternoon as Apollo 11 positioned itself for the first manned lunar landing. They held their collective breaths, and tightly onto each other, when the module touched down in the Sea of Tranquility at just after 4:00 p.m.

They had no way of knowing how long it was going to be before the door would open, and Neil Armstrong would become the first man to walk on the moon. They certainly had no idea that it would be almost seven hours later. Hannah said several times that she needed to go. She just could not pull herself away from the screen.

About eight, they ordered a pizza from the new hut that offered free delivery. Finally, at 10:56 p.m., Walt and Hannah tried not to wake Mrs. Neumann with their celebrating as Armstrong's image appeared on the screen.

Reaching for her purse just before midnight, Hannah said this time she really did have to go. Walt told her that she could stay the night if she wanted to. Hannah intimated that she talked to Phillip every Sunday morning around 8:30. He waited for her call at a payphone in the lobby. She needed to get home.

As Walt turned the TV off to go to bed, he felt exhilarated, exhausted, and exasperated. It seemed light years since he heard President Kennedy say the country would land a man on the moon within the decade. The United States of America did it with several months to spare. Amidst all the tumult and turmoil everywhere else, the country finally had reason to rejoice.

"Othell," Walt said as he put his head on the pillow, "mankind just made one giant leap. But when it comes to my love life, I can't even get one foot off the ground."

When Walt came through Adamsonville on his way up, he went by the college. His old adversary, Dean Rowell, was actually glad to see him. They exchanged a few war stories. The dean admitted that he longed for the good old days with the likes of Walt, in comparison to what he was contending with now.

The former student stopped short of thanking Dr. Rowell for the letter of recommendation that he sent to Ephesus State. That was the dean's little secret.

The people over in the Psychology Department likewise enjoyed keeping up with their graduates. One face was missing, however. Miss

Robbins departed the same year Walt did. She went to the University of North Carolina to complete work on her doctorate. Walt learned that she had earned her Ph.D. She had accepted an assistant professorship at the Outer Banks State University near Wilmington, beginning in the fall of 1969.

On an impulse in late November, he placed a person-to-person call to Dr. Robbins. After the operator jumped through several hoops, she finally got the departmental receptionist who took a message. She said that she would have Dr. Robbins return the call.

The assistant professor was delighted to hear from Walt. She invited him to come and visit her. He told her that his first chance would be during the Christmas holidays. Dr. Robbins said that she was not leaving the area during the break, and for him to come on up.

Walt decided to go to the Outer Banks area first, and then on to Ephesus afterward. Dr. Robbins invited him to stay in her home so they could have more time together.

As he was discussing with his former major professor the dilemmas he was facing regarding his future, she made a suggestion. Since so many veterans were enrolling in colleges on the GI Bill, maybe he should consider applying for a position counseling these irregular students. She even offered to use whatever influence she might have to get him on the faculty of OBSU, if he was interested. Walt had not thought of anything like that.

That night, Dr. Robbins was going to a holiday open house at the home of the dean of students. She invited her houseguest to be her honored guest. The dean was intrigued with Walt's work counseling veterans. He encouraged him to apply for a position that would be open in the fall at this university.

The school acted quickly in processing Walt's application. They did not want a person of his caliber and experience to get away. Besides that, the Veteran's Administration would pay half of his salary. Walt was offered a contract, and he gladly accepted.

Lieutenant Walter O. Williamson received his discharge from the United States Army on August 26, 1970. On September 1 of that same year, he was on the staff of the Outer Banks State University as a counselor working primarily with veterans going back to school, courtesy of their Uncle Sam.

On the move from Columbus to coastal Carolina, it was time to bid Dolly adieu and to say hello to Mary Lou. Earl insisted that Walt get a top of the line Toyota, but his nephew held out for one thing. Mary Lou would have a little help when it came time to shift the gears. He picked out a blue one, almost the color of the ocean. Mary Lou was named after one of his Grandma's sisters, the spirited one who was always the life of the party.

WOWs

Walt had never been one to keep a journal. He admired those who did. He often encouraged his clients to write down their thoughts and feelings. Theoretically, this would help them get a better handle, and then a grip, on their particular situation.

Since he was turning over a new leaf, so to speak, he decided to start scribing some of his own random notions. He knew all along what he would call the notebook. On the front, he wrote in big letters, WOWs.

Walt's first entry was, "When you compromise who you are, to play somebody else's game . . . everyone loses." He was influenced in this assertion by Transactional Analysis, a trendy pop psychology at the time that identified the different kinds of games people play. Little did he know at the time he penned those words, they would become something akin to his mantra.

While that little formula certainly did not cover everything, Walter O. Williamson discovered that it went a long way in explaining why people do and say the things they do. It also shed light on the predictability of the oft-negative outcomes of some behavior. The way Walt saw it, winners were individuals who were true to themselves, and losers were those who compromised who they were trying to please others.

At OBSU, Walt found himself once again a human being trying to stay afloat in a sea of human doers. In this academic setting, merit was so often measured by recognized accomplishment. Those who had received some acclaim for their achievements seemed to get their identity all tied up in what they had done, and not in who they were.

As a counselor for incoming veterans, one of Walt's responsibilities was to help them shift gears from a military mindset, to one where they must think for themselves. He found his work challenging, but not particularly rewarding.

Walt did enjoy the times he spent exploring the barrier islands. He was in awe of how the ocean had carved out such masterpieces along the North

Carolina coast. As a being, he became more and more aware of his connectedness with a larger sense of Being. He continued to spend the greater part of his free time alone.

From sunrises over the shining sea, to misty mountain mornings – Mary Lou made regular jaunts back and forth to his other home in North Carolina. Walt shifted her up and geared her down. The car and driver varied their routes on these excursions, usually going one way and then coming back another.

Walt relished the times he could spend with Mrs. Neumann. She always wanted a full accounting of his activities. Likewise, he also had to find out what was going on with her. She always insisted that it was not much.

He used his how-to skills to keep things patched up around the house. He also took her on outings, since she was getting less sure of her own driving skills.

One day, Mrs. Neumann asked Walt to drop her off at her lawyer's office. She said that it would not take long. She just needed to sign some papers that her attorney had been working on.

Walt waited in the car. When the woman came out, he noticed a little devilish grin on her face. "What?" he asked jokingly.

"Oh nothing," she responded, as she looked forward feigning a straight face.

Time with Hannah was usually limited and guarded. On some trips, he did not get to see her at all. During the second Christmas holidays after he moved back to North Carolina, the two of them did get to spend almost a full day together. Students at her school made little care packages for the residents of an orphanage in Charlotte. Hannah volunteered to deliver them. She asked Walt to go along for the ride.

During breaks in his work, Walt often gravitated to the Psychology Department. He met most of the faculty members. He and Dr. Robbins sometimes had lunch together. It was at one of those midday meetings that she wondered if he might be interested in doing a guest lecture on identity formation for one of her classes.

Dr. Robbins said that she did not want Walt to present material on the various textbook theories. She suggested that he rather share with the students his own concepts of identity. He had given her a copy of his master's thesis, and she really liked what she saw.

The more Walt thought about it, the more fascinated he was with the idea. Dr. Robbins assured him the first time he went before the class that he would not have to worry about filling in the period. While he was not convinced, he was startled when the bell rang announcing the end of the class.

When he could get out of his office, Walt became a regular in Dr. Robbins' classes. He even covered for her on occasions when she had to be away.

A university campus could be like a monastery, isolating its teachers and students alike from the happenings out in the real world. That was not the case at all during the 1970s. Student activists brought the world to the campus.

Walt Williamson usually found a way to be right in the middle of things. As a war baby, he had a distinct perspective. He was raised with old world values. He knew the importance of traditional concepts like thrift, respect, discipline, authority, and accountability.

Yet, he could also see how those with influence and reach could abuse their power. The disadvantaged were often disenfranchised for the benefit of those in control. Walt had sympathy for those with grievances because they have been denied their basic civil and human rights.

As he perceived it, it was up to his age group to bridge what was being dubbed "the generation gap." Walt saw himself with one foot planted squarely on each side of the great divide. He could not come down hard on those earnestly looking for a way to make a better world. He could embrace many of the ideals of the revolutionaries, without endorsing the excesses that were earning for them such negative reputations.

Walt emerged as the unofficial voice for the entire university counseling staff. During campus disturbances, the administrators routinely sent him out as a mediator to try to bring some semblance of resolution. His proposals were rarely greeted with much credence or credibility by those on either side. He found that it was not easy being a peacemaker. The one in this role was often caught in the middle of those entrenched and disinterested in any position other than their own.

Walt struggled amid the growing tensions enveloping the country. In his own personal life, he wondered if he had just been born at the wrong time.

Sometimes he imagined himself a wilderness pioneer. He identified with Henry David Thoreau's *Walden Pond*, but he made note that the writer/philosopher only stayed at his retreat during a small segment of his life. Walt was also frustrated that his own being was so often dominated by calendar and clock.

In his work with students, the counselor was equally discouraged. These young people were trying to decide what they were going to *do* with their lives. Regrettably, most of them had not yet made any serious attempts to figure out *who* they were.

It appeared to Walt that most college students were doing nothing more than carve out little comfort zones where they could work within the system. They seemed eager to become part of the rat race so they could start enjoying more and more of the amenities of affluence. Somewhere about that time, he first heard the expression "the me generation."

After a counseling session on a late spring day in 1975, Walt walked a student out of his office. The receptionist handed him a note. The funeral home in Ephesus was trying to get in touch with him. No matter what, this was not good news.

It was about Mrs. Neumann. She had passed away in her sleep. Walt knew about the agreement she had with her sister that the two of them would talk on the phone every morning to check on each other. When the sister called and got no answer, she knew something was wrong.

Mrs. Neumann had gone to the mortuary a year or so earlier and made her funeral plans. That was why Walt got the call. Her minister was to be in charge of the memorial service, but she wanted him to give the eulogy. He was honored, but at the same time overwhelmed. Walt struggled to find just the right words to say about the woman who had become more like a mother to him than his own.

As he delivered his tribute, he could not tell how it was being received. The friends and relatives were attentive and respectful. Then at the cemetery, a line of people formed wanting to have a word with him. The responses were unanimous. He had delivered one of the most exceptional eulogies that these folks had ever heard.

Walt noticed one man in a business suit not in the line, but also in no hurry to leave. After the others had moved on, the professional looking gentleman approached him. The man apologized for needing to talk business at a time like this, but he knew that Walt would not be hanging around very long.

He introduced himself as Mrs. Neumann's attorney. The lawyer informed Walt that in her soon to be probated will, she had left her house with all of its furnishings to him.

He could just see Mrs. Neumann smiling down on him and saying, "Gottcha, didn't I?"

One other person was waiting for him in the parking lot. "Oh, Walt, she was so proud of you," Hannah said, as she reached for him and gave him a supportive hug. He then shared with her what the attorney had just told him.

Going back to Ephesus would never be the same without Mrs. Neumann. Even so, Walt now had a second home in the mountains. He would be moving upstairs.

Never Mind

Walt had not been back to Mason in several months. It concerned him that his next trip might also be for a funeral. His grandparents were not getting any younger. That had nothing to do, though, with why he did go back during his spring break in 1977. It was, however, a call from his Grandpa that sent him scrambling.

Maude's cancer had returned. The outlook was not so encouraging this time. She had already taken all the radiation she could have. Some other experimental drugs were now available that were showing some promise of keeping tumors in check. In some instances, they were actually reducing them. The doctors admitted, though, that they still had much to learn about chemotherapy.

As Walt was driving into the yard, another vehicle was leaving. One of the women waved to him. She looked vaguely familiar.

This time he did not knock. As he entered the house, he called out to his mother. When he came into her room, she looked startled. She also looked weak and frail. He could see for himself that the malignancy was aggressive.

No one else was around. Walt held back. If there was anything that his mother wished to tell him, she must surely know this was the time. She mostly just lay back with her head on the pillow, wishing for him to leave.

As Walt got up to go, he asked his mother if she was having much company. She did respond to his question. She said a few friends had come by. He inquired about the car leaving when he was arriving. Maude winced. She then said that it was two of her old high school classmates who came together to visit her.

"I wish I had gotten here a few minutes earlier," he said. "I would have enjoyed meeting them."

Maude was caught totally off guard when Millie called and asked if she and Maggie could come by to see her. She had not heard from either of them in years. The house was certainly not spotless, but it would have to do. They could just leave their white gloves at home.

Except for Walt's graduation when they were all in the same auditorium, The Three Musketeers had not been together since Donald Vaughn's memorial service twenty years earlier. Maude had seen Millie a time or two, but she had heard nothing from Maggie.

Maude worked hard to make herself look presentable. When her two old school chums arrived, she ushered them into the living room. Neither visitor had ever been in her home. The "grotesque" jade frog on the mantel was the immediate object of conversation. Maggie looked around. She saw numerous pictures of Emma Lou and her family, but none of Walter.

For the next several minutes, the three of them tiptoed around the obvious. Millie told them all about her children and grandchildren. Maude bragged about little Ben.

Maggie was in the house where her only child had grown up. She could feel his presence all around her. While the others were talking, she was imagining her little Walter running through the house and playing in the yard. She could just see him getting off the school bus, and then going to his room to do his homework.

Eventually, Millie asked Maude how she was doing. She put on a good front, but the other two could see for themselves that the prognosis was not good.

It was soon time for The Three Musketeers to say their tearful goodbyes. Without having to say it, each was painfully aware that this would be the last time all of them would be together. Something else was left unsaid, too. Walt's name was never mentioned.

Maude went with them to the door. Millie gave her a hug, and said that she would be back soon.

Maggie then reached for Maude. As she pulled her tight, she leaned down and whispered, "Thank you" in her ear.

A shudder went through Maude's body. She broke free from the embrace, and then turned to go back in the house. Maggie started to go after her, but Millie stepped in her path. She took her by the arm and said, "Maggie, it's time to go."

Maude made her way to the bed. She listened for the car to start up so she would know they were gone. What she did not hear was another vehicle driving up.

Maggie was stunned by Maude's rejection of her. The whole visit had been very unsettling, but she never expected that reaction at the end. The two mothers of Walter could not even bring up his name. He was everywhere, but he was nowhere to be seen.

Then, out of nowhere, he appeared on the scene. As they were fastening their seatbelts, Millie mentioned that another car was coming up the drive. Maggie was so conflicted that she just wanted to get out of there without having to make conversation with anyone else.

As Millie put the car in reverse, the other vehicle pulled in with a North Carolina license plate. Maggie let out a gasp. It was her Walter. She had not seen him since his college graduation.

The woman started fumbling to unfasten her belt to go to him, but Millie drove away. Maggie waved out the window as he was getting out of his car. It sent a thrill through her soul when he waved back.

After Walt left, Maude wished that he had gotten there before the other Musketeers left. She imagined unburdening herself and handing the boy back over to his mother. Maybe then, she could just die in peace.

Maude considered everything about her life a failure. She was coerced into marrying a mama's boy before she had any chance to figure out what she wanted in life. Her husband seemed incapable of love and affection. He actually admitted to her later that he only married her and impregnated her trying to avoid the military.

The daughter that Maude adored so much turned out to be a daddy's girl. It was obvious to the sick woman that Emma Lou only checked on her mother for appearance's sake, and out of duty and obligation.

Two years into her ill-fated marriage, Maude was then pressured into taking and raising another woman's child. That sealed her doom. From then on, she had no life of her own. Everything revolved around trying to keep a lid on the big secret not many in the family knew.

At no time did Maude ever have anyone with whom she could bare her soul. She had taken a one for all, and all for one vow, but she was then abandoned to bear her burden all alone. She had carried that load about as far as she could. The bitterness inside her was gnawing away at her spirit just as fast as the cancer was spreading throughout her body.

Now, Maude just wanted to die. She was ready to take it with her to her grave. What she failed to see was that the one person she could have turned to years ago was her own father just a half mile down the road.

Grandpa King could hardly contain his excitement when his grandson showed up. He really missed the boy. Grandma was in bed. Nobody else could possibly understand what it was like to have a daughter dying from cancer.

Walt decided to spend the night. This was cause for his grandma to get up and do some cooking. Grandpa said he wished that his grandson had come home a couple of days earlier. He was about to starve to death.

The next day on his way out, Walt knew that he had another stop to make. He had put this off as long as he could. He hoped that he would find his mother alone. Todd let him in the door, and then he promptly disappeared.

Maude once again seemed surprised to see him. He had not told her that he was staying in Mason overnight. After a few awkward moments, Walt knew what he had to do. This might be his last chance.

"Mother, may I ask you a question?" he finally managed to say.

"Well, I suppose so," she responded. "But you are the one with all the answers. So I do not know what I could possibly have to say that you would want to hear."

"Never mind," Walt said. He got up to leave.

The students would not be returning to the university after spring break for another couple of days. Walt had enough time to go by Ephesus and check on things. It was still too early to have to cut the grass. Limbs were in the yard, though, and some shrubbery needed pruning before it started putting out new growth.

This side trip provided a little break that his body needed. In the meantime, Walt's mind had a hard time taking a vacation. He was still pondering what happened in Mason. He feared that was the last time he would see his mother alive. He also found himself wondering about the man who might have been his father.

Then, more and more, his thoughts would turn to the child he never had who would be eight-years-old now.

Walt left several messages on Emma Lou's answering machine. He never heard back from her. About two months after the "never mind" visit,

Walt learned from his grandparents that his mother had gone into the hospital in Mountain Home. She was being sedated for pain.

One morning, his instincts told him that he needed to go. He arranged hurriedly for another counselor to take his appointments. Five hours later, he was in the county seat town.

Walt went to the information desk at the hospital to inquire of his mother's room number. The receptionist who said she had just come on duty could not find her name. The woman left her station for a minute, and then she returned. She wanted to know what his relationship was to Mrs. Williamson. When he informed her that he was Maude's son, she told him to wait right there.

A nurse with a most serious look on her face approached him from down the hall. She introduced herself, extending her right hand. Walt braced himself. The nurse then said that the family was called in the day before, and that his mother passed away just before midnight. The others were right then at the funeral home making arrangements for her funeral. She was so sorry that he did not get the message.

Walt got the message all right. He was no longer considered a part of the Williamson family.

Despite the shock and his runaway emotions, he had to make some immediate decisions. He decided not to go to the mortuary. That would be an intrusion. He drove rather to Mason and to his grandparents' house. He wondered what he would say, what he could do.

Both his Grandpa and his Grandma were in heavy mourning over the death of their daughter. He tried as best he could to comfort them. No one was there to console him.

Walt continued to agonize over what to do. He respected people's right to privacy. If his presence was not wanted, it would be disrespectful for him to intrude.

Late in the afternoon, one of Walt's basic core values made a decided shift. "If you are damned if you do, and damned if you don't, then don't." He had come to realize that even his best efforts were somehow always turned against him. The important thing for him was to be honest with himself, and to be true to his own convictions. The opinions of others mattered hardly at all.

Furthermore, if Emma Lou's assessment was correct, in the eyes of the Williamsons, Walt was responsible for Maude's death. Making an appearance would provide an occasion for them to treat him with contempt. He saw no need to give these folks opportunity to make him their scapegoat.

Before he headed on back up the road, Walt told his grandparents goodbye. Grandpa King seemed to understand, but Grandma said that it made no sense to her. Walt certainly did not have everything figured out yet either.

Walt's absence during the next couple of days did not go unnoticed. When Earl and Mary Beth inquired of his whereabouts, his grandpa said that it was best just to let the boy be.

Two of his mother's classmates also wished to see him. On the night of the visitation, one of them asked Emma Lou about Walt. His sister said that they had not seen or heard from him. Then, she went on. "I certainly hope that he does not have the nerve to show his face. If he does, my father and I have asked that he be turned away. If he persists, we have instructed the funeral director to call the law to enforce our wishes."

Both of these friends of Maude wanted so much to go to Walt. They ached to lie to rest the confusion and the unresolved longings of his broken heart, but they could not. They had taken a vow, and to break it now would reflect upon the one who had so graciously tried to lift the burden of one of them so many years ago.

On the lonely drive, the distraught son did his own mourning. By the time he got to his house near the ocean, Walt was convinced that he had done everything he could. He felt grief, but not remorse.

He just could not understand some things. He got along well with people. Even those who did not always agree with him respected him. He had the esteem and admiration of his coworkers. He had never been in any kind of trouble. He could not think of a thing he had ever done that brought disgrace to his folks.

Yet, Walt was banished and exiled by most of his own family. Todd's disdain he could understand. He just could not make any sense of his mother's rejection.

One thing in particular hit him hard. Whatever his mother meant on D-V Day, she had taken with her to her grave. Walt felt that his birth records were now just as sealed as Hannah's were.

On the long flight back to California, Maggie Hogan was a deeply troubled woman. She had made the trip two months earlier, wanting so much to make peace with Maude. She had been turned away. Now it was too late.

Maggie feared that Maude went to her grave with ill will toward her. So much, she wished to express appreciation to her dear, dear friend for raising her son. She wanted Maude to know how proud she was of the man that he had become, and to thank her for the role that she had played in his life.

Maggie felt so agonizingly helpless. Long ago, she had forfeited the right to be Walter's mother. Now, there was no way to make anything right.

A few days after his mother's funeral, it was time to turn the page in WOWs. Walt inscribed, "On the road of life, there are some interesting twists and turns. It is not always easy to distinguish between a detour that avoids a disaster, a debilitating sidetrack that leads one off course, and a departure from the beaten path that opens up a whole new world."

Walt felt stuck. His own life was sidetracked. He was ready to move on, but he had no idea where or which way he wanted to go.

It did not take Todd long to turn over a new leaf, either. Walt called to check on his grandparents every week or so. About nine months after his mother's death, his Grandpa told him that Todd had remarried.

They knew little about the woman, other than she was a widow of some means. Grandpa King told him he understood that Todd retired from the post office. He sold the house, and he moved in with his new wife. She lived near the country club in Mountain Home. Rumor had it that she was teaching her new husband how to play golf.

Walt wondered if he should send the newlyweds a congratulatory card. Of course, he would have to address it to Mr. and Mrs. "Toad" Williamson. He could always mail it anonymously. He actually looked in the card shop, but could not find one with a frog on it. Maybe that was just as well.

The Renaissance

Walt had heard the expression "reinvent yourself" several times. He had actually used it himself on occasion. Yet, something about that concept did not ring true. He understood redirecting himself, but not reinventing himself. The same person could just change course. Maybe reconnecting was a better way of putting it.

Regardless of how it was expressed, something about that notion was knocking on his door. Walt was tired of trying to counsel other people, even though that was what he was trained to do. He was becoming more and more impatient with students who could not figure things out for themselves.

Client-centered therapy might work if individuals really wanted to find solutions to their problems. If they were just looking for a way to thwart their accountabilities, though, it was inadequate. The therapist was convinced that those who take ownership of their lives need little professional help. On the other hand, those who have defaulted could not be coerced into assuming responsibility. They just found ways to rationalize and explain away their actions.

Walt had also grown weary of working within an institutional setting. That is why he did not go into teaching to begin with. Nevertheless, he now found himself trying to function within a framework fraught with troublesome turf wars.

His mother's death was the catalyst, igniting something inside that told him it was time to move on. He tendered his resignation to the Outer Banks State University, effective September 30, 1977. With no clear path ahead, he packed up what things he had and headed to Ephesus.

With no dependents, and with only modest rent to pay while he was working for OBSU, Walt had been building a little nest egg. Until he could get things sorted out, he could live indefinitely in the house that he inherited from Mrs. Neumann.

After taking a couple of weeks just to unwind, he went by Ephesus State to reconnect. He learned that Dr. Richard Fredrickson was finally going to retire. The distinguished old professional made two things abundantly clear. One was that he did not want his clients abandoned. The second was that it would take two people to replace him.

Dr. Fredrickson had already hired Lynda Boatwright, a recent female graduate who interned with him. However, the other position was still open. Walt paid Dr. Fredrickson a courtesy visit, and he was offered the job.

He had actually never counseled patients in private practice, what he planned to do from the outset. Still not convinced that he wanted to continue in this profession, Walt reluctantly made a two-year commitment with no promises after that.

Walt and Lynda had a couple of sessions together, trying to get a feel for what they would be doing. The clients already engaged were almost equally divided between children with behavioral issues and couples with marital problems. Since neither Walt nor Lynda was married, nor had any children, they decided that they might be the best-qualified counselors in the state.

Being this close to Hannah was more difficult than it was when many miles separated them. Walt did not want to cause her any problems. She had stopped discussing how things were at home, but he knew her resolve. He also understood small town gossip. They rarely saw each other, although they did talk on the phone occasionally.

Walt could honestly say that he had nothing but admiration for Phillip. While Hannah's husband was at Warm Springs, he decided that he was not going to be an I-N-V-A-L-I-D. Inspired by FDR, he determined to operate his own vehicle again. With some government assistance, he was able to get a car equipped with hand controls.

Phillip soon started working in an auto parts place. He was trained to keep up with the inventory. Within a couple of years, he was named manager of the franchise.

Walt did not know if Phillip was capable of fathering a child, or if the two of them just decided to forgo parenthood because of their circumstances. He could talk to Hannah about most things, but not that. Neither did he share with her that he might have been a father, and how he still grieved that loss.

As Walt was adjusting to his new work schedule, there were not always enough clients for two counselors. He was usually in the office first thing in the mornings, but this was when few people could schedule appointments. Lynda came in later. Both of them were busy most late afternoons. He yielded to Lynda when he could, since she was passionate about her profession.

In this setting, Walt found counseling to be somewhat effective. He worked with individuals to help them clarify why they were there. Together, they explored the potential alternatives available to them. Then, they scrutinized the consequences of each. The biggest challenge was getting patients to claim title to their circumstances, rather than blame others.

About a month into private practice, a new client was reluctant to open up. Walt gave the young woman some time to collect herself. With tears streaming down her face, she finally shared with him that she was trying to come to terms with something she had done. Three years earlier, she had an abortion and still could find no peace.

Walt struggled to get through the session. He then suggested that the client talk with Lynda about this issue. Perhaps another woman would be in a better position to help her.

When he got home, he could not get Michelle off his mind. After supper, he dialed the operator and asked for long distance information. Walt had no idea if his former roommate was still working at Walter Reed. The operator could find no listing for a Michelle Bell in the D.C. area. The only thing that was close was M. A. Bell, in nearby Fairfax, Virginia. He wrote down the number.

After pondering the situation for several minutes, he dialed it. He heard someone say, "Hello," but the connection was not good. Phone service away from large cities still left a lot to be desired.

"Is this the Bell residence?" Walt asked.

"Yes, it is," he heard the person say.

Not sure if he was talking to a child or an adult, he asked if this were the residence of Michelle Bell.

"Who is this?" the person on the other end asked.

Walt identified himself. He said that he once worked with a Michelle Bell, and that he was trying to get in touch with her. An awkward silence followed.

Afraid the person might hang up, he said, "Would you please take my name and number, and have Michelle call me?"

"Just a minute. Let me get something to write on," he was relieved to hear her say.

"Thank you," Walt said, before he hung up. No one ever called back.

The transformation was gradual. Walt began to release all the tightness that had been building inside him over the last few years. With no debts, it did not take much for him to live. For the first time since he was in high school, he found himself with some unstructured free time other than a few days off now and then.

Walt's library card was now one of his most prized possessions. He had time to read, and he had a lot of catching up to do. He soon discovered just how insatiable was his curiosity.

Concurrently, he started writing more. In addition to regular entries in WOWs, he dabbled a bit with some short stories. Like his journaling, he never shared them with anyone.

Walt then started reconnecting with the natural world that he knew as a lad. He was soon on a first name basis with the birds that came to his feeder. He talked to the deer when they strolled through the yard. In fact, he had his own patented greeting. "Hey deer," Walt called out to them, waving his hand. They acknowledged his presence by shaking their white tails.

He rediscovered the joys of walking in the woods. Walt began adding to his collection of field guides, learning to identify all kinds of plants and animals. The neophyte naturalist felt embarrassed that he was so ignorant of trees, and wildflowers, and butterflies, and insects, and reptiles. So much, he wished to learn, and he was ready to get going.

When he could arrange a half day out of the office, Walt began exploring more of the hiking trails in the nearby mountains. Half days stretched into two and three days off at the time. Walt also became fascinated with waterfalls. He could sit at their base mesmerized. When he was not at work, he quit wearing a watch.

After one daylong outing, Walt penned into WOWs, "Life is lived somewhere between the four C's – clatter, clutter, chaos, and confusion, and the four S's – solitude, serenity, simplicity, and sacredness."

Two concepts kept surfacing in his mind. One of them was *authenticity*. The lower life forms were all living out their destinies as authentic creatures. They lived in the moment – not shackled by the past, nor fretful about the future.

Walt felt remorse for the human race. His professional life was devoted to helping individuals discover their real selves. Yet, he grieved that society had evolved in such a fashion that in many ways it was designed to keep people from knowing who they were.

Rulers understood this concept well. It kept subjects in their place. Walt had been an eyewitness to how military leaders conscripted young men to go fight somebody else's war by depersonalizing them. In the modern world, he reasoned that it was easy to make consumers out of people by convincing them to be something they were not, and then enticing them to purchase things to fill the voids.

The other term Walt kept exploring was *synchronicity*. He came to appreciate more than ever how all of nature is interrelated and inner connected. He wrote in WOWs, "There is a vast difference between just going with the flow, and being a part of the flow." He then added, "Synchronicity is impossible apart from sanctity, solitude, and spontancity."

Walt had always been intuitive. He was now learning how to trust his instincts more. He was part of a universe alive with energy. The more he aligned himself with the ebb and flow, the more amazing were his insights and discoveries.

Walt Williamson would look back at this time in his life as his renaissance. It was his reawakening, his rebirth. He came to see that life is a journey, and not just a destination.

W.O.W. was a sojourner. His pilgrimage would take him into the inner depths of his own soul. It would also stretch out to points on the earth far removed from his now limited environs. He just did not know all of that yet.

Mrs. Neumann's bequest of her modest little abode proved to be one of the greatest gifts Walt ever received. It enabled him to get his life back.

Hold that Thought

One day when Walt went to the mailbox, he was surprised to see an envelope with a Mason, Georgia return address. Inside was an invitation to his twentieth high school class reunion. He had seen very few of his old classmates since he left for college. It would be nice to see what Alex Oldham and Julian Huffman had been up to. Walt really did need to go check on his grandparents, so he sent in his reservation immediately.

The event was planned around the 1982 Memorial Day weekend. Saturday corresponded to the exact date of the graduation two decades earlier. The reunion was going to be held in the school cafeteria, catered by a local restaurant owned and operated by Julian.

The invitation said the dress code was casual. Walt could not imagine that crowd coming any other way. He wondered if he would be the only one still not married.

Whoops and hollers were coming from all directions as the group was gathering. He might be the only classmate never to tie the knot, but he discovered that he was not the only one there alone. Some of the knots had come unraveled.

Walt found himself going through the buffet line with Mary Jo. Whether it was accidental or not, he was not sure. She did not have a ring on any finger of her left hand. Once seated, those at his table naturally started reminiscing and telling some rather tall tales regarding things that happened long ago.

Toward the end of the meal, someone pointed out that Walt had not really said much. Of all people, he would certainly have some interesting stories. As they urged him on, he asked Mary Jo if she remembered the incident in the gym when Mrs. Webster summoned him to the office. In fact, she did, and always wondered what happened.

The banter back and forth could not have been a better set up for Walt. Everybody was pumped and primed. He recounted what happened leading up to his invitation to accompany their homeroom teacher to the office. Of course, Walt was taking all kinds of liberties as he made the story sound like an epic struggle between male and female, good and evil.

One of the men at the table interrupted him. He stood up and got the attention of the entire group. He said that their classmate was telling a story too good not to share with the crowd. Again, with some prodding, Walt strolled to the microphone that was set up for the later proceedings.

He backed up and started over, embellishing the tale more than ever. The now retired Mrs. Webster was in the audience loving every minute of it. He recalled his fascination with rubber bands. This brought out a few catcalls from other males, relishing memories of their former expertise with spit wads.

The crowd roared with laughter as Walt recounted how Mary Jo yanked his shirttail out of his jeans. Acting it out as he went, he admitted that in retaliation he popped the girl on the derrière with a rubber band. He let the drama build as he described Mrs. Webster soon thereafter standing at the other end of the gym, pointing a finger at him, and then using it to summon him.

At that point, Walt looked toward the table where he had been sitting. The room grew quiet as he blew a kiss in the direction of Mary Jo. "That is exactly what I did that morning," he told the audience. "And then I told her to hold that thought, as I strolled across the gym toward Mrs. Webster. I assumed that she just needed my help with something."

Walt carefully set up the punch line. He had those at the gathering on the edge of their seats. He told his former classmates about having to empty his pockets on the principal's desk. In this revised version, he was packing a lot more stuff than in the original. He did mention rather nonchalantly the two rubber bands. He described how he tried to fib his way out of using one of them just minutes earlier.

He said that Mrs. Webster then read him the riot act. When he got to her assertion that she was not just paddling him for that lone incident, but for all the things she was certain that he had done, but was unable to catch him doing, Walt brought the house down.

As he was returning to his table, something caught him off guard. After almost a quarter century, he could still make Mary Jo blush. "Was M. J. still holding that thought?" he wondered.

After the event was over, everyone was saying tearful goodbyes and already looking ahead to the next reunion. Several classmates congregated around Walt, telling him how much they enjoyed his tale. Others said they still remembered his graduation speech.

Mary Jo sauntered over to him. She then leaned forward and gave him a little peck on the neck. At the same time, she pressed something into his hand.

After the last farewell, Walt started to his car. It was finally safe to open his fist and to see what Mary Jo had handed him. He was standing right there in front of God and everybody holding a key to Room 13 at the Mountain Home Inn. Now, Walt was the one with a red face.

The Calling

It was like a calling. Walt did not remember when he first started receiving it. It kept prodding him. The notion popped into his mind at the strangest times. He had never seen swans in the wild.

In the spring of 1983, Earl and Mary Beth came by Ephesus on one of their adventures. Walt mentioned to them that he was thinking about just getting in his car, and driving as far as he had to go to see swans in their natural habitat.

He shared with his uncle and aunt how he taught himself to read, and about the first fable that he read to himself. Mary Beth said she always knew that he was ahead of his reading level, and now she understood why.

Walt then conveyed that throughout his life, he always had a special affection for swans. He even got brave enough to say aloud that sometimes he felt like he, too, had been hatched in the wrong nest. He stopped short, however, of sharing with these two special people what happened in the kitchen that morning long ago.

"Walt, I have a better idea," Earl injected. "Sitting on my lot is a truck with a camper on it. It is probably worth about the same as your old Toyota. Just let me know when you are ready and I will swap even with you. Then, you can take a bed right along with you."

Earl then chided Walt for driving his vehicles into the ground. He said if everybody did that, he would go out of business. He added that when Walt got back, he could then trade in the camper for a new car. His uncle said that he could go ahead and get the truck title transferred into his name if he wanted him to.

At that point, Walt asked Earl something that he had wondered about several times. He wanted to know what happened to the maroon Dodge. Earl broke out into a big smile. "Walt, I should have told you, and I meant to. An old black preacher came by looking for a way to get around. I sold the Dodge to him for five hundred dollars. I still see him driving it every now and then."

Walt thought to himself, "What goes around comes around."

That trading talk was not what had him so excited, though. Somebody had just given Walt Williamson the little nudge that he needed to answer the call of the wild.

Over the next couple of weeks, Walt got his ducks in a row. He turned the counseling center over to Lynda. He arranged for a neighbor's kid to cut his grass, and to keep an eye on the place. He also went by the university where he shared with Dr. Fitzpatrick and Dean Harris what he was going to do.

Dr. Fitzpatrick encouraged him to take a copy of his master's thesis along with him, and to start considering expanding it into a book. This seemed like a strange request since he could not imagine any time along the way for writing, but he packed it anyway. Maybe just having it along for the ride would give him some inspiration.

His former major professor could envision that this voyage was going to be no ordinary vacation. Walt might not realize it at the time, but he was about to embark on an expedition that would not only take him to points far and wide, but also into the deepest depths of his own being.

Walt's upcoming excursion was bittersweet for Hannah. She was pleased that he was carefree enough that he could be venturesome. At the same time, she had resigned herself never to have that luxury.

On Mother's Day weekend 1983, Walt headed to Adamsonville in his last jaunt with Mary Lou. Since he had no idea how far he would go or when he would be back, she was loaded for bear with clothes and gear that he might need.

Walt took a little detour, went by Mason, and told his grandparents what he was going to do. Grandpa said that if he were ten years younger, he would go with him.

"You crazy old man, you would never get that far from home," Grandma snorted.

"Come here, woman, and give me some sugar," George sang out to Ruby, with that wily grin Walt had seen so many times before.

She turned and went in the kitchen in a bit of a huff. Both men laughed, but not very loud.

His new rig Walt called Nellie. Heading west, he was riding her off into the sunset. Earl told him that the truck had plenty of power to carry the load, but to be careful with the clutch.

According to his field guide, Walt had little hope of seeing swans until he got to British Columbia. He might even have to go as far as the Yukon Territory. Since he was leaving before school was out to get ahead of vacation traffic, he decided to make his trip a true adventure. There were many things to see between the southeastern United States and his eventual destination.

Walt thus headed west across Alabama, Mississippi, and Arkansas, before entering Oklahoma, and then across the Texas panhandle. He had never done any camping before, but he found the bed tolerable. He actually bought a few groceries and did some of his own cooking.

The rambling man pulled into a motel parking lot some evenings where he felt safe. He would then spend the night at a campground or RV park when he needed to dump and recharge.

Walt made his way across New Mexico and into Arizona where the deer and the antelope play. He set his sights on the Grand Canyon. It was at this magnificent national park that he first had the impression that there was no need to keep pressing along every day. He was in no hurry. He had only one agenda, and it had no deadline attached to it.

Walt checked into a camping area, and he stayed three days trying to grasp the marvels before him. As the sun slowly sank behind the rim of the canyon, sunset was a spiritual experience for the pilgrim. He had to agree with something he saw on a sweatshirt. "I dug the Grand Canyon."

Before he set out again, Walt reached for WOWs. He inscribed, "I cannot always tell you where I am going to be. However, I can assure you there are two places where you will not find me. There is no reason to look. One is where I am not wanted. And the other is where I do not want to be." A profound sense of liberation swept over him as he claimed ownership of those words.

After crossing the Hoover Dam, the next stop was Las Vegas. Because the decadence of Sin City was in such stark contrast to the natural wonders he was experiencing, Walt felt no need to hang around very long.

He then circled back a bit to go through Salt Lake City. Walt had a genuine respect for the Mormons, and he wanted to learn more about them while visiting their world headquarters. He chuckled when he recalled the history test question when he suggested that Henry VIII should have organized the Mormon Church a century earlier, to avoid having to get divorces from his wives unable to bear him an heir.

While in Salt Lake City, Walt was able to hear the famed Mormon Tabernacle Choir. What struck him was how much the musicians were in harmony. He wondered if their personal lives were also without discord.

Nellie got Walt to Yellowstone National Park by Memorial Day weekend. The drifter hitched his ride at different points within the vast park for three nights. He worshiped at the waterfalls. He just happened to be at Old Faithful right at dusk one evening with a brilliant sunset to the west, and a full moon rising simultaneously in the east. Wow!

He saw bison, elk, moose, and coyotes roaming freely. Some campers reported bear sightings, but the bruins stayed in hiding from Walt.

The drifter pointed Nellie toward Montana. The sky really did seem bigger. Walt saw his first glacier in Glacier National Park. He then made a run for the border. This was his first time outside the United States.

He camped along a creek in a park in British Columbia. After studying his road atlas, he wrote in WOWs, "The shortest distance between two points is not a straight line, if you are using a flat map." Then, he remembered something that a male nurse once told him at Walter Reed. "Just because you are straight, does not mean that you have to be narrow."

Getting money exchanged, and using different currency was a challenge. Even more so was converting miles into kilometers. Nevertheless, the gregarious Walt found the Canadian people warm, helpful, and welcoming.

When he crossed the Rocky Mountains in the lower 48, Walt found them very different from the Appalachians. It did not take long for him to figure out why they were so named. Now, he was going right along the spine of the Canadian Rockies. He made several passages back and forth across the continental divide. Nellie had to do a little straining at times to keep up the pace.

Glaciers were hanging out in clear sight of the highway. Walt even got out one time and he was able to walk right up to one. Waterfalls that people would drive a whole day to see elsewhere were every few hours along the way. With so much to see, it was hard to take it all in. One thing he had not yet sighted, though, was the object of his quest.

Whoa, Nellie!

Walt did not have a very good camera. He now wished that he had purchased another one. With the Instamatic, he got a shot of Nellie beneath the Mile 0 sign in Dawson Creek, the terminus of the Alaska Highway.

He knew that it would be possible to see swans at any time. Mission accomplished, he could turn around, and head back toward home. Even if he went no farther, this was already the trip of a lifetime.

When he went by huge lakes carved by glaciers, the wayfarer stretched his neck for white objects. He saw many migrating waterfowls heading the same direction he was, but no swans.

As he passed through the Stone Mountain Provincial Park, both big horn sheep and elk were right along the road. Speaking of roads, the farther north he went, the more unpaved sections he came to. It was a good thing that Earl had gotten him an extra spare tire. He would need it.

Walt really enjoyed a stop at the Liard Hot Springs. His muscles and joints were beginning to get weary from so many days on the road. The natural hot sulfur water relaxed him to the bone.

The solitary motorist also noticed that services were getting fewer and farther between. He topped off his gas tank at every little outpost, sometimes a couple hundred miles apart.

Walt took in the Sign Post Forest at Watson Lake. He was now nearing the Yukon, and he had still not seen any swans. He kept thinking that he might need to go down some side roads, but there were not any.

He was amazed by the vastness of it all. Some days he would not see a telephone pole all day. Or a power pole, either, for that matter. He met another vehicle only every half hour or so.

"Othell, you're sure not in Kansas anymore," he said one time. Not that he had ever been in Kansas. He just missed it on the way through. That same night Walt wrote in WOWs, "I'd rather be lost in the wilderness, than to be found in a town."

The man at the service station in Whitehorse said that swans were sometimes very private this time of year. "They are out there," he reassured Walt. "But they often stay out of sight while nesting."

On up the Alaska Highway, Walt started seeing black bears along the road. He soon lost count. Then he hollered, "Whoa, Nellie" as he braked hard when a big grizzly ran right out in front of him.

Nellie had another narrow escape when she rounded a curve, while at the same time coming to the top of a hill. A bull moose was right in the middle of the road. Nellie barely squeezed by without bumping into Bullwinkle. Whew! Walt realized that he could have been stranded for days if he had hit the big bull and knocked a hole in his radiator.

With only a flimsy lock on his door, the camper was a little apprehensive that something might try to crawl in with him while he was asleep. He kept a baseball bat beside his bed, as though that would scare off a hungry bear.

Walt also figured out the hard way that he could not leave any windows open. The peskiest mosquitoes that he had ever encountered were just dying to get a drop of his blood.

When Walt went around Kluane Lake and he still had not seen any swans, he realized just how close to Alaska he was getting. He never imagined going that far north.

The last hundred miles were the roughest roads he had ever experienced. He had to stop and tie everything down to keep stuff from being tossed around in the back. He was more than a little concerned about breaking a spring on his rig.

Holy Ground

Crossing the border was not much of a hassle when he finally got to America's Last Frontier. It was almost inconceivable to Walt that he was again in the United States. The roads were no better. Numerous pothole lakes were in view on the way to Tok Junction. Still, he saw no sign of swans.

There were potholes all in the road, too, but Walt was also experiencing a different kind of driving menace. Sometimes Nellie would take a nosedive in a depression that he learned were frost heaves, created by the ground melting and refreezing just above the permafrost. "Othell, these Alaska roads put a whole new spin on rock 'n roll," he said as Nellie hoisted him out of his seat.

When Walt got to Tok, he turned southwest toward Anchorage. Many lakes were along the rough and bumpy road before he got to Glennallen. The majestic snow-covered Wrangell-St. Elias Mountains were by far the tallest he had ever seen. The air was undoubtedly the cleanest and the freshest that he had ever breathed. Still, there were no swans. "Othell, is this a wild swan chase?" he asked at one point.

The drive into Anchorage was breathtaking. At the Visitor's Center, Walt learned that swans were often in Potter Marsh, at the edge of town on the highway going toward the Kenai Peninsula. None was there that day, however, so he kept driving.

Walt stopped at Beluga Point on the Turnagain Arm of the Cook Inlet. With the binoculars that he bought in Anchorage, he joined others watching Dall sheep high up on the mountainside. He then crossed the train tracks and walked over to a huge protruding rock formation at the water's edge. The wind was blowing briskly.

A strange sensation came over Walt. It was almost as though he had been there before. He did not feel like a tourist, a visitor. He was in a strange land, but he did not feel like a stranger.

Once sitting back in Nellie's saddle, he reached for WOWs. Walt wrote, "You are never totally free until you have absolutely nothing that you have to prove to anyone." He may not have realized it at the time, but he was now part Alaskan.

Walt then looked at his now tattered atlas. There was only one road into Anchorage and one road out. He could turn around and go back, take the fork at Wasilla, and head toward Mt. McKinley, or Denali as the natives called the tallest mountain in North America. From there, he could go to Fairbanks, and then again to Tok, before heading back south. Surely, swans would be somewhere along the road.

On the other hand, he could point Nellie southwest and go all the way to the end of the road in Homer. He had come this far. Why turn around now? Recalling the lesson he learned in that speech class back in college, he said aloud, "Never-the-less – Always."

Just like that, Walt saw his first bald eagle. It came up from the mudflats created by the rapidly retreating tide with a fish in its talons. The magnificent raptor soared right in front of him. What a marvelous sight!

Several more eagles were patrolling the Kenai River at Cooper Landing, as the first run of Sockeye salmon was in. A black bear with two cubs was walking along the bank on the far side of the river, looking to share the bounty of some anglers out in the stream in their waders. Walt wondered how the fishermen could concentrate on what they were doing with the bears looking over their shoulders.

The vagabond had temporarily forgotten what his original purpose was when he set out on his trip. He was in a dimension hitherto unimaginable. In their glorious splendor, snow-covered mountains rose up in all directions. Bright colored wildflowers graced the sides of the roads. The forests were green and lush.

Nearing the little town of Sterling, Nellie crossed the Moose River. Walt looked to the right, and his heart literally skipped a beat. He caught his breath. Two giant trumpeter swans were swimming gracefully along in the current, with three cygnets following close behind.

Walt turned around and went back. He parked on the side of the road and then walked down to the riverbank. The swans seemed not afraid of him at all. They actually posed for some pictures, as if showing off their offspring.

The fuzzy little babies were having no problem keeping pace with their parents. Not one of them was an ugly duckling.

Walter Othell Williamson was standing on holy ground.

Walt could go home now. Job done. Mission accomplished.

He took a deep breath as he looked back toward the snow-laden Kenai Mountains to the south. He figured there was no hurry, so he found a place to hitch Nellie at an RV Park in Soldotna. She was one tired filly.

The next day, not knowing what else to do, Walt decided to drive on as far as he could go. Why not? He had no schedule. He had no further agenda. Anyway, he needed a little break before heading back down the road.

The nomad found Homer an interesting place. He spent some time walking on the rocky beach of the spit, a jutting peninsula created by opposing tides. He tied Nellie up out on the spit and stayed two days. Walt could not believe how many eagles were hanging out in Homer. He immersed himself in the beauty of Kachemak Bay.

The first night after seeing the swans, Walt experienced all kinds of mixed emotions. He had been gone a month, but it seemed more like three or four. There was only one way to go – right back the way he came. He tried hard not to feel dejected. Is this what a dog experiences after the hunt is over?

This was the first time Walt had ever been to the end of a road exactly like this. There really was only one way to go. There were no highways to the left, and none to the right. The Gulf of Alaska was straight ahead. Was this like some midway point in his life? Was this the pinnacle? Was everything ahead now downhill?

The Alaska Woman

The next day, Nellie was turned around, as if a mule at the end of a long row. Walt felt no sense of urgency about anything. He stopped at a couple of viewpoints where he marveled at the ten thousand foot mountains across the Cook Inlet. He took a long walk on the beach and watched the tide as it so rapidly turned.

On an impulse, Walt took a left at Kasilof onto Kalifonsky Beach Road, an alternate route toward the town of Kenai. According to his atlas, this is where the Kenai River empties into the Cook Inlet.

It was getting late in the afternoon, although nowhere near dark. Nellie needed a drink, and he figured he might too. He pulled in at a little store with a gas pump and a neon sign that advertised cold beer.

Just before the tank was full, a tall leggy woman came out and got in her pickup truck. She glanced over at Walt as she went by. His camper almost had her blocked, so he got in her sights and started directing her as she backed out.

Once the truck was clear, the driver raced ahead. She then hit the brakes right beside him. The woman slowly and deliberately rolled down her window. Walt looked at her rather pensively, thinking that she might be about to thank him for his assistance.

It caught him totally off guard when she rather rebuked him. In a mildly admonishing tone, she said, "I'll have you know I am an Alaska woman."

"And I'll have you know I am a southern gentleman," Walt fired right back.

The truck surged forward, slinging a little gravel from the unpaved lot. All of a sudden, the brake lights came on. Whoa, Nellie! As the truck came to a screeching halt, the backup lights popped on.

"The girl, my lord, in the 4X4 Ford is backing up to take another look at me."

"Take it easy, Othell. Take it easy."

The woman with long flowing dark hair ran Walt's retort about being a southern gentleman again through her mind. Umm. As she backed alongside him, she rolled the window down again, this time with a little more gusto.

Walt was frozen. What now?

She surprised him yet again when she said, "I could get used to that. Park your rig and get in."

He explained to the Alaska woman that he had to go pay for the gas, but for her to hold that thought. He chuckled under his breath as he went inside the store, remembering the last time he said those words.

The owner told him that he could park his camper at the edge of the lot for a little while, as long as it did not block anyone from getting to the pumps. He just could not leave it there overnight.

"Othell, has the sound of my own wheels made me crazy?"

As Walt opened the passenger side door, Radar made room for him. Radar was the woman's husky. He acted as if he were proud to see this stranger.

"My name is Virginia Sullivan," she said, simultaneously extending her hand right under the dog's nose. "My friends call me Ginny and my enemies call me Sully. You have your picking choice."

"As for now I will go with Ginny," Walt answered rather meekly. "But I will leave my options open if you don't mind," he added.

"I thought you said you were a southern gentleman," she responded back to him. "First you say something like that, and then you haven't even told me your name."

"Walt Williamson, ma'am," he managed to get out, exaggerating a southern drawl. "I don't have any friends, and fortunately, my enemies hardly ever call."

He had no clue where they were going. For that matter, he did not know if he would ever see Nellie again. What did it mean to be an Alaska woman?

Ginny turned down a street that ended at the beach along the inlet. They got out and started to walk on the gray sand. Radar was in his element. Walt was not sure what he was in.

A few other people were also on the beach. Some had tents set up for camping with a campfire burning. Gin told him that the big mountain directly across the inlet is called Mt. Redoubt. She informed him that it is volcanic. She also said the mountains across the bay were the beginning of the Aleutian Chain.

Walt asked the Alaska woman how to pronounce Kenai. She said it is like "keen eye." She added that the peninsula is named for the Kenaitize Tribe of Native Americans. He then wanted to know why the sand is so gray. Ginny said that it is glacial silt, created from the friction as the massive rivers of ice move ever so slowly downstream, carving and grinding the granite as they go.

When they got back to the F-150, Ginny told Walt that could park his camper in her drive if he wanted to. "But it would be rude of a gentleman not to come inside and make sure that the lady of the house is okay," she added with a sparkle in her eye. "Have you had anything to eat? I'm starving," she continued, before he had a chance to answer.

Walt admitted that he had only snacked since leaving Homer. The Alaska woman offered him some smoked salmon and a brew, if that would tide him over. He had never eaten smoked salmon before. He had no way of knowing it at the time, but a whole passel of other new experiences was awaiting Walt Williamson. This was just the tip of the proverbial iceberg.

The two of them talked well into the night. Walt learned that Virginia came to Alaska with her ex-husband when he was stationed at Elmendorf Air Force Base in Anchorage. Ten years earlier when he was discharged, he returned home to Gig Harbor, Washington. She stayed behind. The woman had fallen in love while they were there, but not with another man. Ms. Sullivan was in the midst of a love affair with Alaska.

Ginny was a nurse. She worked with one of the hospitals in Anchorage when she first arrived. Then, Nurse Sullivan saw a new opportunity. The colossal state was in need of transient health care workers.

Getting personnel and supplies into remote areas was often a challenge. Walt found out that the running of the Iditarod every year is a commemoration of when mushers raced to get serum all the way to Nome during the dead of winter in 1925, because of a diphtheria epidemic.

Folks in the lower 48 finally figured out the merit in having mobile medical professionals. A few years earlier, they started calling what Ginny was already doing a travel nurse.

Nurse Sullivan flew into native villages all throughout Alaska. Her assignments might be for only a few days, or she could be on location for up to a month at the time. In winter, she might be stranded and unable to get out for weeks. Her job also required her to be available to assist in hospitals when short a nurse or two.

Walt was able to tell his story, too. He found out rather quickly, however, that everybody in Alaska has a story. In the grand scheme of things, his was rather lame.

People come to the forty-ninth state for all kinds of reasons. Some are seeking fortune in either yellow or black gold. Others, like Ginny and her ex-husband, are sent because of military obligations. Some are seeking to get lost, while others are searching to find themselves. Many just set out for the spirit of adventure.

In the entire history of America's Last Frontier, though, Walt Williamson might well be the only person ever who made it all the way to Alaska for the solitary purpose of seeing swans in the wild.

When it was finally time for lights out, Walt was about to go crawl in his camper. Lights out was just a figure of speech, of course. The farther north he came up the Alaska Highway, the less darkness he had seen. He was now at Ginny's house the day before the summer solstice. The Kenai Peninsula was just far enough below the Arctic Circle that the sun set for a short time before rising again. Nevertheless, it was so close to the horizon that it would not get completely dark.

Ginny said that he was free to sleep in the house, if he would act like a gentleman. Anyway, if he did not, he would have to deal with Radar. For the first time since he crawled up in the saddle, Nellie and Walt would not be sleeping together.

Gin did some scrambling to find the bed in the guest room. This was the place where she could keep the door closed and let things pile up until she got to them. Walt only brought in his toiletries and a change of clothes.

He took a shower the next morning where he did not have to worry about punching an elbow through the stall. Just as he got dressed, Ginny called him to the kitchen. A moose and twins were in the backyard.

She then told Walt that she needed to do her stretching exercises. She said that she had taken a few yoga classes when she lived in Anchorage. While enrolled, she learned the importance of "balance." He asked if he needed to excuse himself, but she said that she would not disturb her in the least.

As he picked up the local newspaper and started looking it over, Gin spread an old blanket on the living room floor. With her eyes closed, she then began slowly extending her arms and legs in ways that Walt had never seen a person do.

He tried not to look, or at least not get caught looking. The woman really did seem oblivious to the fact that he was in the room. She then lay on her back. She stretched her arms up over her head. After that, she began raising her torso, creating an arch from hands to toes. The sweat clothes that she had on conformed to every curve of her body. This was the most sensuous thing that Walt had ever witnessed in his life.

After about ten minutes, Ginny fluidly gathered herself from the blanket, picked it up, and put it away. Walt folded the paper, but not much of it had been read. She then said that she would fix them some breakfast, as though nothing unusual had just happened.

The travel nurse was just back from almost a month on Kodiak Island. She had earned a couple weeks off before her next assignment. Walt was free to hang out with her if he wished. She could show him around, and take him to a midnight ball game that "night," played without artificial lights. He was in no hurry to go anywhere.

For the next few days, Walt could not absorb Alaska fast enough. It had already gotten into his blood. Ginny became his personal guide. She seemed to be enjoying showing him the sights as much as he was relishing being under her tutelage. Walt became Radar's new best friend.

The Fourth of July was coming up, and Ginny said if he was still around, they could go to Seward. Seward was the place to be in Alaska on Independence Day. This was the setting for the running of Mount Marathon.

When Alaskans do a marathon, they do it their way. The runners go up, and then back down a 3000-foot mountain. Between the time of the women's race and the men's, the city hosts a parade, also Alaska style. Walt was not going anywhere anytime soon. This was something that he had to experience.

After the two-hour breathtaking drive, Gin found a parking place. They headed toward the festivities. Walking beside each other in the direction of the starting line for the marathon, something magical happened. Just like that, they were holding hands.

While they were waiting for the parade, Walt and Gin wandered into a gift shop. She spotted a Russian Orthodox sterling cross on a silver chain. She said that she had been looking for one like that. Walt bought it for her.

On the way back home, she took him on a little detour to Exit Glacier, an immense river of ice that extends for miles back to the Harding Ice Fields. They walked up to the face, and then around the trail beside the beautiful blue spectacle.

As they were standing beside the glacier sensing the cold air coming from it, Gin slipped her arm around Walt's waist. Instinctively, he pulled her into his arms. This was the first time their bodies had touched like this.

The southerner could not believe how easy it was to be around this Alaska woman. She was a free spirit, not trying to impress anybody about anything. He was beginning to get a sense that this was in many ways the spirit of Alaska. It felt good to be among people so unlike the highly judgmental folks that he had been around most of his life.

Walt was beginning to feel right at home. He moved all of his clothes into the spare bedroom.

"Hello"

Walt's camper was still parked in Ginny's yard when she got a call to go to a village well up in the interior. There was an outbreak of some kind of stomach disorder, and she needed to go make sure that it was only a virus.

She told Walt that she would be happy for him to stay at her place while she was away if he would take care of Radar. Normally, she left the dog with a friend. In case he decided to leave while she was gone, she gave him instructions regarding where to take the husky.

After he drove Ginny to the little airport in Kenai, Walt decided to unbolt the camper, jack it up, and free Nellie of her load. Without the extra bulk and weight, getting around in the truck would be so much easier.

He did some exploring on his own while Gin was gone. Radar went with him on some of the outings. He actually had to admit that he missed this captivating woman. He was fascinated by her.

Ginny's house was about a mile out from town on a gravel road. It had been built by one of the many contractors who descended on the area when oil was discovered on the Kenai Peninsula. By Alaska standards, it was a little nicer than many of the homes nearby. All of the streets were unpaved except the main ones. A couple of other houses were on the road, but there was hardly any traffic.

Walt could feel the silence. The occasional crackle of fussing ravens was about the only disturbance other than a plane flying over every now and then. At the same time, he felt no need to fill the void. If he did turn on the TV or put on some music, he often found it a distraction.

Still very much unsure of himself with women, Walt was even less certain of what to make of Ginny. He was enchanted with her for sure, yet duly cautious at the same time.

Just before going to bed the third night she was gone, he was pondering how disadvantaged he always felt when trying to relate to females. Why did they always seem to have the upper hand? He took out WOWs and wrote:

"Cleaverage – the pronounced advantage a woman has in her *double* dealings with a man. And then she uses her leggerage, when she wants to get a leg up on him."

Ginny was able to get a call through to Walt from Anchorage telling him when to meet her at the airport. Normally, she just left her truck in the parking lot. He was not sure what to expect when she got back. Did he only see one side of the woman before she left? Would she come home ready to rid herself of this intruder? Would she want her space back? He could be back on the road again within a couple of hours at most. Walt did not know Gin well enough yet to detect the relief in her voice when he was still at her place to answer the phone.

Late in the afternoon as the twin-engine prop plane taxied up close to the terminal, Walt could see Ginny sitting by a window. She waved at him. He waved back.

Neither of them was prepared for what happened next. She came down the steps carefully, and then the travel nurse walked across the tarmac in lockstep with the other passengers. Once inside the glass door, Walt reached for her tote bag. Ginny was reaching for him. The two stood tightly embraced for a little slice of eternity. She had obviously missed Walt, too.

When they drove into the yard, he started gathering up her luggage. "No, that can wait," she said. She then put her arm around his waist, and they headed for the door. Once inside, Gin led Walt to her bedroom.

She turned to him with a look in her eyes that he had never seen. She then made a simple request. "Walt, will you lie with me on the bed for a few minutes and just hold me?" Ginny started removing her shoes so he did the same.

As she stretched out her body and reached for him, she added, "But no touching." Already befuddled, Walt's eyes registered even further bewilderment. He wrapped his arms around her with his confused mind spinning. "How can I hold her, without touching her? Othell, what the hell did the Alaska woman mean by that?"

Walt was ecstatic as he felt the rises and falls of Ginny's body snuggled against his. What would he do with his hands? They wanted to stroke her hair. They were flexing to run up and down her back. They yearned to cradle the derrière that he worshiped when walking behind her. Yet, the woman he held in his arms said no touching. He obediently clasped his hands behind her back.

This felt so right. But then again something did not feel right at all. How much longer could he go on holding his own two hands to keep them out of trouble?

Walt's whole body twitched as Ginny's right hand started sliding gently along his left arm. He lay motionless. It made its way upward where she began caressing his neck, his ears, and then his forehead. Her fingers found their way to his eyes and his mouth. He turned to face her. Gin's lips were puckering slightly, her eyes closed. Walt leaned in and their lips brushed ever so lightly.

Her body melted. She was now lying on her back. Walt began gently stroking her hair with the back of his hand. Would that qualify as no touching? She did not stop him. Little by little, he then let his fingers venture, but not too far. He got braver and braver. She did not seem to mind.

With no warning, Ginny abruptly sat up in bed. Walt was certain that he was about to get a stern reprimand. But no. She slid slowly off the side of the bed and stood facing him. Then, she started seductively taking off her clothes. One garment after another fell gingerly to the floor as Walt tried hard not to blink. The woman now stood before him, every bit the goddess of his dreams.

Ginny then began meticulously undressing Walt. He was mesmerized as she unbuttoned his shirt, and then ran her fingers across his hairy chest. He yielded as she unbuckled his belt. He wanted so much to reach out and touch what was right in front of his eyes, but he was still not sure if he should. Not a word was spoken as she was soon once more nestled beside him. This time there was nothing between them.

Hearts were racing, as time stood still.

There was no more reluctance, no hesitation. With a slow hand, Walt began stroking and caressing Ginny, getting braver and braver as his hands and his eyes went exploring. She was receptive to his every move, responsive to his every touch.

It was as though every minute of their separate existence had been building for this one moment in time. Bodies merged and spirits melded.

Arched above her, Walt looked down at Ginny. A glow was about her. He searched for a term to describe it, but it was inexpressible. The two of them had crossed over into another realm. They had traversed a threshold hitherto unknown to either of them. They could never go back.

Ginny opened her eyes and looked up at Walt. "Hello," he said, to greet the woman he now knew in the Biblical way.

"Hello," she said back to him, with a serene and loving smile.

Later that night as Ginny's lover lay sleeping so contentedly beside her in her bed, she looked down at him with moist eyes. "Oh, my precious darling Walt, you said 'hello' and I thought you were going to say 'goodbye'."

Radar was not the only one on the peninsula with a new playmate. Walt now had one of his own. He had never met a woman like Gin. She did not step out of character that day at the gas pump. She was just that upfront and straightforward. He did not have to waste energy trying to interpret what she meant when she said something. She let him know where she stood without him having to worry or do any second-guessing. Well, maybe that no touching thing did throw him off a bit.

Understandably, it would take a while for them to get to know each other, to fill in the blanks as they discovered from whence they had come, where they had been, and where they wished to go.

Walt told Gin one night as they were snuggling on the sofa, "I want to get to know everything about you. Even so, how you got from Point A, to Point B, to Point C is not nearly as important to me as knowing that you have connected the dots to Point H and Point N (the *here* and the *now*)."

Ginny's playful side fascinated Walt. The woman who could cut to the chase also knew how to let her hair down.

For the first time in Walt's life, his passion for romance was finding a way to express itself. Ginny was, in his eyes, an incredible blend of the sensible and the sensual.

For the next two weeks, the two of them were inseparable. She took him on one adventure after another, some of which did not involve leaving the house. Walt was having the ride of his life. Both of them knew another temporary separation was inevitable. Gin was on call, and another call would come. When it did, they both felt the enormous pain of separation.

As Ginny was about to go out the big glass door to board the plane, Walt held her tightly. He whispered in her ear, "I love you."

"I love you more," she responded, looking up at him with those big brown eyes.

"I love you no less," he answered back.

While she was gone this time, Walt had some practical matters that needed his attention. He had not planned to be away so long. Bills were piling up back home. If he did not work out something soon, his utilities would be cut off.

He placed a call to his neighbors, the ones whose son was cutting his grass. He did not want to impose, but they were more than willing to help. They agreed to go by the post office and pick up his mail. He forwarded a check to take care of the overdue bills.

Walt also had some business that needed tending where he was. He still had some cash reserves, but they would not last forever. If he stayed in Alaska indefinitely, he must find a way to pay his way. Walt Williamson, the southern gentleman, had no desire to be a kept man.

When Gin returned, she laughed at him when he shared that sentiment with her. She said that if she got behind on her house payments, he would receive a rent notice.

Walt told Ginny about his desire to expand his thesis into a book. Fortuitously, he had brought the manuscript along with him. They both saw this as a unique opportunity for him to get started. He would have lots of peace and quiet while she was gone. When she came back, his mind and body would then be ready for a break. Walt had to pinch himself a few times to make sure this was all real.

Ginny packed a picnic one cloudless day. She, Walt, and Radar drove to the end of another road. Captain Cook State Park was as far north as they could go along the Cook Inlet.

On the rocky beach, Radar entertained himself chasing seagulls. Walt and Gin picked up rocks of different colors. He was fascinated with the red rocks and the green ones. Ginny found an agate, and she explained to Walt what it was. From that moment on, he was an unabashed agate hunter.

Radar's favorite sport was playing Frisbee. He did not understand why anyone would ever get tired.

While the woman and her dog were still going strong, Walt took a perch atop a big rock. He could see oil platforms far out in the water. Mt. Spurr was across the inlet, its snow-covering glistening in the sun.

An eagle was stationed in the top of a tall spruce behind him waiting for the tide to go out. The magnificent raptor was hoping for an easy meal if a careless fish became stranded.

Walt's mind was overridden with his growing appreciation for this thing called synchronicity. This concept meshed well with what Ginny called balance.

Sitting on the big boulder, he started revisiting all of the things that had to come together for him and Gin to be at that store, at the exact same moment. As the tidal waves were sweeping over the rocks, a surge of some force of cosmic energy washed over Walt. More than at any time in his life, he felt an overwhelming sense of sanctioning – something akin to divine grace.

That night Walt made a very simple entry into WOW's. Wow!!!

The time had come for Walt to get serious about his writing. When he reread his thesis, he was amazed at how elementary it was. He even wondered how it had ever been approved. Since his graduate school days, society had undergone a lot of transformation. He wanted to take his original basic premise about identity, and then show how his precepts were so dramatically illustrated in the context of the modern world. That is what the book, *I. D. – The Identity Dilemma*, would be about.

First, he must establish his credentials. Walt took the stance that war babies like himself were uniquely qualified to span the vast gulf between the old prewar principles and standards, and the New Age postwar modern way of thinking which emerged during the 1960s and 70s.

Well into the summer, the loss of daylight was not noticeable. Walt and Ginny were going to bed while it was still light outside, and then getting up with the sun already shining. In the meantime, the amount of darkness was being extended about four minutes every night while they were sleeping. It was a strange feeling to go in the kitchen one late August morning and have to turn on a light to make coffee.

Ginny was especially busy during this time of year. She could be gone for up to three weeks at the time, hopscotching from village to village, giving immunization shots to children.

After the first couple of times when the two of them had rather severe cases of separation anxiety, both of them had to admit that the arrangement was not so bad. Gin had been single for a decade, and Walt had lived alone most of his adult life. Separate space was sometimes a good thing. There was always a beckoning "hello" with every reunion.

When she was home, they packed as much into the time as they could. The warm days would soon be gone. Ginny introduced Walt to the many edible berries growing in the wild. They made jams and jellies, often mixing them with rhubarb. The low bush cranberries would have to wait until after the first frost.

Walt discovered something else, too. He was not just in love. For the first time in his life, he was experiencing what it means to make love.

Before he went to bed one night, he wrote in WOWs, "Some people say the glass is half full. Others say it is half-empty. I say my cup runneth over."

"If You Must . . ."

As Ginny was returning home from an assignment, she had three days of in-service training in Anchorage. Walt drove in to meet her. He was glad that he left early enough to take his time getting to Anchorage. He stopped at various vantage points, amazed at what was before him. He pulled in at Beluga Point, relishing the moments that he spent there on his way through earlier. This would always be a special place, the full extent of which was yet unknown to him.

After being apart, Walt never varied from the familiar and routine way that he greeted his beloved. "Hello" was all that was necessary. Ginny told him later that when he said that word to her after the first time they made love, he found a place that had never been "touched" before. With a devious look on his face, he reminded her that was the same night that she requested no touching.

The lovers shared a WOW moment.

The couple got a room in a motel between the airport and downtown. When he looked out the window the next morning, Walt was amazed to see a big bull moose in the parking lot. During her free time, Ginny showed him around Anchor Town. He learned much about the devastating Good Friday earthquake of 1964.

When Walt picked Ginny up after her work session the next evening, he asked her what she wanted to do. She replied rather unemotionally, "It doesn't matter."

Fortunately, Walt remembered something that his Grandpa once told him. "Keep an eye on a small dog that just stopped barking. Be wary of a rooster when he is not crowing. And you had better be paying attention when a woman says that something doesn't matter."

As he probed a little further, he found that Gin was unusually tired. She just wanted to stay in and chill out. That really did not matter to him at all, especially after she said, "Walt, take me to bed."

The next day, Ginny called Walt and told him that her session would be ending a little early. He drove to meet her, and the two of them headed downtown. Anchorage was still much like a frontier town, but more and more folks from the rest of the country were discovering the Land of the Midnight Sun. On Fourth Avenue near the Visitor's Center, gift shops were springing up to draw the tourists.

Walt and Gin started wandering into some of them. The "express yourself" mentality sweeping the country during the 1980s was making its presence felt in Alaska. Walls were lined with sweatshirts. Many of them were imprinted with Alaska related things.

Some of the stores had only recently started displaying items with clever sayings, however. Oblivious to the fact that it made them look like tourists, they began reading some of them. Simultaneously, their eyes went to one that said, "Real men don't ask directions." Right beside it was one that proclaimed, "Real men don't eat quiche."

"What do you have to say for yourself, sir?" Gin inquired, with a bit of a naughty look.

Without answering, he pointed to a shirt that announced, "Well-behaved women never made history."

Walt turned to Ginny and said, "Well . . ." She cut her eyes and turned her head in that certain way that always thrilled him.

They laughed when they saw one that said, "God's last name is not dammit." The funny meter hit a new level when Walt found boxer shorts imprinted with, "If you play golf in the rain, you'll get your balls wet." Ginny loved the shirt that declared, "I can see clearly now the brain is gone."

It was not that the messages were that hilarious. It was the mood. Before long, they were the main attraction. As they shamelessly cavorted, Walt and Gin were getting more attention than the merchandise.

It did not stop when they went to an outdoor café to sample some salmon bake. No matter what either of them said, it was funny. The other then countered with something just as outrageous. Right when they thought the giggles were over, one of them would snigger again.

On the way back to their motel, they stopped and bought a bottle of Sin Infidel. As Gin went on to the room, Walt stopped at the desk to get a corkscrew. The plastic cups with the ice bucket would have to do for wineglasses. After a few sips, unbridled merriment once again triumphed.

When the bottle was empty, Ginny said that she wanted to take a hot bath. Walt was a bit miffed when she went into the bathroom and then closed the door. What was she doing, and why was it taking so long?

Eventually, she emerged, wearing the sexiest negligee he could ever imagine. Gin slowly and sensuously made her way toward him. As she stood directly in front of him, he fumbled for just the right words. Awkwardly, he managed to say, "You look good enough to eat."

Rolling her eyes yet again, she said whimsically, "If you must . . ."

Walt was on his feet. He grabbed her, and in a flash, they were rollicking on the bed. They were not making love, though. The two of them were again roaring with laughter.

Ginny was home only about a week, and then she had to get going again. This was a difficult and dangerous time of the year for her. Getting to some of the outposts was almost impossible in the dead of winter. Even though small planes could land on the frozen lakes, they still could not get in and out during blizzard-like conditions.

Walt was more than a little apprehensive about his upcoming first winter in Alaska. He had experienced some cold weather in the Carolina Mountains, and he had driven in snow. Even so, he did not know what to expect so close to the Arctic Circle. One thing was certain. He had to purchase some warmer duds.

He knew that he needed to put more antifreeze in Nellie, as well as drain all the pipes in the camper. He thought about putting studded tires on his truck, but Gin said that would be unnecessary. The F-150 would get them anywhere they needed to go. He continued writing when she was at work.

Walt was able to test his four-wheel driving skills while Ginny was gone. The first significant snow of the season blanketed the area on an October day. As he sat by the window watching it fall, Radar got his attention that it was time to go out and play.

Walt had no training as a journalist. He struggled with spelling. Sometimes he could not even get close enough to find the word in the dictionary. The novice author also kept tinkering with what he had already scribed.

First, he wrote in longhand. He then took his scribbling and tried to make it readable, using Ginny's electric typewriter. Revisions followed. When she was home, she retyped what he had written, assimilating the penciled-in changes. She often laughed at the way he had misspelled some words.

Without actually discussing it, the couple had embraced another ritual. Each time Ginny came home, Walt had a candlelight dinner prepared. The routines they were settling into were not the kind that would let a relationship go stale.

All of his life, Walt's birthday was mostly a nonevent overshadowed by Halloween. That would never again be the case, though, as long as Ginny had anything to do with it. On his first birthday in Alaska, she asked him if he wanted her to teach him some new tricks about getting treats. "If you must . . . ," he told her.

By the time Ginny got home from an assignment at Point Barrow, Walt had made significant progress in laying the groundwork for his book. Now, he was ready for a break.

Gin had not been home to Washington State in a while. She decided to go during Thanksgiving, and to take Walt with her. She wanted Christmas to be a very special time for just the two of them. He was a little apprehensive about meeting her parents and siblings.

The well-traveled nurse had enough frequent flier miles for both of them to get tickets to Seattle-Tacoma. One interesting development surfaced as they were making their preparations for the trip. Walt was thirty-nine-years-old, and his feet had never been off the ground.

After boarding Radar with a friend, they left the F-150 in the Kenai Airport parking lot. Walt must now exit the same door that he had seen Gin go in and out of several times. Once again, he yielded to her, the seasoned traveler, to show him the ropes. She even let him have the window seat.

The small, twin propeller aircraft was noisy, and the ride a bit bumpy on the twenty-five minute flight to Anchorage. The sky was clear, and Walt could see the snow on the beautiful mountains and frozen lakes below.

All of that was child's play, however, compared to what he got to witness as the big bird lifted off headed south. The little boy, who was told all of his growing up days that he was worthless and that he would never amount to anything, was seeing spectacular sights few people in the world ever get to witness. The immensity of the endless mountain ranges and ice fields was almost surreal. Walt sat mesmerized, holding Ginny's hand. She sat beaming like a proud mama.

Walt was amazed at how close Ginny's family seemed to be. If there was even the hint of any discord during Thanksgiving, he never sensed it. Her parents appeared genuinely in love with each other. Ginny was a middle child. He could not detect anything but playful sibling rivalry between her and her older brother and her younger sister. Even the in-laws seemed to get along well with each other. Walt wished all families could be that way.

He had told Gin very little about his family. On the flight back to Anchorage, she asked about his parents, grandparents, and siblings. With malice toward none, he said that he and his mother were not particularly close, and that she was deceased. He also mentioned that Todd had remarried. He intimated that he and his sister ran in different circles, and that there seemed to be no room for him in her life.

A big smile then came across Walt's face when he started telling her about his grandfathers. Gin said she regretted that she would never get to know his Granddaddy Williamson, but she was looking forward to meeting his Grandpa King. The prospects of that excited him.

Walt did not get much writing done the rest of the year. Just too much excitement was in the air. Except for a four-day trip to Nome, Ginny was home from Thanksgiving through Christmas. They sipped hot tea, drank hot chocolate, and on occasion enjoyed some spiked eggnog. She did not have many Christmas decorations, so they used their creative imaginations to make the place festive. Walt was disappointed that mistletoe did not grow in Alaska.

When he brought up the subject of exchanging gifts, Ginny was again her straightforward self. She suggested that they spend a weekend in Homer as their gift to each other. That suited him just fine. He had no idea, though, what treats Mrs. Santa had in her bag when they reached their destination. Nor did he have any inkling of the fireworks just ahead for New Year's Eve after they arrived back home.

On the drive to the end of the road, Gin started setting the stage for what was ahead. "Walt," she said deviously. "On one of my trips to a northern village, I noticed how close we were to the North Pole. As we were about ready to leave, I asked the pilot if we could make a landing there. He said that he could do a flyby and check out the possibilities. Lo and behold, he found a landing strip right next to Santa's workshop. The Jolly old Man himself came out to greet us."

Of course, Walt was intrigued with where this was going. Ginny continued with mischief written all over her face. "Saint Nick showed us around the place, and he even introduced us to the elves. Would you believe he gave us cookies and milk?

"Just as we were about to take off, the big guy gave me a bear hug. With a twinkle in his eye, he leaned over and whispered something in my ear. Do you know what Santa Claus said to me, Walt?"

With a look of anticipation as that of a little boy about to go see what was under the Christmas tree, he nodded for her to continue. Gin then leaned across the seat and whispered into his ear, "Sometimes naughty is nice."

Saying goodbye was harder than ever when Ginny got a call after the first of the year to go to Prudhoe Bay. Her job was to fill in for a nurse at the clinic up on the oil slopes who was due some time off. After she left, it took Walt a day and a half to get much writing done. He finally settled back into a groove and began making substantial progress. He was, nonetheless, ready for a break when she got back.

Gin was always eager to see what he had written while she was gone. She was his combination sounding board and number one critic. She kept telling him that what he was writing made a lot of sense to her.

The shortest day of the year had already come and gone right before Christmas. Little by little, the days were getting longer. However, it was still mid-morning before the sun came up, and it was beginning to set by the middle of the afternoon. Walt could understand why some people suffered from sunlight deprivation.

During the winter, the travel nurse was mostly on loan. Some remote areas had clinics with limited staffing. If anyone got sick or had to be away, she was one of only a handful of backups on call for the entire state. She said that she wanted Walt to accompany her on some of her trips, but that would have to wait until summer.

When Walt was able to return to his writing, he took some time to read back over what he had written. He was an eyewitness to one of the most critical and dynamic times in the nation's history. If what he saw was right, what happened during the first two decades of his adult life shaped and shifted the direction the country would take for at least the next couple of generations. The repercussions might well be irreversible.

When Ginny got back from one of her assignments, Walt had a halibut casserole, layered with shrimp and various cheeses awaiting her. As he was getting everything ready, he noticed only one match in the box. He could not find any others in the house.

As Gin was unpacking and settling in from her trip, he was putting the final touches on dinner. When he got ready to light the candles, he had to scratch the lone match three times before it finally sprang to life. Ginny was watching all of this curiously.

The wick of the first candle was embedded in the wax from the last use. By the time he finally got it lit, the match was about to burn his fingers. In his haste to extinguish it, he blew the candle out too.

Walt had just turned over the tickle box. They sat down to a candle-less light dinner, but there was no dearth of laughter.

Mid-February was a delightful time to be in Alaska. The days were already about as long as the shortest ones Walt remembered back where he grew up. The temperatures were mild enough for a windbreaker some days. The snow was still white and pristine. It was the time of "breakup," as the rivers began to shed their ice.

A red-letter day was on the calendar, too. Valentine's Day occurred right in the middle of the month. Ginny was getting home late that very afternoon. Walt waited at the house until she called from the nearby airport before he went to get her. He did not want to be gone long from the house.

Earlier, he had made sure that matches were on his grocery list. As he opened the front door for her, the house was illuminated with candles burning on every table in every room. The luminaries did not even come close to outshining the glow on Ginny's face, though.

Champagne was chilled in the fridge, and chocolates were waiting to be unwrapped. His special valentine did not have to wait long at all to see what else he had in mind. The oil was warm and ready for her gentle massage.

Ginny had big news. During the last half of March and into the first part of April 1984, she was going to be stationed in Juneau working for a hospital. Walt decided this was a good time for him to go back home and check on things. This also gave him a deadline. He wanted to be finished with his book so that he could let his former graduate professors look at it.

Walt was able to get a flight with a three-day layover in Juneau before continuing on to Atlanta. Yet again, Ginny showed him the sights, which included a walk up to the Mendenhall Glacier at the edge of the capital city.

This was the first time that Ginny was the one being left behind. As she was seeing him off, they repeated something that was now so much a part of their lore.

"I love you," he said.

"I love you more," she replied with a twinkle in her eye.

"I love you no less," he responded with a gleam in his own.

A Little Rough around the Edges

Earl met Walt in Atlanta, and they drove to Adamsonville. His uncle and aunt wanted to hear all about his adventures. Earl was pleased that the camper truck had no major problems on the long haul. Walt invited them to visit him in Alaska. He just happened to have a mode of transportation they could use. For now, Earl had a car off the lot waiting for his nephew to drive during his stay.

Walt went through Mason on the way to North Carolina. His grandparents were now on up in their 80s. Grandma King was still "enjoying" poor health. George said that she would outlive him by twenty years. Grandpa King's hair was now snowy white with waves in it, the likes of which would make most women envious.

Grandma had gotten a little rounder through the years. With her ever-present apron and cute granny glasses, Walt thought how natural she would look on "The Waltons" or "Little House on the Prairie." If Grandpa just had a beard, they could be Mr. and Mrs. Santa Claus, he further imagined.

During his short visit, he found out that his Grandmother Williamson was now in a nursing home. No mention was made of Todd and his wife, or of Emma Lou and her family.

As Walt was about to get on up the road, there was one more stop he had to make. It was long overdue. As he drove up, another vehicle was already parked at the Mason-Dixon cemetery. Pulling alongside it, he noted that the sporty baby blue Cadillac had a California license plate. Wanting solitude, he parked some distance away. He sat in his car for a few moments, collecting his thoughts.

A woman was standing alone with her back to him. Walt did not want to disturb her. It was a cold, overcast, windy day. He could see that she was shivering, not properly dressed for the late wintry blast.

Feeling some urgency to get on with his mission, he eventually opened the car door. About that same time, the woman started moving toward her own vehicle. Seeing him for the first time, she appeared to stumble. Walt reacted to go to her, but she regained her step. She nodded toward him in appreciation, and he smiled back.

He had to pass right by the area where the woman had been grieving. He saw her fresh footprints beside the grave of Sgt. Raymond "Little Ray" McDonald, Jr., killed in 1951, during the Korean Conflict. He wondered what the California woman's relation was to the deceased. He looked over his shoulder, and she was now sitting in her car.

Walt pressed on. As he stood at the foot of his mother's grave, the tears flowed freely. They blurred the sight of the other new shoeprints in the damp earth where he was now standing. He begged earnestly: "Why wouldn't you tell me what I had done that was so awful? Why did you never love me?"

Why? Why? Why?

The cold March wind stuttered and stammered its way around marble slabs and granite tombstones. As it howled its way through the bleak cemetery, Walt's pleadings fell on deaf ears.

As he turned to leave, he heard an engine start. The California Cadillac drove slowly away.

Everything was fine when Walt got to his house in Ephesus. He was certainly glad he left a key with the neighbors. They were able to get inside to turn the heat on low and keep the pipes from freezing.

He had to buy a few groceries, and late on a Friday afternoon was not the best time to do it. Everybody and his brother would be there. He at least needed to get coffee and some breakfast supplies for the next day or so.

"Hello Walt," he heard coming from behind him. It was less than a year since he had heard that voice. It seemed more like a decade. Hannah was also picking up a few things for the weekend on her way home from school.

The aisle of a busy store was not a good place to reconnect. She said that she could run by his place the next day. They decided on coffee at ten.

Hannah was excited about getting her hands on the manuscript of his book. She also wanted to know all about Ginny. She was so pleased for Walt. She told him that he was finally getting the happiness that he so richly deserved.

Like others who have never experienced Alaska, Hannah was unable to grasp how and why he was so enraptured with the place. She suspected that it had more to do with his new love than anything else.

Nor did his connection with swans make any more sense to her than it did when he headed out. Walt again considered telling Hannah about D-V Day. That would certainly clear it up for her. He had never told anyone, though, and he decided to keep it that way. This was his own private little burden, and he must carry it alone.

Hannah loved the book. "And it looks like you have picked yourself up a good typist, too," she added.

In his book, *I. D. – The Identity Dilemma,* Walt said in essence that the radical developments in the 1960s and 70s started out as a course correction. The nation's mandated warranties pertaining to liberty and justice for all were in need of some tweaking.

He then theorized that things started getting out of hand. Three "rights" revolutions converged on the country at approximately the same time. Walt identified them as the civil rights movement, the women's rights movement, and the countercultural revolution that declared war on societal boundaries.

The writer postulated that in the process of attaining and expanding rights, gaping holes were left in the self-identifying process. Previous markers such as ethnic, cultural, and religious factors were sacrificed for political correctness. Gender identification also got all muddled. In the meantime, the boundaries that delineate right from wrong became dangerously blurred.

The author further hypothesized that the country, as a whole, began suffering from its own identity crisis. Those obsessed with their rights began losing sight of their responsibilities.

As overindulged baby boomers came of age, Walt saw the American Dream downgraded from opportunity to entitlement within one generation. He furthermore made note of the narcissistic and self-absorbed offspring of "the me generation." He predicted that the entertainment industry would respond with a tidal wave of amusements featuring super heroes, violence, and sex designed to fill the vacuities of those living their lives vicariously.

Instead of concentrating on the common good, the author predicted that sleaze would overwhelm the political system, and that greed would eventually bring the economy to the brink of disaster. Regrettably, the writer also feared that these circumstances would create a culture of corruption and incompetence that would wobble the nation on its axis.

In his conclusion, Walt predicted a rise in conservatism and fundamentalism in attempts to stem the tide. He then forecast that some authoritarians from these movements would usurp power, and pontificate for people what they should think and even how they should vote. The writer feared that this would thwart the democratic principles upon which the country was founded.

According to the author, the combination of all of these factors would initiate a period of decline for the United States as a world power. In light of the teachings of Jesus regarding self-sacrifice, he also questioned whether a country, now bent on consumerism and self-gratification, could call itself a Christian nation.

By no means was the book just a negative treatise. Walt carefully and thoughtfully advanced his own notions regarding how to resolve the identity dilemmas, both for individuals and for culture as a whole. He suggested a rediscovery of:

Honesty: The key to knowing who we are

Integrity: The virtue of who we are

Dignity: The pride of who we are

Morality: The conscience and character of who we are

Civility: The arena within which we rediscover who we are

I. D. – The Identity Dilemma was dedicated to Walt's two grandfathers. The author mentioned that these two men modeled for him the difference between a human being and a human doer.

Dr. Fitzpatrick was pleasantly surprised to see Walt outside her office talking with the receptionist. Two hours later and she would have been out the door for spring break. His major professor was even more amazed when he pulled a manuscript from his attaché case. She said that she would be delighted to take it with her and read it while she was gone.

Dr. Fitzpatrick inquired if this was the only hard copy Walt had. When he said it was, she immediately asked the secretary to make another copy for her, so she could leave the original with him.

The next few days of separation were agonizing for the lovebirds, now on different parameters of the continent, east and west, as well as north and south. Unlike when Gin was in some remote place in Alaska, however, they could talk by phone. With the four-hour time difference, they had to make phone dates so that he could catch her in her hotel room when she was not at the hospital.

Walt decided that he was dreading Dr. Fitzpatrick's critique of his manuscript almost as much as he had feared the scrutiny of his master's thesis. She called him when she got back in town, and they set up an appointment.

"Walt, it is a little rough around the edges," she began. "But then again, so are you." Dr. Fitzpatrick had encouraged him to expand his ideas into a book, but she had no idea what direction he would take. She found it intriguing the way he connected the self-identifying process to the cultural upheavals of the past couple of decades.

"You do know you are saying what a lot of people do not want to hear, don't you?" the professor cautioned him. "You have postulated that the Reagan years have ushered in a new feel-good mentality that is even taking over many churches."

Dr. Fitzpatrick continued. "Your book is a reality check, and I'm not too sure how it will be received. I think you are going to get some negative responses about your conclusion that the American empire is on the decline. And I suspect that you are going to ruffle some feathers in the religious community."

She then wanted to know, "Do you have any thoughts on how to go about getting this published?"

He was fresh out of ideas.

"Walt, the timing on all of this could turn out to be providential," Dr. Fitzpatrick advised. For the first time since he had known her, his former professor felt more like a colleague.

What she told him next got his full attention, too. Dr. Fitzpatrick said that the university was about to embark on a bold new venture with an upstart printing press. The goal was to publish worthwhile materials that might otherwise go unnoticed. She asked Walt's permission to see what the prospects were for having his book considered.

He wondered if it might be done during his brief time in Ephesus, just in case he needed to be around to work out any details. The department head said that she would get right to work on it.

Six days later, Walt was sitting in the new publishing editor's office. After the manuscript had been passed around to some key people, the university press had made a decision. They proposed that *I. D. – The Identity Dilemma* become its inaugural publication. The Ephesus State University alumnus could not be more pleased. Walt could hardly wait to share the news with Ginny.

Two days later, the university's lawyer went over the terms of the contract with him. The press had to be self-supporting. Since there were so many unknowns in how much revenue the book would generate, they could only offer him a mere pittance in royalties.

Walt said getting a good return would be nice, but that he was not writing for fame and fortune. He was more concerned with contributing toward the betterment of humanity, and paying a little rent on the space he was taking up. It sounded like a good fit.

The manuscript had to be professionally edited. If everything went smoothly, *I. D. – The Identity Dilemma*, by Walter O. Williamson, would come rolling off the press by the end of the summer.

Walt's return flight also stopped in Juneau so that he and Gin could fly home together. She was waiting for him when the plane touched down. This time, she was the one who got to say "hello." They both laughed that this was another first.

The two of them now had some serious celebrating to do. "No stops. Straight to the hotel," Walt directed, as she drove the rental car. "If I must," Gin responded, with that devious little smile on her face.

The next day, the F-150 was waiting for them at the Kenai Airport. It sprang to life when Walt hit the starter. Radar was waiting when they went by to pick him up. Most of the snow was gone in the lower elevations, and the days were already longer than the ones Walt left back in North Carolina.

After working for a month straight at the hospital in Juneau, Ginny was due at least a couple weeks off before her next assignment. During the early summer months, the two of them were out and about every opportunity that they had. This was not a Chamber of Commerce kind of summer, however. It rained off and on most of June and July, but this did not dampen their spirits. More than once, the duo came in drenched after hiking in the drizzle. They then took a hot tub bath together.

When Ginny left in late July on another mission, Walt had a project. The galley proofs for his book had arrived. For the next few days, he poured over the pages meticulously, finding a few typographical errors all along. He also had one final chance to do some minor editing.

Ginny wanted to go over the proofs, too, when she got back. Walt was not surprised that she found some things that he missed. They went to the post office together to ship the galleys back to the Ephesus State University Press. The couple celebrated afterward with some fresh grilled salmon, and a bottle of Sin Infidel. Moreover, the day was far from over.

The Accidental Celebrity

Ginny was always full of surprises. This thrilled Walt to no end. However, the one she was about to spring on him would be the biggest yet. On a clear crisp late July day in 1984, without tipping her hand in any way whatsoever, she said, "Walt, let's get married."

Ginny was right up front with him from the very beginning. She tried marriage, and she did not find it to her liking. He also determined some time back that he had passed the customary marrying age.

Walt knew immediately what his response was going to be. He just decided to have a little fun on the way to getting there. "Wait a minute, my darling. Are you getting the cart before the horse?" he began. "Have you forgotten that I am a southern gentleman? I am the one who gets to do the proposing."

Ginny responded, with that look always in her eyes when she was up to something. "Walt, my darling, I am afraid I have to inform you that it is you, not me, suffering from a memory lapse. I can see clearly now the brain is gone. My dear, this is a leap year."

The two of them were at the borough building the next morning applying for a marriage license. That was the easy part.

They agreed that this would be no ordinary wedding. The big question was where to celebrate the nuptials. Walt and Ginny wanted the solemnization to take place at a location that had special meaning for both of them. As they considered several possibilities, they simply could not narrow them down below four.

At exactly the same moment, each interrupted the other with the same proposal. Why not all of them? Like progressive dinners that were popular at the time, where guests moved from one locale to another for the various courses of the meal, Walt and Gin decided to have a "progressive wedding."

Next, they had to choose who would perform the ceremony. They agreed to ask the priest at the Russian Orthodox Church in Kenai to do the honors. At first, he was reluctant to do something so unconventional and nontraditional. Then he agreed, acknowledging that this is after all Alaska.

At 9:00 a.m. on Saturday, August 4, 1984, Walter Othell Williamson and Virginia Arlene Sullivan arrived at the church. The bride wore faded blue jeans and an elegant off-white cashmere top. Her only jewelry was the cross that Walt had given her the day they first held hands.

The groom was dressed in jeans and a blue oxford shirt. They both wore their hiking boots. The priest had decided to forgo the formal robe, and to dress casually as well.

The couple knelt at the altar of the historic church. Father Nicholas prayed and asked God to bless this union.

The three of them then got in Gin's old truck with the groom at the wheel. He drove them to the beach where Walt and Ginny walked the day they met. At a high tide, and with the magnificent Mt. Redoubt as a backdrop, the priest began the ceremony with a discourse on love and commitment.

The next stop was about forty miles up the Sterling Highway past Cooper Landing. It was a secluded spot overlooking the vast and emerald waters of the Kenai Lake. Gin told Walt the first time she took him there that it was where she went when she needed to get in touch with her deepest self. With majestic mountains in every direction, and chickadees singing in the trees, the bride and the groom held hands. Looking into each other's eyes, they uttered their sacred vows.

Afterward, the wedding party took a break for brunch at the Summit Lake Lodge. Father Nicholas was at first quiet during the times of transit, feeling somewhat out of his element. Then, he really began to get into the spirit of things, laughing and joking with the couple along the way. He even volunteered to be the wedding photographer. The priest had already figured out that he would be talking about this wedding for years to come.

The bride's bouquet was made up of wildflowers, starting with pink wild prickly roses picked at the edge of the forest near Ginny's house. Like the progressive wedding, it grew. The groom stopped along the road. He added fireweed, dandelions, yellow paintbrush, columbine, blue bells, lupine, wild geraniums, and poppies. At each pullover, Walt undid the blue ribbon that he had sequestered for the occasion. He tied the knot again as more color was added.

The next station was more than an hour away. The 4X4 Ford lumbered up the Seward Highway to Beluga Point. This was the spot where Walt first felt a strong kinship to America's Last Frontier. The day was so sunny and bright that Denali was clearly visible in the far distance. With the wind blowing briskly, the wedding party reassembled on a rock outcropping. Walt and Ginny exchanged wedding rings.

Going back down the road the way they came, the trio continued straight at Tern Junction. They went through Moose Pass, and then took a right before getting to Seward. Standing beside the gigantic Exit Glacier some six hours after the wedding ceremony commenced, Father Nicholas pronounced the couple husband and wife. Walt took his bride in his arms on the very spot where he first held her. This time he kissed her.

The priest then offered his congratulations. Without saying another word, the wedding party started making its way back to the parking lot. On a rocky ridge, Ginny let go of Walt's hand and wandered off the path. She then knelt at a cavity in the glacier-carved granite. The bride solemnly placed her bouquet in the crevice.

Walt was at her side as she arose. She faced him and spoke. "My darling, I love you so much for picking these wildflowers for me. They were just perfect, but now they have served their purpose. They were meant just for this wonderful day. The flowers are already beginning to wilt, but my precious Walt, my love for you will never wither or fade. It is forever and ever."

Walt kissed her again.

When the happy couple dropped Father Nicholas off at his home, he invited them in for a wedding toast. He then blessed them again, reaffirming that this was indeed the most unusual day of his entire priesthood.

For their wedding night, unbeknownst to Walt, Gin had done some shopping. She had purchased a very sexy negligee, and she planned to surprise him. Once back in the nest, the exhausted bride hurriedly undressed. She forgot all about the nightie, and just fell into bed. It would wait until later.

The next day the newlyweds hitched Nellie back up to the camper, and they headed north for their honeymoon. This was the first time Walt was out on the road with the filly, carrying along another passenger. When they pulled in for the night, the accommodations were small. Gin said that she would have to go outside to change her mind.

From Anchorage, the newlyweds went up the Parks Highway through Wasilla. The couple spent two days in Talkeetna. They went flight-seeing with a bush pilot through the Alaska Range. The clouds parted for them, providing a clear view of Denali. The sights from the small aircraft were breathtaking in every direction.

Walt and Ginny next drove along the Denali Highway, a highway in name only, since it traversed about a hundred miles of unpaved wilderness. Some places were almost impassable.

Wildlife was abundant. In lakes along the way, the baby swans were now almost as big as mama and papa. The humans were dwelling among moose, caribou, bears, coyotes, ptarmigan, bald eagles, and other waterfowl. Walt and Gin tried not to disturb the animals too much. Meanwhile, the honeymooners were enjoying some wild life of their own.

One afternoon, Nellie was tethered near a creek. Coho salmon were making their way upstream. The couple did some hiking, but the relentless mosquitoes soon drove them back inside. While Gin was rustling up some grub, Walt reached for WOWs. After a moment of reflection, he wrote, "Commitment is not all that complicated – I am on your side and you are on my side."

Once at the end of this wilderness highway, it was on to Valdez through Thompson Pass. Nellie was then driven onto an Alaska Marine Ferry to sail to Whittier through the unbelievably beautiful and unspoiled Prince William Sound.

At one point, Walt and Ginny saw an eagle sitting on an iceberg. Both orca and humpback whales were gorging themselves on salmon and haddock at various spots. In a couple of areas, whole pods of sea otters were floating on their backs. Seals were sunning on blocks of ice calved from glaciers.

Sitting on the deck of the ferry, Walt reached for the tote bag. He took out WOWs and made another entry. "A person is not really qualified to use the word 'awesome' unless he has been to Alaska."

Getting communication to and from the university press was not always easy. Even so, everything seemed to be on schedule for release of the book around Labor Day. Finally, the date was confirmed. Since this was such an historical occasion for the educational community, Walt was expected to be present for photographs.

He wanted his new bride by his side. Furthermore, Earl and Mary Beth said that it would not be right if they did not get to meet Ginny. Walt's uncle and aunt met the couple in Atlanta, with Earl providing the now customary mode of transportation.

Walt took his wife through Mason to show her off to his grandparents. He told the story of how he and Gin met. She listened with a sparkle in her eyes. She then told her version of the now larger-than-life tale. Grandpa was all ears.

According to Ginny, she found an abandoned puppy that was totally lost and about to starve to death. When it looked up at her with its pitiful eyes, she knew that she must try to rescue it. The first thing she had to do was get rid of the fleas.

She also discovered that it was not even housebroken. After worming the little dog, and giving it its shots, she planned to find it a home. By this time, though, Radar was enjoying having a playmate. She decided instead just to put a collar on the mutt, and to keep it on a leash.

Grandpa said that it was about time somebody put a leash on the boy. He added that if Ginny had not picked up the stray and taken him home with her when she did, he was not sure that the mongrel would have ever found its way back home.

Ginny was finally able to see Walt's mountain cottage that he had talked about so much. He was thrilled that she went in and made herself right at home. When she went over and picked up the picture of Walt shaking hands with LBJ, she said, "Walt, you never said anything about this."

He just shrugged and said, "Oh, it was nothing."

He had told his wife all about Mrs. Neumann. Ginny asked him to take her to the cemetery where his former landlady was buried. Standing by her grave, Gin said aloud, "Thank you, Mrs. Neumann, for taking such good care of this man that I now love with all my heart."

The release of the first book to come rolling off the Ephesus State University Press was recorded for posterity. Walt found himself in the uncomfortable position of being in the spotlight. Flashbulbs kept blinding him. The new author also got his first taste of a book signing. Both the university bookstore and the local independent hosted him while he was in town.

As the autograph party was winding down at the university bookstore, Walt saw a very familiar face near the end of the line. When she got to the table, he looked up at his wife and said, "Ginny, I would like to introduce you to . . ."

"Oh, you must be Hannah," Gin interrupted. "Walt has told me so much about you. At first, I did not know whether to be jealous or not. It was Hannah said this, and Hannah did that. How is Phillip doing?"

While the two of them were getting acquainted, Walt looked down at the book Hannah handed him to sign. He wrote simply, "To Hannah: She knows who she is."

Ginny had never been east before. She felt an immediate bonding with the mountains of North Carolina. Walt was pleased with everything about the trip except the times he had to wear a coat and tie. With a box of complimentary copies of *I. D. – The Identity Dilemma* in tow, the couple soon headed back to their other home.

On the way to Adamsonville to spend the night with Earl and Mary Beth, the couple went back through Mason. Walt presented an autographed copy of the book to his grandparents.

"Son, the title of this book is most interesting," his Grandpa said, as he started thumbing through the first few pages. When the man came to the book's dedication, his eyes commenced welling up with tears.

The significance of his grandson writing a book about identity did not get by George King. He only wished that the author's other granddaddy could have lived to see it.

Without saying another word, the proud man reached out and embraced his grandson. Walt had a hard time imagining a polar bear hug being any tighter.

I. D. – The Identity Dilemma, by Walter O. Williamson, would have likely been little more than a mere footnote in the annals of history, if even that. That all changed, though, when the Reverend Doctor Billy Sunday Bloodsworth got his hands on the book. Walt was not sure how the televangelist got a copy.

B. S. Bloodsworth was part of the up and coming breed of preachers taking advantage of the new medium of cable television. From his studio church in Roanoke, Virginia, his broadcasts were going out into markets all over the country.

Bloodsworth billed himself as God's anointed bloodhound to sniff out modern-day heresy. He got his authority from the plenary, verbally inspired, infallible Word of God – the King James Bible. While contributions came in from viewers by the buckets full, B. S. could not have stayed on the air without the funding he received from Texas billionaire oilman, Sizemore Hunter.

Rather than see that Walt was actually endorsing many traditional values upon which they would certainly agree, Bloodsworth took offense at what the author said about fundamentalists. The pompous preacher also took Walt to task for suggesting that the United States was not now, if it had ever been, a Christian nation.

B. S. Bloodsworth ripped Walt apart on air, calling him one of the most dangerous men in America. He ripped pages from the book and burned them in front of a large, wildly applauding audience.

The television preacher then invited the author to come to his show, and to debate him face to face. He offered to pay all of Walt's expenses if he would fly in from God forsaken Alaska.

Walt did not see the program himself. He and Ginny could barely get a couple of stations over the air. They certainly did not have access to cable. The first he was aware of the furor was when the NBC affiliate in Anchorage sent a reporter out to Kenai to interview him.

All of a sudden, Walt Williamson was making news. Other people wanted to know more about this menace to society. Book orders went from a trickle to a steady stream. The first edition of five hundred copies sold out, and the university press had to fire back up.

Walt was reluctant to go to Virginia. A celebrity was one thing he was not, and had no desire to be. The university put pressure on him, however, when it realized the potential gold mine in publicity it was sitting on.

Nothing was said about Ginny accompanying him, but two tickets were in the envelope when it arrived in the mail. A chauffeur met the couple at the airport in Roanoke, and they were dropped off at the finest hotel in the city.

On the day of the scheduled appearance, a limousine picked them up in plenty of time for Walt to have some makeup applied. This annoyed him.

He had asked for an advanced copy of the questions that he might be asked, but he never heard back from the request.

On a cue, Walt was directed to walk out on the elaborate stage. Lights blinded him. He heard some hisses from the audience. B. S. mockingly told the audience to be nice to their guest. He took his seat, not knowing what was coming next.

After a polite welcoming to the show, the host startled Walt with a query. "Mr. Williamson, am I to understand that you are living with a woman to whom you are not married?"

Before Walt had a chance to answer, Bloodsworth looked into the camera. He asked the viewers out there in television land how an upstart writer, living a life of sin and debauchery, could have credibility in the eyes of anyone. What right did an infidel have to say that the United States was not a Christian nation? The studio audience cheered their leader on.

All of a sudden, a floodlight came on illuminating the front row area where Ginny was seated. "Is this not the woman with whom you are living in sin?" B. S. bellowed. Boos rang out from the rafters.

Apparently, old Bloodsworth had sent his bloodhounds out sniffing, but they had not followed the scent quite far enough. This old watchdog did not know it, but he was barking up the wrong tree.

Without saying a word, Walt motioned for Ginny to come to the stage. A hush fell over the audience. "Dr. Bloodsworth, let me introduce you to my wife, Mrs. Virginia Sullivan," he said, with a sly little grin on his face. "Her friends call her Ginny, but her enemies call her Sully," he added, now with a definite devilish look about him.

The host, with egg on his face, stood dumbfounded. Walt did not give the man a chance to save face either. Looking into the camera with the "on air" light, Walt began to speak softly and gently.

"Ladies and gentlemen, I have made many mistakes in my life. To my astonishment, God Almighty has always found it fit to forgive me. I have made one this time, though, that I am almost too embarrassed to bring before Him. You see, not long after I got to Alaska, this wonderful woman shared with me some good old sourdough wisdom. I am ashamed to say right here in front of her and God that I have not followed it today."

Walt looked at Gin mischievously, and then he continued. She knew where this was going.

"Honey, you warned me, and I should have listened. Would you please tell this man, and all of those looking on, what wonderful advice you gave me that I have so foolishly ignored?"

Ginny did not answer immediately. She let the suspense build a bit. She then said slyly, "Don't ever get into a pissing contest with a skunk," trying, but not too hard, to contain her laughter.

"CUT!!!" the director shouted. The two of them were ushered promptly off the stage. They never got to see the rest of the program, and they always wondered what happened after they left. Walt and Ginny were taken by car back to their hotel, but they had to call a cab to get to the airport.

The honeymooners flew back to Alaska, cavorting all the way. Book sales skyrocketed. The little press had a hard time cranking out enough copies to keep up with demand.

While on the plane, Walt got up and retrieved WOWs from the overhead bin. He made a little notation. "Would you call a wolf in sheep's clothing out fleecing the flock an imparsonator? Or, would that make him a Phar-a-cite?"

Walt Williamson might not be the most dangerous man in America, but he was soon one of the most on the go. The episode in Roanoke started replaying all over the country. For this unknown writer to take on the high and mighty B. S. Bloodsworth, and to bring him down a notch or two, was fast turning Walt into something of a folk hero, whether he wanted it to or not.

Calls started coming in from all over the country for interviews. He did several by phone. The university press also lined up a series of book signings. This was in the writer's contract, but the accidental celebrity never imagined that he would ever do more than a handful.

Walt signed books at the bookstore on the square in Adamsonville. He felt rather strange, sitting and chatting with his old college professors who showed up to get their own autographed copies. He took great pleasure in signing one for the now retired Dean Rowell. He inscribed, "To a gentleman and a 'scholar'."

On a swing through coastal Carolina, he also did the same at the university bookstore at the Outer Banks State University. Dr. Robbins then hosted an autograph party for him in her home.

Walt was soon flying more than Ginny was. Their separations became more excruciating. His flights were not just hopscotching around Alaska, either. They were long and tiring since they often also involved transit to and from Kenai.

Gin went with him when she could, but it was getting harder and harder for them to coordinate their schedules. Walt often woke up in a hotel room, and he did not remember what city he was in.

He was amazed when television crews sometimes showed up at his appearances. He did not think he looked good at all when he saw himself on TV. Some of the hosts asked Walt to do readings, and to lead discussion groups about the contents of his book.

The best-selling author then started getting calls to appear on talk shows. These productions really unnerved Walt. At least a segment of the Bloodsworth debacle inevitably accompanied his introduction. It was all about ratings. Walt Williamson was the new David who had taken on Goliath.

Out in the marketplace, *I. D. – The Identity Dilemma* was receiving mixed reviews. Just as Dr. Fitzpatrick predicted, the writer said some things that many people did not want to hear. The generation of Walt's grandparents, for the most part, had a very favorable opinion of the book. They were delighted that someone was able to portray the world accurately before the tumultuous decades.

Some social scientists hailed the author for his perceptions into human behavior. A few historians went on record as saying that this interpretation of the 1960s and 70s would become the benchmark from which the period would always be viewed.

On the other hand, Walt's work was meeting stiff resistance within certain circles. A few liberals felt threatened by his warnings regarding how "entitlements" were supplanting human initiative and accountability.

He was also getting dissension from some conservative religious leaders. Those whose message was built on the notion that the United States is a modern-day chosen nation blessed by God were especially rankled.

Walt was not bothered at all by the criticisms. He rather wore them as a badge of honor. What disturbed him was how few people wanted to talk about identity. This concept was at the very heart of his premise. More copies of his book were being sold than he could have ever dreamed. Yet, he wondered how many of his readers had any idea what he was saying.

When people stood in line to get a signed copy of his book, Walt detected that a number of them were what he called seekers and searchers. They knew something was missing from their lives, but they did not know what. He suspected that they were hoping for a quick fix, a painless way to fill menacing voids. He suspected that most of them would be disappointed with his work.

Another thing bothered Walt. People in every phase of the promotion of his book were casting him into roles foreign to him. They kept trying to reinvent him into the underdog now having his day. He was actually contacted by a couple of agents wanting to promote him as the next self-help guru superstar. Walt knew who he was. The hype had no impact whatsoever on turning him into somebody he was not, nor had any desire to be.

The year 1984 was significant for Walt in yet another way. He turned forty on Halloween. Ginny did not let that milestone go by unnoticed, either. She dressed up like a witch, kidnaped her husband, and then held him hostage for three days. When the captive was eventually able to meet her ransom demands, he was finally freed.

Walt's newfound fame began to spread to various parts of the country. The university actually hired an agent to schedule events for him. The popular author did book signings up and down the east coast. He was sent to the Midwest a couple of times.

On one flight, Walt checked his luggage in Asheville and boarded a plane bound for St. Louis. He watched other passengers scurrying around from the time he entered the terminal. Once seated, he observed those coming aboard trying to get as much stuffed overhead as they could.

He took out WOWs and wrote, "It is understandable that individuals will accumulate some personal baggage along the way. Lest it becomes a burden for pilgrims, though, most cumbersome baggage should be checked, with little carry on."

In December 1984, a final tour was put on Walt's calendar that took him to California. He started in the north and worked his way south. The writer rented a car, driving from city to city. Other than visiting Ginny's folks in Washington, he had never been on the west coast. In the span of ten days, Walt did book signings in Sacramento, San Francisco, San Jose, Los Angeles, and Anaheim, enjoying the beautiful scenery along the Pacific coastal highway.

San Diego was the last stop. Walt was looking forward to getting the mall book signing behind him so that he could escape back to Alaska and be with Ginny for Christmas. The line was never very long, and the time was not dragging too much.

The author noticed one woman go by several times without approaching the table. She was nicely dressed and obviously a person of refinement. Yet, she was holding herself in reserve for some reason.

When the two hours were up, Walt started packing up his things. After putting some belongings in his briefcase behind his chair, he turned to leave. The same apprehensive woman was standing in front of him. She said nothing, but from underneath her purse she presented a copy of Walt's book that she brought with her. When he opened it, he noticed that it was not stiff like a new book.

"I suppose you want me to sign it," he said, reaching for his pen. She nodded in agreement. "Is there something special that you want me to inscribe?" he asked.

She spoke for the first time. "Just say, 'To Maggie, who is still trying to figure out who she is'."

After Walt complied with her request, adding his signature and the date, he handed the book back to her. Then he asked, "Did I detect the hint of a southern accent?" The woman smiled. She said she grew up in Georgia, but that she and her husband had lived in San Diego for many years.

"What part of Georgia?" Walt wanted to know. "I was raised near the corner between Georgia, Tennessee, and North Carolina," he volunteered.

"Oh, were you?" she responded, without answering his question. "I'll bet you really enjoyed growing up in the mountains."

"You know that old saying," Walt added. Corrupting a common proverb, he continued, "You can take the boy out of the mountains, but you can never get the mountains out of the boy."

She smiled.

"What does your husband do?" Walt then asked.

"He is an Admiral in the United States Navy," she answered. "He joined during World War II, and then he decided to make a career of the military."

"Do you have any children?" he asked.

"No," the woman answered. "For some reason the Good Lord did not see fit to bestow that blessing upon the two of us." Walt detected a note of sadness as she spoke.

"I'll bet you would have made a wonderful mother," he commented. "I'm a war baby myself," he then continued, wondering why he was taking up so much time with her when he was in such a hurry to leave for the airport.

"When is your birthday?" she inquired.

"It is October 31, 1944," Walt answered, with a grin. "That's right; I was hatched in the big pumpkin patch."

"You just recently celebrated your fortieth birthday then," the lady added, with a little smile coming across her face.

The woman then clutched her book, seeming anxious to go. She thanked Walt again for signing it for her. She told him she hoped that he had a safe flight back to Alaska, and then she was gone.

As he was walking to his rental car, Walt realized that the woman never did tell him where she was from in Georgia. Who was she? She had obviously already purchased her copy of the book. Why did she wait until after everyone else left before bringing it to be signed? Why was she so interested in him? How did she know he was about to catch a plane for Alaska? Why did the lady suddenly get in such a hurry to leave?

Delirious

The Alaskans did not want to be left out either. Walt did two book signings in Anchorage, and one each in Kenai and Soldotna.

But alas, Walt's fame was fleeting, and his fortune was only a bit more than a flash in the pan. By the end of the spring of 1985, he was receiving only a few calls. Total book sales topped the 100,000 mark. Even with the token royalties Walt received, he still pocketed a tidy little sum. He decided to invest the money and let it grow for his retirement fund, especially since he had put very little into Social Security.

The board of directors of the university press did give Walt a $10,000 bonus at Christmas. He and Ginny talked it over, and they decided to use that money to purchase a new Subaru. It was immediately named Brusky. They especially liked it because its color was glacial silt gray. It would blend right in with Alaska muck.

The summer of '85 was the year of the wildflower. With a new 35-millimeter camera and a couple of field guides, Walt and Gin set out every chance they had. They identified and photographed as many of Alaska's countless flowering beauties as they could find. By the end of the season, they had filled a scrapbook with their snapshots.

Walt and Ginny celebrated their first anniversary in August. There were not many fancy restaurants on the Kenai Peninsula that could offer a candlelight dinner. Therefore, Walt decided to take matters in his own hands. He told his wife to take Radar on an adventure for a couple of hours.

Chef Walt went to work. He grilled some shrimp on a skewer, basted with his own sauce. He fixed a tossed salad and cooked some wild rice. It was nothing extravagant.

The hardest part was dessert. Walt tried to bake a pound cake, but it fell flat. Gin would just have to give him E for effort. Actually, it was quite tasty with some of the berry jelly they had made.

Candles were burning throughout the house when she got back. After the slow and easy dinner with soft music playing in the background, Walt took his bride into the living room. He uncorked a bottle of champagne and they celebrated a toast.

He then told Ginny to close her eyes. Walt had purchased "The Jazz Singer" soundtrack, and he had fast-forwarded the tape to a very special song. He went to the stereo and started the cassette player. The sounds of Neil Diamond singing "Hello Again" filled the room. Once again, the two lovers melted into each other.

Celebrating Ginny's birthday on September 13, was the couple's last major outing of the fall. The two of them set out on a daylong adventure, up and beside Exit Glacier near Seward. They followed the trail to the spot where they had been pronounced husband and wife. Walt took his bride in his arms and kissed her again. They then hiked all the way to the Harding Ice Field.

While the two sat eating a picnic lunch in view of the spectacular glacier beside them, a black bear and her two cubs wandered into the little meadow right below. Mama Bear recognized that these lovers were no threat to her babies whatsoever.

Farther up the trail, sentinel marmots sounded like sirens as they signaled the danger of more bears in the area. Another sow and her cubs were off in the distance. A herd of mountain goats crossed the trail at one point up ahead of them.

Walt discovered that he was not only rather good at taking pictures of close up objects, but he was becoming quite the wildlife photographer as well. He was glad he had gone ahead and purchased a zoom lens.

After eight long hours on the trail, the two weary hikers finally got back to the parking lot. Their legs were a bit wobbly. They flipped a coin to see who had to drive back to Kenai. Walt won the toss, so he got to sit in Brusky's passenger seat. Being the southern gentleman that he was, though, he offered to take over at Tern Junction. This was, after all, Ginny's birthday.

The happy couple decided to spend Christmas in North Carolina. Ginny had three weeks off. With a two-hour stopover in Anchorage, they took a cab and went the city center to see Santa come to town in a sleigh pulled by real live reindeer.

The holiday travelers were also able to schedule a two-day layover in Seattle. Walt really enjoyed being around his wife's family once again. They were relaxed and most accommodating. Ginny's folks wanted to know why no book signings were held in the Pacific Northwest. Walt had to get his pen back out anyway. The Sullivans had bought several copies to give as Christmas gifts.

Sitting around the dinner table, Ginny's mother said that she had never heard how her daughter and Walt met. They looked at each other impishly. Walt asked which version she wanted to hear, his or Ginny's. Mrs. Sullivan said probably both of them, but she suspected Walt's was more interesting. He said he was not so sure about that.

Mr. Sullivan indicated that he was worried about his daughter being in Alaska alone after the divorce from her first husband. He said he really would have been out of his gourd if he had any idea that she was going around to gas stations picking up men. Gin's mom put her hand on his arm and said reassuringly, "Just be thankful, dear, that she ran into a southern gentleman."

January was the month Alaskans always dreaded most. The weather was usually the coldest, and those suffering from sunlight deprivation felt it worse at that time of the year. It was not an easy period for Walt. He was not busy writing or even signing books. He missed his wife so much when she was gone.

While Ginny still got much satisfaction from what she was doing, she started contemplating taking a full time job at the local hospital. The downside was that she would not have all of that compensatory time off. Being home every night would be a big plus, nevertheless.

Walt started thinking about perhaps joining the faculty at the nearby junior college, a branch of the University of Alaska. With his master's degree, he could teach freshman and sophomore level psychology courses.

If 1985 had been the summer of wildflowers, 1986 was the summer of Native American villages. Walt went with Ginny on almost all of her expeditions. He could see why she loved her work so much. The residents of these outposts thought that she was really special. He, therefore, had something in common with these folks right away.

To show their appreciation, the natives often gave Ginny gifts of Native American art, crafted just for her. The house in Kenai was beginning to look like a museum.

The vastness of the Great Land still amazed Walt. There was no end to it. His appreciation grew and grew for the people who had lived for centuries in this challenging part of the world.

When the two got home from one of her assignments, things were in a mess at the house. Cabinet doors were open, and many things were in the floor with some of them broken. This was not the work of a prowler, though. A 6.8 magnitude earthquake struck while they were gone.

Walt had been through a few with a lesser punch, but nothing like this one. He was somewhat glad they were not at home when it happened. He did say to Ginny as they were cleaning up the debris, "This time the earth moved, and we were not even here."

The travel nurse continued to mull over her work situation. She was feeling more and more like it was time for a change. In the fall of 1986, she made an appointment to discuss the matter with her supervisor.

While the state understood Ginny's position, her departure would leave a serious gap in health care in remote areas. They asked her to stay on for up to a year until a replacement could be found. She agreed.

With the anticipation that she might soon not have blocks of time off, the couple decided to make the best of it. For the Christmas holidays, they planned another combined Washington/North Carolina trip.

Ginny had become quite fond of Walt's Grandpa and Grandma King. The couple usually stayed at least one night with them coming and going. Grandpa was really taken with her, too. The two of them ganged up on Walt. Although he pretended otherwise, he loved it.

Earl was as generous as ever with temporary wheels. Walt wondered if he would ever be able to repay the bigheartedness of his uncle and aunt.

January was typically the time when Ginny was assigned to a hospital to cover for nurses taking winter vacations. She had to go no farther than the local hospital in Soldotna in 1987. She and Walt got a taste of what it would be like after she started to work full time at that facility.

When the calendar rolled over to February, she was soon on the road again, or rather back in the air. It always unnerved Walt a bit when he saw the plane being de-iced before it took off.

By spring and into the summer, no replacement had yet been found for the itinerant health care worker. Walt once again went with his nurse/wife on several of the flights into remote areas. Immunization shots took much of her time.

Walt missed the spectacular fall colors of the mountains back home, but he loved this time of year in Alaska. He so looked forward to the time when Gin could witness the blaze of color with him in the Smoky Mountains.

He still marveled at how compatible the two of them were. They did not have to surrender their individuality for the sake of the relationship. Neither became an extension of the other. Both were free to be themselves. Separately, they were whole persons, but together they complemented each other in a phenomenal way.

Walt and Ginny did not always see eye to eye. They were both strong-willed individualists. Early on, they agreed to disagree. The first time that they let a misunderstanding get a little overheated, she was the one to ask for some space. Walt was a bit panicky when she said that she was feeling smothered.

An hour or so later, she returned and wrapped her arms around him. He apologized for his part in the argument. After what happened next, Walt suggested that they start having at least one good fuss a week.

More than anything, though, Walt and Gin just loved being together. They enjoyed each other's company. They were best friends, and they were blissful playmates.

As the anniversary of the talk Ginny had with her supervisor was approaching, the travel nurse was asked one more favor. A replacement was being interviewed, and it looked as if he were going to be hired.

In the meantime, there was an urgent situation on one of the Aleutian Islands. An outbreak of some kind had left a number of residents dangerously dehydrated. Two villagers had died. It could be a new influenza strain, or it might be cholera. Gin agreed to go immediately to investigate the situation and to get fluids started.

It was a cold windy day on November 7, 1987, when Walt said goodbye to Ginny at the airport in Kenai. Snow was coming down sideways. "Walt, I have to go," she said to him reassuringly.

"If you must . . . ," he responded.

As they embraced, he said those magical three words to his beloved.

"I love you more," Ginny replied to him.

"I love you no less," Walt finished their special little ritual.

After the plane was de-iced, it taxied out on the runway. Ginny waved to Walt, still standing in front of the big plate glass window in the waiting area. He did not leave until the aircraft was out of sight, which did not take long. On his way to the truck, he said out loud, "Whoever said 'Parting is such sweet sorrow' needs to have his head examined."

Walt considered going with her, but Ginny talked him out of it. There was no need in exposing him to something contagious. She hoped to be home by Thanksgiving.

There was no direct phone communication to the island. Walt would not hear from Gin until she got back. That could be four or five days, or perhaps up to two weeks. He was not looking forward to being out of touch.

Late in the afternoon after his beloved wife left, Walt picked up WOWs and started making an entry. "The word of the day is delirious. I just love the way it tickles my tongue when I say it aloud. I am deliriously happy with Ginny, as she tickles my fancy. I cannot imagine my life without . . ."

Then, the phone rang.

"Is this Mr. Walter Williamson?" the man on the other end asked.

Walt answered in the affirmative, noticing something unsettling in the man's voice.

"This is Sgt. Hayes with the Department of Public Safety in Anchorage. Mr. Williamson, I regret to have to inform you that the plane your wife is on is missing."

Delirium

In a moment . . . in the twinkling of an eye . . . delirious morphed into delirium.

Walt had a hard time focusing on anything else Sgt. Hayes was saying. The plane had simply not arrived on schedule. It was now about two hours overdue. The pilot could have made an emergency landing somewhere on another island, but no distress signal had been received. Search crews were already in the air trying to locate the missing plane. Bad weather was hampering their efforts. He would be informed immediately when there was any news to report.

Walt had trouble taking a deep breath. Had his world just come crashing down around him? He tried to scream, but nothing would come. He went outside and faced the wind, letting the snow pelt his face. Ginny was all right. She had to be all right. How could he live without her?

Where was Radar? He called the dog, and then he sat with his arms embracing Ginny's husky. Radar licked his face, lapping up the snowflakes mingled with tears. Walt was instantaneously transported back in time. Spot and Scout were again consoling a distressed boy. That was right after another plane had fallen from the sky.

Walt eventually went inside and turned on the television. The report of the missing plane was all over the news. He learned little that he did not know already. He wanted to do something. He needed to be somewhere.

After placing a stressful call to Ginny's folks, he had to sit and wait, wanting the phone to ring, but dreading for it to at the same time.

The torturous hours passed slowly. If there was ever a time when no news is bad news, this was it. If the plane did make a successful emergency landing somewhere, it would have most likely been located by now. Then again, there were many Alaska stories of survivors waiting for days before being found and rescued.

Walt never went to bed. He might have dozed a time or two on the sofa. His television was not turned off. About mid-morning, he first saw it on a news bulletin interrupting regularly scheduled programming. Wreckage of an aircraft had been spotted in the Bering Sea. It was presumed to be the missing plane. There was no sign of survivors.

The phone rang. This was the last time Walt would ever again answer a phone with "Hello."

The next few days were like a blur for Walt. Some bodies were recovered. He had to go to Anchorage to identify Ginny's if hers was among them. It was.

Because of Walt's notoriety from his book, he got calls from reporters all around the country wanting an interview. This sickened him. The media would exploit any tragic situation to get a story that might boost ratings.

Just as he put the receiver down after finally getting rid of a persistent news anchor, the phone rang again. He almost did not answer it, but something told him to go ahead.

"Walt, I just heard . . . and I am so sorry . . . ," Hannah said, her voice quivering.

Ginny's parents took the first available flight. Walt tried as best he could to comfort them. They all agonized over the fact that this was her last flight as a travel nurse.

In accordance with her wishes, Gin's body was cremated. Nurse Sullivan's ashes were then turned over to the state to be scattered over the villages where she had served faithfully.

As Ginny's parents were leaving, they assured Walt that he would always be a part of their lives. It was some comfort to hear them say the happiest days of their daughter's life were the ones when she and Walt were together. He assured them that the same was true for him.

Walt could sense her essence in every room of the house. Her scent was strongest in the bedroom and the bathroom. He wished never to wash the sheets or the last towel she used. Everywhere he looked, he saw things his beloved's hands had touched.

Radar knew something was seriously wrong. He was accustomed to Ginny's comings and goings. This time he recognized that it was different. Before Walt came into their lives, Gin and Radar had already been together more than half a dozen years. Like their human counterparts, a dog's life is not always as long in Alaska.

When Radar stopped eating and did not snap out of his despondency, Walt became concerned. One day when the husky wanted out, he saw a certain look in the dog's eye. He remembered the time as a lad seeing that same look in Scout's eyes the day he went off and never came home. As Radar walked slowly into the forest, the grieving widower said goodbye to another part of Ginny.

Walt had not even noticed that it was Thanksgiving Week when his phone rang. Ginny's parents invited him to come to Washington. He picked himself up, and he got the last passenger seat out of Anchorage before the holiday.

The family wished to have a little memorial service for Ginny. Her childhood friends also needed a time to express their own condolences and to say goodbye. Walt understood this need for closure.

Ginny's dad asked him if he would like to say a few words. If he was up to it, Mr. Sullivan knew that his daughter's friends would love to hear the story about how he and Gin met. While he was recounting that priceless episode, he realized that he was smiling for the first time in almost three weeks.

Walt retold the part about Ginny telling him that her friends called her Ginny and her enemies called her Sully. He informed those at the gathering that he could honestly say he never heard anyone address his wife in the adversarial way. With a little glint in his eye that would have made Gin proud, he then said, "I almost did a couple of times, but I thought better of it."

Since she was not there to represent herself, Walt then shared Ginny's version of the tale. He even mimicked sad puppy dog eyes. Everyone laughed when he put his hands around his neck to symbolize the collar and the leash.

On the way back to Alaska, Walt had to start addressing something, whether he wanted to or not. What was he going to do with the rest of his life? He then had his own reality check. He reminded himself that he was a human being, not a human doer. He would just *be*, and let the details take care of themselves. But could he? What did he have to live for?

Some business needed minding over the next several weeks, no matter how devastated Walt was. He had to get a death certificate. Ginny had a will and it had to be probated. She left everything to him. Since she had mortgage insurance on her house, it was signed over to him free of debt. In addition, the state had a life insurance policy on Ginny with Walt as the beneficiary. He was also due a considerable financial settlement from the airline.

Little of this mattered. Nothing could replace Ginny.

He thought about flying back to Ephesus for the Christmas holidays. Since he was going to be alone either way, he might as well just stay in Alaska. He would feel closer to Ginny there.

Walt's grief was immense. He did not try to suppress it, but he did not know how to express it. The friends he had made in Alaska reached out to him. All of his life, however, he was accustomed to helping others with their burdens, while carrying his own alone. Father Nicholas made weekly visits and they established a close bond.

While trying so hard to put things into some kind of perspective, something hit Walt especially hard. The deaths of three women had greatly affected his life. His mother's was the impetus to reconnect with his being, the beginning of his renaissance. When he inherited Mrs. Neumann's house, he gained the freedom to take full ownership of his life. Then, Ginny's death seemed to render everything null and void.

"Othell," he said one day, "Just when I think I might have some things figured out, something always seems to knock the props right out from under me. Who am I? Why me?" The man who wrote the book on identity must now go back to the drawing board.

As the weeks turned into months, Walt gradually began to regain some measure of equilibrium, what Gin called balance. His life had been made so much richer and fuller by her. Going on without her would not be easy. However, he had to go on. He "must . . ."

During the cold winter months, he picked up the pen again. This time he decided to try his hand at fiction. What came out was a succession of short stories with no unifying theme that could be translated into a novel. There was a common thread in all of his compositions, though. They were the musings of a mournful heart.

Well, I'll Be

In 1988, when the first robin of spring announced her presence and started refurbishing the nest under the eve of the back porch, Walt felt a little lilt in his own spirits. One morning soon thereafter, Ms. Robin seemed to be talking to him. "Well, hello," he said. Instantly, he felt a wave of grief roll through him. He had just uttered the sacred word to this lowly bird.

Walt was astounded by what happened next. The robin became very animated. She started dancing and prancing around on the ground, singing a different song.

Over the next several days, he knew what he "must" do. He would go back to his other home for a while, and try to reconnect with his roots there.

Instead of flying or meandering along in Nellie, Walt decided to take Brusky along for the ride. He could save about as much in gas money to pay for his lodging along the way. He and Ginny had planned to take this trip together, but now he would have to go it alone. He could hear Gin saying, "If you must . . ."

On the morning that he pulled out, Walt went around back before he left. Ms. Robin was on her nest. He did not feel silly at all telling her goodbye. As he did, she flew to the clothesline and broke out in song. He wished her well raising her brood. It was time to go.

Walt laughed when he saw a pair of trumpeters at Potter Marsh. Not far above Anchorage, two more were on a lake. Just beyond the Matanuska Glacier, he spotted another pair of swans. By the time he got to Tok, he had seen more than a dozen duos.

It did not stop there. All through the Yukon and Northern British Columbia, swans were swimming along near the shoreline in lakes all up and down. Walt wondered how anyone could doubt a loving Creator. "Othell, God certainly does have a marvelous sense of humor," he said aloud.

The driver decided to vary his route a bit, although there were few alternatives until he got well on down the road. He did have one option before he got out of Alaska. In no particular hurry, Walt took a left beyond Tok Junction and went through the little village of Chicken. Local lore had it that the early settlers of this little gold mining town wanted to name it Ptarmigan, but no one knew how to spell it.

Brusky bounced along on miles and miles of rough unpaved roads. Once into Canada, Walt soon went across what is called the Top of the World. His topsy-turvy world was upside down, though.

A few hours later, he got to Dawson City, home of the big Klondike gold strike. Brusky rode the ferry across the Yukon River. This former boomtown once provided inspiration for writers Jack London and Robert Service.

Sitting on the porch of the poet Service's cabin, Walt had a perception of his own. As he opened up WOWs, he realized that he had not made an entry since the day of the fateful phone call. He looked back over what he was writing when he was interrupted. He had not said, "Ginny makes me deliriously happy." Rather, he penned, "I am deliriously happy with Ginny." He pondered the difference in those two concepts. Walt had lost his lover and his playmate, but not his "I am."

Once back to the Alaska Highway, Walt started recognizing things he had seen on the way up. That voyage seemed so long ago. More roads had been paved in the meantime. Brusky was certainly appreciative of that. He looked over all along at the empty passenger seat trying to imagine Gin sitting there.

When he came to the end of the Alaska Highway at Dawson Creek, he took a picture of Brusky under the same sign where he photographed Nellie. He then decided to take an easterly route through central Canada. The wayfarer eventually crossed the border into North Dakota. He decided to go by Mt. Rushmore one state down. From there, he meandered through the Midwest, and eventually made his way to North Carolina.

Walt was embracing solitude. Some would call him a recluse, but he was not too keen on putting labels on people. With his physical relationship with Ginny now severed, he was connecting more than ever with his being. He wrote in WOWs, "There is a big difference between wholeness and holeness. Those who are struggling with holeness believe that they will be happy if they can only fill all the holes in their life. Individuals who aspire for wholeness, on the other hand, strive to become complete, whole persons from the inside out."

Butterflies Are Free

After he finally made his way back to his little mountain retreat, Walt felt like he was just going through the motions in everything he did. For several days, he was preoccupied with necessary chores to get everything back up to speed. Then, evening would come. How he dreaded the evenings.

During the summer months, he continued trying to put things in perspective. He was in his forties. If someone had told him ten years prior that he would own a house in North Carolina and another in Alaska, he would have asked, "What have you been smoking?"

If anyone else had predicted that he would be sitting on almost a quarter million dollars, he would have said, "Somebody must have left you out in the sun a little too long." To be sure, neither house met current building codes, but you could not beat their location.

Something about his own life mystified Walt. Heartbreak seemed to haunt him on one hand, while good fortune was smiling at him on the other.

Late one afternoon, Walt picked up WOWs and went to the front porch swing. He had no particular thought in mind as to what he might enter. He recalled sitting in that very spot years earlier scribbling on legal pads, trying to hammer out his master's thesis.

He not only missed Ginny, but this place was not the same without Mrs. Neumann. Could a man feel more abandoned and all alone?

Not long after taking his seat, a beautiful blue butterfly came from around the corner. It flitted in and out as though teasing him. He noticed that it had a damaged wing.

Then, an incredible thing happened. The butterfly came and lit on Walt's knee. With its wings flapping very slowly, he gazed right into its eyes. Suddenly, it became motionless. Walt felt a presence, something that he knew, but could not identify immediately.

Just like that, the butterfly lifted off, darted around the yard, and then disappeared.

Lifting his pen, Walt wrote:

"Butterfly, butterfly, how did you come to be?

Were you sent from God Above to come and play with me?

For that moment in time, you were mine; you sat on my knee.

How I worshiped at your shrine, oh, don't you see?

Butterfly, butterfly, now fly away free."

The days were already getting noticeably shorter. Walt got up one morning and a touch of fall was in the air. His restless spirit told him that it was time to get going yet again. He made a trip to Mason to say goodbye to his grandparents. He winterized his mountain home, and he headed back to Alaska.

Walt considered leaving Brusky in Ephesus and flying back. Something about the open road was calling him again, however. He laughed when he thought how he was going about things backwards from what most folks did. They would summer in Alaska and winter outside. He was never much of one to follow the herd.

Just like in the spring, the voyager faced a steady stream of oncoming traffic while he had his lane mostly to himself. Going against the flow was nothing new for him. This was in many ways the story of Walt Williamson's life.

Walt was going to have to do something with some of that money. He could just hear Ginny saying, "If you must . . ." Driving across the country, he decided to go to her alma mater in Washington, and to endow a nursing scholarship in her name.

He formulated some conditions with the financial aid office. It would not be just a simple handout. The scholarship would function more like a loan. For every year after graduation that the recipient worked as a travel nurse, or with one of the government's volunteer agencies like the Peace Corps and VISTA, a year of his or her loan would be forgiven. Otherwise, it would be paid back, but with no interest.

Ginny's parents were overwhelmed with Walt's gesture. They pledged to add to the endowment. After an enjoyable visit, he knew that he had to get on up the road. Otherwise, he might be stranded along the way by an early winter storm.

Three weeks after he left North Carolina, Walt crossed the border into Alaska. The house was dark and foreboding when he got to Kenai. Nevertheless, he burst through the door hollering, "Hi Honey, I'm home."

The next thing he did was light a candle. It lightened his spirit, and he smiled when he blew out the match. He kept at least one candle burning throughout the dark winter months. One morning he awoke, and a candle was burning that he swore he did not light.

Walt had no objection to following Ginny's instructions that her body be cremated. One facet of honoring her wishes, however, he had given no thought to until he had to deal with it. As the first anniversary of her death was approaching, he sat one day trying to capture his feelings. He entitled what he was writing, "The Lamentations of my Soul." The anguished widower ended with, "Where do you go to grieve, when there is no grave?"

Later that evening, Walt wandered outside. The crisp air sent a jolt through his ill-clad body. Something else suddenly grabbed his attention. The night sky was emblazoned with color. The Aurora Borealis was putting on a magnificent light show.

Even though Walt could not go to a grave where Ginny's remains were interred, there were special places that he could go. It was something he "must" do before Old Man Winter blocked his path. The F-150 now stayed mostly in the drive. He had to jumpstart it to get it running.

Walt began his outing by going by the Russian Orthodox Church. He parked, went in, and knelt for a few moments at the altar. He then drove down to the beach. After a few moments, he got out and walked on the gray glacial sand for about half an hour. No one else was around on that late fall/early winter day.

The tops of the Kenai Mountains were already capped with snow as he went up the Sterling Highway. For the first time since Ginny's death, Walt headed the Ford truck up the narrow rough road to the overlook where he and his bride had voiced their wedding vows. First one tear, and then another streamed down his cheeks. Back under the wheel, he would not turn toward home just yet.

The next hour dragged on ever so slowly. It was snowing when he went across the summit. Walt sat alone at Summit Lake Lodge and watched it coming down. He only ordered a cup of coffee. The man at the register said the lodge was closing for the winter later that day.

It was not quite as windy at Beluga Point as he had experienced in the past. The others pulled over were oblivious to the emotions undulating through him.

The Russian Orthodox cross that Walt had given Ginny was not recovered from the plane wreckage. Her wedding ring was saved, however. He had it in his pocket. He reached for it, and he began to sob. He evoked the memories of the day that he placed it on her finger at this very sacred spot. Walt gently rubbed the ring he was still wearing. He placed Ginny's on his pinky for the rest of the day.

One more stop was yet ahead. It was beginning to get a little dark when he got to the unpaved road going out to Exit Glacier. It was rough from the summer traffic, and it would not be plowed again until spring. With the tourists now long gone, the parking lot was deserted.

Walt made his way slowly toward the face of the glacier. He was amazed at how much it had retreated since he first came there with Gin in 1983. A jagged tower of ice was leaning precipitously. He waited for a few minutes, hoping to see it calve as he watched. Something else was more pressing, though.

He hiked up the trail to the place beside the glacier where he first held his beloved in his arms. The silence was deafening. Then, it was broken with a loud crack, not unlike the sound of a high-powered rifle. This was followed by the roaring blare of tons of ice crashing below. Walt managed a smile. Time and tide cannot stand still, even if at times they only move at glacial speed.

The grieving widower then made his way along the exposed outcropping carved years earlier by the glacier. His eyes were searching for something familiar. It all looked so different. He was beginning to think that he might not recognize it.

A little farther ahead, he turned aside from the beaten path. The wind was icy coming off the glacier. He began to shake and shiver, but it was not just from the cold. Could it be near? Walt was not sure. He was having trouble getting his bearings.

A surge of something raced throughout his body and soul as he then looked to his left. Nestled in a seam of the rock were remnants of the dried wildflowers that he had picked for his beloved bride on their wedding day. They were still bound together by the now faded blue ribbon. The words that his precious Ginny had uttered to him on that very spot reverberated throughout his soul. Her love for him was indeed forever and ever.

Tears ran down Walt's cheeks, only a tad faster than the nearby glacier was moving. He carefully removed the ribbon. He clutched it in the same hand that also cradled Ginny's wedding ring all the way back to the house. The next day he tied it in a bow and put it in a frame.

Walt could have easily become a hermit. On the drive back to Alaska, he had let his beard grow out. His hair was longer than it had ever been. He kept making an effort to mix and mingle, but his reclusiveness usually kicked back in and took over.

In time, he was able to start reading again. Once more, he became a regular at the library. When it came to ordering books, the director soon found that he must do little research. Walt's routine requests for upcoming publications alerted him to what readers would be wanting. The newly organized Friends of the Library also tapped him to be one of its volunteers.

When one book was released that Walt recommended, the front desk called and told him it was in. *How to Be Your Own Best Friend*, by Mildred Newman and Bernard Berkowitz jumped to the top of the bestseller lists for nonfiction. He read it in one sitting. Walt could not understand why the content was not common knowledge to everyone. He and Othell had been best friends all of his life.

After reading the book, Walt wrote in WOWs, "An optimist is someone who says that he is his own best friend. A pessimist believes that he is his own worst enemy. A realist knows that he is both."

One day in the spring of 1989, Walt read a newspaper article about the need for volunteers on the peninsula. Aging pioneers sometimes required a lift to get about. Widows in the area were often in need of a helping hand with simple maintenance projects around the house.

He was good with his hands, so he signed up, and he soon started getting calls. Walt had always felt a certain fondness for senior citizens. He found them a treasure trove of rich experiences. He already knew that some unpolished gems were among the old sourdoughs in Alaska.

The handyman did not mind at all fixing a leaky faucet, or repairing a broken step for elderly folks. Stories from the past would be pay enough. One woman said that she was a charter member of Soldotna's first social organization. It was called the Malfunction Junction Bitch and Stitch Club.

Walt started telling people jokingly that he guessed he had come full circle. He was once again concentrating on the 3 Rs. This time, though, they were Reading, 'Riting, and Repairing.

When the phone rang about the middle of January 1990, the person on the other end was asking for a different kind of assistance. It was Walt's old counseling partner, Lynda, back in Ephesus. She was now married and expecting her first child at the end of the month. Lynda wondered if there was any way he could come and keep the office open while she was out on maternity leave.

There really was no reason why he could not honor her request. He got a ticket to Atlanta, and then placed a call to Earl. He would need his own wheels to leave in Ephesus, so he might as well go ahead and let his uncle set him up. Mrs. Neumann's worn out old Oldsmobile was still under the shelter, but Walt had not started it since she died.

He intended to get a nice used vehicle, but Earl insisted that he could put him in a new Toyota for not that much more. Walt drove off in Yo, declaring himself now a local yokel. Enough of the drab colors. Yo was a little redder than Dolly's dull maroon.

Walt stayed in Ephesus well into the spring. The practice had grown to the point that one person was having a hard time keeping up. Lynda thus made Walt an offer. She knew how important Alaska was to him, but if he could swing it, she would like to have him on board during the winter months.

Over the next couple of years, Walt settled into somewhat of a routine. He returned to North Carolina after the cranberries were picked and put in the freezer in the fall. He then went back to Alaska when the rivers were flowing again after breakup. He could earn enough to pay his keep without having to rely very much on his savings. When the country entered an economic downturn and business fell off, Lynda took the practice back over.

With every visit to Mason, Walt found his grandparents aging more and more. He was especially concerned about his Grandpa. It appeared that wonderful man was right about one thing. Actually, Walt never knew him to be wrong about much of anything. It did seem that Grandma King might make the century mark. Her husband told her that she would need to have her tombstone say, "See, I told you I was not well."

During his visit over the Christmas holidays of 1991, Walt could not quite figure out what was going on. It seemed to him that his Grandpa kept trying to tell him something. He would start to speak, and then shy away from it. Walt made sure he gave the grand man whatever opening he might need. No amount of prodding was successful, though.

When he was back in Mason a month later, he took his Grandpa for a ride. While they were out, the old man wanted to go by the cemetery. The sun was shining brightly, but winter was yet to do its disappearing act.

Standing at the foot of Maude's grave, Grandpa King began to shed some tears. Walt was soon weeping right alongside him. What he had no way of knowing was that his Grandpa was trying so earnestly to find a way to tell him something. More than once the man tried to speak, but he would then let out a deep sigh, and just continue to sob.

He Took It with Him to His Grave

About the time the dogwoods were at their peak in the spring of 1992, George King got up one Saturday morning feeling restless. He kept squirming in his tattered old recliner. When Ruby brought him a cup of coffee, she noticed a strange look in his eyes.

About mid-morning, George finally put on his overalls. He went out in the garden, now long neglected and overgrown with weeds. He wandered over to the orchard, wondering if there would be any apples and pears this year.

Ruby made cornbread, and then warmed up some vegetable soup for their little lunch. While they were still sitting at the kitchen table, George started reminiscing. Ruby had always known her husband to be sentimental, but this caught her a little off guard. He told her how much he loved her, and what a good wife and mother she had been.

George then said if he went first, he hoped that she would be able to get along okay until she joined him on the other side. His companion of many, many years rebuked him and said, "Why, George King. The only reason I'm still around is to take care of you."

As Ruby was washing up the dishes, George went to the bedside table and got his Bible. She watched curiously, as he ran several references. Then, he put the Good Book back where he kept it.

After a nap in his easy chair, the old man stood up. Without uttering a word, he went out the backdoor. His wife kept an eye on him as he ambled toward the old mule barn. She then busied herself cooking a beef roast with onions, carrots, and potatoes. Earl and Mary Beth were coming for Sunday dinner to help celebrate a very special occasion.

George eventually made his way out behind the barn where his old GMC truck had been parked for about three decades. When he no longer needed the vehicle, the kindly old man could not part with it. He just put it out to pasture.

George trudged through the bramble, and he tugged on the door handle. As the weary old man and the rusty hinges were both making grimacing sounds, the door grudgingly gave way. With considerable effort, he climbed up in the cab, clearing spider webs out of the way with his left arm. The tires were flat, which made the step up not as steep. The key was still in the ignition.

As George settled into the seat, he felt a sharp pain run up his left side. He tried the window, and with a grinding sound, it went down slowly, letting in a cool breeze. Sitting in the driver's seat, the erstwhile mule trader took hold of the steering wheel. Memories surged. The longings in this devout man's heart began to spill out.

> Dear Heavenly Father, it has been many years now since I first lifted my grandson up before your throne of grace. Sitting right here in this seat one hot and sweaty day, I implored you to make that little war baby into something really special. Thank you, Lord, for so wonderfully answering my prayer.

> No man could ask for a finer grand boy. As it turned out, he is the only grandson I have. I thank you for allowing me to live to see the man he has become.

And you know God, it did not get by me that the man who does not even know about his own mammy and pappy is now an expert about people knowing who they are.

Lord, I admit I don't understand everything in his book. But what I do know is that Walt Williamson believes with all his heart that people should just be the best folks they can be. That boy has certainly overcome obstacle after obstacle to be who he is. You must be just as proud of him as I am.

(George King paused. He was struggling to get his breath. Then, he continued.)

"You know my Heavenly Father that my time on this earth is short. I am not going to be around much longer to keep an eye on Walt. I hope my efforts on his behalf have found favor in Your sight. Watch over that boy for me after I am dead and gone. Prepare him for whatever is still ahead."

(Once again, the saintly old man stopped praying aloud for a few moments.)

"Dear Jesus, I'm now ready to go, whenever you decide to come get me. I have had a wonderful life on this old earth. And one more thing Lord – please also take care of my faithful wife, Ruby."

"Amen."

The shadows were getting long, and George had not come back to the house. Ruby was concerned, and she called out to him from the back porch. When she got no answer, she carefully made her way down the path. Many years had passed since the old woman had last walked to the barn. The lingering smell of manure still hovered in the air. She continued to call George's name, all the while looking into the dusty stalls and the corn cribs. Her husband was not in the barn.

Just as the worried wife got back to the house, her son and daughter-in-law drove into the yard. Earl hugged his mother. He told her that they decided to come a day early because he was concerned about his dad. Ruby then told him that she did not know where George was.

Mary Beth took her inside while Earl went to look for his father. He had a notion where he might find him. As he turned the corner behind the barn, he could see that someone had already traipsed through the weeds and the vines. The trail led straight to the old GMC. Slouched in the driver's seat, George King had gone to meet his Maker, one day shy of his ninety-fifth birthday.

Walt got the call just as he was about to sit down to dinner. Food would have to wait. He quickly packed some things and said, "Yo, let's go."

When he got to Mason a little before midnight, Mary Beth was lying down with Grandma King. Earl was waiting up for him in the kitchen. He filled Walt in with the details. The coroner determined that George died of natural causes. His body was at the funeral home.

By sunrise the next morning, neighbors were already bringing in food. After breakfast, Walt went into his grandparents' bedroom. He reverently gathered up his Grandpa's Bible. He then slipped out unnoticed, heading for the place where his mentor and hero all in one breathed his last breath.

The weeds and briars were all beaten down now, and there was a clear path to the truck. Walt stopped beside a blackberry patch that was all decked out in white blooms. His mind took a little detour as he remembered picking blackberries with his Grandma. He could almost taste the cobblers and jam she made.

Walt went around to the passenger side, dusted off the seat, and sat once again where he had ridden many miles with his Grandpa. He did not feel worthy to sit behind the wheel.

He then carefully opened the leather-bound Book that he held in his trembling hands. He saw on the presentation page where his mother had given the Scriptures to her daddy for Christmas in 1961. That was the year Walt was a senior in high school. He looked at the family history section, and he saw where his own name was entered. Walt smiled when he observed W.O.W. inscribed after it.

What was his grandpa reading the afternoon before? His Grandma said that he kept going to the concordance in the back and looking up verses. Did he leave any kind of a clue?

Walt gently lifted the red ribbon. He opened the Bible to the pages it marked. Underlined, were two verses from the Gospel of John:

"When Jesus therefore saw his mother, and the disciple standing by, whom he loved, he saith unto his mother, Woman, behold thy son! Then saith he to the disciple, Behold thy mother! And from that hour that disciple took her unto his own home."

What did this mean? Why would his Grandpa highlight these two verses?

Walt's mind then drifted back to his most recent visits to Mason. How he wished for another chance to sit and talk with that great man. Whatever it was that he was trying to tell his grandson, Grandpa King had now taken it with him to his grave.

Walt thought back to his last conversation with his Granddaddy Williamson. Right before he died, that man also acted as if he were trying to tell him something. This beloved grandson could not help but notice the similarities in how these two great men had passed away. On their last day, both read their Bibles, and each marked passages.

In Walt Williamson's eyes, no two finer men ever walked this earth than his Granddaddy Williamson and his Grandpa King. They taught him so much about life. Both of them were now dead and gone. He knew that he was incredibly blessed with a storehouse of wisdom and lore imparted to him by these gentle giants. Yet, so much was still left unsaid.

He Saw It in Her Eyes

Hannah was now teaching at the university. The school continued to add postgraduate programs, and she kept climbing the degree ladder as each new rung was added. Walt occasionally went by and had lunch with her.

She was increasingly anxious about Phillip's state. She said that about all doctors knew how to do any more was write prescriptions. She added that the medicine cabinet in their bathroom looked like a pharmacy. Every time a new drug came out for depression or pain, Phillip returned home from his regular appointment with yet another bottle of pills.

During one of their infrequent chats, Hannah suggested to Walt that he needed to write the story of his incredible life. His longtime friend conveyed that characters in a Greek Tragedy had nothing on him. "And she does not even know about D-V Day," Walt thought to himself.

He then said to Hannah that if he did it, he would have to write it as fiction. Nobody would believe it was true.

"Well, you already have a title," she suggested with a twinkle in her eyes. Even after all these years, that sparkle still sent a thrill through him.

"And what would that be?" he asked, with a little boy mischievous look on his own face.

"Walt, it is so obvious. Your book would be 'The War Baby'."

Walt was not prepared for the impact that his Grandpa King's death had on him. Yet another connection was now severed, creating more vacantness that could not be filled. All of his reclusive instincts began to kick in again.

Elijah Pierce, one of Walt's former graduate school classmates, was now the chaplain at the hospital in Ephesus. Chaplain Pierce also served as the assistant rector for the St. Elizabeth Episcopal Church. They occasionally had lunch together.

At Eli's insistence, Walt started volunteering some of his time for inpatient counseling. He even agreed to be on call when his colleague was unavailable. Walt did not mind being around a hospital. It made him feel closer to Ginny.

The first patient that he looked in on was an interesting old man with terminal prostate cancer. They hit it off right away. As Norman Ferrell described his condition, he said that if "prostrate" cancer was not enough to deal with, he was also suffering from "mascular" degeneration.

Walt noticed his misuse of words, but he did not attempt to correct the unassuming man. He rather replied, "I hear there is a lot of that going around," trying hard to be impassive. The patient grinned slyly, but he looked away so Walt could not see him.

On his next visit, Mr. Ferrell laughed when Walt entered his room. "I really had you goin' last time, didn't I?" he said.

"What do you mean?" Walt asked.

"About prostrate cancer and mascular degeneration," the patient responded. "When you didn't flinch, I knew you wuz okay."

When Norman was being transferred to a nursing home, he asked Walt to come visit him. First one thing and then another hindered him, though. Realizing that this old man did not have long to live, Walt set out one day to find the Pleasantdale Nursing Home on the outskirts of town. He was surprised at how much ground the man had lost since he saw him last.

Walt listened as the crusty old mountaineer spoke bravely of his courageous fight with the disease. The professional counselor was amazed at how Mr. Ferrell was facing his impending death with such peace and tranquility. Rarely had Walt been in the presence of a person with this kind of faith. Something about the man reminded him of his Granddaddy Williamson.

While he was at the nursing home, Walt looked in on a few other residents. He introduced himself, and said that he would come back from time to time when they could just sit and talk. Over the next couple of visits, he chatted again with some of them.

One day when he got to Mr. Ferrell's room, the aides were almost finished giving him a bath. Walt waited in the lobby as they were getting him dressed. Meanwhile, a new patient was checking in. The woman had no family with her so he offered his assistance.

After she finished filling out the forms, Walt escorted the new resident to her room. Her belongings were left on the front porch, so he retrieved them for the rather frail woman. He then offered to help her unpack. She said that she could manage, although he could see that she was crippled with arthritis.

On his next visit to Pleasantdale, Walt went by to check on the woman. He looked at the name on the door, Margaret Hogan, to make sure he got it right. "Hello, Mrs. Hogan, are you all settled in?" he asked.

"I'm getting used to things," she answered. Walt did not stay long, but he promised to come back soon. The woman said that she would look forward to his visit. He sensed something about her that was different from the other patients. For one thing, she did not speak with a parochial brogue.

When Walt returned to the nursing home a week later, Norman had lapsed into a coma. He met with family members, keeping a vigil in the chapel. They all knew that it was only a matter of hours. Even though he had known Mr. Ferrell for just a short time, Walt was asked to be a pallbearer at his funeral. He felt truly honored.

After he got home, Walt was thinking back over his nursing home visits. The residents were really enjoying the time he was spending with them. That he was not there because of some sense of obligation or duty seemed to make a difference. Mrs. Hogan in particular appeared to appreciate him coming by. He decided that he would go by every week or so. That was the least he could do.

For some reason, he always found himself heading to Mrs. Hogan's room first. He had introduced himself to her as Walt Williamson, but he noticed that she always addressed him as Walter. Mrs. Neumann used to call him that, too.

He could not get Mrs. Hogan to talk about herself very much. He did find out that she had been a naval officer's wife, and she had lived in San Diego most of her adult life. Walt mentioned to her that he was in San Diego once, but he did not explain why.

After Mrs. Hogan's husband died of a sudden heart attack, she decided that she wanted a change of scenery. She told her new friend that she had always loved the mountains. She said that she felt fortunate indeed to get a room in Ephesus.

One day, Walt asked the woman about her arthritis. She hesitated, but felt compelled to offer some explanation. Mrs. Hogan told Walt that when she was a young woman, she worked in a factory during the war. Her hands were under great stress running a stranding machine making war materials. When she started having problems with her fingers, the doctor told her that she had most likely damaged them at that time.

She then said something that Walt did not understand. "This is just my little cross that I have to bear as a painful reminder that life is not without consequences."

Mrs. Hogan wanted to hear Walt's stories. This was a bit awkward for him. In his profession, he was accustomed to getting others to open up, while keeping his own personal life out of the conversation. But then again, he was not visiting these residents as a counselor, but as a friend. Reluctantly at first, he began to recount for her some of his boyhood adventures.

Mrs. Hogan seemed genuinely interested. He told her all about his dogs, Scout and Spot. He described how the three of them played together in the wagon.

Walt told this nursing home resident about the time when in the fourth grade he learned the importance of drinking lots of water. When she found out how he had gotten around doing his homework, a big smile came across her face and she said, "Oh, Walter, that is so clever."

With a playful look in his eyes, he told her about the paddling he got from Mrs. Webster. "And just what were all those things you did that she could never catch you doing?" Mrs. Hogan wanted to know.

"I'll never tell," he answered, impishly.

Walt thought about telling her about his high school graduation. He was just not sure that he could find the right words to explain the significance of his speech to someone who had known him for such a short time. Maybe later.

The woman could see the pride in Walt's eyes when he spoke of his grandfathers. He recounted helping his Granddaddy Williamson in the woodshop and at the fruit stand. He told about going fishing with his granddaddy, and about how Old Gus made him cuss. He said that if he had only followed all the wonderful advice his granddaddy gave him, he would be a much better man.

Walt also voiced genuine appreciation for all of the things that Earl and Mary Beth had done for him. He said nothing about his parents and his sister, though, and Mrs. Hogan did not ask.

He described for her what happened the night of the storm, and how his Grandpa King winked at him around the kerosene lamp. He told Mrs. Hogan about the double barrel shotgun his grandpa wanted him to give a try. "I think it rattled my brain, and that's the reason I'm so crazy," he added. Mrs. Hogan just rolled her eyes and let out a sigh.

On another visit, Walt told his special new friend about hog killing days. He described the time he learned how to tie his shoes. He recounted for her the conversation he had that morning with his Grandpa King about being a war baby. The storyteller did not quite understand her response when Mrs. Hogan said, "That's what you are Walter, a war baby for sure."

He then told her all about the tenderloin biscuits from the Rusty Hinge Grill. Mrs. Hogan said that it made her mouth water just thinking about it.

This was getting to be fun. Walt had thought that his nursing home visits might cheer up the residents. Mrs. Hogan's interest in his life was having a different effect, however. By revisiting these character-building episodes in his life, the counselor was experiencing a measure of catharsis. Some of his own wounds were beginning to heal.

The nursing home visits with Mrs. Hogan soon became a part of Walt's routine. He started thinking ahead of time what he might talk about on his next visit. One session was devoted entirely to the prayer meeting in the principal's office.

"What was your prayer again?" she asked.

"Dear God, please forgive us Christians for acting like the devil in front of all those sinners," Walt not so reverently repeated. Then he added, "I'm no saint."

"How could you be?" the woman thought to herself.

On another visit, Walt told her about his encounters with Dean Rowell when he was in college. He added that he would have never gotten into graduate school except for the letter of recommendation from his old nemesis.

Walt then told the woman about the anonymous gift that he received the day he graduated from college. He said he would not have been able to go to graduate school without it, and that he had never been able to thank the person who was so generous. He did not seem to notice when Mrs. Hogan turned her head toward the window for a moment.

As he shared with this willing listener about his days at Walter Reed, he explained why Sin Infidel was his favorite wine. He did not volunteer how the nurse who gave it that name could have become the mother of his child. That was just too personal.

Walt told this gracious lady about his association with Mrs. Neumann, and how he came to have a home in Ephesus. He even described his lengthy friendship with Hannah. His new friend said that she would love to meet the woman who meant so much to him.

On his next visit, Walt parked beside a car from Fulton County, Georgia. When he entered Mrs. Hogan's room, she already had another visitor. The woman was introduced to him as Millie Hancock, a lifelong acquaintance who lived in Atlanta.

Soon, Mrs. Hancock rose to leave. She said that she had a long drive ahead, and she needed to get started. The woman then told Walt that she already knew all about him. He looked surprised. She said that she and Maggie talked on the phone at least once a week. That was the first time he had heard Mrs. Hogan addressed that way.

Mrs. Hancock then came toward Walt with her arms extended. She gave him a big hug that was a bit awkward for him. Then she said. "Walter, I doubt that you will ever know how much you mean to Maggie. I want to thank you for being her friend. You will never regret the time you spend with her."

He did not know what to say.

When Walt was having lunch with Eli one day, he told him about the rapport he was developing with Mrs. Hogan. Chaplain Pierce was pleased. He told him that there was no way to put a value on what something like that might mean to a woman with no immediate family in the vicinity.

When they were conversing one day, Mrs. Hogan asked Walt if he had ever met anyone famous. "I guess that all depends on how you define 'fame'," he answered. "In my book no one was ever more famous than my two grandfathers."

That did not satisfy her. He then acknowledged that while he was in the army, he met a number of high-ranking officers. He added that when he was stationed at Walter Reed, many dignitaries came through the hospital.

"Who was the officer of the highest rank you ever met?" the woman queried him.

"Well, I guess that would be the Commander-In-Chief," Walt responded.

"You met the President of the United States?" Mrs. Hogan quizzed him. "Which one?" she wanted to know.

Walt then proceeded to tell her about his encounter with President Johnson. "Would you bring the picture with you sometime, and let me see you shaking hands with LBJ?" she requested.

On his next nursing home visit, Mrs. Hogan asked Walt if he played ball when he was a kid. He told her all about being the first baseman for his Babe Ruth Baseball team. He did a play by play of the opening day. He then conveyed to her how the words of his coach, "Hey, Williamson, get in the game," had stuck with him throughout his life.

Walt paused. He dropped his head. Mrs. Hogan could see how his demeanor had suddenly changed. Was something wrong? What should she do? She wanted to reach out to him.

Walt had been replaying in his mind what happened right after the season was over. For a few moments, he was back in the kitchen of the house where he grew up. He had just come into the room and found his mother crying.

The secret that had been locked away in Walt's heart all these years began little by little to leak out. What he had been unable to tell anyone else, he was now sharing with this sweet woman.

His eyes welled up. Like his words, his tear ducts also started releasing drops only a few at the time. All of a sudden, the dam burst. Walt was so overcome with emotion that he got up to leave. He apologized to Mrs. Hogan for his abruptness, but said that he had to get some fresh air. He would come back again soon. As he went out the door, he mumbled that he had *never* told anyone else what he had just shared with her.

As he and Yo headed out of town, Walt's emotions were every bit on the roller coaster that the vehicle was experiencing, negotiating the ups and downs of the precipitous mountainous road. What possessed him to do such a thing? He thought about the woman's circumstances, and he decided that he did not have to worry about her safeguarding his secret.

As the miles began to add up, Walt felt a sense of unburdening. He had presumed that he would take what his mother told him that day with him to his grave. Just to say the words about D-V Day aloud to another human being, however, was so liberating. He wondered if Mrs. Hogan would have any questions. He hoped not.

Because Walt was so blinded by his own tears, he was unable to see the look on Mrs. Hogan's face when he was telling her about Maude's slip up. Nor did he have any clue what happened to her afterward until a couple of days later. He was again having lunch with Chaplain Pierce. Eli asked him if he had been by the hospital room to visit the woman from the nursing home. Walt was confused.

Chaplain Pierce explained that she was brought to the emergency room barely conscious. An attendant found her passed out when she looked in on her. Eli understood that the woman's blood pressure went out the roof, and that she narrowly averted having a stroke. Walt was beside himself with concern.

He finished his lunch hurriedly, and he headed to Mrs. Hogan's room. In syncopation, a look of relief came across both their faces. "Oh Walter, I was so worried about you," she said. "I hope you are all right."

"I'm fine," he responded. "But the question is, are you okay?"

"I just gave the folks at Pleasantdale a little excitement," she answered, with an aura of resignation about her. Walt wondered if she was on medication to keep her calm. She said that she would be released the next day if her blood pressure remained stable. He promised to get by to see her again soon.

Walt kept replaying the conversation about D-V Day in his mind. Why did he feel so free to share this extremely personal information with Mrs. Hogan? He had always shied away from the subject with everyone, including Hannah, and even Ginny.

While he was still reeling from the effects of what he had done, he realized that he had no regrets. Never once had he doubted what his mother said in the kitchen that fateful morning. Yet, by opening up to another person, there was a different kind of validity. It was no longer something just bottled up inside him. It was released to the universe.

All of this impelled Walt to revisit his feelings toward his family. He had long ago forgiven Todd for the whuppin's.

Poor Emma Lou – she just parroted all kinds of positions and postures projected onto her, with nary a notion that there was something seriously wrong with the picture. Walt remembered something that he had written in WOWs. "Sometimes the hardest thing for a person to see is what is right under his nose."

Then, there was his mother. How could a mother not be proud of her son?

Mrs. Hogan looked a little tired and a bit fragile when Walt dropped by the nursing home later in the week. Nothing was said about what happened the last time he was there. He did not stay long.

On his next visit, Mrs. Hogan was back to her old self. She told Walt that she wanted him to tell her all about Alaska. To help her understand, he shared with her how he taught himself to read.

"I'll bet Maude was a good mother," she interrupted him.

"She is dead now," Walt responded, not really wanting to comment on what the woman asked him. "She died of cancer," he added. "They say cancer runs in my family, but it seems to be mostly on the female side."

After the awkward interlude, Walt told the woman about "The Ugly Duckling," the first story he read to himself. He then explained that it was because of his fascination with swans that he set out on the journey that took him all the way to Alaska. He even went so far as to say aloud that like the baby swan, he too, just hatched in the wrong nest. He was puzzled when she frowned.

To lighten the mood, Walt asked Mrs. Hogan if she knew what it was called when a moose makes a mistake. She shook her head. "That would be a moose-take," he said slyly. She liked his humor.

"What happens when a caribou does something wrong?" he continued. Again, Mrs. Hogan had no clue. "A cariboo-boo," he explained cunningly, both of them now laughing.

Walt never fancied himself much of a storyteller, but he had to admit that he was enjoying this as much as she was. He told her about the mama moose he named Lucy Moosey that raised her calves in and out of his yard every summer. She smiled with delight. He then recalled a few rather up close and personal bear encounters, going into some graphic detail. Mrs. Hogan just shook her head.

Walt shared with the woman his enthrallment with eagles. With a bit of a swagger in his voice, he said that he even spoke a little "eagle-ese." He then made a few mimicking sounds to illustrate this expertise. He could tell that she was pleased.

Walt then said that he had also been known to carry on conversations with loons. Mrs. Hogan laughed out loud. "Does that make you a loon-a-tic?" she asked, showing a little pizzazz of her own.

Walt said that Ginny once said to him, "Lots of folks talk to animals. But you are the first person that I have ever known that the critters talk back to."

"Who is Ginny?" the woman asked.

Walt choked up with emotion.

"I'm so sorry," Mrs. Hogan said. She reached over, took his strong hands, and started rubbing them with her gnarled fingers.

As Walt was pulling into his driveway after the visit, something struck him. He did not ever remember mentioning his mother's name to Mrs. Hogan.

During his next visit, the now willing narrator told the nursing home resident about seeing salmon jumping up cascading waterfalls on their way to spawning beds. He explained how these fish travel for thousands of miles out in the ocean, and then they mysteriously find their way back to the very streams where they were hatched.

Walt depicted the beauty of the wildflowers. He promised to bring the scrapbook of photos he had taken. He tried to portray the magnificence of the snow-covered mountains.

He could see a glow about Mrs. Hogan, as though she were seeing Alaska through his eyes. It made him feel especially good inside to think that he might be adding some sparkle to this woman's life.

Walt tried as best he could to describe the awesomeness of what it is like to be present when a glacier calves. He even asserted that a person is not really qualified to use the word awesome unless he has spent some time in Alaska.

Mrs. Hogan objected with such forcefulness that it startled him. He turned and looked at her just as she said, "Walter, you are awesome." He found himself blushing from such an affirming compliment. Their eyes remained fixed on each other for a couple of seconds. Walt felt a wave of warmth wash over him.

Of course, Walt eventually told Mrs. Hogan all about Ginny. He was touched that this sensitive and caring woman was shedding tears right along with him. She never tired of Walt's visits. He was also rejuvenated each time he left.

One day after a lively visit, Walt told Mrs. Hogan that he would soon be returning to Alaska for a few months. He assured her, however, that in the fall when he got back, he would come to see her.

The woman told Walt how thrilled she was that he was getting to go again. As he was leaving, she said if she were a few years younger, she would get on that plane and go with him. He thought it, and then he said aloud, "Mrs. Hogan, that would be really nice."

Walt spent a day or so getting all of his loose ends tied together before Eli was to take him to the airport in Asheville. He needed to cut the grass one more time. When he was almost finished, a butterfly sailed right over his left shoulder. It landed on a bright yellow dandelion just ahead.

He paused, beholding the spectacular sight and wishing for his camera. For some mysterious reason, the butterfly caused him to remember a forgotten promise. He had told Mrs. Hogan that he would leave the wildflower scrapbook with her while he was gone, and he had forgotten to take it to her.

Walt soon put the mower away, took a shower, and headed toward Pleasantdale. As he unexpectedly entered her room, the woman was sitting in a chair beside her bed. She tried to conceal what she was holding in her contorted hands, but it was too late. He got a good glimpse of the tattered book jacket of *I. D. – The Identity Dilemma.*

"You never told me that you had read my book," Walt said to her curiously. In fact, the modest author had not yet gotten around to mentioning the book. He had thought about bringing her a copy, but he was afraid that she could not turn the thin pages.

Walt put the scrapbook down, and he reached for the book. Mrs. Hogan reluctantly surrendered it to him. He thumbed through the well-worn pages. He then did a double take when he turned to the title page and looked down at his own handwriting.

"To Maggie, who is still trying to figure out who she is."

Walt's mind was racing, trying to process it all.

San Diego . . . ? Maggie . . . ? The woman in the mall . . . ?

The wheels were spinning, but they were getting no traction.

Mystified, he then turned to face Mrs. Hogan. He could see angst in her eyes, and fear written all over her face. Her feeble hands were trembling.

The woman then took a deep breath. For a few moments, she bowed her head and closed her eyes.

Walt's gaze was riveted on her. His heart was pounding.

When Mrs. Hogan looked back up, something had shifted. Her panic-stricken expression had given way to a look of peaceful serenity.

He saw it in her eyes. Why had he not seen it before?

"Are . . . you . . . ?"

"Oh, son, I am so *proud* of you . . ."

"And Walter, I am *so* sorry . . ."

Walt missed his flight.

In Appreciation

The author would like to thank a number of individuals who offered candid advice and invaluable support for *The War Baby*. They include, but are not limited to those whose initials appear below. Full names are not listed for fear that some of them might have to go into the Witness Protection Program if publicly linked to this writer. Thanks a bunch, E. P., D. P., K. H., B. H., B. B., M. W., M. K., L. N., L. T., J. H., A. H., E. E., and especially L. H., and L. W., my best editor ever.

About the Author

Larry G. Johnson devoted periods of his life to ministry, college administration, and counseling. He also owned one of the oldest bookstores in the United States, and then he became a newspaper columnist. The author is now a self-unemployed journalist who migrates back and forth between his little lakeside retreat in northwest Georgia, and a special place at the edge of the wilderness on the Kenai Peninsula in Alaska. This wandering writer's other interests include woodworking and winemaking.

thewarbaby@mindspring.com

Made in the USA
Charleston, SC
12 January 2013